Just Doll

the fiction of Janice Daugharty

Novels

Dark of the Moon
Necessary Lies
Pawpaw Patch
Earl in the Yellow Shirt
Whistle
Like a Sister

Stories

Going Through the Change

Just Doll

a novel

book one of the Staten Bay trilogy

by

Janice Daugharty

BASKERVILLE
PUBLISHERS

Baskerville Publishers, Inc.
2711 Park Hill Drive
Fort Worth, Texas 76109

Library of Congress Cataloging-in-Publication Data

Daugharty, Janice, 1944-
  Just doll : the first novel of the Staten Bay trilogy / by Janice Daugharty.
      p. cm.
  ISBN 1-880909-72-3 (alk. paper)
  1. Plantation owners' spouses—Fiction. 2. Plantation life—Fiction. 3. Married women—Fiction. 4. Mistresses—Fiction. 5. Adultery—Fiction. 6. Georgia—Fiction. I. Title.

  PS3554.A844J87 2004
  813'.54—dc22

                                                        2004000969

Manufactured in the United States of America
First Printing, 2004

Acknowledgments

Thanks to Kristin Lewandowski, of The Writers Shop, for sorting and salvaging my numerous revised manuscripts, and for her friendship; a posthumous thank you to David Norman, for teaching me all I know about Stockton pottery; thanks to the Agrirama, in Tifton, Georgia, for inspiration and reaffirmation and the hottest day excursion of my life; thanks for understanding to my neglected friends Rheta Johnson, Cynthia Shearer, Mary Hood and Judy Long; general thanks to Dave Eden, Delores Parrish, Billy Raulerson, Ruth Salter, Deborah Davis, Diane Howard, Bobbie Warren, Robert H. Boyle ("Bookend," NY Times Book Review, July 23, 2000), Ronald E. Moore, Charley Reese, Jerry Greene, Robert Davis, Angela Daugharty, Seward Daugharty, Stacey Daugharty, Laney Dowdy, and Dr. Thomas Dasher. Researching for Staten Bay I consulted many books, newspapers, magazines and other sources, such as The Internet and Encarta Encyclopedia, but none was as practical, precise and dependable as *Roots, Rocks and Recollections*, by my friend and neighbor Nell Roquemore. Other regional books used as resources were *The Chinkypin*, by Dot Price and her students at Echols County High, and *Judge Harley and his Boys*, by Dr. John Lancaster. Thanks too to my friend and favorite turpentine man, Harley Langdale, Jr., for setting me straight on the subject of turpentine and its peculiar language and evolution. My daddy and Aunt May's old tales of family struggles and traditions are at the soul of this book. I am especially grateful to Margaret Ann Levings for allowing me to use a letter she wrote to me while on vacation in Key West, Florida, and for all her advice and work on Staten Bay. Above all, I am indebted to Jeff Putnam, editor at Baskerville Publishers, for his patience, faith and hard work on JUST DOLL.

For Frankie Mae Levings and her granddaughter Margaret Ann, who honored me by posing for the portraits of Little Doll and Sara Ann. And for the tough but tender men in my family who served as models for the composite characters of Daniel and his sons. Without their example, I could never have mined the inherent strengths of these characters, their bearing and dignity, and details as seemingly insignificant as genetic gestures and speech patterns.

Doll was picking squash next row over from her older sister Sheba, who was scrapping through the sprawl of vines for pickling cucumbers. Both went still at the same time, listening to horse hooves clopping down the road toward the long, low house.

In the flatwoods of Southeast Georgia, Doll Baxter was raised knowing that when she heard somebody coming, they would likely be coming to see the Baxters. Otherwise, they would have taken one of the other few connecting roads leading to the houses of the Baxters' few neighbors, who were likewise walled in by pines. Land so flat and swampy it turned to crawfish dirt when it rained and sand bogs when it didn't rain, and the roads alternated between mud gullies and swollen sand. But scattered as they were, the neighbors seemed within hollering distance; when somebody had a house fire, got sick, or died, they would pop up out of the woods like squatters on your property. Sunday meetings at Bony Bluff, Doll could see them all in one bunch and count no more than seventy-five head, including children by the dozen belonging to a single household.

Doll often thought of the eastern section of Echols County and her spot in it as the wheel that makes a clock's hands move and the hands themselves pointing north at twelve o'clock to Homerville, east at three to Fargo and the Okefenokee Swamp, west at nine to Statenville, and south at six to Jasper, across the Georgia/Florida line. Commonplace were the spotty was-towns in between that thrived when the sawmills moved in and withered when they moved out, except for those living on as lumberyards. Time had a lot to do with the distance from Doll's place to any place, all within a day-ride radius of twenty miles by buggy or wagon, and all born of roving sawmills for sawing lumber and railroads for transporting farm produce, timber, turpentine and cotton to the riverport in Savannah or to the seaport in Jacksonville, both a day away by rail, then on to the rest of the world, which hadn't yet figured into Doll's perception of time and space.

Sheba stood with her white apron bundling cucumbers. Her eyes were fixed on the left front corner of the picket fence where horse and rider would show any minute around the blind of pines. She was wearing her faded yellow dress and a hickory-stripe bonnet belonging to her mother. Her eyes were wide set, her breasts wide set, broad face red from bending.

Doll watched too, but kept picking the smooth yellow crookneck squash. She broke one off at the throat and had to crop the neck separate, dropped both into the oak stave bucket.

The sun at eleven o'clock was beating down on the square garden, on the shingle roofs of the house to the right of the garden and the barn behind the house, and sliding back the shadows of tall loblolly pines from the white sand road. Smoke gusted from the brick chimney of the wood stove—a reminder that it was hotter in the kitchen than outside. Smells of burning oak, baked earth and steeping greenery. A wonder—so much green—given the fact that they'd had no rain for weeks, had been watering the garden straight from the well.

The cattle grazing the woods across the road raised their heads, then registering the source of the new sound nosed into the fountains of wiregrass again.

Doll lifted her heavy hair from her neck. It was black as fur of otter, glistened as if it were wet, and rippled down her back in loose spun curls. When it grew past her waist, she got her mother or Sheba to trim it, and she used the excuse that it was too dense to bunch on back of her head, because at seventeen she'd already learned that boys were drawn to her hair like hummingbirds to red.

The horse was now clipping at a smart eager trot. Closer but not close enough yet.

Doll stooped to pick another squash from the prickly bush. Still Sheba stood watching.

From the kitchen at the rear of the house, their mother, Mrs. Baxter, clanked a spoon on a pot rim. Across the woods, the turpentine men dumping gum from their dip buckets into the barrels rapped them as if in answer. The rumor of a timber train at the turpentine camp called Tarver was followed by a series of clear brass whistles and bells. Locusts droned, crickets sang in the grass, and bees harmonized in the pear tree at the far end of the garden rows. All backdrop to the rhythmic trotting of the horse.

A breeze hassled the corn leaves at Doll's back but she could feel no breeze. Her blue eyes teared from staring at the bright sand road, then spangled when she looked down at the green bushes.

Guineas, a dozen strong, cried out and scooted like shadows across the yard.

"Daniel Staten," said Sheba. "Oh my God, Doll, it's Daniel Staten." She let fly the apron full of cucumbers and began hopscotching through the cucumber vines toward the back yard. Her yellow skirt filling with air as she hiked it above her knees, old brown shoes picking up and putting down. The bonnet sailed from her head to the swept dirt yard. Ducking under the well sweep, she crashed through a gathering of butterflies nursing on the soured mud from the watershelf runoff, and climbed up on the back porch. She stood and began washing her face and arms in the water bucket, not even having bothered with dipping some into the wash pan.

"Doll," she shushed, "don't mention we got a bear in the barn, swear to God you won't." Then quick as the sun when it went down behind the treeline each day her yellow dress vanished from the shadow-capped porch.

Doll could tell when she passed the kitchen, going up the hall. "What in the world?" asked Mrs. Baxter.

"Daniel Staten." Sheba's flat voice sounded throughout the house. "Help me dress."

"For goodness sake, Bathsheba!" said Mrs. Baxter. "He's not God. Besides, he's too old for you. Not to mention too experienced. We may be poor but we are still ladies?"

"Go! Go talk to him on the front porch while I get dressed." Her voice raveled out. "Honest to goodness, if he finds out about the bear, my chances are ruined."

"I wish those beekeepers would come on and cart that thing off to the Okefenokee or kill him, one."

"No, not *kill* him. Hush, Mama."

"Well, he's gone be right back in our honey if they don't. And after us going to all the trouble of trapping him."

Big shush. "Mama, Daniel will hear you."

"Who ever heard of a girl making a pet out of a bear?" Mrs. Baxter clicked her tongue on the roof of her mouth.

They'd been at this same row for days. As for Daniel Staten, none of them really knew him, only who he was, some bigshot plantation owner from down around Statenville, west at least twenty miles, who had for reasons of the heart suddenly become important in their lives. Sheba had taken a shine to him at Sunday meeting a while back and had laid claim solely on the grounds that she couldn't live without him.

Nothing new about that. Sheba was forever falling in love, and her mother and sister both had given up trying to prevent her falling and saved their energy for her rescue. Mrs. Baxter never said, Do like Doll and ignore the boys and they'll be swarming all around you. She never said that because it encouraged comparison—and didn't they get enough of that from neighbors and strangers? Besides, she feared what worked for her pretty younger daughter wouldn't work for her plain older daughter. So far Mrs. Baxter felt she had succeeded in teaching the girls that pretty is as pretty does, and the proof was in how close they were despite the difference in their personalities and looks. What really evened things up though was Sheba's whopping sense of humor. Except where boys were concerned and Mrs. Baxter, blessed with a funny bone or two herself,

4

made it known that in her opinion boys will be boys and for the most part their brains are located in their unmentionables.

Doll watched the sleek black stallion and the tall bearded man, fair as the horse was dark, both proud with their heads high. He had on a white shirt, black pants, hat and boots. His hair was gold brown, his beard gold brown, green eyes set deep in a prominent brow. He rode up to the paling gate with an iron bell hanging from the notched and rotting hinge post. As he started to dismount, swinging his long right leg over the pommel of the saddle, the horse stepped sideways and Daniel had to leap to the ground. He landed on both feet, just short of a squat and backing, then caught on his left leg and spun round like a dancer.

"I'll break you from that if I have to break your damned neck," he said, speaking low and for the stallion's ears only. Which meant he hadn't spotted Doll yet. He switched him across his face with the reins and reset his hat. The horse neighed, reared, then stood shuddering away its mantle of mayflies.

Daniel tied the reins to the brace of the picket fence, right side of the gate, and stepped inside. The yard bell overhead rang, dull as a cowbell. He stilled it with one hand, took off his hat and smoothed his hair.

From the garden, Doll could hear the bear rattling his cage in the barn. Then his "unh unh unh" substitute growl. Sheba claimed he grunted like a gator; Doll thought he sounded more like a hog. But get downwind of his sharp wild scent... Doll laughed to herself and picked another squash, dropped it in the bucket. She would give that old fence about two minutes to stay standing and that horse smelling bear.

"Morning, Mr. Staten," said Mrs. Baxter, stepping from the hall to the porch.

"Mrs. Baxter," he said. "How are you this morning?"

"Fine, and you?"

"Been over to Four-mile Still with a load of gum. Thought I'd check on you ladies out here in the flatwoods before I head home."

The horse yanked on the reins; the entire section of fence to the right of the gate rattled and shook. Daniel scolded the stallion.

"Sheba'll be out in a minute. Come on in and have a glass of tea."

"I'll just wait out here, ma'am." He didn't say that he had to mind the stallion, but the horse was swinging his fine head and prancing in place.

"Well, have a seat, won't you? I've got to see to my corn before it scorches."

He sat in the swing on the south end of the porch, his back to Doll, who was gathering Sheba's cucumbers in her arms.

Inside, Sheba sounded like she was slinging a coil of haywire. A door clapped shut. Dull thumps—her old shoes slung, one here, one there. Bare feet padding room to room, then the light, quick clicking of her Sunday shoes.

"Just June and hot already," said Mrs. Baxter, done stirring her corn and out on the porch again. "And dry, my gracious!"

"They say it's the same all over. Cattlemen from Texas to the Dakotas are selling out."

The bear in the barn growled feebly, the stallion whinnied. He jerked the reins, the fence rattled, shook and quivered like wind-blown broomsage from picket to picket, gate to corner posts.

Daniel stood, scolded him, and sat again. "I'm sorry, ma'am. I don't know what's got into him."

Mrs. Baxter laughed weakly. "No need to apologize, Mr. Staten. Animals will be animals, we all know that."

Doll almost laughed out loud. Poor Mama! First she accidentally announces that Sheba is in love with him by saying she'll be out in a minute; and now Daniel Staten probably thinks they have a mare in heat in the barn out back and has to be cautious mentioning the antics of the stallion, now rearing, snorting and walling his eyes. "Two minutes up," Doll whispered. "Look out fence!"

"You will stay for dinner, won't you?" Mrs. Baxter asked.

"The girls would just love hearing all about President Cleveland's wedding at the White House."

"I'd like that, ma'am, but I've still got a good long ride ahead of me." He said something about turpentine that Doll couldn't make out clear. Only that slow, thoughtful, commanding monotone. She heard mention of the Savannah Cotton Exchange, which was responsible for setting market prices all over the world. He said he was sorry to hear about Mr. Baxter dying and to let him know if he could do anything.

On the front porch too now, Sheba spoke out in a breathy put-on voice.

The horse stepped side to side and back, gave one last mighty snatch on the reins, and the right fence panel collapsed intact to the ground. The stallion reared, bringing with him a two-by-four and about a dozen snapped pickets and the hinge post with the bell dangling chest-high and wobbling side to side. He made a forward lunge toward the porch where Daniel stood waving both arms and shouting as if to head him the other way, which happened to be south and around the house. Bib of pickets harvesting pink frilly blooms of crepe myrtle and boughs of sweet shrub, and all to the tumbled donging of the tarnished iron bell, like the climax of a one-act circus.

Meaning to keep him out of the garden, Doll dropped the cucumbers for the second time and flapped the tail of her white homespun dress at the horse, now passing in a whorl of dust between the back porch and the well, headed mistakenly for the barn just over the picket fence in the back yard. She lit in behind him with her dress tail caught up at the waist.

"Doll!" Mrs. Baxter yelled out the kitchen window, keeping safe inside while following the progress of the horse's destruction of her yard.

Doll slowed as the horse slowed, then skidded to a halt, heaving and snorting with nostrils flared. The dust cloud overtook him at the northwest corner of the back yard and settled on the honeysuckle vines over the fence. The wall-eyed stallion appeared anchored by the flower-laced palings, the two by four and the post with the dead bell that had somehow wound up apeak. In his wake were splinters, green leaves and deep gouges in the swept dirt like after a storm.

The bear in the barn was pawing wood, trying to tear out.

Daniel crept around the red brick chimney, north side of the house, arms out to keep the spooked horse from bolting past. "Hoo now," he crooned to the horse, but his eyes were on Doll easing closer to the stallion. She placed her left hand on his slick right rear flank and began stroking, switching hands as she reached the saddle, stroking all the way up to his neck, then down his muscular sculpted jaw and caught the reins in both hands.

"Mind he doesn't step on you," Daniel said low, moving closer. "Stand back."

"Doll Baxter!" Her mother was shouting from the back porch now. "Get away from that animal, hear me?"

Doll unwrapped the reins from the brace and began stroking the stallion's forehead. He smelled salty, of leather, but young-horse sweet. "Here," she said to Daniel and handed him the reins. She had never stood so close to him, except when she had brushed past him in the doorway of the tax collector's office at the Statenville courthouse a few weeks before, and several times after that when she spoke to him like any Christian would at Bony Bluff Church. She had thought it odd, his being at Bony Bluff, since he lived so far away. He scared her more than the horse did.

"Thank you." He snatched the horse from the corner. "Hoo now."

Her mother yelled from the back porch, "Doll, you get away from that horse this minute!"

"Good thing you didn't hitch him to a porch post," Doll said to Daniel.

"Doll!" her mother scolded again.

"Mrs. Baxter, I sure hate it. Here I've got your hogs all riled up too." He nodded toward the brittle old barn, alive with the bear's snuffling and snorting. "I'll send one of my men over to put up a new fence soon as I get home. Meantime I'll just patch up the old one."

Doll figured he was either dumb or his nose was stopped up if he couldn't smell bear.

Sheba, wearing her two-piece black dress with pink floral stripes, her church dress, stood next to her mother on the back porch. One young and anxious, the other old and anxious, but feature-wise almost identical. Trying for curls, Sheba had twisted damp wisps of her fine brown hair each side of her face.

"That old fence was barely standing anyway," she said.

Daniel laughed, lifting chin, eyes and voice. "Wouldn't be much to me if I was to leave you ladies where the cows and hogs could get in your garden, now would it?"

Sheba winked at Doll. "Doll, go help Mr. Staten prop up the fence so he can come eat."

Doll would have as soon not helped, but for her sister she headed out to the cellar-dim toolshed to the left of the barn and took down from a shelf on the back wall a claw hammer and the fruit jar of rusty nails they had salvaged from rotted-down outbuildings or just found here and there on the homeplace.

She would have liked nothing more than to stay there, soaking up the dank coolness of the earthen floor. Her face felt hot and had to be red, just like when she'd faced Daniel Staten, a nosy, bothersome stranger then, at the courthouse in Statenville. Her mission that morning had been to gently persuade—cajole, charm or whatever the circumstances called for—the Yankee tax collector to give her and her family more time to catch up their back taxes before the county took over the Baxter place, five hundred acres more-or-less of row crop and timber land; they would auction the dirt she loved—and had slaved to keep in the family like a mule—before the courthouse door. She promised the tax collector, a soft, pale, loose-limbed man with his hair wiped across his bare crown, that she would have the money by the end of the summer. She had a white family coming to chip boxes and dip gum and following the peak of the gum-running season she should have enough money from turpentine sales. Pretty please with sugar on it.

He had explained with his pink tongue pushing between posts of top, side teeth that he would do what he could but the matter wasn't altogether up to him. She had leaned forward, hands flat on his desk, Pretty please with sugar on it. She was dressed in a wine waist and skirt, her mother's wine drawstring bag hanging from her wrist, and her sister's tattered petticoats geared up at the waist to keep them from falling down. She could see her own black shiny hair falling forward on each side her face, an offering of hair.

"You know," she said, standing straight and fixing him with her blue-blue eyes, "I was just saying to my sister Sheba just the other day how I was surprised you'd stayed a bachelor all these years. Said you must get lonesome, being from up-north and all, and living way down here away from your kinfolks."

"Well, I do sometimes. It's a long way from Boston and..."

"Then you just come on out to see us anytime. Mama'll fry a chicken for you and I'll show you around the old place."

"I might do that. I just might." He reared back as if to escape her. His lips were pale and flat but stretched across the bottom half of his face as he began to speak again and his eyes lit up. "What about your sister, Sheba, I think it is? How's she doing?"

"Oh, Sheba!" So, it was Sheba he was interested in and who could tell? Sheba might like him too; she'd liked worse. She might like him and marry him and solve all their problems, temporarily at least. "Well, Sheba is doing just fine. Mama's always saying what a good hand she is with children. She's definitely the marrying kind."

"Marrying?" He sat forward, arranging papers on his desk. "I figured to court for awhile."

"Court, my goodness gracious, Sheba would just love to have you come courting." Maybe this was true. "I guess you heard we're having a big shindig at Hamilton Fletcher's in a few weeks."

"I did hear that. Heard the governor is coming all the way from Atlanta. Is that right?"

"Yes, sir. All the way from Atlanta. And we'll be expecting you too. I'll make certain that Sheba saves every dance for you. Okay?"

His slit eyes roved around Doll. She turned and saw Daniel Staten leaning in the doorway with his arms crossed, amused and not trying to hide it.

"Good morning, gentlemen," she said and headed for the door. Staten tipped his hat, smiling. Brushing past him in the doorway, she had felt light and hot and furious. Of course she was embarrassed having somebody—some man—witness her flirting, then practically promising her sister's hand in marriage to this dimwit tax collector. She stopped to listen to the two men talking inside the office now, pulling in her skirt and tucking her shadow close along the dark wall. Vague light, cigar smoke, and men's voices spilled from the other open doors along the hallway.

"You old dog, you," Staten said to the tax collector.

"Staten."

"Wasn't that one of the Baxter girls?"

"The one they call Doll, yes."

She covered her face with her hands.

"That gal's after you," Staten said and followed it up with a mocking laugh.

"After me to give her some leeway on her taxes. Their father left them land-poor and the girl has taken it on herself to hold onto the old homeplace. A fine family, so they say. Girls come from fine stock, despite their father's drinking."

"She's sweet on you though, I can tell."

"No, no. You've got it all wrong. Besides, she's too hot-blooded for me. Too many men after her. She'd keep you in trouble and you never would have any peace. They say there isn't a man in the county can get within two feet of her and every single one of them dying to. Her sister will make the better wife."

"That so?"

"I guess you heard about Doll Baxter beating that fellow up a while back."

11

"Yeah, seems like I did hear something about that."

"They say he was trying to have things to do with her."

Now she was mad, hearing them talk about her, and had to fight back the urge to go in there and tell it her way. Then Staten told it.

"Way I heard it, he was rustling some of her cows. I don't blame her."

"Anyway, she sailed in on him like a man. Little woman like that, it's hard to believe."

Doll left the shed with the jar of nails, cutting around the south side of the house. Through the open windows she could hear Sheba and her mother talking in the kitchen and smell the smoke of the wood stove and the corn, which after all had scorched. At the front of the house was a broach of space made up of yard and road in the absence of the fence Daniel was now piecing together from the wrecked pickets.

For punishment, and for practical purposes, he had roped the stallion to a black pine across the road. Low, so that the flat of his head butted up to the tarry base of the stout trunk. The stallion still stamped and walled his eyes, left rear hoof cocked in case the bear approached from behind. All around, cows grazed toward the spent shadows of the road.

"He keeps that up, I'll sell him first chance I get." On his knees, in the open sun glancing off sand like glass, Daniel hammered a fractured picket to the brace.

"How much?" Doll stood before him, holding the fruit jar of rusted and bent nails. She didn't want to get too close.

He sat back on the heels of his black boots, wiping sweat from his eyes with his shirtsleeve. "What?"

"How much do you want for the stallion?"

"Not for you I hope."

"Whyever not?"

"You're a girl—a mite on the little side at that. That's *whyever* not."

Smells of steeped tea, frying ham and bear rode the heated breeze down the hall.

"By the way," he said, "how much longer will it be before

you're out of school?"

"For good or for the summer?"

He laughed. "For good, I guess. You did go to school, didn't you?"

"Not that it's any of your business, but I did. Tenth grade, far as I could go at Hickman's, other side of Four-mile Still. Then a teacher boarding with us learned...taught...me Latin." She cleared her throat, set the jar on the dirt and stood the panel of pickets against the posts for him to nail. "I'm hungry—nail or hand me that hammer."

He walked on his knees to the post on his left and had to reach through the pickets to get a nail from the jar. The nail was bent and he had to get another one. Held it, point to wood, and hammered. The rapping echoed out over the woods.

"You can let go now," he said, shaking the panel. His hair and beard had threads of gold like the looped chain of his pocket watch.

She no longer feared being near him; he didn't matter.

The cows were grazing closer, seemingly oblivious to the sudden open space of road running to yard, but drawn to it like children to water. A scrub cow with scur horns crept across the road. Doll ran toward her, clapping her hands. "Get on back away from here!" The cow stopped, swinging her head, then turned and scuttled off into the woods.

Doll went back to the fence, crossing her arms. She had been dying for a reason to put the nail jar down, to cover her breasts. Her nipples had to be showing through the sweat-damp bodice of her worn white dress. Besides, she didn't like the direction things were going, could feel herself heating up from more than just the sun, though not at all like she had at the courthouse. In about a minute she would sic Sheba's bear on his stallion for him making light of her. Well, that's what she felt like doing.

The stallion stamped, tugged at the rope, stood still. The scaly brown tree shook all the way up to its green bushy top; pine cones, mast and short needles rained down.

"See what I mean," Daniel said and tipped back his hat

13

with the hammer handle. "He's about half-wild."

"I'll go on in now, Mr. Staten. I'm too little to be fetching nails and working fences." Out of habit, she started toward the panned place where the gate had been, now a queer abyss created by the stallion.

"Hey"—he laughed—"I didn't go to hurt your feelings." He bowed his head, spacing two pickets on another panel. "How about bringing me that piece on the other side of the walk there."

She crossed the brick walk and picked up the brittle splintered picket in the trampled petunia border, carried it to him. Shadowed on the dirt, she looked as if she were about to slam him upside the head. She dropped it next to his crooked leg.

He looked up at her, green eyes so focussed they seemed to spring from their sockets. "Actually, I came here hoping to have a word with you," he said.

"With m*e*? What about?"

"I hadn't planned it exactly like this." Sitting on his heels again, long legs folded, he wiped his face on his sleeve again. "I have a feeling you don't like me."

"I don't."

He hammered a nail, talking. "Well, that's too bad because I intend to marry you."

"Marry! You're crazy." She laughed out. "I don't even know you."

"What do you want to know? I can tell you everything you need to know here on the spot."

"For one thing—why me?" She was speaking too loud, too shrill, had to lower her voice. "Ask Sheba—Sheba's the one so anxious to get married."

"I'm afraid she's already spoken for."

"She is not."

"What about that Yankee tax collector?" He laughed.

"No, it's you she's set her cap for, and if she knew I was even talking to him about her, she'd have a fit."

"Well, he's about to take you up on the offer. He aims to marry Sheba."

14

"You're picking at me now. He's so shy, he'll never even show up here, much less mention what I said. And I do hope you'll be gentleman enough to do the same."

"Your little secret's safe with me. But if I was you I'd be more careful who I bargained with and for what. Your own sister!"

"I do what I have to."

"Regardless, I want to marry you," he said. "I want you to be my wife."

"You mean like that horse is your horse, right?" She nodded toward the horse, broke and at rest now but with one hoof set to strike.

"That's not what I mean." Daniel stood, left foot forward and hands on his hips. "I'm new at this. I've never asked anybody to marry me before."

In the kitchen, either her mother or Sheba was setting the table—tinkling silverware, clattering dishes.

"Let me get the straight of this," she fairly hissed, "you thought you could just stop off on your way home from Fourmile Still and pick up a wife to take back with you." She eyed the curious cows inching toward the road, the stunned man before her. "I'm sorry, Daniel...Mr. Staten...but that's the most puffed-up thing I've ever heard."

His face blazed around his shaped beard. He held his right hand palm down and out before him and waved it to aid his explanation. "I've always been one, once I make up my mind to do something, to just go on through with it. Land, cows or women."

"How humble of you."

"I don't have to be humble. Maybe you don't know this, but I could have any girl from here to Fargo and back to Statenville."

"Word is you already have, and I imagine you will again."

Sheba wasn't the only girl eager to marry the rich bachelor, and even the women here lately were whispering behind their hands. Doll felt giddy but guilty thinking that out of all of them she could have Daniel Staten. Not that she would do anything about it, but she did wonder why, out of all the others, he had picked her. Maybe for the same reason she felt giddy—like him, she was rumored to be a prize.

A week later, he showed up again, but this time at the party for the governor of Georgia at the huge old many-gabled house belonging to Hamilton Fletcher, about a mile across the woods from the Baxter place.

The once-prosperous gentleman farmer, Fletcher, was now broke in all but spirit and alone since the death of his wife. Well, actually he wasn't so alone; his sister Grace Burkholt, who had married a well-off jeweler, and her son and daughter, from Homerville, ten miles west through the woods, made sure that Hamilton was seen to and often. Hardly a weekend passed without either Adam or Brice staying with their uncle, to keep him company and visit with their flatwoods friends. Besides, Uncle Hamilton was fun; blessed with humor and not cursed with the ordinary contrariness of the aging. He was always holding fish fries or square dances, at the close of which those invited sometimes found that they'd been lured over for a working. He called the workings corn huskings, peanut shellings, pea pickings, stump burnings, as opposed to husking corn, shelling peanuts, picking peas, and burning stumps.

Doll was talking with Adam and Brice, her dearest friends, when she saw Daniel Staten step through the front door and stop, eyeing the shabby but decorated parlor where the main party was going on. He had on a black vested suit and black hat and his thumbs were hooked in his pants pockets, exposing the looped gold chain of his pocket watch. He wandered over to the halltree on his right and hung his hat, then on through the crowd in the middle of the room to the long table full of food, lit candles, and a silver bowl of cherry punch spiked with 100-proof gen-u-ine shine.

"Who is that?" Brice asked.

"Daniel Staten." Doll turned her back to him. Facing Brice and Adam, she fanned the candle smoke and perfume of magnolia and roses. She could feel a blush rising from her chest to her face, easy to blame on the heat. But all week she'd been blushing at the mention of his name, often and loud from the lips of her sister, who had stayed home from the party in case Daniel should drop by, and her blushing then could only be blamed on guilt. Sheba was starving herself, even refusing her favorite fried okra, after torture of cutting the spiked pods from the nettlesome stalks, so that she could fit into her mother's wedding gown.

When the okra came in it was generally the hottest part of summer, but Doll and Sheba had to wear their daddy's oldest thinnest long-sleeved shirts and trousers to keep from being flayed by the broad star-shaped leaves and thorny stems. The okra plants often grew as tall as young trees—the taller the thornier it seemed—and the girls even wore work gloves to part the leaves and get to the pods, but one thing they didn't wear was their corset bodices, because they'd found it was cooler without them. Last week, Doll had looked up from cutting and seen Sheba, next row over, in a thin white shirt with twin spots of blood where her nipples had been lashed by the leaves.

Such were the sad sisterly thoughts Doll was trying to maintain while she stood and smiled and swished the silky skirt of the yellow-sprigged dress with a giant yellow bow on the bustle. Dress on loan from Brice, like all the other accumulated props in the room, and on the entire property, in fact, on loan from various neighbors and the Burkholts of Homerville to confuse the visiting governor who was prospecting for areas of rural poverty for his annual report. Word was, he was planning to recommend to the state legislature that a cotton mill be located in this "utmost impoverished area of the rural southeast." Like that was some honor!

All week the church-bound community, and even those like Hamilton who didn't go to church, had worked to make ready the old falling-down house for the big party. Everybody coming together with hammers, nails, saws, and buckets of whitewash to slather on the brittle outer walls of what was still considered the biggest, finest house in the flatwoods. Yesterday Grace Burkholt had brought a full wagonload of precious vases, tissue-wrapped china and silver, had nearly cleaned out her new two-story house in Homerville. And all for a party that the suspicious, prideful flatwoodsers hadn't wanted in the first place, except to escape being labeled poor dirt farmers in need of state handouts. Now all their hard work could go for naught if Daniel let on that that was exactly how he saw them (poor, proud dirt farmers).

"So that's Daniel Staten," said Brice, following him through the crowd with her blond-lashed eyes. "He's every bit as good-looking as they say. Isn't he, Doll?"

Doll turned and looked again, turned back. "I've met him before. He was at Bony Bluff Sunday before last, the day you missed." Usually she told Brice everything, but Daniel's marriage proposal had to remain secret to insure that Sheba didn't get hurt. Doll felt dishonest for not mentioning his visit to the Baxter house though.

"Don't go getting any notions, Brice." Adam latched his square hands behind his back and swayed. "The way I hear it he's one of the biggest rounders in these parts."

Adam was always bossing his younger sister, but she never listened. Seemed not to hear him now, but instead some muse in her head. "I wonder if it's true that Statenville was named after him."

The other girls at the party had spotted Daniel Staten and were making eyes at him and sashaying his way.

The band, set up before the rubble-brick fireplace stuffed with flowers and woods ferns, struck up a lively tune and the crowd started clapping, chief among them the governor with his paunch strutted and his white cat-whisker beard stained red with cherry punch. Hamilton Fletcher, big-man handsome with a head full of hair white as his shirt, took the Governor's almost-drained glass and parted the crowd around the punch bowl and filled it again. The Governor's wife, a tall and gauche but elegant woman with towering black hair, stood next to him, turning a fine crystal ruby-tinted glass in both hands while talking to Grace Burkholt, obviously the only other woman in the room with a little money and class, so a safe place to stop and seem to chat, except for that Mrs. Baxter, who kept butting in and wouldn't quit laughing. She looked geared up in a girdle under her best dress.

She looked tipsy and hot. Everybody looked tipsy and hot, because it *was* hot. But only Mrs. Baxter wore a dangling wad of hair on back of her neck. One of her "rats" as she called the matted hanks of hair kept on her bedroom dresser for special occasions to be rolled and pinned up, ear to ear, filler for her own pale thinning hair.

"No, I think that was Staten's dead brother, the senator, they named the town after," Adam said. He was the only man there dressed in his own tuxedo, and at least a couple of other men in the room were squeezed into tuxedos tailored to fit the compact young lawyer from Homerville. Adam had no beard, like most of the other men, and his red face was made more heart-shaped by the widow's peak of his coarse black hair. His hairline had started rising shortly after he came home from Atlanta last year with his law degree, both of which made him seem older than a mere twenty-four.

"I just hope he doesn't tell the governor that we're as down-and-out as he thought before he came here," Doll said.

"I don't think the governor's in any shape to think at all after so much punch." Brice had what was called red hair but was really more coral, almost the color of her dress.

"Speaking of the governor, here he comes," Adam said and changed the subject for his benefit. "I hear the Malloy and Fender boys are going to wrestle after Sunday meeting tomorrow."

Doll kept fanning, didn't look, but braced herself by stiffening. She had already been one round with the governor, up close, all hands, and hot in a gray wool suit. Sort of like wrestling.

"There you are," the governor said to Doll, stepping between her and Brice, rocking on his heels with a glass of punch in his right hand. His left hand slipped around Doll's waist

19

and settled on the small of her back. "Doll Baxter, isn't it?"

"Yes sir," Doll said and fanned him, laughing.

He roared. "You're the one whose family's in cattle, right?"

"Yes sir."

Suddenly Daniel Staten appeared between Brice and the governor. "Governor," he said and stuck out his hand. "I heard you were coming to Echols County. Welcome to the flatwoods."

"Why, Staten, you old son-of-a-gun." The governor had to let go of Doll to take his drink in his left hand and shake with his right. "It's been a while, hasn't it?"

"A while," Daniel said. He nodded to Doll. "Doll." His full but trimmed beard dipped to his starched white collar.

"Mr. Staten. Meet my friends Brice and her brother Adam Burkholt, from Homerville. Adam's a lawyer there." The last part she added for Daniel's benefit—show him he wasn't the only man around with influence. If he concluded that Adam was her boyfriend, that was okay too though not her fault.

Daniel spoke to Brice, shook with Adam.

The governor guffawed as if somebody had told a joke and again sneaked his left arm around Doll. "So you know this fine-looking gal here, Staten?"

"Quite a while in fact, Governor. Did cattle business with her daddy for years before he died."

"Oh, he died! I'm sorry." The governor drank. "I had to pull a little rank with the boys here tonight"—big guffaw—"they were thick as flies around Miss Baxter here. Course, who could blame them? Lovely lady like this."

Behind them, something slammed the rickety floor. Women squealed. The governor's wife had toppled like one of the rotted columns on the porch and the women were gathering around her.

"She's a little on the frail side," said the governor, turning to look and turning back. "Not used to good whiskey." He sampled his. "Staten, may I have a word with you? On the front gallery if you don't mind."

He wheeled, walking carefully, one foot ahead of the other,

along the edge of the crowd toward the open door. Daniel shrugged, followed.

"Do you think he'll tell?" Brice whispered.

"I wouldn't put it past him." Doll fanned her glistening face.

"Oh, no!" Adam said, gazing over her head at the crowd. "They've got the governor's wife on her feet and aimed toward that cane chair with the broken bottom."

When the governor came back in to refill his glass and check on his wife, Doll made her way through the crowd and out the door where Daniel was standing alone on the north end of the porch, drinking from a pewter flask. "Well, well, well, if it's not the Southern belle."

Two girls Doll knew from church stepped to the doorway and stopped, watching them. Then turned back inside. Men and boys were grouped and talking in the yard. Spotty fires burned along the lane of bushwhacked weeds leading up to the dilapidated but shored-up farmhouse. Horses whinnied and stamped in the dark. The air was ripe with citronella and oak smoke. Dressed-up children chased in and out and tumbled over the groaning white spindle banisters. Their hands came away white as new gloves.

Or the moon-white blossoms of the twin magnolias hiding the front of the house. They looked stuck among the large waxy leaves, fake, and they smelled fake, too sweet and too loud and about to turn brown and drop from the too-straight branches.

"I guess you told the governor we're a bunch of fakes," Doll said.

"No ma'am, I didn't." Daniel capped the flask and eased it into his coat pocket. "Actually he had me mixed up with my brother, like everybody else does. He's so addled he didn't even remember that Jimmy had died." He leaned into a porch post; it creaked and he pulled his hand away. "You know, last time I passed Hamilton's house, I could of swore it wasn't painted."

Doll looked at the watered-white porch wall lit by citronella candles in the row of door-sized windows. Moths and beetles swirled around the flames.

"I bet you folks have been holding your breath it didn't come up a rain. Then again, if it don't rain, y'all run a danger of setting the woods afire, don't you?" He laughed. "What did Hamilton do when he picked the governor up in Fargo? Hand him a drink the minute he got off the train?"

"Well, how would you like to be written up in every newspaper in Georgia as a pauper?"

"You'd rather starve, right?"

"We're not hungry in the least, not a one of us."

"If I was y'all I'd be more worried about killing the Georgia governor and his wife with that rot-gut whiskey in there. Talk about making the news!" He made a pained face.

"It's not rotgut whiskey, and besides he asked for it, coming out here to use us for political purposes. We've got our pride."

"You're right about that. But still and all he's got it in his head to put up a cotton mill out here. 'Break that cycle of rural poverty,' as he says." Daniel swung his head.

"What, and give ten, fifteen people jobs? Bring in all the riffraff. We don't want a cotton mill; we're doing fine the way we are."

"Yeah, a cotton mill might draw moonshiners and liars, who knows what kind of *riffraff*. Might even draw hypocrites to your church."

A magnolia blossom dropped to the dirt and lay glowing like a cluster of lightning bugs.

"You're making fun of us, taking me for a fool." Doll spun around to go back inside. "That put-on cracker talk of yours and the governor's is more fake than we are."

He grabbed her arm. "Hey, I was kidding, I'm on your side. It's just so funny, this whole thing, you've got to admit it. Come on, sit in the swing with me for a minute, will you?"

Inside, the fiddler was fiddling wild. Somebody whooped, sounded like Hamilton. Or the governor. A woman laughed shrilly.

Daniel tested the braided swing ropes, then sat, holding it still for Doll to sit and situate the swishy ruffled skirt of her dress. Through the window on her left they could see into the north bedroom. The governor's wife was laid out like a corpse on a bed placed parallel to the porch wall. One long pale foot was stuck dangerously close to the lit candle on the sill nearest Doll's end of the swing.

Doll caught her breath. "You don't really think she'll die from drinking that shine, do you?"

"Nah, she's just a little on the frail side, like the governor said. Not used to drinking whiskey." Daniel was leaning over Doll as if to get a better look at the woman's feet through the window, breathing in the scent of her hair. "Is the lawyer the reason you won't marry me? You're planning to marry him?"

Another bed on the other side of the room was full of sleeping babies.

Doll sat back, forcing him over to his side of the swing, but he placed his left arm across the back behind her head.

She waited for that heated feeling, like at the courthouse, and didn't have to wait long. "I've already told you, I'm not marrying anybody."

"Doll, I hate to put it like this, under these circumstances. But if you stay out here, now your daddy's dead and gone, you're likely to starve."

"For your information, we've got land and cows."

"Correction: cattle."

"Cows. Eight or ten."

"How long? How long can you hold on without letting the land go? And the cows."

"Till the end."

"Listen, Doll, I admit it—I went about this business all wrong the first time." He leaned closer, so close she could smell his whiskey breath. "Let's start over; I under-estimated you. For starters, I know your folks haven't paid the taxes on their place in better than four years."

"I know how you know and I don't appreciate it in the least."

The toes through the window wiggled; the flame of the candle flickered.

Daniel kept the swing moving by pushing from heel to toe, his boots tapping in time to the fiddles and banjos sawing out another tune inside. "It's my business to know that."

"So you can take advantage of people down on their luck?"

"Sometimes, I won't lie. But right now, I'm just offering to pay your taxes up to date and ever after. Pay off your mortgage."

"We don't have a mortgage."

"Yes, you do. I checked. Sorry."

"My daddy would have told us."

The fiddler inside wrapped up with a fierce quick swipe of his bow across the strings and everybody clapped and Doll had to wait to hear Daniel's response.

"Listen, Doll, I'll take care of Mrs. Baxter and Sheba as long as they live. You'll have a good life with me, and don't tell me that doesn't matter to you, because I know it does." He lifted her ruffled skirt tail with his boot. "You're too fine to be wearing borrowed dresses."

"How do you know it's borrowed?"

"I'm guessing."

"I don't even like you; in fact I think I hate you. And speaking of hate—Sheba would hate me forever. I guess you should know she stayed home because this...this business with the governor goes against her principles. That's the kind of fine Christian person she is. Besides, she's crazy about you." Thinking of all that prickly okra Sheba had cut and wouldn't eat, Doll felt the urge to rub the tops of her hands.

"What if the Yankee tax collector shows up and she's not here."

"He won't. Don't start that again. It's you she's in love with."

"I've never encouraged her. I hardly know her. She'll get over it, and you don't even have to like me especially."

The toes in the window wiggled. The woman snored, developing a percolating pattern.

"I hope you don't think I'd marry somebody I didn't love. I hope you don't think I'd do something like that to my sister, close as we are. Anyway, I like my good times; get married and the good times are over."

"Don't play your games with me, Doll."

"What games?" She whipped open her fan, fanned him and laughed, then quit laughing. "So, I'm not marrying you or anybody else. I'm not leaving my home, my mother, my friends. You'd lose interest in me if you married me anyway. I know how men lose interest in women once they're married to them, I've seen it all my life."

"That's ridiculous, and women like you have to get married."

"What does that mean?"

"It means you're not the old-maid type. You've got that extra-hot skin. I felt it when I took your arm a while ago and I can feel it like sunshine coming off of you right now."

"I think you've gone just a little too far, Mr. Staten." She started to rise.

He caught her right arm, squeezing, testing. "I haven't insulted you and you know it; I've paid you a compliment and if you're honest you'll admit it."

She stared into his eyes. A hollow formed on her brow above her left eye. "I honestly don't know what you're talking about."

"Good," he said. "But you do know what I'm talking about when I say I'll take over the mortgage and the taxes on your place." He held up one long jointed finger. "Plus...take care of your family for the rest of their days."

"So, that's it, that's your offer?"

"That's my offer. On top of that, I'll get you a fancy way to go and you can come see your mother anytime you like. I'll give you your freedom."

"My freedom is not yours to give, Mr. Staten." The toes in the window wiggled. Doll stood and blew out the candle. "But if that was the case, Mr. Staten, then I could give you your freedom too."

Chapter 2

Doll's plan to save her homeplace had seemed simple enough, and profitable, before she had learned about the mortgage. Before she had hired on the family, four grown boys and their rascally father, to work the Baxter's turpentine timber. But so far, mid-summer, height of the turpentine season, the men had managed to dip only a few barrels and half the time she either couldn't locate them in the woods or she would ride up on them taking a break from the heat under some shade tree.

She had to admit it was too hot to work. Her riding breeches were wet in the saddle and scalding her buttocks. Staring up at the noon sun flaring white in the blue sky, she could see no sign of relief. Black buzzards with fringed and faded wingtips circled overhead, dipping, rising and gliding. She tried to recall when they had last had rain and couldn't remember. Only that it was too long and according to the weather-wise old men of the community it would be a good while longer.

Even the locusts in the oak thicket up ahead sounded hoarse and weary, more a monotonous unnerving drone than a familiar summery brattle. She rode on through the still flocked shadows of the oak grove, toward a pool of inky water corralled by the beavers from the main channel of Toms Creek— Big Arm of Toms Creek, this spot was called. On the south curve between banks of palmettos, gallberry bushes and willows, they had built a dam of twigs and branches, creating a musical spillway. The level overflow turned to a honey-tinted tunnel, sheer and lilting and tumbling into the main flow of the creek and out of sight around the curve over small white pebbles and sand.

Doll dismounted and let the mare drink while she kneeled and wet her neckerchief and mopped her face and neck.

"Hot enough for you?"

She looked behind and saw Daniel Staten on the black stallion in the spotty sun and shade of the oaks, the stallion and Daniel's light pant legs accented by the sunlight, his face in shadow.

"You're always where you're not supposed to be," she said, trying to hide that he had frightened and excited her. "For a little bit, I'd think you're following me."

"I am. Sort of." He rode forward a couple of feet and stopped and now she could see his face—coppery skin, coppery beard and that smirky grin. "Run up on your gum crew nooning beyond that cypress flat yonder, lil ole cathead of a bay." He pointed east. "Wanted to know if I'd seen their boss lady. I say, What does she look like? She's real pretty, one of them says, but ain't a sweet bone in her body. I say, Oh, that would be the woman I'm going to marry. Doll Baxter."

She stood, facing him square. "You didn't say that."

"Not exactly," he said, shifting in his squeaking saddle and leaning, resting his right forearm on the saddle horn and flip-flopping the reins while he talked. "Had a little business with Hamilton Fletcher."

"He said you've been trying to buy him out. Well, you can forget it; he won't sell. He's been out here, his family has, since back before the war."

Daniel reached behind him, taking his time, and unlatched one pocket of his saddlebag and took out a folded white paper and waved it at her. "And he'll stay out here long as either one of us is alive. Right there in that old whitewashed house and just as cuss-fired ornery and handsome as ever, chasing the ladies. Only difference is, he won't have to bother with taxes and timber and such. Same deal I made you."

"I'm not interested, and Mr. Hamilton has never chased the ladies."

"All men chase the ladies."

She started toward her horse now grazing in fountains of wiregrass along the north rim of the oak shade. "Why don't you go on and leave me alone?"

"I don't think so, not yet." He swung down from the saddle, fluid and easy and all of one motion, looking suddenly serious and charmed beyond point of reasoning. "Don't move, Doll."

"I most certainly will. I don't know what you're up to but…"

Like a cat he sprang at her, slamming his body into hers, sending both of them flying, crashing into the creek. The lick had knocked out her breath before the water rose over her head, suffocating her. She came up thrashing and sputtering, fanning her arms. Then she stood, about waist deep, facing him and waiting for him to stand too so she could get a good swing at him. But when the water quit snapping in her eardrums and she could hear clear what was going on around her, she heard behind her on the bank the dry singing of rattles, almost a smell, and looked to see about a foot away from where she had been standing a coiled canebrake rattler, head and tail scudded and bright hide glinting in the sun.

The stallion began rearing and snorting, eyes walling, then hopping front to back hooves like a wild horse in the act of being broke. Doll's mare merely lifted her head, frozen and watching the fool dance, then went back to grazing again.

"Hoo now," Daniel said to the horse as he waded out of the water with both hands up and his eyes down at the snake. "Keep a close watch on that fellow there, will you, Doll? Don't let him get away." His pants and shirt were plastered to his slim body and dripping. He stepped wide to the left of the snake and eased up on the frantic stallion and caught his bit shank close to his mouth and led him toward the oak grove, sweet-talking like he would to a woman.

Doll couldn't take her eyes off the snake. She sank to her knees, chin deep, tasting the cool sweet water and smelling the tart willows, eye-level with the snake only a yard or so away on the bank. Rattling like castanets in time to the gurgling of the waterspill over the beaver dam of the creek.

Moments later, Daniel appeared from the oak grove without the stallion. He was holding forth a long stout branch, creeping up on the snake. Standing over it he brought the limb up and slammed down on the teetering pitted head, sending it writhing and wriggling, belly up and over, almost braiding. Then he lifted the snake, a good five feet long, on the end of the limb and pitched it out into a cluster of fan palmettos north of the creek bank. Rattles still sounding, but fading out to a phantom chatter.

Brushing bark from his hands, he started back to the point of the creek where she still knelt, water bobbing under her chin, eyes level with his black boots now.

"You okay out there?" he called.

"Okay," she said, but didn't move.

"I think I'll go on back to Staten Bay then." He laughed. "This place is too rich for my blood."

"Thanks," she said, savoring the cool water and the peace now. The snake had ceased rattling and the drone of locusts filled in. She couldn't come out until Daniel left or he would see her breasts through her wet blue shirt.

"Here," he said, stepping closer and holding out one hand, "let me help you out before I go."

"No, thanks."

"Will you marry me now?"

"No."

"Will you kiss me for saving your life?"

"No."

He turned around, walking toward the oak grove. "You will, boss lady," he called back. "You will and you'll be begging for more." Again he vanished into the oaks, leaving behind an afterimage of his sure solid striding.

He was stuck in her head. She felt her knees would buckle if she tried to stand; it was a delicious, raw feeling that surely must be a sin. "Oh Baa!" Doll said, sighing her sister's nickname. "Baa, I'm drowning."

They had been ten and twelve, the two sisters, racing toward the creek, Doll ahead dropping her skirt to the ground, running out of it and on in only her bloomers and white blouse, and Sheba behind, laughing, scolding. Doll stripped off her shirt, laughing, both of them laughing, and jumped holding to her feet into the pool of black water. Sheba eased along the bank with her skirts lifted, yelling, "Doll Baxter, you're gonna drown if you don't mind out. Hear me?" Doll was hiding behind a fallen pine log, peeping over. Watching her sister drop the skirt and shirt belonging to Doll that she had gathered up along the way, then tip timidly out into the water. "Doll, where are you? Doll?" Suddenly she stepped into a washout and dropped neck-deep with her skirts burbling air and billowing up to the surface like ruffled mushrooms. She shouted, "Oh my God, Doll, I think I'm drowning!" and began slapping at the water and stepping toward the nearest bank which dropped off deeper than the place where she was standing before. Doll watched her go under, then bob up, strangling, and began swimming, hand over hand and straight for her. She knew Sheba would drown her if she tried to rescue her by swimming up to her and grabbing hold. So she sloshed out and up the bank and grabbed her own overskirt and laid it out over the churning water in front of Sheba. She caught it and Doll reeled her in like a giant fish.

The next day was hotter still when Doll rode the woods checking behind the turpentine crew. She rode all morning, looking for them and listening for the sound of their dip irons rapping on their tar buckets, though generally what she would hear if she heard anything at all was their hollering at one another or the old man threatening to whip one of them—doubly troubling in echo. She'd hired on a sorry lot, to be sure. Men who worked cheap, she had learned, turned out cheap work.

A lordgod woodpecker, laying-hen-size, cackled out over the woods, then another. She found fresh signs of where the crew had worked a stand of timber on high ground next to a cypress slew; the slew had gone to crusts of mud from the drought and not one crust had been broken. Any woodsrider knows the signs: a sorry crew will work the trees on higher ground and avoid the mud and moccasins of the slews. Wagon and mule tracks had disturbed the dead pinestraw of the high ground, but the men were long gone.

Even telling herself that maybe the men had moved on to another drift of timber, she knew better. They were gone for good, this time. But they had taken her mule and wagon, plus the tools she had loaned them. Even the empty barrels and what dab of gum they had dipped. Not owning tools themselves should have been a clear sign they were shiftless and lazy. She'd thought that the man having a family meant he'd be dependable, less apt to cause trouble in the flatwoods than a single man would.

She rode on out of the woods to the beaming sand road and headed south a mile or so toward the shack where they'd been batching since they came to work for her. Her scalp steamed under her hair she was so furious.

When she got to the shack, wading the mare through the high grass and weeds of the shallow yard to the sloped wood porch, she found the front door standing open. From where she sat, looking in, she could see a shirt here, a sock there, and centerwise of the front room a charred circle on the floor, meaning they'd almost set the house afire. The heat of the sun, now overhead, made the burned spot seem more ominous—a miracle they hadn't set the dry woods on fire—and strengthened the odor of rancy lard and piss.

She heard what sounded like the neighing of a mule coming from the back yard, and rode on around the house, through the thick grass, dog fennels and briars. Guiding the mare over the scattered clay bricks from the collapsed chimney on the north end of the house, she spied her gum wagon loaded with barrels still hitched to the mule, shifting hoof to hoof in full sun in the heat of the day. Left to thirst or starve to death. She unhitched the mule from the wagon and led him over to the crumbling brick well, drew a bucket of water and set it before him to drink. While he drank, she went over to the rotting corncrib east of the gum wagon, opened the door and picked among the leavings of snaggled corncobs, some with black-hearted kernels, and bundled it out to the mule.

Doll was small but she was strong, and she had dipped gum before. She'd helped her daddy. Or was it the other way around? Now she would need help.

Sheba was ready to quit before her first bucket was full of gum. Actually, she kept lugging it half-full to one of the empty pine-stave barrels on back of the wagon and dumping it.

"You girls don't strain yourselves now." Mrs. Baxter was scooping gum from the bowels of a pine like soup from a tureen, with the same tender concentration. "My daddy, bless his soul, used to say you could tell if a box was cut right by rolling a fifty-cent piece across the bottom of it."

A "box" was a sloped pocket routed out of the fatty heart of the pine trunk, hip-high to a man, for the purpose of collecting the resin or gum seeping and running down from the skinned and streaked patch above it. The whisker-like vee streaks resembled the face of a cat, so came to be called catfaces, a craft born of need, but like the boxes themselves symbolized the turpentine man's industriousness or slack.

Doll's daddy had pulled the very streaks over her head and she had to admit they were as crooked as she'd ever seen.

Sheba set her bucket next to the barrel, took off her straw hat and fanned with it. "Doll, I say we ride over to Mr. Hamilton's and talk to him about who we can hire to dip."

Doll was dipping boxes a few yards from the wagon. "I've already done that, Baa. He's the one sent me to the Dempsys. Just think taxes and dip, Baa." She didn't want to tell them that the men she'd hired, the Dempsys, had stolen the Baxters' tools and she'd had to borrow from another neighbor.

"They seemed like such nice boys," Mrs. Baxter said, holding up her dip iron by the handle for emphasis. "Of course, their daddy didn't look like there was much to him, which just goes to show—a man without a wife..."

"I'll bet she didn't die like they said," said Sheba. "I bet she left the whole bunch."

"Smart woman," said Doll.

"Oh my." Sheba sighed. "Aren't you *tired*, Doll?"

"We just got here two hours ago."

"Well, it feels like ten hours to me."

"Take a break if you want to." Doll lugged over a brimming bucket of gum, set it on the wagon next to a barrel. Then she stepped onto the wagon and dumped it into the barrel. The gum oozed like honey over the barrel bottom. Usually the mule would haul up the wagon on command to accommodate the workers, but Doll, feeling sorry for the mule, had staked him out in the shade after the wagon was situated in the drift of pines they would be working—a kind of triptych of women and timber. On high ground.

"And let you do all the work?" said Sheba. "Of course not." She set out with her round pine-stave bucket swinging.

Mrs. Baxter, stomping wiregrass to keep from tripping on the long stringy blades, getting set to dip from another tree, said, "I'd give a pretty to happen up on that pine that runs green gum, wouldn't y'all?"

"Oh yeah." Sheba set her bucket down, peering around. "I remember that. Don't you, Doll?"

Sheba never could talk while she worked. Doll kept dipping, as example. "I remember."

"Green as a gourd," said Mrs. Baxter. "Never seen anything like it."

"Did you actually see it, Mama?"

Mrs. Baxter stopping dipping, thinking. "No. No, I didn't, come to think of it. Your daddy just told me about it." She laid her iron carefully across the rim of her dip bucket. "Strange how something like that you picture in your mind for so long, afterwhile you believe you really saw it."

"Well," said Doll, "we might just find it if we keep dipping."

"Yes," said Sheba, feebly picking up her bucket and walking toward another tree. "Poor Doll's doing all the work."

33

Thirty minutes later Sheba was sitting against a tree near the wagon, bracing her back. Hat on her lap. She looked like a fat hen setting eggs in the nests of wiregrass. Miserable, duty-bound, wishing to be somewhere else.

Doll would have liked to think that the other two women were lazy or weak but she figured they were smarter than she was, that they would last longer, because of pacing themselves. No time for pacing.

"Keep an eye out where you step, girls—snakes are crawling."

Doll kept dipping, even knowing they were about as far away from getting a load of gum to take to the nearest fire still, Four-mile Still, as they were from catching up the back taxes. Not to mention the mortgage. If not for her sister sitting there under that tree, she would have been tempted to take Daniel Staten up on his offer. Thoughts of him yesterday made her insides nettle. Or was it her blood boiling from the heat? The sticky pale gum had turned dark on her hands, like permanent dirt, and she could barely free her fingers from the sappy wooden handle of the dip iron. Thinking about it made her torment herself with crazy incessant longing to tap her fingers, to scratch her nose where a bead of sweat clung to the tip. Gnats sipped from the bead. Each swing up of the iron to the box cut into the tree, she felt her right elbow wrench; her right shoulder socket felt enlarged by the pain of lifting the bucket. Add to all that the fact that her misery had caused her to forget to look down at the ground for snakes.

"Try not to ruin your hands now, girls," said Mrs. Baxter. She lugged her bucket to the wagon, left arm out for balance, set it on the ground and leaned on the wagon facing Sheba under the tree and Doll dipping gum a few trees east of them.

Doll could tell they were intent on practicing gracious living regardless—porch talk after noon—to the shrill of katydids and drone of locusts and the clicking of crickets in the russet pine straw.

Mrs. Baxter led off: "Aunt Tee used to swear by vinegar. She would dab it all over the tops of her hands to get rid of the liver pieds."

"And couldn't she make the best crabapple jelly!" Sheba replied.

"Bless her heart, she suffered though. That old heart dropsy from sleeping in the moonlight."

"If that was the way of it, Doll would be dead, Mama."

"Doll never sleeps in the moonlight. Do you, Doll?"

"Sometimes I do, Mama. I really don't believe that about heart dropsy."

"Well, it's true and it runs in the family."

"Then it stands to reason," Doll said, stepping to the next tree with her bucket, "that sleeping in moonlight has nothing to do with it."

"I am so hot," said Sheba.

"All this heat," said Mrs. Baxter in a drawn-out longing tone, "it's bound to rain by and by." She stared west, in the direction of the gulf, known locally as Peter's Mudhole.

"I wish it'd come up a shower." Sheba peered up through green pine needles at the sullen white sky. "Course, then we'd have to worry about lightning."

"And us out here in the woods at the mercy of the world!" Mrs. Baxter crossed her arms over her massive bosom. "I do wish the Dempseys had of spared our weather shelters."

For no reason that anybody could ascertain, the Dempseys had kicked or knocked over the many scrap-wood lean-tos scattered about the woods for shelter from sudden violent weather. Though Doll never believed for a minute that the single slanted tacked together four-by-fours really offered much protection, their having destroyed them made her fume. Next time she would hire on a single man. If he rambled, so be it.

"Did Cousin Catherine ever re-marry after her first husband died?" asked Sheba.

"Not as I know of, sugar. She just moved on back home and took care of Aunt Tee till she died."

"I'll be glad when I get married," said Sheba. "I'd marry the man in the moon if he asked me. Long as he didn't have turpentine timber."

"I could use a man around the house myself."

"Mama!" Sheba laughed and flapped her hat at her.

"No," she said, wiping sweat from her red face with the tail of her old faded gray dress, "I won't marry again; I don't trust men anymore." She stood straight, staring off at the neat pinewoods, tree upon tree forming a brown fortress. "Your daddy plain wore me out with his drinking and rambling. But you girls should know he wasn't always like that; he was industrious and true-blue as they come when we first got married. Many a good boy lost heart after the war, I can tell you."

Before she spoke, Doll had considered telling them, then and there, about the mortgage. Get to work! But she could imagine their shocked faces, or worse, her mother making light of the situation—we will manage. She never lost heart, couldn't afford to—this woman was the one who uplifted and held the family together—and Doll would do no different. She would do what she had to for her mother now. She would take hold.

"Let's knock off," she said and walked off toward the wagon, leaving her bucket and dip iron next to the last tree she would ever dip.

The following Sunday, at Bony Bluff meeting house, a thirty-minute buggy ride across the woods from the Baxter place, Doll was sitting between her mother and Sheba when she saw Daniel Staten stroll in during morning preaching and sit directly across the aisle on the men's side. Same white shirt, black string tie, coat, vest and pants he'd worn to the governor's party, as if he'd decided what to wear courting with the same unwavering mindset used to decide which girl he would court.

Doll could tell Sheba saw him too by the way she stiffened and sat straight and smoothed the gathers of her black and pink dress, though her eyes stayed on the weak-eyed young preacher in the pulpit. He was new, and nobody had gotten attached to him yet, which meant that if he didn't put some fire in those sermons, he'd be looking for another church soon. When the congregation stood to sing the last hymn, "When We All Get Together," Sheba's fake-cultured voice rose above the country whang of the other voices. And then her wide-set brown eyes began darting at Daniel Staten, who was standing without singing, not even humbling himself by mouthing the words.

Sheba had pitched a fit when she found out that she'd missed him at the dance, and she was now turning up the volume, intent on making him sit up and take notice.

If not for the fact that Doll had not set out to get him to ask her to marry him, she would have felt guilty for betraying her sister instead of just guilty for not telling her he'd proposed so she could start eating again. How long could she last without eating? She didn't look famished, or even slimmer, only hollow-eyed. Doll felt guilty too for not discussing his "offer" with her mother. If she had, if she had left the matter up to her mother, Mrs. Baxter would have forced her to choose between the pride and virtue of the Baxter household and the homeplace of that very household. No, Doll would have to make this decision on her own—make it and then live with it the best way she could. She knew what her answer would be because there was only one answer.

Fifth Sundays, and on Sundays before and after spring revival, Bony Bluff Church would wrap up the morning service with dinner-on-the-ground. More people than at regular services, coming from far and wide, and all of them bringing food. Except for the bachelors. Like Daniel Staten. Still, he didn't stand out, Doll decided, coming to Bony Bluff on Fifth Sunday. She wondered how early he had to get up that morning to make it to Sunday meeting at Bony Bluff on time. Had he come just to see her? She knew he had. She felt the skin on her forearms and it did feel hot.

After serving their plates from the tables set up outside and loaded with food, Doll and Adam Burkholt sat under one of the old longleaf pines surrounding the lofty frame meeting house, called Bony Bluff. A mellow breeze hummed in the pine tops and scattered their spurred shadows. Legs folded and plates of food on their laps, they watched Sheba in line behind Daniel leaving one of the food tables between the building and the cemetery. Mrs. Baxter, in a happy straw hat with a red rose center of the brim, and Aunt Millie, her sister-in-law, were fanning flies from the food with trimmed palmetto fans, laughing and talking with everybody passing by and dipping from the bowls to their plates, forking pink slices of smoked ham and brown crusty fried chicken. Aunt Millie and Uncle Lester had come on Friday from the Wrights Chapel area, thirty miles west, across the Alapaha River, to help Mrs. Baxter and the girls shore up the old barn and dredge sand from the well. Being smallest and youngest, Doll was the one who was lowered down into the well to dip buckets of sand for the others to haul up.

Not that Doll had minded the icy water or the sand—Sheba said she looked like a mealed fish—but she did mind looking a mess. Today she felt fixed-up: She was wearing an ankle length green skirt cinched at the waist with a wide brown belt borrowed from Brice, her own white blouse with puffy sleeves, green plaid bow at the neck borrowed from Brice, who had begged her to wear her straw hat with the matching band. No, she would not cover her hair.

Holding plates of food out before them, Daniel and Sheba made their way through the crowd, appeared to be heading straight for Adam and Doll. Daniel stopped, eyes locking on Doll. Adam was telling her about a landline case his law firm in Homerville was working on. She bit into the juicy white meat of a wishbone, nodded at Daniel.

Adam quit talking. "Let me know if I'm boring you."

Doll laughed, dropped her chicken to her plate. Watched Adam watching Daniel followed by Sheba after they had passed from her view to the pine shade behind her.

Adam picked up his wedge of cornbread and broke it in half, placed the crusty end on her plate. "Friends?" he asked.

"Friends," she said, smiling and flipping a lock of black hair from her face. "Forever," she added and bit into the bread.

He stared at her, smiling back, then beyond her. "Don't tell me Mr. Staten Bay is courting Sheba?"

"I thought it was Statenville that was named for him."

Adam drank from his glass of tea. "Right. Staten Bay's his plantation." He set his glass down on the mat of dead pine straw and nodded west toward the on-going pinewoods. "South of Statenville, near the Florida line. What he doesn't own already from the Suwannee to the Alapaha, he's looking to own—that's what they say." Again his eyes strayed beyond her, over her head. "I guess you heard about him buying out Uncle Hamilton."

"I heard." She wouldn't say how she'd heard.

"Looks like he's trying to scoot his landlines eastward, buying up the flatwoods."

She looked down at her plate. Waiting.

"So, is he courting Sheba?" Adam asked.

"No. Me."

He set his plate down by his glass. "But you're not marrying, are you?" Sudden katydids shrieked tree to tree, woodside of the iron cemetery fence. "That's what you always say."

"Is that why you never asked me?"

"And what if I asked you now?"

"I'd say friends don't marry friends." She tossed the wishbone over her right shoulder for the raccoons to eat that night, and for luck.

"But it's okay to marry a stranger—like Staten there?" He butted the hot breeze with his dark head.

She started to tell him about the secret mortgage and the not-so-secret back taxes, about Daniel's offer to take over both and take care of her and Mrs. Baxter and Sheba forever. But she didn't want Adam to think she'd been bought, for one thing; and for another she didn't want him to think that for the right price he could have bought her, and that by not buying her, by not coming up with however much money it would take, he was out of the bidding, relenting to the next highest bidder. But finally, when all was said and done, that's exactly what she would want Adam and everybody else to think, rather than guess that at only seventeen she was already going back on her vow never to marry. That every time she saw Daniel Staten she felt flushed all over and more than a little curious about what it would be like to be loved by this rogue-hearted stranger, who even at a distance behind her excited such sinful thoughts. "Yes," she said, "it's okay to marry a stranger."

A young lad in patched gray knee britches, one of Adam's Sunday school students, was sneaking up behind him. He tapped Adam on the head. Adam whirled, still seated on the pine straw, and grabbed the boy around the legs and wrestled him to the ground. Both laughing, wrangling, till Adam let go and the boy loped off, grinning back.

Smoothing his ruffled black hair, Adam turned to Doll. "Tough as a litard knot," he said. "Boys like that are the hope of the New South. Reminds me of that Confederate soldier Cousin Henry Grady made reference to in New York City back before Christmas. Said he was headed home after the war, he and a couple of other soldiers; they'd stopped along the road to parch some corn, and the soldier said, 'You can leave the South if you want to, but I'm going home to Sandersville. I'm gonna kiss my wife and raise a crop, and if the Yankees fool with me anymore I'll whip them again.' Sherman was right there in the audience, and Cousin Grady acknowledged him, said he guessed the old Union general was okay but he had a bad habit of burning.'" Adam laughed.

"Is it true they have electric lights in New York?" Doll asked.

"In the city, yeah. But that wasn't the point; the point was rebuilding what the war destroyed."

"I'm sorry, Adam. I just get tired of hearing about some old war before I was born."

"Barely before you were born. Anyway, it's over and we're on the way up, and I doubt we'll be throwing another party for the governor anytime soon." Adam laughed. "Sick as his wife was the next morning, she insisted they catch the early train. The governor told Uncle Hamilton it looked to him like we were holding our own."

"What did that mean?"

"I guess it meant we can make a living without his cotton mill. Who knows? Maybe he got afraid we might sabotage it." His eyes roved over Doll's head, to where Daniel and Sheba were standing. "So, does Sheba know yet?"

Talk of the governor had squashed Doll's notion of squaring with Adam. "Nobody knows yet. Not even me for sure."

Adam leaned back against the pine trunk, one knee up and the other leg crooked under. "I believe you will ...marry. I believe it'll be some swaggering joker like Staten there."

She leaned forward, shook his slim booted foot and laughed.

"Yeah," he said and didn't laugh. "And he'll make you miserable and you'll come crying to good old dependable Adam."

"I won't...I mean I probably won't marry. I'm too much a mama-girl for one thing." Even saying it she knew she was lying, on the church grounds at that.

"Don't say you won't. I hope you will. If I can't marry you, I'll take you for my mistress. I'll take you any dang way I can get you."

"Adam," Doll squealed and laughed out, "Mama would kill you if she heard you say that." She searched the grounds for her mother, located her and Aunt Millie and a couple of other older women passing through the spiked-iron gate of the cemetery where the sun shone harsh among the leaning shadows of headstones.

"Just remember, a man like that gets bored real easy, even with a beautiful woman like you."

She started to speak, he placed his hand on her arm. "Don't look now, but I think Staten's just broke the news to Sheba that he prefers her pretty sister."

Doll turned quick, regardless of Adam's warning. Sheba was standing with her arms crossed, staring down at the ground while listening to Daniel. Her face was red; she looked pouty-thick and misplaced.

"You think he's telling her about you or just telling her to get lost?" Adam asked.

"To get lost." Doll continued to look at them. "Oh, Baa," she said, guilt-ridden even knowing that she hadn't stolen her big sister's beau—Doll would never have done something like that—and sad because Sheba didn't have the insight to know that Daniel Staten never was interested in her, or the pride to hide her private feelings.

Strangely, on the way home in the buggy with Mrs. Baxter guiding the snuff-brown gelding along the open sunny roads and around shady curves of vine-bound blackgums and scrub oaks, Sheba said nothing about what Daniel had said, but the fact that she didn't even mention his name for the first time in weeks said it all.

Doll felt like crying, but reasoned that even should she refuse to marry Daniel, he wouldn't marry Sheba in her sister's place. Then there was their good strong mother to think of— more important than saving the homeplace, more important than sparing Sheba's feelings. No more scrimping. No more dipping gum.

Still, Sheba's unhappiness stanched Doll's own happiness.

At home, Sheba changed out of her Sunday dress and put on her old yellow gardening dress, the hickory-stripe bonnet and a white apron and headed out the back with her oak stave bucket swinging from the bail.

"Whatever in the world, Sheba!" Mrs. Baxter called through the open kitchen window. "It's Sunday."

Doll standing beside her mother placed a hand on her arm to quiet her. The kitchen still smelled warm of chicken and dumplings and gingerbread taken to Sunday meeting.

"What's going on?" Mrs. Baxter asked Doll.

"She's going to cut the okra."

"I can see that." Then, "Sheba!" out the window.

Stiff, sullen and justified, Sheba started cutting the okra and kept cutting the okra and didn't look up. Moving along the heat-warped row like she was deaf and set in motion and couldn't stop till she reached the end of the row or the end of whatever was playing out in her head.

"Leave her be, Mama," Doll said. "She's just found out that Daniel Staten's not interested in her."

"How do you know?"

"He proposed to me."

She took off her hat. Her faded brown hair was matted to her head and comical looking. "Well, I hope you set him straight." She held her hat to her bosom, rose facing out. "My mercy! Poor Sheba."

In the kitchen Sheba washed the spikes of okra, dried and sliced them in perfect thin rounds, then mealed them and heated up some grease in a black castiron skillet and fried them. A full two-quart blue shoulder bowl of gold-crusted okra, which she sat and ate leisurely at the kitchen table while Doll and Mrs. Baxter rocked on the front porch and thought their own private thoughts but didn't tell. They often talked at night after Sheba went to sleep to keep from riling her. You never could tell what might rile Sheba, but they knew talk of Daniel proposing to Doll would rile Sheba. It could wait till night.

But not that night.

As the sisters lay in the muggy hot dark, that night, in their side by side double beds, Doll heard Sheba sniffling, sobbing into her pillow.

"I'm sorry, Baa," she said low.

Her voice turned Doll's way. "Sorry for what?"

"Not for anything I've done, but I know you had your sights set on Daniel Staten." She figured then that Sheba didn't know he'd proposed to her.

She started crying again, turned away. Muffled crying.

Doll propped on one elbow. "Listen, Baa, you'll marry somebody else, and then you'll laugh about this."

"I won't marry."

Doll laughed. "That's what I always say, not you."

"Well, are you going to marry him or not?"

Doll was wrong about her not knowing. Didn't answer.

"He said you are."

"He said that? I can't believe him!" Doll sat up, silhouetted in silver in the dresser mirror at the foot of her bed: a glowing figment of one-part giddy elation and one-part numb despair. "I never said I would, I said I wouldn't."

43

"But you will." Sheba was no longer crying. "And I'll hate you till my dying day."

"I love you, Baa. I'll always love you. I never set out to betray you with Daniel Staten. I won't say I'm not flattered to have a handsome man like that wanting to marry me, but I never set out to make him like me." Doll bunched her pillow under her head and turned facing her sister's bed. "I would never hurt you if I could help it, you know that."

"Well, you have." Sheba started crying all over again—linking sobs.

"Please quit crying, Baa. Please."

"Not till you swear you won't marry him."

"Answer me one thing, Baa, will you?"

"What?"

"Would you really want to marry him now? I mean, knowing he doesn't want to marry you?"

"No. But I wouldn't want my own sister marrying him either, not after the way he's treated me. Embarrassing me to death in front of my friends."

"Would it have been kinder of him to marry you to keep from embarrassing you?"

Sheba laughed then, actually laughed out in the dark. Doll laughed too, then quit when her sister's laughter turned to violent sobbing, scraped from the heart.

Doll's wedding day broke hot and hazy. By noon, August 2, 1887, she would be Mrs. Daniel Staten, a married woman at seventeen. Leaving the flatwoods on the fringes of the Okefenokee Swamp for the first time, traveling west to Staten Bay, twenty-odd miles that would feel like a thousand miles from home because she would be leaving her mother and Sheba for the first time. With a stranger she didn't particularly like but liked better than she let on to everybody concerned. She had always said she wouldn't marry and now she was marrying. Still, she would hold forever in her heart who she truly was—Doll Baxter.

The wedding was set for eleven o'clock on Saturday morning, at Bony Bluff Church, to allow time for the bride and groom to travel to his home before dark.

Mrs. Baxter had altered her once-white satin wedding gown with its stained appliques of roses to fit her tiny daughter. More than a tuck here and there on the bodice; she'd had to completely remake the dress, had pressed the train to flow like water behind the bride. Not a happy day for Mrs. Baxter or Sheba, but necessary to hold on to the old homeplace. Leave it at that.

Finally Doll had confessed to both women about the mortgage, but only after she'd told Daniel she would take him up on his offer.

This time when he had come, in the cool of the evening, after suppertime at the Baxter's, Doll and Sheba were picking peas. A long time hearing him coming, like before, and when Sheba saw him clear the blind of pines and suddenly appear on the stallion in the dusky open stretch of road in front of the house, she simply picked up her bucket of crisscrossed peas and walked down the row to the back of the house. Set the bucket on the porch and went out to the barn to check on her bear.

Mrs. Baxter had gone to take cornbread and pot liquor with fresh field peas, just coming in, to a sickly neighbor lady, so Doll was alone when she took her bucket and headed out of the garden and across the yard. He had stopped at the gate, still sitting on the edgy black stallion with about a zillion yellow flies swarming around them. Doll set her bucket down and leaned on the gate, waiting while he circled the horse in the road to calm him. Lightning bugs twinkled like stars in the woods across the road and the cooling pines smelled tart. Whiffs of bear came only at intervals when the breeze switched from east to west. The white sand of the road seemed to have soaked up the heat and glow of the sun that day.

When at last Daniel had the horse aimed in Doll's direction, she spoke. "I'd ask you in but Mama's not here." She smushed a yellow fly siphoning blood like a vampire under her chin.

"Good evening to you too, Doll." He took off his hat.

"Good evening, Mr. Staten."

The horse swung his head and champed at the bit, jangling it. Daniel snatched the reins, circled, came back. "Well?"

"Yes."

"Yes you'll marry me or yes I can come in."

"Yes, I'll marry you and no you can't come in. Sheba's out at the barn, all upset over this."

"It never was a contest, she has to know that."

"She does. She's just hurt."

The yard was growing up in shadows, closing in, and a whippoorwill struck up a steady harking, distant but distinct across the woods. The horse whickered. A rumble of buggy wheels sounded down the road out of the south.

"That'll be Mama," Doll said.

"I guess I'd better come in then."

"No. I'd rather you didn't. I'll tell her myself."

"So, Doll," he said, "when are we getting married?"

The buggy was getting closer, bucking over ruts and rattling like a peddler's wagon with pots and pans hung on the sides.

"I'll talk to Mama and let you know."

Daniel turned the stallion, trotting north. But when he got to the start of the pines at the north corner of the new fence, he turned again, galloping the horse with glaring eyewhites, and skidded to a stop at the gate. "You won't be sorry," he said and swung down, holding to the reins and leaning over the gate, close in her face as if to kiss her, but all at once the horse reared, yanking him back. He laughed, wheeled and placed one boot in the stirrup with the other following, hopping along, then swung up again. "You don't reckon my horse is smelling bear, do you?" He laughed, sawing back on the reins. "Maybe he's just trying to warn me about getting married after all this time."

He didn't wait for an answer, just trotted up the road in the stallion's fusing tracks.

Again, Doll felt that giddy elation mixed with numb despair. When he'd leaned over the gate—to kiss her?—she had felt that heat like sunshine coming off of him.

She went up on the porch, down the hall and into the front room on her right, lit the lamp on the table by the door and waited for her mother to unhitch the buggy and send the mare out to graze the sparse but dewy grass beyond the lot. Doll turned as the lamp flared and saw Sheba sitting in the cattycornered chair by the farthest front window over the porch.

Doll knew she had heard. "Sheba, I have to marry him. For us. All of us."

"Do me a favor and let me just guess." Sheba's chin was resting in one hand, elbow propped on the stuffed chair arm, staring out the window where white moths floated through to the furry yellow light. She had on her long white nightgown and her dark hair around her face was damp. She looked pure as Mary, mother of Jesus. Her coarse face shone of soap-washing and youth. Pretty skin on a not-so-pretty girl.

"Please, Baa. Please forgive me."

"Yoo hoo, I'm home," Mrs. Baxter called from the back porch and came on up the hall and into the parlor removing her straw hat.

"Mama," Doll said, "come sit down."

"What's going on?" She plopped into the chair next to the table and lamp and placed her hat on her lap. Her tan-checked skirt and bulk overflowed, covering the worn tapestry.

"I'm marrying Daniel Staten," Doll said, eyes roving from one woman to the other. Tonight they didn't look alike. Sheba looked like somebody else, a stranger, or the way she might look dead in her casket.

Mrs. Baxter sat forward. Silent, figuring Sheba.

"I want you both to know why." And then Doll told them about the mortgage, which seemed not to surprise Mrs. Baxter, and Sheba appeared not to care.

When Doll was done, Sheba got up and walked out and down the hall to the bedroom she shared with her sister, went inside and closed the door softly.

Mrs. Baxter followed her, went into her room and came out and on into the kitchen where she lit the lamp on the square table in the middle of the room. When Doll came through the door, she saw her mother slicing the jellyroll she'd baked that afternoon, then sitting with a fork and saucer, eating. "Poor Sheba," she said low, forking the cake to her mouth. It was filled with blackberry jam they'd put up the week before.

Doll sat across from her. "What did she say?"

"Nothing, which says more than anything she might have said."

Doll started to get up.

Mrs. Baxter stopped her. "Let her sleep. This is one of those things only sleep or a good jellyroll will cure."

After they had got ready for bed and snuffed the lamps in Mrs. Baxter's bedroom, she said, "I wish you'd have let me handle this."

Doll was lying beside her under the gauzy white tent of mosquito netting. Always afraid of the dark, she had started slipping into her mother's room when she was a child, and still, most nights, she would sneak out to sleep with her mother after Sheba fell asleep. This night she hadn't had to sneak. "And how would you have handled it—what would you have said?" Doll asked.

"I'd have said, 'Mr. Staten, I'll have you know my daughter is not livestock to be bargained for. Come courting her proper or don't come courting atall.'"

Doll, speaking to the dark, said, "But really it all amounts to about the same thing, doesn't it? I mean, a woman marries for love or for convenience, but still it boils down to the same thing."

"I've seen people who married for love start hating each other in a couple of months. And I've seen people fall in love who married for convenience. Six of one, half-dozen of the other. It's chancy either way."

In summer, they always threw open the wood shutters after dressing for bed, swapping off their safety from uncertain human menaces, certain snakes and mosquitoes, for a bit of air. Now the mosquitoes whined and went silent in the folds of net. Through the windows each side of the bed came the call of an owl backed by the seesawing ring of katydids. Kerosene fumes and smoke lay thick on the smothery air, but the rough muslin sheets smelled of sun, felt cool when Doll moved an arm or leg to a fresh spot.

"Well, I feel a whole lot more sensible marrying for convenience," Doll said.

"Seems like a fine enough man, this Daniel Staten. Quit wiggling. At least I'm not worried about him taking you off to starve. It's like they say—money's just a fact of life and not all that important if you have plenty. Still, it's all a matter of balance."

Doll propped on one elbow, gazing at the ghost of her mother's familiar bulk encompassed by the net. "I'm coming home, you know that. I mean, he said he was getting me a fancy way to go and I could come and go as I like."

"That's how come I'm not crying the blues over this marriage; I know if things don't go to suit you, you'll come home if you have to walk." She shuffled and shifted onto her side—bed frame groaning—facing the far wall. "Now go to sleep," she said.

"Mama, I don't think you're supposed to say that to me about coming home." Doll laughed. "I think you're supposed to say, 'you made your bed now lie in it.'"

"That's the good in getting old: You have more authority, don't give a hang about the rules. Another thing, you can eat all you want because fat looks as good as skinny on an old woman." She moaned. "But I do wish I hadn't eaten that whole jelly roll. I am a weak woman. Go to sleep."

"One more thing," Doll said, knowing now that she had worried her mother awake, she would talk her younger daughter to sleep. "What about the mortgage and taxes if I leave Daniel?"

"So, the old place goes. We'll move in with Lester and Millie, we'll go begging if we have to. I could use a change ever now and then."

"I don't think I could stand to lose this place. I mean, I'll be gone but I need to know this land stays in our family. That I can come home when I take a notion."

Mrs. Baxter threw her night voice over her left shoulder. "You want to live a short sad life, start giving in to the notion that there are things you can't stand."

The morning of the wedding, Daniel arrived on his black stallion, wearing a dark coat and gray-striped trousers, black bow tie and white shirt, bringing with him the same wagon drawn by the brindle mule-faced gelding that had brought the lumber to mend Mrs. Baxter's fence. One of Daniel's hired men, Oscar Bowen, a swarthy, stocky man, in a brown felt hat, was driving the wagon.

Almost everybody in the flatwoods showed up at Bony Bluff for the wedding—all of Sheba's friends and Doll's friends and Mrs. Baxter's friends, plus family. But only Oscar Bowen attended for Daniel Staten. As if, Doll thought, this was business, not pleasure, and not to be made much over. And it *was* business. She wouldn't have married him for love—if it was love—because of her sister.

In spite of the heat Doll felt shivery, walking up the aisle with Adam, whose face was red with nerves. Shoe soles scraping on the hardwood floor. Maybe she shouldn't have asked him to give her away; maybe she should have done like Mrs. Baxter said and asked Hamilton Fletcher, but she'd asked Adam to include him and to announce publicly that all along they'd just been friends and not lovers like everybody thought. This whole wedding suddenly seemed so wrong, what did one more shouldn't-have matter? A man in the congregation cleared his throat as if to correct her.

At the altar, decorated with woods ferns and white candles in branching wrought-iron candelabras, shaped like trees, Daniel was waiting on the preacher's right, Sheba and Brice, dressed all in pink, on his left. Doll and Adam were getting closer, passing the standing congregation. Mrs. Baxter on Doll's right was smiling, turned toward the bride, almost there, almost hung for her crime of agreeing to marry Daniel Staten.

Why was he marrying her anyway? She had her reasons and excuses but what were his really?

Their shoe soles stopped scraping on the floor. Adam and Doll were facing the preacher, whose thin lips were moving way too fast, it seemed to Doll. Getting it said and over with.

"Who gives this bride in marriage?" he asked.

"I do," Adam said and kissed Doll's cheek and lingered with his left arm about her waist.

Daniel with his hands clasped behind hesitated as Adam turned and sat next to Mrs. Baxter, then he stepped forward, green eyes pinned on Doll even while repeating his vows. There were comb-marks in his coppery hair. In a minute, in less than a minute, he would be kissing her for the first time. She thought about Adam's kiss on the cheek, other kisses on her lips, preparing herself for her first time being kissed by Daniel Staten, this tall handsome stranger with the deep-set eyes and shelf brow. She thought about Sheba on her right, slightly behind, watching her and hating her. Then she was yanked away from all thoughts, feeling shock, stabbed by light, as Daniel hugged her to his hard body and covered her mouth with his, parting her teeth with his tongue. She bit it. His eyes flew wide, he let go of her and covered his mouth with one hand. They stood staring at each other until somebody in the congregation laughed, then they marched up the aisle, side by side but not touching.

"You bit me," he whispered.

"How dare you kiss me like that in public?" They were at the door now, crowd following, laughing.

"You didn't bite your lawyer."

"Adam is too much of a gentlemen to do something like that in public."

"*In public?*"

At home, with the wedding guests eating, laughing, talking throughout the house, Doll changed clothes in the traveler's room, north end of the front porch.

Sheba unbuttoned the numerous tiny buttons on back of the wedding gown, then buttoned Doll into the new pink-sprigged white dress Mrs. Baxter had made for her. It had a wide pink satin sash that tied on the side and pink satin bows on caught-up scalloped gathers in back.

Sheba turned to leave the small stifling room. She looked thicker in her pink glossy cotton dress, though frail to the point of sickly. Her pale skin was flushed, red as a stove flue on fire.

The narrow rope bed was full of dress. Children were chasing and squealing around the house.

"Baa," Doll said, "you know why I had to marry him. Just say you understand."

Sheba came back and stood before her. "I don't hate you if that's what you think."

Doll hugged her, felt her stiff body give, her arms going up to hug Doll too. Felt her shaking. "I am sorry, I'm truly sorry," Doll said. "You have to know that I wouldn't have married him for love if I'd been in love with him. I wouldn't have done that to you."

They both cried, hugging each other and swaying. "I do believe that," Sheba said.

"Mama makes it sound like some kind of adventure if we lost the place, saying we'd go live with her kin. But you and I both know she doesn't really feel that way. She'd feel like a beggar. She'd go on laughing like she does, making light of it, but her pride would be hurt."

Sheba stepped away, wiping tears from her eyes with the back of her hand. "Are you scared?"

"Of Daniel, no. I could do a whole lot worse and I won't lie. I'm every bit as attracted to him as you and a dozen other girls I could name. But I am a little afraid of why he married me and what comes next, and I'm afraid of going so far away from home."

Sheba hugged her again. "You can come home and we'll go visit you."

"I'm sorry about your bear."

52

The beekeepers had come yesterday and taken him to the Swamp.

"He'll come back; really I'm not crying about that bear or even Daniel Staten. It's just that it's hard being ugly." She cried harder.

Doll laughed, then cried, held her away to look at her miserable face. "You're not ugly, Baa, you're not. Is Mama ugly? You look just like her."

"Doll, hurry up!" Brice opened the door. Her wide smile drooped when she saw them crying. "Oops!" she said and closed the door.

Sheba laughed. "Go on. Finish dressing. Once you're out of here I'm gonna look a whole lot better."

Doll stood before the tilted mirror of the small oak dresser while Sheba tied her sash. Then tied back her long black hair with a length of pink ribbon left over from the sash. Done, Sheba stood behind her—a head taller and twice as broad—looking with her in the mirror. "I do wonder sometimes where you came from, whose cabbage patch."

They both laughed.

"I don't have to tell you how proud I've always been of you. You know I'm the one named you Doll, and you know how come—I had a real-live doll baby, and I still do."

"Baa, I don't think I'm pretty; I don't even think pretty is all that important. But I believe it's just as hard to be pretty as ugly. I mean, people don't always like you for the right reasons if you're pretty. Leaves you forever trying to figure who to trust and how to get people to take you serious." What Doll had just said was true, but it was true too that she wouldn't want to be less pretty; she would have no idea how to even up the odds, especially male to female, without her looks.

Beyond the door, Mrs. Baxter called out in her cheeriest, high-pitched voice. "Yoo-hoo! Where's the bride?" and rapped twice on the door. "Let's eat, girls."

"Baa, will you see to it that Brice gets her book back?" Doll said. "It's *Jo's Boys*, on the dresser in our bedroom."

"After I read it." Sheba clapped the puffed sleeves of Doll's dress, then squeezed her shoulders. "This thing with Daniel Staten did open my eyes to one thing."

"What, Baa?" Doll sat on the edge of the bed and began slipping on her brown hightops.

"Doll, don't wear those old shoes with that dress."

"I have to; they're my something old." Doll finished tying her right shoe, put it down and picked up her left. "Not really. I don't care about that. I just need to wear these shoes; I can't think if my feet hurt."

"Honey, you're not going to war," Sheba said. "Were you really mad as you acted about him kissing you in church like that? And why was he covering his mouth?"

"I bit his tongue."

Sheba laughed. "His *tongue*? How...why?"

"I don't know. I thought maybe you would know—I mean why somebody would stick his tongue in your mouth?"

Sheba's face was even redder than normal. "I've never heard of such."

"I know about...you know...from the cows and all, but I never figured on some man sticking his tongue in my mouth."

"Doll, I don't think you're supposed to bite anything. I mean, he's your husband and you just don't go around biting your husband's tongue."

"I figure he did that to show he can rule over me. I'm not taking anything off of him, Baa."

"Okay, so you are going to war." Sheba went to the mirror, leaned in and twisted the hank of hair on her right temple. "His *tongue*? That does it! I think I'll be an old maid teacher like Miss Muffet who used to stay in this very room."

Doll laughed. "God, if she'd ever heard us calling her that!"

Sheba laughed. "I'm serious, Doll. If a man likes me, he can come courting. If I like him, he can keep coming. I might marry, I might not." She spotted Doll watching her in the mirror with those pure blue eyes, doing a quick tally of all the boys her sister had been in and out of love with and starved for since she'd started walking. But for now Sheba was back to her naturally happy self—comfortably out-of-love, free to take off her corset and eat like a preacher.

After a dinner of chicken purlow, cooked by the men and women of the church in the iron wash pot in the back yard, everybody, laughing and talking, followed Daniel and Doll out to the new raw-pine gate.

Dubiously shy, sullen or patient, Oscar was sitting with his elbows on his knees on the front bench of the old wagon pulled up to the left of the gate. The brim of his brown felt hat pulled low against the sun balancing on the peak of the shingle roof and bronzing the flat frowning face with its radiating mouth wrinkles marked by brown tobacco juice. The drab white gelding stood dozing, Oscar-like, in the droning heat with one hind leg cocked. Without batting an eye, he switched his tail at the flies on his swayed back. Mrs. Baxter's old hump-lidded wood trunk looked strange in back of the wagon. Right side of the gate, a bright-eyed neighbor boy stood holding the reins of the sleek black stallion, liquid fire in the sunshine and perfect foil for the mulish gelding and man.

Doll started through the gate, behind Daniel, then came back to the rectangular shadow cast by the long low house, and going down the line, kissed and hugged Brice, Sheba and Adam. "I'll be listening out," he whispered, holding her about the waist and grinning. "Silly!" she said and laughed with a note of near-crying, then started toward the gate again. She looked back at her mother standing on the porch, fanning her rosy smiling face, and waved. Mrs. Baxter waved her away with a pleated fan and stepped down the sun-purged hall. One more minute and Doll would be crying; Brice and Sheba were already crying, huddling close, while the church ladies shushed and shamed them.

Daniel, minus his coat and tie, but wearing his black hat, was waiting on the other side of the wagon to help her up on the bench next to Oscar. Suddenly she felt slapped by the fact that he meant for her to ride like the old trunk in the old wagon, while he strutted alongside on the smart stallion.

"You ride in the wagon," she said to Daniel, wheeled and took the reins of the stallion from the boy holding them. "I'll ride your horse."

Everybody in the yard and on the porch got still and quiet. Somebody laughed, then another. Daniel smiled, tipped his hat to them as if Doll were joking.

"Get in the wagon, Doll." Daniel chuckled low, stepping off the distance between him and his new bride. "You've seen firsthand how crazy this horse can get."

She looped the reins over the stallion's sculpted head, hiked her white dress up above her shapely dark knees, stuck her left brown hightop into the stirrup and swung up. The horse stepped back, reared, then settled under her like a shook rug.

"Hoo now," said Daniel, approaching the stallion with both hands out. "Get down, Doll, before you break your neck."

"I can handle him," she said and turned him circling in the road to distract and defuse him. She could feel the power building and surging beneath her, the lit stallion set to blow like dynamite.

"Doll," Daniel said, easing toward her still. "You've seen how he can act up, now get down."

"Oh that," she said, pointing the stallion northbound, prancing but on hold. "He ripped up our fence trying to get away from my pet bear in the barn. Mama and Sheba were ashamed to tell you we'd trapped a bear."

Chapter 3

In the lead by several yards, on the parched dirt road west toward Statenville, she would look back and see Oscar Bowen scratching his shaggy brown hair under his hat, smirking between spits off the slow rattley wagon. And Daniel looking off at the deep shady turpentine woods on his right as if taking keen interest in the fresh vee streaks cut in the amber catfaces to make the gum bleed down into the boxes of the pine trunks. Dust churning beneath the wobbling, squeaking wheels of the wagon. The sun was now in their eyes, shining like a ball of fire set to roll down the clear open road. Steel-rimmed wheel tracks were woven and overlaid from the time of the last rain, from the last wagon along the road. Wide shallow ditches gave way to the everlasting rise of tall pines; vine-tented slews and branches were announced by the ringing of katydids and the chirruping of frogs, phasing out to the phantom clicking of grasshoppers in the dry weeds and grass, and always, always, that lonesome song of crickets. They passed through Needmore and the crosstie camp, men and oxen about to knock off for Sunday after a full week of hauling logs from the woods to the sheds for hand hewing. And out over the woods, like spotty wildfires, smoke rose from the random floating sawmills. This was still familiar territory for Doll; she could close her eyes and find her way home by smell— sharp pine and snuffy deer tongue. Soon all that would change.

At Tom's Creek, with the sun at four o'clock, Doll loped the stallion down the steep ditch next to the wood bridge, checked the reeds and watergrass for moccasins and rattlesnakes and dismounted. Two hours straight riding in the sun had left her stiff and shaky and drained. She led the horse over cobbles of cracked mud to the edge of the black water and its skirling minnow bugs and let him drink till his head lifted and stayed for a couple of minutes. Then she led him upstream, under the wooden bridge, to a clear spring dribbling from rocks and sand between the crossed bracing of thick hewed struts. She geared her dress tail up, tucking it into her pink waistband, knelt and wet her handkerchief in the spring, swabbed her face. Then she scooped water in her cupped hands and drank, hearing above the dabble of water the wagon approaching with its buck and trundle rhythm.

From underneath the bridge she watched the breaching of horse and wagon pass overhead, then stepped out to see the two men seated in the wagon staring straight ahead. She swung back into the saddle and trotted up the bank and along the dry grass shoulder till she drew level with Oscar Bowen. Still smirking, but on the verge of grinning, dingy brown eyes staring beyond at the sun floating above the pine tops. It was impossible to tell how old he was but Doll guessed thirty, thirty-five, not all that old but hard-worked and sun-cured, tough as cowhide. Daniel reached back and picked up a buggy jug from the bed of the wagon, pulled the stopper and brought the spout of the jug to his lips. The pottery jug bellied out from a flat base and was the very dun color of the dirt spinning to dust under the wagon wheels.

Doll galloped on ahead with pink ribbons flying, dress tail up above her knees. Getting farther and farther away from home and her mother. What would happen if she hauled on the reins and headed back home? Nobody could stop her, for a fact. She may not have known that if she hadn't taken the stallion and forced Daniel to ride in the wagon. *The wagon* which symbolized his first in a string of attempts to make of her a settled married woman, contented or discontented with being set up in a house on Staten Bay, birthing babies, while Mr. Daniel Staten gallivanted about unchanged.

Besides, he had lied about getting her "a fancy way to

go."

From a dot, to a smoking box, to a wagon chased by dust from under the sun, came the first travelers Doll met on the way to her new home: dray horse, man and woman up front and about a dozen white-headed cracker children swapping benches on back for a closer look at the beautiful black-haired girl on the headstrong black stallion. Piled high on the rickety wagon were beds and chairs, pots and pans, folded quilts and a slat pen full of frantic butternut chickens. A crosscut saw was strapped to the outer sideboards of the wagon, and a ringstraked goat teetered behind on a short rope leash.

The woman sat forward, clutching the closure of her bonnet under her chin. "You don't look out, honey, the Indians'll get you," she called out.

"No ma'am," Doll said. "What Indians are left are in the Okefenokee."

"That's where we're heading," said one of the boys on back.

"Pa's going to haul timber off Billy's Island," said another one, standing tall.

"There's a treasure in timber there, that's a fact," Doll said, adding, "problem is, all that water."

The man tipped his hat—"How do?" and drove on. "Lil ole gal like that don't know nothing," he said to the wife when he figured Doll was out of hearing.

"Let's go back to Moultrie, Mama?"

Doll rode on, listening to the quarrelsome wagon wheels and meek voices fading out behind her. She had to laugh to herself, thinking about the vast lonesome swamp wilderness with its floating peat islands, a few miles southeast of Fargo, still fifteen miles or so for the travelers. Rumor, myth or fact Doll couldn't say, but the Okefenokee, so named by the Indians, meaning Land of the Trembling Earth, had been home to Indians since 2500 B.C. All 400,000 acres within the bowl-shaped depression of islands, prairies, pine forests and choking vegetation. Gators, bears, snakes and panthers could be dangerous for a fact, but the few Indians there now were Creek

Indians, as harmless but mischievous as children. One might sneak up to a house in the middle of the night and snitch a sack of cornmeal or flour, but after the final skirmishes at Troublesome and Cow Creek, in Echols County, in the late 1830s, those who were left had been humbled and driven into the Okefenokee for the duration.

The wild tales of those battles would outlast them.

"Men and their wars!" she said, but checked behind her for reassurance that her husband was on the lookout and was reminded of women and their fears.

On the outskirts of Statenville, passing a train depot and a couple of shanties with barking dogs, the stallion neighed, trotted faster. "Hoo now," she said, and the stallion slowed, but champed at the bit. The bridle jangled. She waited for the wagon to come up alongside. Staying to the left, on Oscar's side, with her sour-faced groom on the right, staring right. She knew they had only a couple more miles before they would reach Staten Bay. Already the sun was going down, but the heat seemed to simmer from the blistered earth, the body of the stallion steamed and the air lay still and thick following the wind of the stallion's own making.

The mule-faced gelding plodded sensibly on, an inherent pacing gait, undeterred by the dogs and people gathering along the road to watch. A black and tan hound waggled out from the yard of a log house with double galleries. The stallion shied and pranced, and Doll patted his neck and leaned down and talked to him low. It seemed ages since she had spoken. She felt the first real pangs of homesickness—too far to go back, too close to go on.

At the crossing, in Statenville, barely more than a crossing itself, but boasted as the county seat, people stood in the sharp leaning shadows of the two-story white courthouse, and in front of the steep-gabled post office across from it. Cow followed cow down a narrow tramped out path through the courtyard, coming together under the great live oaks for the night.

From the courthouse porch, an old man with a walking

stick called out to Daniel. "That the new bride, boy?"

Everybody laughed. Daniel tipped his hat. Doll sat higher on the horse, feeling more naked than she ever had on washdays when she and Sheba would bathe in the leftover sun-warmed wash water in the back yard.

"Looks like you come by a wife but lost your horse," somebody else said.

"Y'all go on about your business," Oscar spoke up in a spit-thick voice.

"Well, she's a pretty little thing," said a woman in a bonnet to two other women.

"She can flat ride too," said a man. "See that horse sweating?"

"How'd you come by the horse, honey?" asked a toothless man walking along the string of frame stores, left of the crossing.

Oscar veered south and whipped the horse up from a dead mope to a slow walk. He clucked air in at the corners of his chew-tobacco lips. "Hum up there," he said. The stallion with its head high pranced in a circle as if to exhibit the bride, then fell in line with the wagon—hooves smartly clopping, tail raised to the spectators.

Daniel sat slumped and sullen till they reached the edge of town, then sat up and shouted, "We're getting off to a good start, Mrs. Staten."

Doll leaned forward and jabbed the stallion's tight undersides with her heels. He shot off like a star. Bugs beat against her face and body and snagged in the webbing of her hair. No dust, which meant that the southwest section of Echols County had had rain while the southeast section had not, which meant that she had now passed some God-mark delineating the known from the unknown, home from not-home. The sun showed hot and bold across a field of corn, ears already filled out and turning down, then hid quick behind the maze of huge hill pines where night would come stalking like a panther. Smells of cooling earth like green peanuts. Already the road appeared closed up ahead. No houses, left or right. She looked back and saw the wagon angling down a ditch at the creek she had just passed.

She slowed the horse for the wagon to catch up, thinking what her daddy would have done if her mother had humiliated him by taking his bay gelding and galloping ahead with her knees showing. She could not imagine it. Only her mother sitting at home, keeping house and children, while Wayne Baxter loafed and drank with his buddies off hours from the crosstie camp where they worked. She tried to imagine other women she knew from church, all over the flatwoods, behaving as she had done and was doing and found not one with enough spunk, or maybe foolishness. Well, she'd never intended to marry in the first place.

"This is business," she said to the stallion.

Developing out of the dusk, two timber carts drawn by six mules each rumbled out of the south. Double wheels at their top-most points high as the head of the stallion and groaning under sixteen-foot logs. The ends of the massive pine logs, hanging from the carts, looked limber as switches. When the two men driving the carts got to the wagon, they stopped to talk to Daniel, then the carts rolled on.

Eastside of the road, bound by blackgums, scrub oaks and old-growth pines, stood a bare-dirt settlement of shacks, Negroes and dogs rambling the run-together yards. The air smelled suddenly of brass. Of brass and wild meat in the frying pan and moss smoke drifting from random yard fires. The yatter of women's voices, grownups' scolding, children laughing, a baby crying, harmonica music and a cow bell. A large brown woman in a brown rag dress was drawing water from the red brick well, front and center of the camp. She set the bucket on the rim of the well and called out in a guttural voice, "Mr. Daniel, that you?" and craned her neck to better see.

A man stepped up, said to the woman, "Some lady riding his hoss," then hollered out, "You snakebit, bossman?"

Daniel bellowed from the wagon, "Not exactly, Isaac."

Rawboned and hollow, the bandy fice and heart-faced curs came on, yipping at the spinning wagon wheels and wambling between the legs of the horses. Genuinely put out, Oscar reached beneath the bench and hauled out a braided cowhide whip, hied it above his head and brought it down off the side of the wagon with a loud crack. The dogs yelped and scuttled back toward the shacks with their tails tucked. Daniel didn't even blink—green eyes lit, chin lifted, a slight smile. He looked satisfied at having arrived home at last, somewhat defeated but home at last.

Ancient live oaks on the other side of the road were hung with smoky tatters of moss, sheer as lace in the afterlight of sundown. Then the rail fences, miles of rail fence, chest-high to a man and rickracked, and over the fences, acres of uniform, tasselling corn running out to pure green where the starring sky met the treeline of the Alapaha River. Then abruptly, cotton: clean hoed middles between thistle-like shrubs, all the way south to a pine-lined lane leading to a large white farmhouse with lights burning in many windows. Lowing cattle with white faces and solid red ranged the edges of the east woods, some straggling across the road and along the lane. A small log cabin sat diagonally in a clearing facing the lane to the big house. On the low porch of the cabin, nearly swallowed up by shadows, stood a stooped woman in a bonnet. She waved. Oscar nudged his hat high on his pale lined forehead—his exposed skin was dark and tough as saddle leather—and turned the horse down the lane.

Everywhere there seemed to be somebody doing something: four strapping Negro men were walking up the lane, one with a bush hook, two with grubbing hoes, and another with a railsplitting maul. Their muscular arms were hinged and swinging from blocky shoulders. Other Negro men and boys were leading horses and mules and yoked oxen toward a large barn leftside of a cluster of live oaks and the house. The lane branched south past the barn and on, with a stop-off at a one-room raw-lumber commissary, dimly lit. Men, women and children, all Negroes, idled from the porch to the yard. A large woman who looked formed of circles—eyes, nose, cheeks, head and body—wearing a red headrag and a bustle of buttocks, crossed the commissary yard lugging a gallon syrup can and set out toward the lane. In the sideyard of the big house, a small black boy with a square head was splitting stove wood with an axe. More misses than hits and the stood stick of wood would tumble with each blow.

The woman with the syrup can stopped, eyed the boy, then waddled toward the gate and through it and turned along the south side of the house and stopped again in the woodpile where ricks of firewood stood drying in. The boy leaned on the axe, then ducked as her hand flew up and caught him in the jaw. She walked away with an air of having finished her business, and the boy started chopping again.

As the wagon reached the four men walking up the lane, they spoke to Daniel. "Bossman," they said and kept walking, not even glancing at Doll and the stallion.

"Come Monday, y'all get what fodder you can in now," Daniel said. "Rain last week's a good sign we might get more."

Doll didn't know what she had expected but she never expected to see so many people at Staten Bay. Especially Negroes. In the flatwoods, houses were scattered out—some with big families, most with big families—but the only time she saw what she considered a crowd was at Sunday meetings and other social gatherings. And the only Negroes were the turpentine hands, who by day kept to the woods, and at night kept to the camps, territory off limits to Doll, who rode the woods and kept her distance as they did.

To her knowledge, Staten Bay, one of the few plantations in the county, was the only plantation with a Negro quarters. But in most of the other little, surrounding towns, usually on the south end, turpentine and farm-labor quarters were commonplace, with subtle but certain demarcations—porches suddenly running out to stoops, maybe—designating white from Negro row shanties. The most common race lines drawn, however, like fences or trenches, were the railroad tracks.

She could now see beyond the rail-fenced yard that the house stood a good three feet off the clean swept dirt. Leaf piles about the yard were smoldering to level red ash. A wide open hall divided the house in exact half, and there were one, two, three candles burning on tables, plus several hanging lamps backed by glimmering brass plates. Who had lit them? She could smell burning oak and either roast beef or pork and wondered who was cooking.

She felt lost. She didn't know a single person on this strange place. Oscar and Daniel no longer seemed like strangers, and that was the strangest feeling of all.

The wagon pulled up to the gate. Doll sat the stallion next to the wagon and waited. Eyes traveling point to point, ears plugged into the combined sounds of laughing, talking, low-ing, stamping, chopping. A wagon with a brace of gum bar-rels labored down the lane and south along the fork, loading the air with tangy raw gum.

"Your new home, Mrs. Staten," Daniel said and stepped down from the other side of the wagon.

Oscar eased down, holding his bent back.

A man in indigo overalls came out of the barn, walking pigeon-toed, and headed their way. He looked to be about thirty, abnormally tall with a long body and long face and droopy, pale eyes. Lightning bugs sparkled under the oaks as he waded through them. "Mr. Daniel," he said, smiling. "I see you made it back." His voice was meek and his face too mild for his stature.

"Joe," said Daniel, walking around the front of the wagon. "Meet my new wife."

"How do," said Joe and reached for the stallion's reins.

"Pleased to meet you, Joe," said Doll, springing in the saddle she felt grown to.

"You don't have to help Mrs. Staten down, Joe," Daniel said. "She can do for herself."

Doll swung down. Handed the reins to Joe. Her knees al-most buckled, her behind was numb.

A tall buxom woman wearing a black skirt and white blouse stepped out on the porch and stood slant-eyed and smiling with her hands clasped behind. Her soft brown hair was parted in the middle and loosely bundled on back of her head. The cream skin of her face glistened with sweat. She looked older than Doll but younger than Daniel, Doll thought, then looking closer decided it was impossible to tell because she was so large and queenly and serene.

Daniel opened the gate and Doll stepped through and started up the red brick walk.

"Joe, how bout giving Oscar a hand with that trunk, will you?" Daniel said. "And I'd appreciate it if you'd wash the stallion down before you knock off."

Doll lifted her skirt high, going up the tall doorsteps. Through the door-sized windows, draped with sheer white curtains, she could see a lit room on the right with a fluffy high bed draped in white mosquito netting. The covers were turned back and there were four pillows plumped and resting against a spindled brass bedstead. Through the net-draped windows on the left was another bedroom with a high bed crowned with a hoop of gathered mosquito netting. That room was lit only by the citronella candles in the hall. The lemon scent lurked in the smothery light, along with the smell of roast beef and onions.

"Doll, this is Maureen," Daniel said, stepping around Doll and standing shoulder to shoulder with the dreamy-eyed woman. "Maureen's the best cook and housekeeper in these parts," he added.

"Maureen," said Doll.

"Mrs. Staten." Her voice was rich but husky as a man's.

"Just Doll," corrected Doll.

"You boys can carry that trunk on in my room," Daniel said to the Oscar and Joe bringing the trunk up the steps.

Doll turned. "I'll have my own room, please," she said. "This house looks like it's big enough for two rooms."

Maureen went into the room on the left and lit the kerosene lamp on the nightstand. Then she began parting the shirred net drapes and closing the louvered shutters on all eight windows. She turned back the covers on the high fluffy bed and released the mosquito netting from the hoop and spread it around the bed like a skirt. Like some kind of ritual, she stepped up to the hump-backed clock on the mantle between the south windows, took the key next to the clock and began winding it. The room smelled of lavender and beeswax overlaid on citronella.

Oscar and Joe carried the trunk in and set it at the foot of the white iron bed. Looking down and not at each other and especially not at Doll standing before Daniel in the doorway.

He stepped closer, laughing, and whispered, "Just Doll." He pinched her sore right buttock.

She had never ridden so far, was sore from head to foot, the bones of her groin felt broken. His pinch made her mad as fire.

Alone in her room, Doll sponged off with the water brought by Maureen, along with a stiff white sunned towel and a bar of sweet soap. Doll had never used sweet soap before, and she wanted to lie on the high bed with the plump pillows and fall asleep smelling the soap on her cooling skin and listening to the clock tick. But the oak smoke and food smells from the kitchen—onions and roast beef maybe—were more of a lure.

From the hall, she could see Daniel standing other side of the watershelf on the back porch. He had changed into a green shirt and work boots that laced up to the calves, light pants stogged into the boot tops. One hip cocked, hands on his waist, he was talking to two men in the yard—Joe and a giant Negro man. The boy who was chopping wood earlier came up the doorsteps with an armload of oak.

The Negro man in the yard said, "Next time you do like you belong to and won't nobody be sending you out in the snakes after dark." Joe and Daniel laughed.

The boy went through the door to the kitchen at Daniel's back. The wood tumbled to the floor, shaking the house.

A French door facing the hall led to the dining room where the table was set for two with china in patterns of roses and green leaves with gold borders. White damask tablecloth and napkins. A brass chandelier of white candles was hung over the long table filled with bowls and platters of food. Moths were stuck to the window lights of the door.

67

At home, the Baxters cooked only the noon meal and ate leftovers for supper when the heat set in.

Doll passed quickly through, closed the door. Listening to the woman named Maureen talking to the boy in the kitchen, from which emanated a dense but fragrant heat. "Tell Fate I said to be here first thing Monday morning. Get the washing out in case a cloud comes up later."

"Yes um." The door from the porch to the kitchen opened, closed.

The men laughed, talking louder, wrapping up.

"Here, Bo Dink," said Daniel.

"Thank you suh," the boy said.

"He be lost that fifty-cent fore he get to the house." The Negro man laughed.

The kitchen door opened, shut, and Daniel stood looking into the dining room. "Well, Mrs. Staten, you don't look like a lady's been riding half the day."

She stared down at her blue dress, old and faded but respectably ironed before wrinkling in the trunk.

"Have a seat," he said. "Make yourself at home." Then, "I believe I'll have another little drink with my supper."

Doll sat in the cushioned high-back chair at the end of the table, listening to the beetles bat against the glass at her back and the gurgle of a bottle in the kitchen. She sipped from the glass of cool tea before the plate on her left. She was thirsty, starving, couldn't wait to taste the fluffy mashed potatoes and tiny acre peas and the browned roast garnished with pearls of onions.

Daniel was standing in the doorway from kitchen to dining room when she looked up. He walked in, set the squat glass down before the plate on her left. "I'd offer you a whiskey," he said to Doll, "but I'm afraid you'd take it."

Maureen came in, still smiling, and placed a dish of small round evenly-browned biscuits on the table and a square of butter with a "Staten Bay" imprint. In the light, Doll saw that she was even more beautiful than she'd first thought. Her white blouse was more beautiful, store-bought, trimmed in lace. Her skin creamier, lips fuller, eyes darker. The bundle of hair above her fine neck and ears looked like poured water. But most outstanding of all were her lingering mannerisms, and she was lingering now, holding to the back of the chair at the far end of the table, cat-eyeing Doll, then Daniel, face lit as if laughing but not laughing.

For the first time in Doll's life she felt little. She had always been small—didn't mind it, didn't suffer because of it—but now she felt little. And inept. Mousy even.

"That'll do," Daniel said to Maureen and sipped his whiskey. The light from the candles made his hair and beard look gold.

Maureen lingered, walked to the kitchen door, looked back again. Closed the door easy.

"Maureen's kind of surprised to see somebody sitting in my place."

"Your place... I..." Doll started to get up.

"No problem. Not from a man's been bit by his bride and had his horse taken, all in one day. Pass the peas, please."

"You had no right to kiss me like that in front of everybody."

"Preacher said I could. Your lawyer kissed you."

Figuring there would be no grace said before eating, unlike at home, and feeling more in the mood for arguing than praying anyway, she passed the white bowl of peas, then held her plate out for him to carve her some roast. "Is it true you still have slaves?

"That's what people say, huh?" He eyed her, carved the roast and forked a juicy slice to her plate. "Well, truth is, I got stuck with the overflow, you might say, from my Daddy's slaves. He had fourteen back around 1850. Before he died, he deeded what was left living to me; my brother got the old homeplace, north up around Alapaha. I stumped and cleared Staten Bay from scrub and virgin pine, a place nobody else wanted—a Yankee wouldn't have had the grit and neither would any of those soft-handed plantation gentlemen of the Old South. They wouldn't of had the hindsight to appreciate how our ole tough straggly wiregrass makes for such prime cattle grazing."

"Mr. Hamilton Fletcher always says it's the making of these woods."

Daniel eyed her as if she had butted in on what he was saying. "Anyhow, my inherited slaves have long ago either died or gone off up north." He was eating now, fork and knife in cutting position, glowering, pausing as if waiting for comment, then laboring on, chewing and talking. "Most people around here didn't have slaves; the whites were about as poor as the Negroes along then. One worked as hard as the other. What interest the rednecks had in the War Between the States had more to do with secession—separating the south from the north. Wasn't much to do with slavery. Just another fracas, like the Mexican and Indian wars." He drank from his glass of whiskey, set it down. "So, the truth is I've never *owned* a slave, don't own the descendents of slaves—they can leave when they like, live where they like. By the way, I'm twenty-seven, ten years older than you."

She cut her meat, ate. Drank her tea.

"Hard to beat this ole wiregrass-fed beef. So tender you can cut it with a fork."

Actually, the beef was too stringy and strong for her taste.

So far, they hadn't touched on a single subject of which they were in agreement. Even the tea was too sweet to suit her.

At home, when they butchered a beef, the flatwoods community would turn out to help and to share the meat, a rare treat. After three days the beef would begin to spoil, so sharing was a necessity as well as an act of giving.

This man before her was no giver.

He drank his whiskey. Growing sterner looking, his long brow and deep set eyes. "Negroes live on my place. They work for me; I pay them. Same as Oscar, Joe and Maureen."

"Joe and Maureen?"

"Yeah. They live down that road past the commissary, south of the house. Lil ole place back there by the cotton house."

They ate quietly then, listening to the beetles pelting the glass door, to the katydids shrieking in the oaks. Forks and knives clinking on plates. Doll had never tasted such fine, light cooking. Though she preferred the heavier cooking of the flatwoods—a bit more seasoning meat in the peas, more salt, denser bread.

Head bowed and brooding, Daniel said, "The little *slave* boy, Bo Dink, belongs to my right-hand turpentine man, Elkin. Elkin and Fate came here from South Carolina some five, six years ago. They *are* descendants of African slaves, part of the Gullah tribe that settled on the coastal islands from North Florida to the Carolinas. You can see the Geechee coming out in Bo Dink—never will get up any size."

"I didn't say you own slaves." She placed her fork on her plate. "I heard..."

"You probably heard that I have babies all over the quarters too." He emptied his glass. "Not true. *But*, Mrs. Staten, it is true that I'm a rounder. Meaning, occasionally I take a notion to wander and chase the ladies."

"Why did you marry me?"

He laughed out, chin up and head back and the light overhead filtering through his beard. "Why did I marry you? Why does anybody marry? Why do rivers run?" He turned suddenly sober and his eyes fixed on hers, the jewels of both their bodies, hers blue and his green, an unlikely mix it seemed all at once. "Take your pick: I married you because you're from fine stock and you'll have fine children for me; because you're the most desirable woman I ever met and I couldn't have you any other way; because it was time I got married."

"Or my land—you couldn't have my land any other way either. Could you?"

"I could have waited for the auction and I wouldn't have had to wait long." He drank from his glass, the last dram of his good brown whiskey. "Don't flatter yourself, Mrs. Staten. Right now your piddling farm and timberland is more liability than asset."

"What about me—unbred—asset or liability?"

71

He reached for her plate. "You're being silly now. More roast?"

"Thank you, no." She stood, placed her napkin on the table. "I'll say goodnight, Mr. Staten." She went through the French door and down the hall, smelling of citronella and parched bugs. The wide heart pine boards were stained mahogany with a waxy sheen that bowed up in patches of light from the big squat candles.

"Maureen," he called. "You can finish up now."

In her new room, Doll blew down inside the smoked glass chimney of the kerosene lamp beside her bed and a cloud of smoke rose to her face. Her eyes burned. She hated that. But remembered as a child trying to snuff the lamp flame with her hand cupped over the top of the globe and burning her fingers. Not much of a choice: burned eyes or burned fingers.

When she could see in the dark, she went to the tall windows over the front porch and began unlatching and folding back the louvered shutters, each one letting in more and more moonlight and night air. The cool air could hardly be called a breeze, just winey night filtering through the sheer white curtains. Four windows on front and four windows on the side, the south featuring an expanded view of Staten Bay. Moonlight accented the shingle roofs of the barn and commissary, and several other buildings she hadn't noticed when she got there, then swept across the open fields to the ragged dark woodsline and a single light—Maureen's and Joe's house?— no brighter than a struck match.

Tomorrow she would go home.

There was a small stool for stepping up onto the high plump bed, but she used one knee and hoisted herself up and under the tent of mosquito netting and lay on the cool smooth sheet. Not rough muslin, like at home, a finer weave, silky but not silk. White sheets, white gown and netting glowing in the moonlight like mist. Sounds of the clock ticking, katydids in the oaks, frogs in the swamps, and lone shouts from the quarters, Maureen rattling dishes and pots in the kitchen, then closing the door of the kitchen and going out, down the back porch steps, into the yard, head high and gliding right past the moonlit span of south windows in Doll's room.

The door to either the kitchen or the dining room creaked open, clapped shut; then footsteps sounded along the heart-pine floor of the hall, stopping at her door, moving on toward the front porch and halting—Daniel Staten, her new husband, of course. Then walking again, stopping at her door and turning the knob—locked. Trying again, knocking softly, pacing the hall, turning the knob, knocking softly. Then LOUD. So loud, Doll bunched the feather pillows up to her ears and held her breath.

"Just Doll"—that was what it sounded like he said, then laughed, then walked toward the porch, onto the porch, and sat in one of the large rockers before the first two windows of her bedroom. Not even looking in, but drinking from the same squat glass he had at supper.

Doll lay still. Breathing easy. White gown, sheets and netting, waffing and aglow. She could actually smell his whiskey through the window draping. And what kind of protection was netting from this monster-stranger with the smirky face lifted and one long leg crossed over the other? Not even looking in or ripping through the curtains. Not saying a single word on their wedding night—after leaving no doubt that he was marrying her for one thing and one thing only—except "Just Doll."

Sunday morning she came alive from a dead sleep to the large ivory room bowling over with sunshine, heat hanging just off the edges of morning. Every safe dark corner and shadow was gone. The only sounds, a faint tinkling like bells in the kitchen, and outside the murmur of insects, and now and then a horse neighing, a cow lowing. She sat to step down off the bed and her pelvic bones and buttocks seized up with pain. It had been so long since she had ridden her own horse—the mare had an infected frog—and never for so long, and she had forgotten the teeth-gritting ache, but remembered that tomorrow would be worse should she give into the urge to lie sick all day.

She got up, slipping on the blue cotton dress from last night. The lid of Mrs. Baxter's trunk was open and Doll's poor dresses and shoes looked fit only for rags and patching in the fine room: white cut-lace scarves on the oak chest, dresser, and chiffonier; towels to match on the oak washstand with its white porcelain bowl and pitcher set; even the white cotton coverlet on the bed had cutouts like bird tracks in sand. Two white wicker chairs in the southeast corner of the room. They had cushions of blue flocked chintz. A plush blue rug the color of the sky with a green border like grass covered the lavender-waxed floors to within a foot of the ivory bead-board walls. She stood on the spongy rug, then sat to slip on her small brown hightops. Lacing them as she had yesterday and all the days before when she was home. Then she stood and went to the trunk and tucked the pink grosgrain sash of her going-away dress inside and closed the lid. The pink ribbon from her hair she left on the washstand.

She opened the door to the hall and looked out at the sunny front yard and lane. Everything looked so different emptied of all the people she'd seen when she got there. So quiet she could hear the mourning doves—a high lonesome hollow sound. Through the open door of Daniel's room, she could see that the louvered shutters were closed, horizontal straws of light on the mahogany floor. But the covers of the high brass bed were turned back in a triangle—proof he'd not slept in it. In fact, except for Daniel's black suit laid across a rose velvet chair by the fireplace, he might never even have set foot in the room since he got home.

From the kitchen came a rapid chopping sound, like a knife chopping vegetables on wood. She walked down the hall to the watershelf on the back porch. The woodpile looked farther away from the house in daylight, and what she'd thought were plum trees was instead a half-acre grapevine arbored with stout posts. Lacy sunshine on the loamy earth below, and martins flitting under and out to the blare of sunny sky. Home of the martins was a wooden cross of hanging gourds, like human skulls. Set back, to the left of the woodpile, stood an open shed with a black iron washpot and two wooden troughs like at home. Off the west end of the porch was a chickenyard enclosed with diamond-mesh wire; and another pen grand with strutting turkeys; and one with gray and white geese, parading and honking, some bare-chested as babies, their down sacrificed for pillows. And beyond that, what looked like a smokehouse. And beyond that another outhouse, and then a thicket of mulberry and chinaberry trees, giving way to the cotton fields and pine woods. She dipped water from a red-rimmed white metal bucket into a matching pan, scooped it to her face, then washed her hands with a bar of lye soap like at home. Like at home. She dried the water and tears from her face with a rough white towel hanging from a nail.

When she turned to go to the kitchen, she saw Maureen standing rod-straight in the doorway. She was wearing a gray-striped skirt and another white blouse, plain but starched and ironed. Over the skirt she wore a white apron-wrap, like a bed sheet doubled and snuggly drawn over her hips. A folded blue-striped towel hung from her waist on the right. The smile from last night was gone, and with it that discomforting beauty. She looked merely broad and irritable in the morning light.

"I kept your breakfast warming on the stove," she said and stepped into the kitchen again.

Doll talked to her from the doorway. "I'm not hungry, but thank you all the same. I wonder, could you tell me where Mr. Staten is at?"

Maureen was standing with her back to Doll, washing dishes at the counter along the north wall. "I expect you can look for him when you see him coming."

Was she joking? "I don't understand. I..." Doll paused, took a deep breath, said, "What about Oscar Bowen? Where can I find him?"

Maureen turned to the bulky black stove in the left corner of the square white room. She opened the warming oven on top and removed Doll's plate of sausage, eggs, grits and biscuit and dumped it all into the slop bucket at her feet.

Then Doll was hungry.

"Oscar and Estelle live in that little cabin just across the road," Maureen said and faced the counter again and dunked the plate in the dishpan of sudsy water. The long window over the counter featured bands of blank green and blue. Green corn and blue sky and nothing else.

"Listen," said Doll, stepping across the hewed-wood threshold, "I don't know what's the matter with you, but I'm just asking for a little information. You won't have to cook for me or clean up after me, so you have nothing as I know of to be puffed up about."

Maureen looked at her then. Long and easy and unbelieving but with only her head turned, hands busy in the dishpan.

"Tell Mr. Staten I decided to go home and the deal is off," Doll said. "Understand?"

Maureen nodded once, smiling that obnoxious, all-purpose smile Doll had found so charming last night. Doll walked off the back porch and down the tall steps to the foot-tracked dirt.

It was hot now, at least eleven o'clock, and the heat seemed to draw the sweat to her skin as she started around the south side of the house. A Satsuma orange tree with waxy leaves grew close to the chimney, and farther out on the clean swept yard was a fig tree with fat ruddy brown figs bursting through their skins. In the fencejamb to the right of the gate, a pomegranate tree hung with orbs of fluted fruit the color of sunset. Crepe myrtles with ruffley cerise flowers lined the rail fence each side of the gate, and purple petunias bordered the brick walk.

Starting up the lane she could smell cows and horses, pine and crushed dog fennel. Green so bright it made her blink. On her right was the horse barn with what looked like the wagon Oscar had brought for her to ride in parked under the shelter. Several other wagons under the shelter and around the lot, and if she cared enough to check, if checking served some purpose, it would be interesting to see if, as she suspected, Daniel Staten had picked the crudest, ricketiest wagon on the place to put her in her place. But the bones and muscles of her pelvis and buttocks balked at the notion of walking to the left or right and even straight.

At the end of the lane, she crossed the three-path road to another path angling toward the little side-set cabin hemmed in by a rail fence, palmettos, pines and tittering birds. One bird she'd never heard before sounded like it was scaling a flute. Up the road, in the quarters, she could hear the Negroes singing, clapping and stomping on the floor of what she figured was their Sunday meeting house. Where would her own church be now? Maybe Daniel had got up to go to Sunday meeting nearby, found her sleeping and hated to wake her and went on without her. If that was the case she should feel ashamed, but she didn't believe it and anyway wouldn't feel ashamed after the way he had behaved last night.

Holding to the mounds of her aching buttocks, she stepped onto the low porch of the log cabin and could hear a clock ticking and nothing else. A dove cooed in the east woods. Another dove cooed from the north woods. The porch smelled of coffee grounds and snuff.

The front door was open and Doll started to knock. But then she spied in the gloom of the shuttered room a warped-looking woman in a gray dress and bonnet watching her. She looked like a witch doll that glides in and out of a toy house predicting rain or sunshine.

The long room smelled musty. Was dark as a chimney, coming in out of the sun. There was a single bed covered tight as an iced cake with a homemade white sheet.

"You must be Mr. Daniel's new wife?" she said, ambling, then backing like a crawdad. She looked hatched from the chinking of the log walls. "Come on in. Or we can set on the porch if you want to." She stopped, gazing hard at Doll. "Why, you're just a little-bitty thing, ain't you?"

When the woman reached the light of the doorway, Doll was shocked at how young she was—maybe thirty, but she could go for seventy she was so stooped and wrinkled.

"I'm looking for Oscar Bowen," Doll said. "Maureen told

me he lives here."

"He does," she said and stepped out to the edge of the porch and spat snuff juice into the russet dead pinestraw. Piled pinestraw hung from the shingle eaves like thatch. She took a handkerchief from her bosom and wiped her screwed mouth.

"That Maureen's a sight, ain't she?"

Doll didn't answer

"Honey, I'm Estelle," said the woman and collapsed into a small cowhide rocker that looked as if her body had shaped the hide from the day it was cut and tacked.

"You can call me Doll." Doll eased down onto the straight chair with a flat wood bottom facing her. She groaned low with pain and shifted her weight side to side. "Miss Estelle, I came to get Oscar to take me home."

"Well," she said and spat off the porch again, wiped her mouth again. "That didn't take long." She hummed a laugh. Her face was dry brown, wrinkled like brown paper.

She rocked, hands balling the handkerchief in her lap, eyeing Doll curiously. "I reckon you're wondering how come me so stove up, huh?"

"No ma'am, I..." Doll placed her hands in her lap too. She was hot, hungry, homesick. Her buttocks ached so that she had to sit sideways, tried to cross her legs but couldn't.

"Well, old buggy run over me in Jasper, yonderside of the Flordie line there." She nodded south.

"How far?" Doll asked. "To the Florida line, I mean."

"Couple, three miles maybe."

"I guess people live all along the road between here and there, don't they?"

Estelle cackled out. "Not so you'd notice. Just driving long the road. Get off the road apiece and you'll run up on a farm now and then. Lord, it gets lonesome here sometimes. Course, another ten miles or so and Jasper's overrun with people."

"I didn't know Jasper was a big town."

"Is to me."

Doll listened to the doves again, way off and lonesome and not another sound save for the church in the quarters.

Sounded like drumbeats.

Estelle seemed to read her mind, tempering down and sweetening her bitter voice. "Honey, I was just like you when I come here from Alabamie. Couldn't stand the place, and to this day, I ain't got a bit of use for that man brung me here."

Doll stood to straighten her skirt, then sat easy to keep from breaking.

Estelle cackled out again. "Gal, you need to go soak in some Epsom salts."

Doll said, "Why do you stay with him if you don't like him?"

"Ma'am?" Estelle cupped the large hairy ear turned toward Doll. "I hear you right?"

Doll spoke up. "I said, why do you stay?"

"I heared you." She rocked looking out at the woods, her horrible face shortened with concentration, or fury. "Go on over there to the horse barn and tell Oscar I said take you home to your mammy. You'll find him trimming the mules' hooves. You too frail for married life. Mr. Daniel's too much man for you; this place is too much for you. Now run on."

She shooed Doll off the porch like a bandy hen.

Doll was halfway up the lane when she wheeled around and marched back, walking as stove-up as Estelle, she imagined. Across the road she marched, then down the double path, stopping at the shallow porch. Estelle quit rocking.

"Not that I have to explain *anything* to you," Doll said, "but I'm not some spoiled mama's girl. No, I haven't been run over by a buggy, but I've suffered in my own way. I've worked like a man to help feed my family and hang onto our homeplace. And I've fought wildfires to save our house and timber after grown men had given up and run to save their hides." Both hands were down by her side but they itched to rise and cover her body against the raw glare of the older woman. "I may be little, but I'm tough as they come—there's not a soul in the flatwoods doesn't know that. And *Mr.* Daniel is a long way from being too much man for me to handle."

Again she wheeled, behind her hearing the rocker sweeps

creaking under Estelle's chair.

On the back porch of the big white house, she had every intention of announcing to Maureen that she would have her breakfast now, but she smelled chicken frying, heard it sizzling. And instead spoke from the doorway. "Maureen, in view of the fact that I can expect Mr. Staten when I see him coming, I will have my dinner alone. Now." She felt strange and uncertain giving orders to an older, larger woman.

She knew he was coming at about five o'clock that evening when she saw him riding up the lane on the black stallion who had ruined her entire lower body. Yes, the pain had spread from her pelvis to her thighs to her calves. But when the man she had married only yesterday and considered leaving today got to the fence and dismounted to hitch the stallion to the post—probably having learned his lesson about fences—she was lounging in the porch swing with her back to him, facing the windows of her bedroom while reading an essay by Catherine Beecher in *Scribner's Magazine*, which as best Doll could gather had to do with women being duty-bound to bow down to men, king of the home, and forget voting for other kings.

Earlier, she had found the magazine in Daniel's bedroom, come out and sat in the swing, swaying it with one bare foot pushing against the swing chain, and not even Oscar with those all-seeing eyes could possibly have known she was in pain. All day, he had watched her. Like a good dog—slow, friendly, always there. She had considered putting him in his place, just as she had Estelle and Maureen, but she decided that Daniel had told him to watch her. So, she'd kept him curious and busy while she moved about to prevent being doubly sore tomorrow, to prevent dwelling on home and Mama, Sheba and Adam. There was always something going on at home: candy pullings, barn raisings, fodder pullings, log rollings, peanut shellings, chicken bogs, corn huskings—play conjured from work, like at Hamilton Fletcher's, with Mrs. Baxter as chief magician. She could turn even death into a celebration with one of her food-plied wakes. Doll really needed to see her mother and talk through this mess she'd gotten herself into; to hear her mother tell her one more time that if all else failed they would let the homeplace go and move in with Uncle Lester, though she was bound and determined to stay. At one point in the afternoon, she got so homesick, she started to leave re-gardless—Oscar, Estelle, Maureen and Daniel bedamned!—but she was too sore to ride even in the wagon he brought for her to ride in yesterday—the honeymoon wagon.

"Just Doll," Daniel said and laughed and stopped on the top porch step, holding to one of the square columns for bal-ance.

Gnats were driving her crazy, swarming around her face, but she only blew at them. She pushed the chain hard with her bare foot. The swing squeaked.

He stood watching her read without reading, then walked across the porch and leaned against the wall at the end of the swing. "Been out trying to save my reputation," he said. His beard was mangled, his eyes crossed, his clothes wrinkled—same green shirt and light pants he wore for supper last night. Suddenly he lifted her foot from the chain and kissed the sole.

Pain shot from her calf to her groin. She groaned, yanked at her foot tight in his grip. He dropped it and shoved off from the wall. "This marriage is now consummated," he said.

He stumbled out, back to the stallion, saddled up and rode past the oaks, past the barn, down the south fork of the lane, the clomping hooves of the stallion fading out to the drone of locusts. She had thought at first that he was riding the horse to the barn, then thought he was checking on the crops, then talking to Joe, thought maybe he was just out riding and drink-ing, till he didn't come back and didn't come back and sun-down turned to dusk and dusk to dark. She went into the kitchen and served her plate from the noon meal leftovers Maureen had placed in the warmer of the stove: fried chicken, field peas, creamed corn, okra and cornbread.

In the dining room, so silent and dark it creaked, she lit the citronella candle on the table and sat in Daniel's chair, eating alone. At least Maureen had asked if Doll would need anything else before she left after noon. That was something, that Maureen had asked. But Doll was not at all sure she'd made her point—that she would not be made to feel like a stranger in her own house.

Her own house?

Yes.

In bed, she lay listening to the same night sounds carried over from last dark: katydids shrilling in the oaks, frogs chirruping in the swamp, an owl hooing in the woods. The heat was as thick as the dark. She had closed the shutters and they snapped and popped on the windows till she got up and opened them. Moonlight and a stiff breeze, and in the south the muted orange light of the cabin where Joe and Maureen lived.

She heard footsteps on the dirt before she could figure a man's shape from the trees and weeds and moon shadows.

Her husband.

She got back into the bed, under the white tent in her white gown and waited for him, for the certain repeat of the night before—footsteps on the hall and him turning the doorknob.

But he simply went into his room and closed the door softly.

Chapter 4

A knock on Doll's door woke her, and opening her eyes she saw that it was daylight, beyond daylight, maybe seven o'clock in the morning. Monday morning—hellish Monday after heavenly Sunday, as Hamilton Fletcher would say. Outside a Negro woman was bawling at somebody to fill the washpot with water. Hollow donging of bucket down the well, squeak of teakle. Horses neighing, wagon wheels trundling, clink of metal, men talking, shouting. Somebody knocking on her door.

Seldom sleepy at night, always sleepy in the morning— either Mrs. Baxter or Sheba having to rouse her from the bed— Doll felt ashamed, groggy, irritated. Her lower body was one keen ache from riding on Saturday. She lifted the mosquito netting and slid from the high bed to the spongy blue rug, went to the door and opened it just enough to peep through the crack.

Big bad Maureen. "If you got clothes needs washing, I'll take them out to Fate."

Doll started to turn and gather her clothes, but instead said, "It'll take me a minute; I'll carry them out."

Maureen closed the door. "Suit yourself," she mumbled halfway down the hall.

"Rake my breakfast in the slop bucket again and I'll suit myself by sending you down the road," Doll said low but loud enough. She hoped.

She got dressed, then bundled up her two dirty dresses and stuffed her bleached flour-sack bloomers inside to hide them.

Outside, the Negroes were passing to and from the barn and the commissary. Would Fate hang Doll's underwear on the clothesline for everybody to see?

Going up the hall, she saw that the door was open to the narrow, one-window room between the guestroom, east of the dining room, and Daniel's bedroom on the front. Yesterday she had tried the heavy paneled door and found it locked. Was it really snooping to explore your own house? A wide oak desk sat on the north end of the room, under the window, a brown leather wingback chair behind the desk and a smaller matching chair before the desk. Shelves lined the wall on the right, neat green and wine clothbound books giving way to loose stacks of tablets and papers, vellum and white, and drab-green ledgers, like the kind she'd seen in commissaries.

Along the left wall was a blocky black safe with a dial of numbers and another chair, mahogany with a green and white striped padded seat, and above it two gilt and mahogany framed, lead-tinted portraits of lit-eyed but solemn and distinguished people, all of whom resembled Daniel or the other way around. Especially the bearded younger man with inset eyes and a shelf brow—had to be his senator brother—alone in the portrait on the right. The man in the other portrait, standing behind a severe but smiling woman seated in a chair, could have been an older brother, but Doll guessed the father of James and Daniel because to her knowledge that there wasn't another brother. Then it struck her that in the absence of memory aging stopped at the moment an image was struck on paper. Daniel would be about the same age as this senatorial older brother if he had his picture made now.

She felt on the verge of getting to know Daniel—something in the neatness turning to mess and the leather and musk smell of him she'd not noticed before, that and the smell of paper, old and new, the dry old-trunk smells of books and bookwork, and the family pictures—how it all mixed and yet didn't mix at all, only close, a thought slipping away like water through a crack in the floor. She stepped over to the desk, looking down at a sheet of white stationery with careful writing in blue ink over watermarks. It was a letter from Daniel to his attorney in Valdosta advising him to transfer the mortgage on the various plat numbers belonging to the Baxters to his own name.

Really that was all she should need to know about Daniel Staten.

A southerly breeze carried the smoke from the pedestal of flames under the round black washpot to the back porch where Doll sat watching Fate put out the wash: shirts, pants, dresses, underwear, towels, sheets, washrags and handkerchiefs of equal importance when she slapped them onto the washboard stood in a wooden trough of lye water.

"You, Bo Dink!" Fate hollered, rubbing out Daniel's green shirt on the washboard. "You better have that second water to me fore I get down there."

Bo Dink, at the well, located between the barn beyond the fence and the washshed in the yard, came running with the pine bucket of water sloshing onto his short thin legs. He dumped it into the number two trough on the far right of the washpot. Then he slunk off again with the bail of the bucket screaling.

Fate slung the shirt into the cast iron pot of boiling water, picked up a bedsheet from the basket on her left, dunked it into the melted lye and water solution and lay into it on the washboard. Her round face looked smithed from the same iron as the washpot. Huge eyes bogged in fat, pouched cheeks, and blisters of lips. She wore a red rag tied around her head and knotted in front. She was humming—not a happy tune, but a tune of deep thought or maybe hope—eyes on the washboard, the washpot, the lined up troughs of water, the one on the end half full and twinkling in the morning sun. Waterlights danced on the dirt and spiraled up the shed posts. The air smelled of boiling lye, potash, and woodsmoke.

"Get a move on, boy," Fate barked.

Bo Dink dumped another bucket into the trough and headed for the well again. He stepped around to the offside, looked at his mama, then pulled a coin from his pocket, turned it over in his pale palm, and pocketed it again.

All clothes in the pot, Fate took up her battling stick, a long wooden paddle, and began stirring the clothes like the stiff batter of a fruitcake. Checking the sky for clouds and the boy for mischief. Waiting for the clothes to boil clean, she stepped back into the shadows of the washshed and sat with the tin pie plate of food brought from home that morning and began eating with fierce concentration from the pone of cornbread and sweet potato.

Next bucket of water from the well, she called Bo Dink over, scooped out a fruit jar of water for herself and broke an end off the cornbread and handed it to him. All quiet now while the clothes boiled and the smoke drifted toward Doll on the porch.

After Fate had rinsed the clothes through the first and second waters, she wrung them tight with her great hands, then carried the piled-high basket out to the clothesline, shook and hung each piece: Doll's floursack bloomers with the crotches tucked inside, like tiny skirts, next to Daniel's fine white boxer shorts, shirts with shirts, pants with pants, sheets with sheets, towels with towels, handkerchiefs with handkerchiefs, an art of hanging wash.

Then she popped Bo Dink upside the head for good measure and sent him to sweep the backyard with a bundle of gallberry switches.

After dinner, alone in the dining room, same as yesterday, same as at breakfast, Doll sat on the front porch fanning the hot noon air. Her lower body was aching worse than yesterday; she needed something to do. What was she supposed to do?

She saw Estelle when she hobbled down off the cabin porch across the road and started up the lane, a long time coming in her drab gray dress and bonnet. Up the brick walk and onto the porch and sitting in the high-back rocker next to Doll.

Doll passed her a cardboard fan from a stack on the floor by her chair.

"Mighty dry, ain't it?" Estelle said, fanning.

"It'll rain by and by." Doll wondered if it had rained in the flatwoods yet.

An empty wagon rumbled from the barn, up the lane. Dust gathered, scattered and settled like a gnat swarm.

"Strange how a little bit of rain can seem like a whole lot till it dries in," Estelle said, and spat off the porch. "Course, in this heat..." She finished her sentence by fanning her face. Already the snuff had dried in on the baked dirt in the shape of a rat's tail.

Bo Dink had swept his way from the side yard to the front. Erasing tracks with the gallberry switches and drawing fancy swirls and lines fit for the finest penmanship. He looked up with squinched gnat-inflamed eyes, saw the two women on the porch, and began sweeping southside of the house again. The swishing of the broom stopped and started and meshed with the dry shuffling rattle of locusts in the oaks.

Fate showed around the corner of the porch, carrying the metal pie pan with a white rag over it. "Get that broom agoing, boy. And see you dump that wash water under the grapevine fore you head home," she said to him, then to Doll and Estelle. "How do?"

"Hot, ain't it?" Estelle said.

"Sho nuf hot, yes ma'am." Fate laughed from the gullet and walked on under the flocked shadows of the oaks toward the gate.

"You met the new missus yet?" Estelle asked.

"Sho have now. Done and met and washed her clothes." She opened the gate, stepped through, closed it.

The swishing of the brush broom stopped.

They watched Fate labor up the lane, turn left at the road and vanish beyond the cotton and the tall rail fence. Doll expected Estelle would apologize for yesterday, or at least mention yesterday; but weather aside, she began talking about Daniel and the men rounding up the cattle and hogs in the woods, marking and branding. Oscar was keeping the commissary while Joe was gone. Well, she could talk or not talk or go home, but Doll really couldn't think of a thing to say to

87

her.

"You still ailing, ere you?" Estelle asked.

Doll stared at her. "Not exactly...I'm sore...I..."

"Well, I brung you some salts to soak in." Estelle stiffened with a game leg stretched before her, dusty brown hightops like Doll's but longer, and pulled a square blue box from her apron pocket and handed it to Doll.

She leaned close, speaking low and muffled through her snuff. "The worst is over, honey." She winked one terrible eye. "Say some women even get to where they like it. Big man like that, and you just a little-bitty thing." She sucked in her breath and made a face to show commiseration. "Bout the best advice I can give you is to make water quick as he's done."

Finally rid of Estelle, Doll went into the bathroom—a stifling narrow room between her own bedroom and the one at the end of the hall—latched the shutters on the single window, closed both doors, and emptied the whole box of salts into the long zinc tub filled with the sun-warmed second water left over from the clothes. Bo Dink had been on the verge of dumping it under the grapevine when she caught him and had him carry it, bucket by bucket, into the bathroom. She ordered Maureen to give him a slice of pound cake, then told him to sit on the back porch davenport till she was done, so he could carry the water out again. He took his cake out to the doorsteps and sat instead.

She undressed and stepped into the tub, sitting, then lying into the curve of the raised rim. Her long black hair floated over her small pale breasts. She slid lower, dunking the back and sides of her head, hearing the drumming of the water, then sat again and begin lathering her hair with the sweet soap from her washstand. And again she lay back, lowering her head till the water covered her ears and wobbled around her cheeks, forehead, and chin. Her eyes caught some motion behind her and she sat up quick, looked around, and saw the bathroom door leading to her bedroom closing. She jumped out of the tub, opened the door and stuck her head through and saw through the front windows Daniel striding down the porch steps and across the yard.

Almost sundown, pumpkin sun slanting across the brush-marked yard, and the smoke from the burned-down wood under the washpot was blending with the dust from the gum and fodder wagons passing along the lane. One of the wagons stopped under the oaks, and Fate stepped down, laughing but holding her paining back. She waddled off toward the gate and along the south side of the house to take in the dried clothes. The long line of clothes had been raised high on two split rails and now furled in the light breeze like strange flags. Long-horn cattle crept and grazed under the tall yellow pines along the lane. Horses and mules kicked the stall walls of the barn. Sound of iron pounding on an anvil. Joe was trying to coax a mule with blinders into the dark maw of the barn door. Other men going in and coming out and calling to each other nodded at Doll on her way to the commissary following her bath. Her hair was still damp, cooling her head, neck and shoulders. Either side of the foot-tracked path from the fork to the commissary, bush-hooked weeds and grass smelled like citron. A hedge of plum trees grew off the left end of the store porch behind a raw plank bench nailed from post to post. Two Negro men in black rubber boots came out the door, spoke, and stepped aside for her to go in. She could smell croaker sacks, cottonseed meal, kerosene and cheese.

Oscar was seated on a tall stool behind the wood counter. When he saw her he tipped his hat up on his pale lined forehead. 'Howdy do," he said.

"How're you, Oscar?"

"Ain't much." He was whittling on a fat litard stick with his pocketknife. The heart of the wood looked like fire.

Along the north wall behind the counter were shelves of white pots and pans rimmed in red and castiron, startling in its new gray cast; pottery jugs and glass jars with metal clasps and leather seals; kerosene lamps, like the castiron, startlingly new; tall white hatboxes of "Lion Hats;" bolts of material in plaids, stripes and checks, blue, green, brown, indigo and hickory stripe, even a bolt of black cotton with pink floral stripes like Sheba's Sunday dress, which made Doll want to cry. Ladies' black and brown ankle boots and men's work boots, both slender as wooden shoetrees. Left to right on top of the counter was a coffee grinder, a screened cheese box with a round of cheddar inside; a glass case of vari-colored sewing thread on tiny wooden spools; packs of sewing needles; cards of buttons; lamp wicks; bottles or boxes of Swamp Root, Quinine, Lump Alum, Sassafras, Asafetida, Elm Bark, Sienna leaves, Bitters; and on the end of the counter, a standing roll of brown paper for wrapping it all up to take home.

"You needing something up at the house?" Oscar asked, coming round.

"No," she said, taking inventory with amazement. Could she really have anything she wanted?

She had shopped in commissaries before, in Fargo and Tarver, but never had she shopped knowing that she could have anything she wanted; unlike the workers at Staten Bay, she didn't have to have coupons or credit. She wouldn't have to work off her debt, like the others, which was next to impossible to do. It was a poor girl's dream of Christmas, and almost, almost, a cure for homesickness.

Along the south wall were bins of garden seeds and kegs of everything from nails to cornmeal; hanging hames and harnesses and plowlines—you name it. But what she absolutely couldn't take her eyes off of was what looked like a small blanket of crocheted leather strips draped over a sawhorse.

"What is that for?" she asked, pointing.

"What you put on a mule or horse's back to keep the flies off," he said.

"How does it work?" She stepped forward and ran her hand over the leather mesh.

"Old mule goes to walking and the leather strips move." He demonstrated by bringing his stiff hands together just short of clapping. "Flies ain't got time to settle."

She started to ask how much it cost then changed her mind when he went to the door—broad flat backside in indigo overalls—spat off the porch and came back, saying, "Go on and get whatever you want, but next time send Maureen."

She stood still as if waiting for further explanation.

He obliged. "Mr. Daniel, he wouldn't cotton to his wife hanging round the hands coming in here."

"I don't have to ask Daniel if I can come over here or anywhere else." She crossed to the door, speaking back. "But while I'm here I would like to know when you've got a gum wagon going back over to Four-mile Still."

He lifted his brown felt hat and scratched his head. "Well, Mr. Daniel, he…"

"Tell Mr. Daniel *he*, I intend to keep my part of the bargain and I expect him to keep his." Head high and fuming, she walked out.

So far, she had learned that all she had to do was eat and sleep and sit on the porch, and that Daniel wasn't always gone when he was supposed to be gone.

That night, she left her door unlocked and lay in her white gown under the white net tent with the shutters closed, listening to Daniel's footsteps along the hall. She thought she heard him pause at her door, but immediately heard the door close across the hall.

Just as she started to get up and open the shutters, to let the hot room cool, she heard his door open, the doorknob to her own room rattle and the door open and close. So she lay back waiting. It was too dark to see, but she could tell where he was by his bare footsteps and his breathing: inside the room, at the foot of the bed, standing next to the bed on the right side. Sounded like he was removing his clothes, unbuttoning his shirt, then his pants. Yes, removing his clothes; she could tell by the whisper of his shirt to the floor. Dropped pants with clinking change, keys, pocketknife. One knee on the bed, pressing down.

"Light the lamp," she said.

The knee moved, foot on the floor. "What?" he said.

"Light the lamp," she said. "You've seen me, now I'll see you."

He fumbled the globe, overturned it, felt it all back into place like a blind man. The matchbox shook, rattled. He struck a match, touched the tiny flame to the wick. It flared. And there he stood—all shadows and hollows and hair—naked and at her mercy.

But when he placed his knee on the bed again, lifting the mosquito netting and reaching for her, she froze. Words were one thing, actions quite another.

On all fours, he laughed, panting and crouching over her. "You're full of surprises," he said. "I never expected…"

She still had on her gown. He tried to take it off. She'd expected him to maybe pull it up, do his business and go. She stayed, dead in one spot, while he tried to work the gown over her head.

His green eyes glowed. "Could you sit up a bit…while I?"

"Just get on with it?" She closed her eyes to make it dark. "I don't know how."

"This is not a dance, Doll. Not something you have to learn."

The two of them together smelled starchy and hot.

He seemed to be rethinking his strategy. He let the gown go and kissed her. Not like the kiss in the church at all, but a warm gentle kiss more like the kisses of other boys, and not all that bad. She pressed her lips to his and ran her hands up and down the long muscles of his back. Of its own volition, the rod between his legs began pushing at her gown. He reached beneath and tried the tail of the gown this time. Raising it only enough to allow for skin contact.

"You scared the hell out of me, my shy little wife," he said. "Thought I'd married some kind of hussy."

She would have to pay, she knew she would, but she was tough and resilient and couldn't resist it. She bit his shoulder and arched her body toward the assault that was coming anyway.

Slow days and long nights at Staten Bay, and Doll found herself falling into the routine of her new home. Now that they'd gotten beyond the physical initiation rites of marriage, they could laugh and talk. Doll couldn't stand for long not-talking, not-laughing, after the fun of growing up in the flatwoods, and she liked the easy off-hand joking of this country brother to the dead state senator. She warmed to the visits of this virile man in her bed, who came after dark and left before dawn— long before dawn—to sleep in his own bed. If he fell asleep in her bed, she would nudge or knee him till he woke up.

"Are you doing that in your sleep?"

"I'm awake."

"You want me to go, right?"

"It's too hot for two in this bed."

He would leave but come back for another visit before morning.

She could feel herself softening and yielding, body and spirit.

What she knew about sex was what she'd learned from watching the bulls mount the heifers. Unlikely couplings with the bulls so big and the heifers so small—how did that work? She thought she understood now. What she hadn't expected, the beautiful mystery, was the part she played in reassuring Daniel that he was powerful, that he was in command. In nature the coupling had been short and brutal, the bull's thrusts were never slowed to make time for thinking. Part of her husband's power over her, she had found, was in the way he knew how to make the act last and enable her to savor it.

Still, there was something bull-like about Daniel's part in the act—maybe all men's. She was the one being done to and him the doer, her taking it all in in thought and calling it love and him staying on the surface, struggling toward an end. Not that his arousing of her wasn't paramount, a test and triumph of power, but he seemed to remain outside while she went inside, alone.

Sitting next to Daniel over dinner, she would smile shyly. Who was this man?

She was a stranger finding a comfortable corner in a new place. But in all the huge house, with all its many corners, there was no space that Maureen didn't invade.

On Tuesday morning, the third week in August, Doll watched through the east windows of her bedroom the mailman on his brown horse stop outside the gate and hand down a shallow stack of letters to Maureen.

"This dry weather's got the cattle ranchers all over going bankruptcy. Tell Mr. Daniel he can pick up cows for a song anywhere he takes a mind to."

"I'll tell him," Maureen said, turning toward the house.

Again Doll had slept late and felt pointless and lazy. Daniel had left on Saturday for Louisiana, taking Oscar with him, to buy some red polled cows he'd read about being auctioned off in New Orleans (the mailman was always relaying old news, hoping to score with the local big shots). At least when he was home she felt that her pointless days were moving toward some point if nothing but night and the thrill of loving this man she now liked enough to miss. Actually they got along fine, till they tried to talk business. Each time she reminded him of his promise to get her a fancy way to go—his words—he said he intended to, that he hadn't got around to it yet. She said that she would catch one of the gum wagons to Four Mile Still, and he asked, "And back? Would you come back? I'd probably have to end up going after you, and right now I'm too busy." She watched Maureen sorting through the mail, coming up the walk. When she got to the hall, Doll opened the door, surprising her.

"Maureen, did I get any mail?" Doll asked.

Maureen pulled two letters from the bottom of the stack and handed them to Doll.

Doll closed the door. She no longer said please or thank you to the two-faced woman who ruled her house. Had quit feeling spoiled and impolite. She wouldn't even dignify Maureen's behavior by mentioning it to Daniel. He knew—he had to know—otherwise why had he bragged so on her cooking the night before he left. Stewed squash with onions and cream, juicy pork tenderloin, blackberry pie and biscuits so light they seemed cut from the air itself. Doll couldn't quarrel with that. And too, since that first morning, Maureen had kept Doll's breakfast warm till dinnertime if she slept late.

Doll slipped on her old thin white dress—the one she'd had on the day Daniel's stallion snatched the fence down—and took the letters out to the front porch and sat on the doorsteps to read them. One from Adam, the other from her mother. The sun had already cleared the top steps, leaving a straight edge of shadow on the bottom one.

There had been only a couple of night rains since Doll came to Staten Bay, but the hot centering sun soaked up the moisture each daybreak. Across the woods and fields a soft haze hung like distant rain in sunshine. The cotton plants were wilted but the blooms shone like bolls. The corn had dried into bent beige stalks as if struck dead in blowing poses by the steady hot breeze. Still, the ferny dill dog fennel and split-tipped grass, bordering the forks and patches of baked white sand, were rank green and gaining on the men who slung the bush hooks weekly.

Already the Negroes were harvesting the corn in the north field beyond a ridge of black pines separating the fields, and Doll could hear the slow creaking of the wagon wheels and women and children calling out to one another. Most of the men at Staten Bay were gone, either to the gum woods or to check on the hogs and cows now forced deeper into the swamps and hammocks to suck what water could be found from the slews, or to the Alapaha River which had been reduced to a pale yellow stream that lured the cattle out on the exposed riverbottom of boggy sand.

Listening to the riveting buzz of locusts, broken only by the clatter of pots and pans in the kitchen and Joe's soft plundering at the commissary, Doll ripped open the letter from Adam.

Dear Doll,
Supposing you didn't receive the letter I wrote on your wedding day, I'll repeat: I miss you. Your loving friend, Adam.

P.S. I cannot help wondering about Staten's reaction to your emasculating him on his wedding day.

She read it twice, word by word and then whole, because Adam always said much by saying little. Okay, so he still loved her. Then why hadn't he come right out and said it before? Because now he was safe from having to marry her himself?

The next letter:

Dear Doll,

I hope you know how lucky you are to have married such a fine, honest man as Mr. Staten. That said, I doubt those qualities alone make for a good husband, a happy marriage. But you should know that since my last letter to you, he has taken over the mortgage on our place like he said and had delivered from Fargo a wagonload of groceries. Cornmeal, flour, lard, coffee, sugar, cheese and cloth on the bolt, even store-bought hats and shoes for me and Sheba, which as you know have been scarce as hens' teeth around here these past few years. It seems like everywhere in the house there's color where there wasn't much before. Of course I'm talking about bright color, like spring and fall flowers, or yellow squash and green and red peppers, speaking of which we have always been blessed. Looks like this old house is fading right along with me. I guess color is something you don't think about money buying until you get ahold of a little and then all of a sudden color is there. I just wanted to tell you that, to give you a picture of the old place with new things in it, to let you know that Mr. Staten has certainly done his part. With all my heart I hope you'll come to respect him even if you don't love him. Just don't wait for him to make you happy, that's up to you. By the way, Sheba is fine. She's got her eye on our new preacher, and is as excited as I am about us coming to visit you in a couple of weeks. No word from you about that, so I'm guessing we'll be welcome. But welcome or not, I need to see you and know you're fine.

Love, Mama

"A couple of weeks?" Doll searched for a date on the front of the envelope, but the stamp was smeared, unreadable.

From where she sat, Doll could see Joe standing on the commissary porch with his hands in his roomy overalls pockets, talking to a drummer in a long suit coat. She waved. Joe waved. The drummer watched as she got up and started down the hall.

"Maureen," she called.

The racket in the kitchen stopped and Maureen stepped out to the back porch. Just standing there in her white blouse and white apron-wrap over a gray skirt. Poised as ever with her arms loose by her sides and the hanging blue-striped towel like a sash.

"Maureen, did you see any other letters for me? Maybe a week ago."

"Who from?"

"Anybody—my mother."

"No." She stepped back over the threshold and was gone.

Doll went to the watershelf, took the metal dipper from the bucket now shimmering with noon sun. One dipper, two dippers into the white pan with the red rim, and she was scooping it to her hot face with her hands. The water was luckwarm and smelled of minerals and brass. The white towel she dried on smelled of sun and harsh lye washing. Of Fate. Fate.

She tossed the water out to the crimson princes' feathers where butterflies lit batting their wings—black and white striped and yellow—just being butterflies. Butterflies.

It seemed important that she name off simple things, the understandable. No, she wasn't accusing Maureen of hiding her mail; she suspected that she had—maybe to force Doll to leave out of loneliness, or to bait her into a quarrel—but she wasn't accusing her. She'd simply had enough.

From the doorway to the kitchen she said, "Maureen, I'm not accusing you of hiding my mail," and stepped inside the dim hot room smelling of stewing chicken and steeping sweet tea.

Maureen turned, holding out her white hands glistening

with chicken fat. A huge ham with moldy rind lay on the counter next to a blue and white stoneware shoulder bowl.

Doll sat at the cook table in the middle of the kitchen and pushed damp hair from her temples. "I'd like to know what your problem is, why you don't like me," she said.

"So far I've seen nothing to like. You're flighty, childish..."

"Childish?" Doll's face felt hot, a bright spot flared in her chest.

"You asked." Maureen didn't even stop stripping meat from the bones, didn't even look at her

"You're fired."

Maureen laughed, facing the window full of noon light. "You can't fire me; I don't work for you. I work for Daniel."

"I'm his wife."

"Wife's a title, dear."

"Get out."

"I will." Maureen began wiping around the green bowl of boned chicken with a cloth. "But not because you've ordered me out and not for long."

Doll stood and walked out, feeling she'd just proved Maureen right—that she was flighty and childish. But really she felt like a coward, fearing Maureen might not go and she wouldn't know what to do next.

Sitting in one of the wicker chairs in her bedroom, Doll waited, watching through the south window left of the fireplace for Maureen to pass. One minute, two minutes later, Doll heard her footsteps cross the back porch, then saw her walking—gliding—past the window. She looked up, locking eyes with Doll, then walked on. No apron and her hands regally brushing the folds of her gray skirt as she walked along the fork, past the barn and the commissary and vanished beyond the field curve.

Doll's first skirmish won as Mrs. Staten.

In the kitchen again, Doll forked from the green bowl some of the white meat of the chicken, took a boiled egg from the simmering pan of water on the stove. She sat and ate at the cook table, taking measure of the cattycornered black iron stove; the various tall, short, fat, squat pottery jugs, all South Georgia-dirt colored; castiron and copper pots, hanging from the beadboard wall behind; shelves of jarred peaches, pears and pickled cucumbers; and in the left corner, near the back door, a clunky dark lard press and sausage stuffer and a butter churn next to an oak pie safe with hammered tin panels and holes that breathed out scents of cinnamon, cloves and nutmeg.

So, Doll didn't know how to cook. She could figure what was in the pottery jugs—lard, sorghum, sugar-cane syrup—but not how to use it. So, she had worked in the fields and woods instead of the kitchen at home. Her mother and Sheba would come to visit—maybe today, maybe tomorrow—and she would show off for them by feeding them hog slop. Or let her mother cook. But when Daniel got home on Friday or Saturday, what would she do? The huge moldy ham on the counter looked intimidating.

Fate. She would go get Fate to come cook.

Leaving the small white bowl on the cook table with eggshells in it, she set off down the hall and up the lane. Through the flaring white sunlight, she could just make out Estelle rocking on her front porch under shelter of steeping pine, enveloped by smells of moldering deer tongue. At the three-path road running north to Statenville and south to the Florida line, Doll waved and kept walking toward the quarters and didn't look back. She got along fine with Estelle—her only company other than Fate and Maureen—but still felt Estelle thought she needed looking after. Doll had accepted that she was here to stay at Staten Bay, and now it was time to order her household.

When she got past the ridge of pines separating the fields, she could see the mule-drawn wagon plugging down the dusty corn and peanut rows across the ten-rail fence. Trailing Negro women in bonnets or headrags, plus a couple of old men and boys, were cropping ears of corn from the stripped stalks and pitching them into the wagon.

Doll stopped, trying to pick Fate out from among the

women, listening to them laughing, shouting, wagon wheels screaling, the SCHLP SCHLP of corn ripped from the dead stalks, and overlaid on the myriad sounds, babies crying and mourning doves purling. Curious, she crept through the high grass and weeds along the left road shoulder, checking for snakes, climbed over the fence and started toward the pine ridge where the crying seemed to make up from.

A slim, leggy young woman wearing two long shiny braids pinned on top of her head, who had been tailing the wagon, came loping down the cornrow and across the patch of humped green melons at the end. When she got to the pine shade she knelt and lifted a tiny wriggling baby in a rag diaper from a panned place in the dirt. The hole was lined with a scrapwork quilt, and as Doll got closer she could see a half-dozen or so other holes with babies kicking and squalling inside or either sleeping. Dog flies and mosquitoes swarmed in the shade and lit on the babies. The woman opened her indigo shirt and clasped the crying baby to her cream-brown breast. One less baby's crying now.

Her face looked more Indian than Negroid: like the skin on her breast, cream-brown; symmetrical features and high cheekbones marked by brighter blades of skin and clear eyewhites. Her quick black eyes said it all, that her refined look set her apart from the coarser, darker women and she had to be on guard asleep and awake, a condition since childhood maybe which had resulted in a lonesome, wary quality. A mean scar on her fair neck was her only visible flaw.

"I'm looking for Fate," said Doll, holding up her skirt tail to keep it from dragging over briars and sandspurs at the end of the cornrows.

Her eyes darted over Doll, assessing her. No smile. "Aldean!" she called out, still nursing the baby on her knees. She didn't sound at all like she looked; her voice was as harsh as the other women's. Made Doll flinch.

A short black man with white hair was stomping down a peanut vine. He stopped and cupped one ear.

"You seen Fate this evening?"

"At the house," he hollered and pulled up the vine, shaking the dirt from the halms of dangling green penders. He plucked one off and cracked it open, checking to see if the nuts were filled out. He dropped the vine—pops. Meaning not filled out yet.

"How old is your baby?" Doll asked.

In the flatwoods, she would never have asked that; at home you didn't associate with the Negroes, but that was then and this was now, this day in this lonesome place. Here, she didn't know the rules, only that this woman was about her own age, almost as fair, and not Maureen.

"She be a month, come new moon." The woman looked down at the suckling baby. Her little round head was tufted with black wool.

Doll gazed up at the waning moon like a chalk mark on the blue sky and figured the baby for only a couple of weeks old.

The woman switched the baby to her other breast, a pale melon ripening in the blowing shade. Crows cawed overhead and ricocheted from the short-leaf pines. Another baby, penned in a hole not three feet away, peeped out with huge inky eyes.

"Well, I guess I'll go look for Fate," Doll said.

"She be at the house." The woman was still on her knees.

Doll started to turn, then said, "What's your name?"

"Lottie."

"Lottie," said Doll. "Is that your first baby, Lottie?"

"Nome." Lottie laughed. "I got two more at the house." She broke the suction of the baby's scar lips from her perked nipple. She was sleeping, her mouth still pursed and sucking, as Lottie lay her back on the pallet in the panned dirt.

"Who minds the other children while you work?"

"They mind theirselfs." She stood, buttoning her shirt over her milk-heavy breasts.

In the quarters, a fat black moccasin with a white ridged underbelly hung on exhibit from a forked pole near the well. Green-hooded blowflies swarmed, glanced and lit. The snake smelled like goat. Dogs barked and lunged and near-naked children with legs sore-crusted as lepers stood off and watched as Doll walked past the well and the snake display and along the open berth of tracked dirt between the facing shanties of the quarters. Broken furniture on broken porches where deer tongue, a type of wild tobacco cropped and sold cheap to be cured for snuff, lay drying on croaker sacks and ancient ladies sat fanning in the midst of filth as if born to leisure.

A guinea boy was riding the back of a large yellow dog with lit eyes. A puss-filled carbuncle stood on the child's ribby chest. Another boy was riding a stick horse.

"Where's Fate?" Doll asked a doll-sized girl with sprigged plaits and red mattered eyes.

"Fate!" one of the boys in the lineup hollered. He set off running with his heels kicking high along the row of shacks on Doll's right.

A slow labored creaking came from inside the shack at the end of the row and through the open door the silhouette of a heavy round woman backlit by an opened door behind. "You younguns go on now," Fate said and ambled out on the porch.

Doll walked over and stood in the ragged shadow of the shingle eaves. "How you, Fate?"

She laughed without opening her mouth. "Ain't no good today," she said. "How come me here at the house stead of the cornfield."

"Well," said Doll, "I wondered if you'd come cook for me and Mr. Daniel."

"He done back from New Or-leans?"

"No, he won't be back till Friday or Saturday, but I got company coming any day now."

"Law, Miss Doll!" Fate said and dropped into a rocking chair with a broken sweep. "I tell you the truth, Mr. Daniel done sample my cooking, say I ain't no count for nothing but to wash. Can't work in the fields half the time," she added. "Old back trouble."

"But you can cook, right?"

She laughed again. "I can cook, shore can. Just can't cook

to suit Mr. Daniel. Me, I feed this whole bunch half the time and ain't nobody starved to yet as I know of."

"Fate, I had to let Maureen go."

"Law, Miss Doll. Mr. Daniel gone take a stick to me and you both, he come home and find you run off his pet cook. He *some* picky bout his eating. Picky bout who-all in his house too."

"I'm kind of picky myself," said Doll.

"Ma'am?"

"Nothing." Doll looked around at the grouped children. "Are you the one looks out for all these children?"

"Some, I do."

"Then maybe you ought not..."

"Nome, they's a couple old aunties ain't able to work belong to do that."

"Okay. Talk it over with Elkin and ..."

"Shoot! Elkin ain't studying what I do." She stepped down the porch steps, hanging to the handrail, and walked next to Doll through the thronging children and dogs.

"Fate," said Doll, "what're these children doing with impetigo—all those sores?"

"Dog days," she said.

"You got any Methiolate?"

"Nome, none as I know of."

"Well, I'll see to it you get some. And they look wormy to me. Tapeworms maybe."

"Sho do now."

"I'll have Estelle look into it, but these children need a bath at least a couple times a week."

"Sho do now.

When they reached the field again, Doll could hear the babies crying from their panned pallets.

"Nussing babies," said Fate.

"I talked to Lottie," said Doll walking slow to keep pace with Fate, stepping heavy, foot to foot in her black flat shoes with walked-down backs.

"Huh!"

"You and Lottie don't get along?"

"That Lottie, she spread her legs for ery buck in rut."

Ah! So, the other women were jealous of Lottie. "How did she get that scar on her neck?"

"What scar that?"

Chapter 5

The bowl of eggshells on the cook table was still there on Wednesday morning, the ham was gone, and a seasoning can of runny lard sat in the center of the filthy stove. Fate didn't show up till after ten.

The fast-talking mailman on his slow horse came and went, leaving mail for Daniel only, along with a message that some bully from Waycross was coming to town and looking for a fight.

Every since she married, it seemed, Doll had been daily jolted by some surprise information concerning Daniel, piecing together who he was. Could he be the local bully that the reigning out-of-town bullies sought out to enhance their reputations? She laughed to herself, imagining asking him and him saying as usual, No, that was my brother the senator who was the bully. Truth, evasion, or convenient excuse, she never could tell. But really she didn't think Daniel was a bully; he didn't seem the type. He was too industrious and homesteaded, no fool like the old man in Statenville she heard about who was down on his hands and knees in the courtyard, pawing like a bull and begging for a fight.

Doll took the mail to Daniel's office, lay it on his desk and started toward the kitchen to tell Fate to clean up after cooking, to ask what happened to the ham. This could be the day that Mrs. Baxter and Sheba showed up.

Heading up the hall, Doll heard shoe soles brushing on the doorsteps, and turned to see Estelle standing on the porch.

"Good morning to you," she called.

"Estelle, hey," said Doll. "Come on in."

Huge racket in the kitchen, glass breaking, a stove lid clanked over a hole. Smoke streamed from the doors to the kitchen and dining room. Fate popped out to the back porch, fanning her apron. A yellow cat slipped through the door to the kitchen. "Git yoself out from here," she yelled. Much shouting and meowling as Fate chased the cat around the kitchen. The cat shot out the door, followed by a stick of stovewood.

Fate stepped out behind the cat. "Moaning, Miss Doll. Miss Estelle." She went back into the kitchen, fanning smoke.

"You training you a new cook, I see," said Estelle.

While the two women visited on the porch, Doll couldn't take her eyes off the wide pine floorboards. She should be up sweeping in case her company was coming today. How did the house get so dirty overnight? With only herself and Fate around. Well, Bo Dink had come by, then Elkin, plus dogs and cats. It was as if Maureen had cursed the house with her absence.

At the moment Estelle was talking around talking about the new cook, which Doll figured was the purpose of her visit. "Had a sister was bad to read," she said. "Daddy told her it's crazy people reads all the time."

A loud VLAM! from the direction of the kitchen, like killing a housefly with a frying pan.

"Have you ever been to New Or-leans?" Estelle asked.

"Not yet."

"Did he ask you?"

"No."

"Would you of gone if he'd asked?"

"Probably." Where was this interrogation leading? Doll thought she knew. Estelle had to be trying to tell her that this New Orleans venture was as much about women as cows. If so, Doll had been wrong to feel safely married, to think that Daniel had given up yearning for his bachelor days, that she was all to him and enough. But why? She, herself, couldn't imagine wanting any other man except Daniel. She longed for him just thinking his name.

If not for her pride, her trying to hold her place as Mrs. Staten, she would have prodded Estelle for more information. "New Orleans must really be something," she said instead. "Next time I might go."

Estelle paused rocking: she stared at Doll like a foolish child in need of correction but not ready for it yet. "Oscar says it's just crazy people everywhere you look."

"So, he's been before with Daniel?"

"Couple times a year." Estelle spat off the porch, a cord of brown snuff juice. "Course it's business." The way she said it meant it wasn't business. Then, "Look out, honey, " she said, "if he brings you a pretty."

"A pretty?"

Now Fate was humming in the kitchen.

"You know, a present of some kind."

"Why?"

"Just look out."

Enough. Doll had to drop it here or risk making a fool of herself by begging for more information about her husband. Yes, she'd married him for business reasons but it was more now. Whether love she couldn't say. "My mother and sister ought to be here any day now."

"That a fact?"

"I haven't seen them since I got married."

"That's the way of it generally. You get married, move away, don't hardly see your folks no more."

"You don't have children, do you, Estelle?"

Big spit. "Two in the graveyard."

"What about your family, your mama and all?"

"In the graveyard."

"I'm sorry."

"Look out she don't oversalt what she cooks. Lard in everything she sets on the table."

"Fate?" Doll was beginning to warm up to Estelle, but sometimes she reminded her of the mailman with his outdated messages.

"They say the way to a man's heart's through his stomach." Estelle stood then, crossed to the porch steps, held to the railing and stepped down.

Was she implying that Doll had better learn to cook? Or warning her that she'd better get Maureen back before Daniel got home.

"By the by," she added, turning for emphasis, "I seen your ham dressed up in a white apron, walking off down the lane yesterday."

Come Thursday, the bowl with the eggshells still sat on the cook table. Houseflies everywhere. Splinters from the firewood brought in by Bo Dink were scattered on a trail from the doorsteps to the kitchen. The white kitchen walls were smoked. The rest of the house Doll had cleaned up yesterday, but a runaway mule pulling a wagonload of corn had churned up the dust in the lane and now it lay like crocheted dollies on every piece of furniture in the house. On the floors like gauze mats.

Fate's mangy black dog had camped out on the front porch, smelled dead. The yellow barn cat slept on the back porch davenport.

But worst of all was Fate's lard-spiked cooking: collard greens sobbing in grease, a great cake of dry white rice, stringy stew beef, fried okra so salty your tongue clenched and tea so strong and sweet your throat closed up. Her cornbread was heavy and damp with a glazy charred crust.

After dinner, Doll had a talk with her: clean up after you cook, go light on the lard, forget the salt.

"You reckon I best go get that Maureen fore Mr. Daniel get home?" Fate asked.

"No. I'll go get Lottie to help out."

Doll headed out to look for Lottie. She'd been dying for an excuse to rescue her and her baby from the fields, and this was it. But there were other babies, other women, and she couldn't rescue them all.

Actually, Lottie didn't seem all that glad to be rescued— Doll could almost see her heart beating in her fair smooth throat—and of all the babies on their panned pallets at the south end of the corn field, Lottie's cried loudest and longest.

Back at the house, Doll was sitting on the front porch, barefooted and dusty, rocking the baby for Lottie to clean up, when she saw her mother's old boxy black buggy turn down the lane. The baby was gnawing her fist, crying and grunting. Colic, Fate said.

Doll dashed from the porch with the baby bobbling on her shoulder, meeting her mother and Sheba halfway down the lane. "Mama, Baa! You're here," she shouted.

Mrs. Baxter hauled back on the leads and the old brown mare stopped cold. "What in the world, Doll?"

Doll was kissing the mare's neck, sweet-talking her. "Oh, this is Lottie's baby. Girl who's cleaning up the house." The baby whimpered, knotted with her knees in Doll's chest. Doll swayed her, walking. "Come on," she said to her mother and sister.

The mare plodded on with her head hung, following Doll to the hitching post.

Sheba stepped down in her homemade yellow dress, new shoes and flat-brimmed straw hat. They hugged, almost crying; the baby was crying.

"You hateful old thing you," Sheba said into Doll's hair, "leaving us like that." She pulled back, straightening her hat and looking around.

Mrs. Baxter got down and grabbed Doll, rocking and hugging both her and the baby. Laughing, both of them, while the baby cried. The older woman's corseted body felt like a skinny woman's ribs. Doll longed to feel her soft mama. She smelled of new cloth—the two piece green-checked dress with tailored bodice, tight sleeves, ankle-length skirt and bustle. Her face was red.

"You're too hot, Mama," Doll said, then called out to Joe on the commissary porch. "Joe, come get this buggy and bring these things inside."

He stood a minute, then strolled over, nodded at the two strange women. Doll introduced them, then walked off toward the gate, while he reached in back of the buggy for the two tapestry bags. Joe had surely heard about Doll's run-in with Maureen, but he hadn't shown it.

A timber cart drawn by six mules passed along the fork to the south woods leaving a rattle and tumble of dust. The baby was crying good now, constant bawling.

"Daniel's gone to New Orleans to get some cows, he and Oscar," she said to the women behind her, going up on the porch. "He'll be back tomorrow or the day after."

She stopped in the hall where Lottie was flirting dust with the sage broom. "Lottie, maybe she's hungry," Doll said and handed over the baby. Lottie sat in a chair and opened her shirt letting a ripe brown breast out.

Joe stepped up behind the three women.

"Joe, put those bags in the bedroom next to mine."

He started into the room across the hall next to Daniel's room.

"No, not Daniel's," she said, walking on down the hall. "Put them in here." She pointed to the dim tidy room on the left at the end of the hall. And then to her mother and Sheba, "Oh, I'm so happy to see y'all."

Smoke was boiling out of the kitchen.

Doll yelled, "Fate, your cooking's on fire!"

Gone from the fine, ordered house, were the close smells of beeswax and lavender and mellow cooking; and in their place, harsh bleach and collard greens, like swamp mud. A hectic commonness covering the ordered calm—how Doll liked it. People talking all at once, a baby on the place. Things going on.

After dinner, Mrs. Baxter took off her corset and her relieved belly rose up under the new green dress. Earlier she'd taken off her hat and her thin graying hair was smashed flat on top, but the rats of fake hair tucked in the fat roll on her nape kept their shape. Fate was ironing clothes in the kitchen while Lottie cleaned up her cooking mess. So far, not a cross word, only the squeaking of the ironing board as Fate pressed down with the flatiron. Smells of hot lye and starch barely distinguishable from her scorched corn.

Things were looking up—except for the food.

Mrs. Baxter said the baked sweet potatoes were the best she'd ever eaten. She went on and on about the potatoes to make up for her lack of comment on the greasy chicken, salty corn, and soda bread. Maureen's jarred peaches had been transformed into a cobbler that floated like cork in a pool of butter. Then Mrs. Baxter ambled out on the back porch and sprawled on the davenport next to the yellow cat, bare feet up and new brown shoes paired on the floor. Leafing through a magazine while watching Sheba trim Doll's hair, now well below her waist. The cat purred and curls whispered down like tassels of silk.

Doll was sitting in a straight chair facing out. The new shoots of vines and tendrils had drooped atop the arbored acre of grapevine, glossy purple scuppernongs like shining eyes. Doll picked up a lock of hair from her lap. "Cut it, Baa," she said.

"Doll!" said Mrs. Baxter and clapped the magazine shut.

"Just do what I say, Baa. Cut it." Doll lifted the mass of hair from her sweaty neck. "Cut it to my shoulders at least. I want to wear my hair up like you and Mama."

"Well, it *would* be becoming, I guess." Mrs. Baxter sat up straight and crossed her big warped feet, looking at the magazine again. "I want you girls to see this picture of the Statue of Liberty. It says here it was a gift from the French, 'symbolizing the independence both countries fought for during the American Revolution.' President Cleveland dedicated it in New York last October."

"I can't picture it," Sheba said and posed with the scissors.

Mrs. Baxter turned the magazine picture out for her to see.

"Not that, Mama. I meant Doll with her hair cut."

"Mama, the Statue of Liberty looks like you," Doll said. They laughed.

Lottie in the kitchen mumbled something. Fate didn't answer but sounded like she dropped the flatiron.

"Cut it," Doll repeated, eager before she changed her mind.

Sheba raked the hair from around Doll's chair with a bare foot. "Yes. You'll look darling with it up. Especially in hats."

She began snipping at Doll's right shoulder. Doll caught the lock and felt it into strands, single hairs. She was a married woman now.

Earlier, Mrs. Baxter had cornered her and asked if she and Daniel were getting along. "Yes," Doll said, "I think it would have killed me to lose our place." "He's a fine man," Mrs. Baxter had said. "Has done good by us. But is he good to you?" "You mean does he beat me, no. I just miss home."

Mrs. Baxter dozed with the magazine on her lap. Doll watched the chickens pecking the dirt of the back yard, pecking and stepping and scratching and yanking their rag heads. This morning when Fate had gone out to the chicken pen to wring the neck of a chicken for dinner, she had somehow managed to let all the chickens out on the yard, and even the first one with the wrung neck had somehow escaped and flopped away. Every so often now Doll thought she heard it fluttering its wings and clucking weakly under the house.

Estelle came walking around the south side of the house, limping up the steps and onto the back porch. Doll introduced everybody and Estelle sat watching the hair cutting with Mrs. Baxter. As usual no comment till she had sufficiently charmed them all with her sour silence and that knowing set look of her vicious little face. What was she thinking? Doll smiled. She would tell Sheba about the Epsom salts episode later. Well, maybe not since Baa wasn't yet married.

After several more lunges in the rocker, Estelle sitting at full attention got up and hobbled over to the watershelf and drank water from the gourd dipper in the white bucket. Then she shoved the yellow cat from the davenport, settled in next to Mrs. Baxter and launched in on one of her one-sided, disjointed conversations, starting with her accident with the buggy in Jasper, then on to her milk cow dying from eating poison felder, and somehow meandering into instructions on how to sand a breadtray with a piece of broken glass. Eyes ever on the haircut now progressing toward Doll's centerback.

Lottie's baby, napping on the sideroom bed off the back porch, began fretting, then crying, and Lottie came out through the dining room door and crossed the hall to check on her.

Haircut done, Doll stood and brushed the clippings from her shoulders and hefted her hair. Then turned toward the two women on the davenport.

"Well, it's precious as can be," said Mrs. Baxter.

"I can't believe all this hair!" said Sheba, gazing down at the rug of black hair. "Where's the broom?"

"See you don't sweep it out in the yard," said Estelle. "Do, a bird'll build a nest with it and give you the headache." Wagging her head at Doll, she stood to spit off the porch edge.

Why didn't she just come straight out and say that the haircut had been a mistake? That Daniel would hate her hair cut? The warning look cast Doll's way as Estelle headed back for her place on the davenport made Doll furious.

"By the way," she said, changing the subject in her mind, if not Doll's, "I went to the quarters and doctored that infitigo on the picaninnies. Give em some sulfur old Doc Hill left with me. Clear em up if they take it reg'lar." She spoke up. "Y'all listening, Fate and Lottie?"

"Yessum," Fate called out from the kitchen.

"Don't give it, it won't work, hear me?"

"Sho do, now."

"What about worming the children?" Doll asked.

Mrs. Baxter and Estelle began batting back and forth their remedies for worming, which led off to talk about dysentery which both agreed could be headed off with better hygiene. As for malaria, Estelle pointed out, at least the men with syphilis benefited from the high fevers which seemed to burn the disease out of their bodies.

"Doll," Mrs. Baxter said, "you be careful, you hear?"

"Mama!"

"I mean the dysentery, of course."

Suddenly Doll looked up the hall and saw Daniel riding down the lane ahead of Oscar in the wagon. Horse hooves clopping, wagon wheels screaling. The mangy black dog on the porch set off barking across the yard and bellied under the fence where he'd dug a tunnel.

"Here they come, straggling in," Estelle said and stood and began hobbling up the hall with the others following.

Joe, on the commissary porch, took out up the lane after the dog, slung a stick at it, then walked alongside Daniel and the stallion toward the house.

From the fork of the lane, Bo Dink appeared in the oak shade at the hitching post, as if he'd been there all along. He was grinning and scarifying the dusty dirt with his bare toes.

"He ain't brung you nothing, boy." Estelle cackled out and sat in the rocker left of the doorsteps with her fingers laced in her lap.

Mrs. Baxter took the chair next to Estelle's and Doll and Sheba stood near the hallway watching.

Squinting in the sun Daniel's eyes roved over the women on the porch, then locked on Doll. He tipped his hat, grinning, dismounted and handed the reins to Joe.

Oscar stopped the wagon alongside the stallion.

Daniel sauntered into the oakshade, rubbed Bo Dink's head, boxed at his sucked in stomach. The boy dodged, laughed, then stepped up to Daniel as if asking for more should that be the price.

"You awright, boy," Daniel said. Then he yelled to Oscar. "Oscar, see if we remembered those firecrackers for this knothead here, will you?"

Bo Dink slunk off behind the stallion toward the wagon. Oscar handed him a long red narrow package, then got down. Bo Dink wandered off up the lane, digging in a pocket of his patched black shorts, brought out a box of matches and shucked a firecracker from the pack. Lit it and threw it up the lane. Loud crack. Then another.

Daniel and Joe laughed. The spooked dog cowering in the pines, left side of the lane, ran bow-backed with his tail between his legs toward the house, trying to escape the wrath of Bo Dink's fireworks.

"Betwixt them old firecrackers and that dog there," Oscar said, "won't a calf be left on the place."

"Get rid of the dog, Joe," Daniel said, walking on toward the gate. Then without changing tones he spoke to them all, "Don't look like any rain to speak of since we been gone."

Another firecracker popped off as Daniel stepped through the gate with the dog on his heels. He hollered back, "Bo Dink, I catch you shooting those things off where the woods'll catch fire, I'm gonna take them back. Hear?"

He stopped midway on the walk, speaking to each of the ladies: Mrs. Baxter, Sheba, Estelle and finally Doll.

The chicken with the wrung neck flopped from beneath the edge of the porch; it looked like a bait chicken being twitched by a string. The black dog sprang forward and scooped it up with his mouth and scuttled under the house. The other chickens squawked and ran, running squawks spreading from front to rear of the house. The baby on the back porch cried full blast. A firecracker popped.

"What happened to your hair?" Daniel asked Doll.

"I had Baa cut it."

Without turning around, he shouted, "Oscar, you and Joe, bring in that trunk of pretties for Mrs. Staten, will you?"

"A whole trunkload!" Estelle cackled. "Honey, you married now."

"Yes," he said, standing before Doll. "You do look right wifey. Now if you can just cook."

That evening, supper was a disaster that Doll didn't even try to make less disastrous. She was too mad. She couldn't wait for her hair to grow out. Her head felt fuzzy and light. She'd almost cried when Lottie had sacked up her hair to take to the quarters for one of the aunties to sew on the girls' cloth dolls. Mrs. Baxter had suggested that Doll save the hair for rats, like the kind she used for filler, but couldn't come up with a single needy woman who would benefit from hair so black. Could be of course that later Doll herself might find that the hair would come in handy, she said, trying to helpful. Wrong thing to say, given Doll's mood and such volatile circumstances.

First Doll had left her hair down, but she started thinking she looked too girlish. Then she'd pinned it up in a rich loose bundle but it kept spitting the pins. And too Doll decided Maureen would think she was trying to look like her. She checked and checked before the mirror in her room for signs that her cropped hair might also be thinning.

They ate early to keep the night bugs from fogging to the lights. Still, houseflies clouded the scorched limas floating scored fatback, Fate's same old cake of white rice, hand-rolled lard biscuits shaped like rocks. Heavy as rocks.

"I guess the peas and butterbeans dried up in the garden," Daniel said, dipping limas to his plate and passing the bowl to Mrs. Baxter on his left.

"It's dry all right. Thank you."

"Pass the biscuits, will you, Mrs. Staten?" he said to Doll.

Doll, next to Mrs. Baxter, lifted the platter of biscuits with one hand, brought the other up to support it. He took the platter passed on by Mrs. Baxter, picked up a biscuit, looked at it and let it drop to his plate with a loud thunk.

"Fate," he called toward the kitchen, "bring the butter please."

The late sun streaked through the kitchen to the dining room; the heat was mesmerizing, almost ticked.

In a few minutes Fate waddled in—her white apron was filthy, her flat feet bare—and offered him a bowl of yellow butter marbled with white. The red headrag made her round chocolate face glow like the sun.

"That lard in the butter?"

"Yassuh." She looked ready to run.

He handed the bowl back. "Plain butter will do."

She took it, left the kitchen.

"Sheba," he said, "you're looking fine in that yellow dress."

"Thank you," said Sheba and looked at her sister. She shrugged.

Daniel laughed, small-talking. "You ladies don't still have that bear, do you?"

Mrs. Baxter laughed. "No, I'm glad to say we don't."

"It was my bear," said Sheba. "Not Doll's." Not trying so hard, Sheba did look fine, her scrubbed face open and shining with sweat. Sheba being Sheba and nobody else.

Changing the subject, Mrs. Baxter said in a cheery voice, "Now, I for one would like to hear all about that wedding you went to at the White House, Mr. Staten."

"I didn't go," he said, chewing carefully, suspiciously, then adding, "I got invited through connections of my brother, the senator. Don't mean to cut you short, ma'am, but I often get credited and blamed for Jimmy's doings. My folks sent him off to Cornell, and sent me to a business school in Jacksonville, Florida. Guess we had to be sent somewhere and I opted not to go where it was cold or much was expected of me."

Outside, Joe and Bo Dink were rounding up the chickens. The dog barked, head bumping on the floor under the house. Chickens squawked. Lottie was eating in the kitchen with the whimpering baby on her lap. Doll had tried to send her home but she'd insisted on cleaning up after Fate, now yelling out the kitchen door for Bo Dink to take that dog home if he wanted him alive.

"Tell him I'll take those firecrackers back if he doesn't," Daniel spoke up.

Doll said, "Are there always conditions to your gifts?" Behind Daniel's back, she had warned Joe he'd better not get rid of the dog.

Daniel only smiled at her. "How long will you ladies be staying?"

"Oh," said Mrs. Baxter, "I expect we'd better start on home tomorrow morning. Take care of the livestock."

"You get the supplies from Fargo this week?"

"Yes."

"Be careful," Doll said, "he'll take them back."

"Doll!" Mrs. Baxter said and pushed her glasses up on her nose.

Sheba shook her head, then bowed over her plate. "My, at the flies!"

"Fate, get in here with that fly flap." Daniel said.

Doll stood, picked up her plate. "I believe I'll eat with the help in the kitchen."

"Sit down, Doll," he said. "We have company."

Fate came into the dining room with the fly flap, meeting Doll with her plate going out.

Daniel stood. "Well I hope you ladies will excuse me." Speaking louder. "If anybody needs to discuss another household matter with me, I'll be in my office."

The sun was still shining after supper and the three women went out on the north end of the porch to rock and talk. Dusk seemed a long time coming while the two women from the flatwoods filled Doll in on news of the neighbors. When dusk did come, the heat seemed to gather with the grains of darkness making up on the porch.

Daniel came out later, drinking whiskey from a glass, and sat in the empty rocker next to Mrs. Baxter, nearest the doorsteps. Four in a row with Doll on the other end. He seemed over his mood or as if he'd come to some conclusions how to set his household right again. He told them about the cows he'd bought in New Orleans—two hundred head of red poll heifers and brood cows to be delivered by train to Haylow tomorrow—started in on some story about the ranch where he had bought them.

Doll stood. "Goodnight," she said, passing behind the other chairs. "Mama, Baa, if you need anything, just call."

Daniel was reared back with his feet crossed and propped on a porch post and she had to hug the wall to keep from brushing the back of his head with her left arm. An awkward moment and she was almost clear of his chair when he reared farther back and touched her with his head. It felt like shock, like the time she was washing dishes and seeing through the window heat lighting way off and suddenly felt a shock zinging up her arms to her shoulders and rippling through her chest. Not exactly a jolt but memorable and useful as future warning.

She got ready for bed in the dark so she wouldn't have to close the shutters. Besides, she didn't want to chance a glimpse at her hair in the mirror of the washstand or the chiffonier. In bed, she lay listening to them talking on the other end of the porch. Who had died recently, what was going on in the world outside—Daniel's department—which led to a one-man oratory on something called the American Protective Association and immigration restrictions, targeting polygamists, contract laborers and people with diseases.

Mrs. Baxter said she thought it was a crying shame how the Chinese were treated in the US of A after all the work they did on the railroads. Daniel agreed and Sheba said you couldn't find cleaner people than the Chinese, and used as an example the Chinese family in Homerville who stayed to themselves and worked hard, then narrowed in on them by trying to recall their names.

There had been a dross fire at Four-mile Still, Mrs. Baxter said. The gum-sopped cotton batting used to filter trash from the resin should have been hauled off instead of piled, Daniel said. "That fool stiller likely lit a lantern—what caused the fire." All agreed.

After fifteen minutes or so, Sheba and Mrs. Baxter announced they were going to bed. Daniel walked them down the hall to their room, offered to get them anything they needed. Apologized for the uproar at supper. Doll thought she heard her own name.

Daniel started back up the hall. He stopped at Doll's door, turning the knob, found it locked. Went out to the porch and sat in the rocker before her window. Still not dark, and she could see him silhouetted in the runner of dusk between the porch wall and the oak.

"Have you even looked in the trunk yet?" he said low. So low she wondered if he were talking to her or somebody else.

"No."

"Why not?"

119

"I don't like *pretties*. And I especially don't like being treated like a child."

"All women like pretties. Who was it borrowed a silk dress to impress the governor?"

"I wasn't trying to impress that old goat, you know that."

"Well, you did, lady. Couldn't keep his hands off your pretty little ass."

"I hate it when you talk like that."

"No you don't." He laughed. "What about this one: who wouldn't ride in a plain old wagon on her wedding day?" He drank from his whiskey glass. "Open the door, Doll. I need you. I haven't had a woman since I left here."

"Oh, really!"

"Swear to God."

"Me either."

"*Me either*, what?"

"I haven't had a man since you left here."

"That's no way for a lady to talk. Now open the door."

"No. And I'm not sure I want to be a lady." That was true. If all a lady did was wait at home for her husband, she'd rather be a hussy. Not that she would ever shame her family by becoming such.

"I'd hate to raise a ruckus with your folks here."

"You already have. So go ahead, kick down the door; you can always blame it on the ghost of your senator-brother." She absolutely couldn't recall having sat up under the hoop of mosquito netting. Her head felt light, and not only because of her haircut.

"Doll, you know I can't have Fate and Lottie around here. You know that, don't you?"

No answer.

"For one thing, Fate's liable to jump on Lottie over Elkin. You must have noticed how miserable Lottie gets shut up in the house. All the women in the quarters are jealous of her; out in the open she stands a better chance of dodging them."

"I'm not sending her back out in the fields with that baby. And that's that."

120

"Long as I'm the boss, I'll say who works where; I know these people and it's up to me to place them on the jobs that suit them." He paused, then said, "I guess I should tell you right now that I've sent word for Maureen to come in the morning."

Doll scooted out under the netting, breathing hard, rooting her toes into the rug. "I can't believe you'd do that to me; you never even asked me why I had to fire her."

"Well, she's not fired now." He drank. "You may as well accept it."

"Then you can give Maureen the trunk of pretties. I'm going home with Baa and Mama in the morning."

The rocker stopped. His voice leaned into the window. "You'll do no such thing. We're married, remember? You go where I say go, when."

He got up and went into the hall and she thought he was going to bed. She started to climb back into her own bed, but stopped, hearing—feeling—his footsteps light along the hall, then she saw the curtains parting on the left east window, him stepping inside.

She reached for the lamp on the nightstand, waiting till he reached the foot of her bed, aimed and threw it. Glass shattered. Kerosene fumes filled the room.

"What the...? My shoulder, hellfire!"

"Oh, I'm sorry!" she said sweetly. "I was aiming for your damn head."

Doll was getting dressed the next morning when she saw Maureen walking past the south windows of her bedroom. She was carrying a small stave bucket heaped with pods of okra. The small bucket looked odd swinging from the hand of so large a woman, and the okra didn't mesh with her queenly bearing.

Still in her room, later, Doll smelled coffee brewing, sausage frying and biscuits baking. Heard Sheba and Mrs. Baxter talking to Daniel in the dining room. Glass and kerosene on the blue rug, on the east wall. To get to the chiffonier, to pack her clothes, she had to put on her old brown hightops. The new wood trunk with its brass latches and leather straps, at the foot of the bed, seemed more dangerous than the spears and splinters of glass.

Through the front window she watched Daniel and Oscar and several Negro men ride up the lane to meet the shipment of cattle in Haylow and drive them home. Thunder of hooves, cloud of dust. She waited till the dust cleared, then unlatched the new trunk for a peek. Just a peek. It bloomed with perfume of roses and lemon, new paper and cloth. Pastel dresses frothed up like meringue on a pie—yellow, blue, pink with bell skirts and bustles and ruffles on the tails. Matching petticoats and under garments. Boxed hats, fans, lace-edged parasols and handkerchiefs. There was even a lace-up corset, like Mrs. Baxter's, only satiny, and a white cotton A-line gown with lace panels. But what she loved most, what she would wear till she wore it out, was a straight brown paisley skirt with a silk cream blouse and matching cummerbund that fastened in front with a pearl and rhinestone brooch.

She started to drop the lid, but instead took out the pink dress. It had a high, banded neck and a bodice overlay that reached from the shoulders to the tapering waist, puffed sleeves likewise tapering to the wrists, and enough material bustling out into a shirred skirt for two dresses. She had to take out all the dresses to get to the papered hatboxes with carrying cords on the bottom. Layered in rustling white tissue was a flat-brimmed straw hat sporting a pink grosgrain band and bow. Next to the hatboxes were three pairs of shiny, hard-leather shoes—white, brown and black with buttons up the side. Hurrying now, she sorted through the trunk for undergarments and a handkerchief to match the pink dress to take with her to the flatwoods. Heart aching to take it all, but not giving into her weakness—where would she wear such, to Sunday meetings at Bony Bluff?—feeling consoled by the fact of taking the pink dress and dressings by letting lay in its white velvet case an etched gold locket, the real pretty from New Orleans.

Out front, Joe had brought around Mrs. Baxter's buggy

with the brown mare. Two oxen, double yoked, stood stolid and drowsy-eyed in the sun north of the barn. Doll stepped outside to the porch and called him to come get her trunk. He acted as if he carried her trunk out every morning and brought it in at night—part of his job at Staten Bay. Nothing seemed to faze him, not even the weight of the trunk. He was a big man, a sweet man. He had pale, kind eyes. Not the man in the story she would hear over and again: how he had gone out bear hunting with the other men, and the dogs had surrounded a great black bear in a cypress slew in the east woods. When Joe got there, slipping through the woods with his rifle, he found the bear raring on its hind legs on a small island with its back to Joe, the dogs swimming in the black water, circling the bear and barking and snarling. The bear would reach out, pawing at them; all but one, a yellow cur, circling out and away from the growling bear. With one giant paw the bear had grabbed the head of the cur, pushing it down under water and pulling it up. Over and again, trying to get a grasp on the dog. Joe eased out into the water, barrel of the rifle pointed straight ahead and breath on hold. The bear growled, the dog's head popped up above water. So close he could smell the wild musk of the bear, Joe stuck the barrel as near as he could get without touching the center back of the bear, pulled the trigger and the bear dropped with a single grunt.

Doll tried to imagine this mild man killing the bear; she tried to imagine how he had told Daniel about her firing Maureen; she tried to think back to the point and place of him pacing down the lane next to the stallion and couldn't recall seeing him speak. Had Daniel hired him because he was so passive and obedient but gutsy? Had he made him that way? Was Maureen only part of the deal? Or the other way around. To understand Daniel, she felt she'd have to understand Joe and Maureen, how they came to be so dedicated to him and him to them.

When Mrs. Baxter and Sheba got to the porch, they stopped, staring at Doll on the front bench of the wagon, leadlines in hand and ready to go.

"I'm just going home for a visit, Mama," she said. "I'm lonesome for home." Her shoulder-length hair hung loose, crinkling and curling in the dank dewy air.

Mrs. Baxter came out the gate and climbed up on the wagon next to Doll and took the leadlines from her. Sheba got up on the other side, looked back at Mrs. Baxter's old trunk, at Doll.

"A *long* visit," Doll said.

Mrs. Baxter patted her knee. "Let's go home," she said.

Going up the lane, Doll could see Estelle sitting on the shady cabin porch. She scooched low between the two large women to keep Estelle from noticing her. Heading north, on the straightaway to Statenville, she could see the fresh hoof tracks stamped over stale tracks in the powdery road. Her only regret was giving Estelle the satisfaction of knowing she was right, that Doll was a mama-girl and Daniel Staten was too much man for her. Here she was, giving into Daniel and handing over her household to Maureen. The haircut had been a big mistake. She should have learned to cook. She was giving up by leaving Staten Bay.

Still, it was good to be going home.

Chapter 6

It was mid afternoon when they got to the flatwoods, heat clamping down on the long low house. There was a Stone Mountain watermelon on the porch, left by a neighbor; there was a Georgia Boy grasshopper on the gate. The same dull-gonging bell, and cattle grazing the wiregrass across the road. The raw fence lumber was drying in; the branch was drying up. Because of the drought, there was a sere quality to the land even with all the green pines, palmettos and wax-berry myrtle. Doll was everywhere, taking it all in: the dense heat and silence of crickets. The parched garden steamed. The dirt at Staten Bay smelled richer, less salty. Had Bo Dink set the woods on fire with his firecrackers? Had the men come in with the new cows yet?

It was too quiet in the flatwoods, left too much room for the din of memories in her head. Thoughts bumping into each other, but a hollowed out heart. She missed Daniel, which made for her longest evening yet.

Then night:

"You awake?" she said, easing up to Mrs. Baxter's bed.

No light, but she could see the bulk of her mother under the mosquito netting, could see one arm rise to her forehead as if hiding her eyes. "Don't tell, let me guess."

Doll laughed. "Move over," she said. "You're on my side of the bed."

"Well, forgive me if I never expected you to use it again."

They both laughed.

"Shh," Mrs. Baxter said. "Don't forget the visiting

preacher's sleeping in the room off the porch."

Doll slid into bed, kicking back sheets to feel the breeze through the windows—a fake wind portending rain that hadn't come, wouldn't for another week or so.

"I guess Mr. Staten couldn't handle all that bossy business in bed. How come you to be sleeping in another room."

"You never slept with Daddy."

Laughing. "I must have."

"Twice," said Doll. "Once for me and once for Baa."

"More than that but too much. Glad when your daddy, rest his soul, went on about his business."

"You mean, he did his *business* elsewhere, right?"

"I suspect so."

"I hate that; I never will stand for that."

"Some women don't, you know. Like a man in their bed I mean." Mrs. Baxter held her breath as if hoping for death to stop her from saying what she would have to say next in order to maintain her reputation with her daughter as being a truthful woman regardless how it hurt. "If a woman does like it...you know...she's blessed with a man understands...that sort of thing."

Doll could feel the heat of her mother's blushing. "I didn't say that, but I'd kill a man if he dumped me for another woman because I got old."

"You've got a few years yet."

She almost told her mother just how much she liked a man—Daniel—in her bed, but thought better of it. It was okay to talk around sex but not about it, though Doll felt that something so blissful and miraculous should be allowed, if not shouted out. Or at least the mystery of sex should be opened up and analyzed with somebody close. Since it was something that apparently just happened, however, a random miracle, maybe it shouldn't be talked about. Just kept warm inside until ready to explode again.

Moving away from the not-okay to an okay topic, Doll told her mother about the essay by Catherine Beecher in *Scribner's Magazine* espousing the view that it's a woman's

126

duty to be inferior to her man, to the best of Doll's understanding. Leave the voting to the male head of the household. "She went on to say that it's unchristian for a woman to vote."

"There's a real flaw in that, to my way of thinking. I mean, what about widow women and old maids? Don't we cease to be represented in church and government without men in our households? Still, we have to pay taxes on our land; we have to provide for our families all the same. And besides, you, me, Sheba, we're just as capable of good judgment as that preacher in there, or Adam, or Daniel for that matter."

"So you think women should vote."

"I think women *will* vote." Mrs. Baxter paused as if pulling from inside some deep surprising thought that had never occurred to her before. "Women will vote when men conclude that it's in their best interest for women to vote."

Doll rolled toward her. "I missed you, Mama."

"Me too." Mrs. Baxter placed a hand on top of Doll's head. "I missed my dollbaby. Like to killed me when you left."

"I didn't know…"

"Ah, you know me—I exaggerate."

Quiet while the breeze billowed the white net. Katydids sawing in the oaks.

"I've got a secret," Doll said.

"Oh, no. Your secrets keep me up all hours."

"Two secrets; I have two secrets."

"Two'll keep me up all night."

"Remember how we used to talk till out in the night? I mean, it was like we had to wait for Baa to sleep before we could really talk."

"The secrets. I'm sleepy."

"No, you're not. You're just as happy as a pig in sunshine cause I slammed Daniel with that lamp…"

"A lamp!" Mrs. Baxter sat up. "Why a lamp?"

"Shh, the preacher. Remember." Doll spoke low. "He came into my bedroom through a window."

"A window? Does this go on all the time?"

"Off and on."

"You're sorry you married him, aren't you?" Mrs. Baxter lay back.

"Not all the time, no. But sometimes I wonder if he's really true to me."

"Don't wonder, honey. Just outsmart him. If I had it to do over that's what I'd do: keep him wondering."

Wondering herself, Mrs. Baxter's voice trailed off, then: "I ever tell you about Amos Simpson, big timber man over round Fargo? Got caught with his pants down, so to speak, by Lois, his wife. After that, she made him clean her cookstove for the rest of their lives. Her only power, you might say."

"Is that a lesson?" Doll asked, propped on her elbow.

"I don't think so. Not a good one anyway."

"Yeah, her only power." Doll lay down. "One problem."

"What?"

"Maureen cleans the stove."

They both laughed, rolling side to side. Muffled laughter. Finally: "At least while you were gone, I got some rest." Mrs. Baxter was still laughing, sounded like she was crying. "Didn't expect to have you back."

"Are you crying, Mama?"

"A little bit, I won't lie."

"Because you feel guilty for me marrying Daniel to save the place."

"Something like that."

Doll hugged her, feeling her soft and mothery, breathing in her clean talcum smell. "Well, you didn't. By now, you oughta know, I don't do what I don't want to do."

"And that's the truth?"

"Well, I might rather be on my own. And someday I will be. Just me and you."

"Oh, no, not that joint headstone business again."

"That too," said Doll. "Now secret number two."

"No. We've got to get up for Fifth-Sunday preaching tomorrow and I've got to cook in the morning. You'll take all night."

"Shush! Remember the trunk Daniel brought from New

128

Or-leans?"

"What was in it?"

"Would you believe I was so mad I didn't look?"

"I know better."

"It was full of fine store-bought dresses and stuff. All kinds of stuff." Doll's voice rose and she stroked the netting over the bed.

"And you just left them there?"

"I brought one; fluffed the others up so it'd look like I hadn't been into it."

"I thought so."

"I'm planning to wear it to preaching tomorrow. I can't help it, Mama. I just have to wear it. I'll stick out like a sore thumb and people will say I think I'm better than them, but I have to wear it."

"People who matter won't say that; it's as good a way as any to cull them. But could be the preacher'll look down on you for fixing up for somebody other than your husband."

"That in the Bible?"

"Oh, Lord! I forgot the preacher."

They laughed again.

"Okay, enough secrets. Now go to sleep." Mrs. Baxter rolled onto her right side, facing the wall.

"That's not the second secret."

"Make it quick."

"I'm gonna have a baby."

"You're making that up to keep me talking."

"I'm not. Cross my heart I'm expecting."

"Well, I'm not ready to be a grandmother."

"I'm not ready to be a mother either."

"Doesn't matter whether we're ready or not, does it?"

"Not a bit."

"Go to sleep." Mrs. Baxter sighed, breathed. They lay there. "A baby."

"You ever wish you were a man?"

"How many times have you asked me that?"

"A couple hundred at least."

"The answer's still no."

"The answer's still yes for me."

"Well, you're not, so forget it."

"If I were a man, I'd be just like Daniel, I bet."

"He's a fair man, handsome too."

"Just curious. About the time I think I've got him pegged, he changes on me."

"How's that?"

"Well, no, not *change* exactly. I mean that's the point—that's the problem. He hasn't changed. I think maybe he's still like he was when he was a bachelor. He seems to cling to that while at the same time acting settled down and married when he's home. It's me he wants changed and settled down. My changing makes him feel changed, I guess."

"That's called having your cake and eating it too, what I think." Mrs. Baxter yawned, patting her mouth with one hand. "Men like variety, way I see it. Other way around a woman would be tarred and feathered."

"Is that in the Bible too?"

"Yes. It's called submission."

"Anyway, I wish he was more like Adam. Adam's easy to figure."

"I didn't hear that, not from a married woman."

"Adam's sweeter, will make some girl a fine husband."

"Just not you."

"I'd of been better off, I think. I mean, I doubt he'd break into my bedroom and boss me around about the help. I doubt he'd let somebody like Maureen lord over me all the time."

"Be smart." Mrs. Baxter yawned. "Use your head."

"Like a woman's head is all a man wants."

"I'd like to meet the man would want a woman without a head.

More laughter, then silence. Then, "Mama, you asleep?"

After Sunday meeting at Bony Bluff, Doll in the pink dress rode home with Adam and Brice. Adam drove the buggy slow but the dust still lifted from the plodding hooves of the dappled

horse and flowed over them. The sun seemed to hang up at
midday in the hazy sky. A long day—neither morning nor afternoon—of white heat. Dog fennel, bullous vines, pines all
powdered with dust, pale as the dead weeds and grass in the
straddle of the road. Brakes of bamboo and willow bracken
speckled yellow and dropping leaves to the cracked mud of
creek beds. *The* dress was a nuisance. It was itchy, tight, hot,
the object of whispers. Doll had been wrong to wear it, though
she'd worn it for the right reason—because it was pretty and
she liked pretty things. She had ended up feeling overdressed
and uppity among her own proud hardworking people. Nobody had turned out to be puffed up or spiteful though. Sheba
had told Brice, who told Adam, about Doll's big blowup with
Daniel—the lamp-throwing incident specifically. As a result,
Adam was around every time Doll moved, trying too hard to
be the opposite of Daniel, young, gay, polite, and coming off
as too sweet, silly, verging on obnoxious. A dozen times, at
dinner-on-the-ground, he asked her why she had cut her hair,
the real reason. Then again, she'd be talking—just talking to
ward off feeling faint, sleepy, and removed—and he'd seem
distracted. And now, after noon, laboring toward evening,
about half the church had gathered on the Baxter's long front
porch. Every bed full of napping babies and old drab hats,
every chair occupied by grouped men. The women were in the
kitchen dishing up berry cobblers and making lemonade. The
lemons had been the latest surprise in Daniel's regular delivery of provisions from Fargo.

Fair game out of the pulpit, the young preacher had been
cornered by Sheba in the parlor. Legs crossed and fanning on
the davenport, she talked low and laughed every time he spoke
and seemed not to notice people wandering up and down the
hall. He sat shy, slumped and flushed, his reddish hair like
copper in the dim rosy room.

Sidetracking to the watershelf, on her way to her bedroom,
Doll dipped her linen handkerchief in the water bucket and
dabbed her face and neck. Adam and Brice were sitting on the
front porch. She looked up the hall while opening her bed-

room door and saw everybody thronging toward the yard.

"Daniel Staten," somebody said.

Whether from the damp handkerchief or the sound of the name, she felt instantly less wilted, started up the hall with her heart twitching and other feelings held back.

There at the gate sat Daniel on the black stallion, holding to the leads of a bay mare that was harnessed to a red surrey with fringe around the top. He was wearing his usual white shirt and black tie and hat. He swung down from the saddle and started to hitch the stallion and the mare to the gate, but instead handed over the reins to two of the boys heading up the crowd that poured from the yard. Everybody laughed. He smiled, tipped his hat and shook hands all the way through the gate and up the walk into the eave shadows of the porch. He spoke to Adam and Brice, to the ladies in the doorway, then Doll.

"Mrs. Staten," he said, "you're looking mighty fine today." He posed—right boot on the top step, hands on his cocked hips.

"Mr. Staten," she said, fanning gnats from her face with one hand. "I guess you got that buggy from New Orleans too."

"*Surrey*, Mrs. Staten." He looked around at the surrey, then set his eyes on her again. "Another pretty for you."

Lingering for emphasis, he stood a moment or too. Finally he strolled on across the porch and up the hall, speaking to the ladies on the back porch and in the kitchen. Sheba, in the parlor, was now cranking out a lively hymn on the foot pump organ, to show how pious and talented she was, or maybe because her conversation with the preacher had dulled out to silence.

Doll ate her blackberry cobbler on the vine-shaded end of the front porch with Adam and Brice. Growing cooler in the warm breeze blowing off the woods. Yellowflies, gnats, tiny black mosquitoes that bit quick. She caught only glimpses of Daniel talking with the men, with Sheba and the preacher, and the women in the kitchen when she carried her bowl inside. Outside, everybody was parading around the surrey, touching the padded red leather benches, stroking the poplar frame and feeling the red fringe, all except Doll who kept seeing it too bright, too rich, against the drab greens, grays and browns of the flatwoods under siege of drought and hard times. Stunning as a diamondback rattler in the grass.

By sundown, the crowd began to thin. Come dusk, everybody was gone. And Daniel led the black stallion out to the barn lot and came back for the prissy mare and surrey.

Naked except for her old sheeting bloomers, Doll watched from her bedroom window till he started back toward the house. In the kitchen, Mrs. Baxter and Sheba were fixing supper—roast beef hash and grits. The smell of browning onions filled the house.

Doll pulled on her blue-flocked sackcloth shift, feeling the smooth worn cloth mold to her rounding body, and left the bedroom just as Daniel was stepping up on the back porch. The cooling air smelled bitter from the steamed dead plants rotting in the garden.

"I do wish it would rain," she said, leaning in the doorway.

He crossed over to the watershelf. "All this moisture, it's bound to by and by."

"The surrey—is it really mine?"

"Only if you stay home." He dipped water from the bucket to the pan with precision.

"Then why would I want it?"

"Good point," he said, staring out at the dark woods where insects keened. "You are going home, aren't you?"

"I am home." She crossed her arms. The sky above the shingled roof of the barn was a curious filmy plum color.

Lathering his long hands, he said, "I mean home with me."

"Not if I wasn't expecting I wouldn't."

He looked at her, green eyes dulled by the going light. "*Expecting.* You're pregnant?"

She went on into the kitchen to help put supper on the table.

That night Sheba slept with Mrs. Baxter and Doll slept in the same bed with Daniel, finding that she'd missed his long firm silky-haired body, his leathery scent. Still, she dreaded leaving the flatwoods the next morning, but was eager to ride in the surrey that would bring her back.

Dreamlike, on the verge of dreaming and satisfied, both of them, she spoke up in the dark, "I do like the surrey."

He gathered her in his arms, sighing, "Good. I like making you happy."

"I want to go to New Orleans."

He laughed low. "You can't go to New Orleans in the surrey."

"By train. I want to go by train. I want to see what you do there."

He loosened his hold on her but lay still, talking into her hair. "Afraid you'd find it mighty boring, lady. Looking at cattle to buy. Noisy, nasty streets."

"I hope you're not expecting me to believe New Orleans is nothing but ranching country and filth. I know better. I've read better."

He gathered her close again. Tight. "Okay, after the baby's born, when I get time, we'll go."

With him or without him she would go. It would be too easy just to give up and give in and forever lie in his arms, forever sleep.

It was late afternoon on Monday when they passed through Statenville on the way home. Doll in the surrey and Daniel on the black stallion. Moccasins hung from poles all along the courtyard in superstitious hope of bringing on the rain. Doll had seen this before; country people were forever hanging dead snakes on poles as a warning to look down at your feet while working in the gum woods. But this display of hanging snakes was like a pagan offering to the rain-god or to discourage the evil spirits responsible for the drought. Which didn't make a lot of sense for Bible-believing folks. She supposed it was something that could be *done*, something hands-on and eerily evident, aside from prayer.

The men on the courthouse porch waved to Doll in the surrey and Daniel on the stallion, keeping pace alongside. An old man called out: "See you got her back again, boy." The other men laughed. Doll waved and smiled and whipped up the mare, trotting the surrey south. Daniel sat higher in the saddle, then galloped on to catch up with her. Everybody seemed friendlier, expectant, banding together along the brief storefronts facing the courthouse, as if in celebration of the peak heat and drought which had to be nearing its end: yes, it would rain, it would have to rain, it was too hot not to rain and God being a fair god would see to it soon. Women taking in clothes in the backyards or sitting on their porches waved Daniel and Doll past. Out of town, a bent man in a straw hat was lugging buckets of water to his hogs, thick hectic shadows in a slattered pen.

Still the haze hung thick on the smothery air. The sky was no longer blue but white. An easterly breeze stirred, so slight that Doll had to check the moss in the oaks along the edge of the woods to see if it was truly blowing. The red surrey was gray with dust, the bay mare and the black stallion were sweating mud.

Daniel stopped the stallion and rose in the saddle, tilting his hat brim up. Doll followed his gaze over the southeastern section of woods and a mushroom of gray smoke forming above the ragged treeline.

"I don't like the looks of that," he said without looking at her. "I'm gonna ride on."

He snapped the reins on the withers of the sweating stallion, heeled him in the flanks and spirited ahead, the stallion cross-stepping in dust of its own making.

Doll sat watching the smoke rise, trying to gauge its distance and direction, while drinking the last of the warm water from her buggy jug. No white in the smoke meant there was no moisture in the cypress bays and slews.

"Rain," she said, searching the mean white sky for clouds feeding out of the Gulf. Then she rode on, feeling frivolous and foolish in the fancy surrey.

By the time she reached the Negro quarters at Staten Bay, the smoke had spread and settled till the low sun looked like the ball of fire that had set the east woods. Only women and children roamed the yards, speaking in frantic coarse snatches at sentences, while staring at the woods, that point from which the fire would come razing tarry palmettos, pines and people. Nobody noticed Doll passing, and even the dogs didn't hear the gentle creshing of the surrey or couldn't scent her through the smoke.

Not a man on the place when she got home, and she had to unhitch the surrey under the barn shelter and lead the mare into the lot. When Doll slipped the harness from the horse's head, she headed straight for the wooden trough of green moss-lined water.

Grimy from head to toe, Doll started for the house. Fine white ashes drifted like gnats up the lane and in the yard. The wide boards of the front porch floor were gauzy with ash. The tops of the pines across the road appeared to be burning, but it was only the upcast of the fallen red sun.

Maureen stood in the hall entrance, wan and wraithlike, peering out.

"How far away is it?" Doll said, going up the doorsteps.

"I don't know yet. They all left a couple of hours hour ago and nobody's come back."

Doll stood on the edge of the porch, gazing at the woods. No lights at Oscar and Estelle's cabin. "What about Estelle? Where is she?"

No answer. She looked back and Maureen was gone.

She went on into her bedroom, closed the door, undressed and bathed with the warm water from the pitcher on the washstand. The glass on the rug from the broken lamp was gone, but the kerosene splotches were still there. The fumes were still there, raw and furious. Another lamp sat on the table by her high white bed.

She had left her trunk in the surrey, so had to put back on her dirty, sweaty dress. She could have worn one of the new dresses in the new trunk at the foot of her bed, and it would have been fine, understandable, but not fine by her, not while other people were fighting fire—she'd fought fire, she knew the heat and fear and simple thirst. She went out into the hall filled with smoke and the muted light and muffled scent of citronella candles, then on into the kitchen.

Maureen was on her knees, shoveling dead ash and dust of live coal from the belly of the bulky cattycornered stove into a bucket. The ash heap in the bucket fumed up in marl of potash and spent heat.

When Doll had come in she'd had every intention of ordering the other woman to get her a glass of tea, but not now; she figured Maureen was cleaning the stove to get her mind off Joe out fighting fire. She got her own glass of tea and went out to sit on the front porch. She hadn't eaten since lunch—the picnic lunch of fried chicken, deviled eggs and biscuits Mrs. Baxter had made for her and Daniel—but she wasn't especially hungry, just thirsty. She stood and poured the tea off the edge of the porch.

If she looked at the dark smothered woods a certain way, she thought she could spy the fire through the pines. The wind was blowing out of the east now, not as strong as the west wind earlier, but almost as hot, as if the fire itself was heating the air. Still no yellow kerosene glow from the cabin across the road, which had to mean that Estelle was gone.

Suddenly Maureen was standing at the hall entrance again, holding by its bail the lighted blue bonnet lantern she always carried after dark.

Doll said, "They say after a wildfire the wiregrass will come back twice as rank and green."

No answer.

"They'll have to backburn," Doll said.

Maureen walked down the doorsteps and across the yard, swinging the hooded lantern by her side. "Not till everybody's rounded up and accounted for, they won't," she said. The light of the lantern beaming out past the oaks to the barn turned hazy then fused into the smoke.

Just as Doll had started to go inside, to lie down, she saw a line of slow fire growing south to north deep in the woods. Thought she could hear the fire crackling and men shouting but listening harder heard only katydids and whippoorwills. A lone owl. Staten Bay. Home.

When she could no longer stand the smoke and was so sleepy she itched all over, she went inside and lay fully dressed across the bed. She thought she'd only dozed when she heard the metallic clinking and dry squeaking of saddles, horse hooves clopping quick along the lane, and men's voices, lunatic and hoarse. But dawn light filtered through the louvers of the shutters.

She got up and headed for the kitchen to help make breakfast for the men. Maureen was already there, rolling out biscuits while the coffee brewed on the stove. Like a military officer in formal dress she was wearing the tightly wrapped white apron and the blue-striped towel hanging to her right. Doll was glad to see her for the first time, glad she was in charge, and glad for her familiar clatter and the food smells, for the routine day she represented.

But that day would be anything but routine.

Together Maureen cooked and Doll served the men throughout the day. Not only Daniel's people, but fire fighters from connecting counties and Florida. The fire had spread south, across the Florida line. No stopping it without backburning. But Maureen had been right, there were too many houses scattered about in the woods, too many men fighting fire on foot and on horseback unaccounted for.

Cows and hogs, ranging the woods, had been hazed by fire and driven by thirst into the Okefenokee Swamp in the east, or the Alapaha River in the west. The cattle's powerful bellowing and ponderous hoofbeats along the lane grew apocalyptic, a sign of the coming fire and backdrop for the human frenzy inside the house at Staten Bay. Like gusts of smoke deer loped across the fields, white tails signaling their escape. Sandhill cranes seen only twice a year during migration stormed west with lost squawking. Gates flung wide, razorback hogs and rattlesnakes came to be as common as chickens on the yard.

Queasy, weary from the smoked light, that level dusk-to-dawn anti-light casting a dusty-rose smear over dirt, house, barn and people, weary from the bitter smoke itself, Doll watched whole platters of biscuits vanish, baked hams devoured to the bone; a chicken could be walking around live one minute and the next minute be dead, disjointed and mixed with rice, then like magic, gone, never-was, except for bones piling up in the slop bucket to keep the wild hogs, coons and possums from feeding at the back door. Teapots were emptied into pitchers, pitchers emptied into glasses and glasses into mouths and then it all started over again with boiling water.

Doll's house was now headquarters for the warriors of fire, and her enemy Maureen was her only ally.

Strangely, the two women found they could talk to each other about food and fighting fire. Could alert each other to another battalion marching down the lane. Once they even laughed when another battalion showed up before the dishes from the last locust-like foray had been passed from water to water.

Finally Estelle, who had been away in White Springs, Florida, soaking her warped bones in the sulfur waters, came over to help in the sweltering heat of the kitchen; then Fate and Lottie and the crying baby, who made the chaos seem more chaotic. But the easy ambling routines of the two Negro women soon tamed the wild house. Later, the baby's wailing became only one more voice in a chorus of wailing when Lottie's man was carried in—his rawboned body plumped up and rosy-brown as a roasted turkey's, flesh peeling away from bones. Estelle placed a saucer of salt on his chest and a drop of turpentine on his tongue to keep the body from bloating and rotting till the men could get around to laying him out for burial. All men were black, all ate without distinction at the dining table, on the porches and in the yard. Resting for a minute with their heads hung. Maybe praying.

Bo Dink and several other Negro boys gathered buckets

and barrels and tubs of water from the well—anything that would hold water was filled—with orders to douse the house if the fire reached the road.

Life centered around water.

Lord, let it rain!

Daniel seemed to be everywhere and nowhere. When he did come in to eat, at last, his fair hair and beard were singed, his white shirt was soot-streaked and briar-torn, pant legs stogged in his boots and laces decorated with sandspurs. Not a word directed to his wife, rooted to the dishpan with red-mackled arms from the greasy lye water, only to Maureen, rooted to the stove with the snood of hair on back of her head worked loose. Her white apron was filthy and so was the blue-striped towel always hung from the waist on her right.

By the third night, the fire was clearly visible in the east woods beyond the road, its crackling and gusting no longer something imagined. It seemed to sweep the men forward along its battleline, closer to the house, closer to the women.

Nobody slept.

Throughout the night, men were brought in who had collapsed from heat and exhaustion and the women cooled their parched hides with wet cloths, fed them water, treated their burns with Estelle's aloe extract. Put them to bed between sheets of strangers with no present need for them.

It was daylight at night, like a war-time hospital with no opening or closing time.

Every man brought up the steps between two other men Doll expected to be Daniel. And when by dawn of the fourth or fifth day—either Friday or Saturday—he hadn't been brought in, she expected the worst: that he'd been burned alive in the woods.

Unable to bear not knowing, she asked two hoarse stumbling men bringing in another, who looked like the First Man formed of soot, if they had seen Daniel and one said, Yes, last night, and she couldn't recollect whether she'd seen him before or after.

Leaving the household to the other women, she set out the

next morning to find him, to help him, almost relieved to be outside and about to take part in fighting fire—a job more suited to her nature than washing dishes and doctoring the burned and collapsed men. Riding up the smoke-choked lane with ashes raining down like snow onto the over-sized head and brittle mane of the old grass-bloated gelding she'd found stabled in the barn, she stopped to adjust her kerchief over her nose. Behind she heard the slow solid clopping of old spread hooves and turned squinting through the smoke to see somebody in indigo pants and shirt riding loose-limbed toward her on a shambling sway-backed brown mare.

"I'm going with you," Maureen said, stopping on Doll's right. "I need to check on Joe." She looked strange outside of the kitchen and more a stranger with the brown felt hat pulled low over her eyes and the red kerchief covering the bottom half of her face. "I had to get out of there, you know?" she added, arching her back and rubbing her neck.

Doll rode on up the lane with Maureen riding low in the saddle alongside.

"Have you ever fought fire?" Doll asked her.

"The only fire I've fought is in some kitchen," she crooned, muffled by the kerchief. "But I doubt a woods fire could be any meaner than some of the people I've fought. At the café where I used to cook in Louisiana men customers kept mistaking me for the regular help. Even the owner never quite understood that without me his place was just like any other place. To him a man was a chef; a woman was a cook."

She looked behind her at the folds of smoke. "I had some bad settling up of accounts after a run-in over that last chef. Then Joe got in trouble…"

Doll waited for her to finish, but she only shrugged. Her tone as well as what she said sounded vaguely like a warning to Doll—don't cross me, don't take me for granted. But this was neither the time nor place for such ruminations. The fact that Maureen was a trained cook though might help explain why even when Daniel was gone Maureen continued to cook and serve her best to Doll alone. Even though she didn't like

her.

"What about you? You ever fought fire?" Maureen was eyeing the two water jugs in croaker sacks hanging from Doll's saddle horn.

"All my life, seems like."

"And men?"

"No. Not like that." Doll laughed. "I beat on a fellow I caught trying to rustle one of our cows, if that counts."

"It counts. Wrassling a rustler, huh? I never would have thought it."

They both laughed, but it seemed to smother in their throats with their breathing.

Crossing the road, heading toward the woods, they could see rosy creeping flames like flowering bushes banked by smoke. Jagged rows of low flames and then towering flames like maples and sweet gums changing color in fall. The hot wind was switching west to south and whipping the flames and the hoarse calls of the men in the woods, and now and then hair-raising shouts, a lone cow bellowing, a deer blowing and stamping and the crashing of trees to the ground.

They entered the still-green, unburned woods from the point along the tram road just south of Estelle and Oscar's cabin, though Doll considered riding the main road till she came to a good wide burn and riding over it into the woods toward the fire. Fire wouldn't back over a burn, she knew that.

Her eyes smarted and teared and the smoke stole under her kerchief making her cough. Maureen, trailing a few feet behind, had taken off her hat and was flicking live ashes from the brim. She reset the hat and caught up with Doll pushing on through a dried up drain toward the voices she had pinpointed in the east.

It was midmorning but looked like daylight or sundown. Puffy leaden clouds swagged with pent-up rain and smoke, and dry ashes turned to mush in the humid air. Flames shot up in the trees north and ahead. They were in the heart of the fire and any moment now they might look behind or to their right and find themselves blocked. Doll knew all about that and wondered if Maureen knew that. Doll figured she did when she spied her looking behind more than ahead.

"I heard about this fellow one time fighting fire," Maureen said. "He got hemmed in and tried to bury himself to keep from burning alive."

"I've fought fire in the flatwoods with men who got cooked alive." Doll didn't want to know what had happened to the man who tried to bury himself. "Listen," she said, stopping and sitting forward in the saddle, "can you hear voices?"

"No," Maureen said, stopping. Barely breathing, she looked back. "We'd better head south, I think. Try to outrun that fire closing in on us from behind."

Doll looked. Two, three, four treetops were burning, fire jumping to number five as they sat watching, but still a good distance away. Hard to tell with the firelight standing out in the smoke, but Doll judged that taking the route southward wasn't the answer either, because the wind was now whipping northward, and before she could speak to suggest to Maureen the probability of fire cropping up in the south, they both spied it and headed east toward a narrow-looking gap in the row of flames, either slowly filling in with fire or grazing outward and overlapping in the direction of the two women.

Then came the shout of a man who sounded like Daniel. "Back burn. Let's head it off with a backburn and that ought to wrap it up, boys."

"Okay," Doll said, leaning forward again on the prancing gelding, suddenly come to life as if understanding that a backburn would mean his doom, "this is where they separate the men from the boys. Or maybe I should say the spirited horses from the half-dead ones."

"Why do you think these old nags got left at home?" Maureen said and tugged her hat low. "Let's make a run for it."

Doll shot off with her gelding not even slowing to pick through the brush and logs. He would stumble and right himself on the verge of buckling. She could hear Maureen behind her, the hesitant cantering of the mare and her snorting.

Doll looked back and saw fire jumping treetop to treetop, maybe razing the very spot where they had sat their horses moments before, and ahead the cold dark gap closing in, end to end, with fire.

She could hear Maureen gagging and coughing. "Don't panic!" Doll yelled, then gagged too.

Smoke was swirling now, over and around, with the heat from the fire, north, south, east and west.

Maureen shouted, "Doll, wait!"

Doll wheeled the gelding around and saw her sprawled on the fire-lit ground, then on her feet and running toward Doll and the gelding without her hat.

Doll caught her right hand to tug her up, but Maureen was too heavy and Doll lost her balance and landed on the ground next to her, still holding to the reins to prevent the snorting, sidling horse from bolting toward the opening which he had apparently located during all the commotion. Maureen placed her right boot in the stirrup and swung up into the saddle and Doll wondered if she was planning to ride off without her, to save her own hide, until she shifted back from the saddle to the rump of the gelding to make room for Doll in the saddle. After all, Doll was the one in charge, the one holding to the reins. It was only a thought and a fleeting one in the heat and firelight and smoke that threatened them both. Safe in the saddle, Doll felt Maureen's strong arms go around her waist and grip tight, the oddest embrace she could imagine, but somehow a comfort, an anchor, as the horse leapt ahead. Only a thought.

They were moving now, one.

"Look!" Maureen shouted and pointed ahead.

Men in hectic silhouette, still yards and yards away, were swatting with pine tops along the line of fire, opening the gap like a gate for them to pass through, it seemed. Yes, they'd been spotted.

The cow that had been lowing all along was now lowing closer and visible on the northeast curve of fire. Her small calf was sidled close and blatting. Eyes wild with fear, tail and ears raised.

Doll dodged left, toward the corner of fire, almost slinging Maureen off the rump of the gelding. "What are you doing?" she yelled. "Let's go!"

Doll didn't answer. She whipped the gelding around, out of his single-minded dashing for the lone break in the fire, and faced the addled red cow and calf facing west and home regardless. Doll had seen this cow, an old mammy cow, wandering up the lane in the evenings, coming home for the night. Her speckled droopy eyes and long curved horns glowed like coals, and she was chewing her cud, a bit fearful looking but accepting or waiting for a break in the fire gnawing east through the woods.

"Hie up there!" Doll shouted.

The cow wheeled facing the fire behind and kept a wide berth between her and the fire but followed the rim of it as if seeking an opening or just running to be running, running till she ran out. Doll galloped left then right, herding, hazing the cow and the toddling calf toward the opening she could not see now but had faith would be coming up. Already the men's voices sounded nearer, only slightly ahead and to her left, but she couldn't see them either.

Maureen was silent, but she was squeezing Doll so tight she could hardly breathe. They had to duck under the low branch of a glowing hickory and both grunted.

The gelding kneeled suddenly, almost gracefully, on his forelegs, and just as gracefully sprang to his feet, running now and game for the chase. Ahead, the cow and calf passed shambling through the opening in the fire.

"You scared the shit out of me," Maureen hissed.

Shutting their eyes against the spiraling smoke and giving the gelding his head, they passed through the gap behind the cow and the calf, men shouting at them as if they had just won a race. Only mad-sounding, incredulous. One of them Daniel.

Doll reined in the gelding by turning him to face the fire,

him twisting and surging toward the cooked and cooling woods at his rear. Daniel ran forward and caught the bit in one hand. His beard had been set fire and was singed to the skin in patches. "What's the meaning of this, Doll, you and Maureen? Didn't y'all have enough to do at the house?"

Doll dismounted, standing before him, kerchief down around her neck. The fire was snapping and crackling like ice. Gusting like a storm.

"We needed to do more. I brought some water." Doll turned her back on him and took down the water. Then she walked off to crop a sapling to fight fire with.

"Where's Joe?" Maureen asked, swinging down.

"Joe!" Daniel shouted behind. Then to Doll, "You can't do that." He was still holding to the bits of the bewildered wild-eyed gelding. "What about the baby? Now, get back to the house this minute."

"How, Daniel?" Doll shouted and nodded west toward the rising fireline rushing eastward and already clashing and twisting up to the sky at points. The baby—she had forgotten about the baby. It made her crazy. She laughed out loud and he took it for a sign of something worse.

"Okay," he said loudly. "But you women stay back and beat out the spots you see blazing up behind us."

Daniel lifted the horse's head high by the bridle and let go with a snatch. "Hoo on away from here!" He clapped his hands and the gelding trotted off east into the wilderness of blackened woods where the saved cow was standing for her calf to nurse. The other horses had been set free, to wander or go home, to pick their own safe passage through the fire, after the men had given up trying to negotiate fallen logs on horseback and fight fire astride.

Smoke on the new burn feathered up from slow burning stumps and cradled logs, and wisps of smoke like springs seeped from the leveled brush and broomsage stubble—blackened and peaceful almost, as if the worst that could happen had happened. By contrast, in the west, the fire—the worst that could happen—was happening, and it sounded like the very earth was being ripped up by its roots.

Joe, sweet-smiling as ever, limped away from the wall of flames and stopped next to Daniel. His overalls were in tatters and his face and arms looked scalded. His eyebrows were gone, making him look mad, gone-mad. A retard whose body had gotten a jump on his brain. Maureen stepped forward and hugged him. They talked only seconds before he rejoined the firefighters to the right of the growing gap in the east line of fire. Maureen walked over to where Doll was swabbing down flames climbing a large pine like a flowering vine. If it reached the lower branches, about halfway up the pine, it would catch and jump top to top of at least two spared pines that Doll could see and who knew how many more beyond that. The flames were following a trail of bleeding sap, eating at the bark and almost out of reach of Doll's sapling when Maureen, now wielding a pine sapling herself, appeared around the other side of the tree, reaching high and beating wildly at the flames Doll had chased out of reach. Then they moved on, smothering sparks that flared up in the palmettos, gallberries and wire grass. Maureen's long dark hair loose and swinging about her shoulders, both of them safe on burned ground and working onward toward the men and home.

Doll would wonder later about this crisis she had shared with Maureen, about the two of them together, alone and close. And she would wonder whether women maybe thought too much and wouldn't they be better off just to act. To have something primal and terrible like fire to fight instead of each other. And she would conclude that it amounted to about the same thing—fighting fire, fighting each other. Both primal, fire and women.

When there seemed no end to the cooking and the fighting and the smoke and the charred skin and the panic and lowing and racket and heat, the rain came swift and slanting out of the Gulf, a tropical storm that would rage till the last ash dissolved.

Chapter 7

With the same ease of calving as the red polled heifers from New Orleans, Daniel would later boast, on March 10, 1888, Doll delivered her first baby.

"I want my mama!" Doll screamed, whipping her head left and right on the pillow, while gripping the cool iron spindles of the headboard because she'd been gripping the iron spindles for so long and was afraid to let go: so far she hadn't died and holding on must be helping. Besides, if she let go, it would be down into darkness, down where the pain couldn't go and then she'd be dead. She couldn't believe she'd taken such pleasure on this very bed, taken pleasure from something that could cause such pain. "I want my mama!"

"Well, you just gone have to make do with me, honey," Estelle said from the foot of the bed. "Now push when the next pain comes."

"No. I'm tired." Doll had been pushing and pulling since six o'clock last evening and the clock on the mantel said six again, as if her hard labor hadn't changed a thing or had stopped the clock. Another contraction started and grew, tumbling and ripping her insides from stomach to groin. She groaned, bit her lip, then let go and screamed, crying.

"It'd go easier on you if you'd squat and breathe like I told you to," Estelle said loud and accusing.

"I don't want to squat; I don't feel like breathing."

"The Indians squat."

"Well, I'm not Indian. Where I come from women lie flat out on the bed to have their babies." Doll had seen iron spindles on headboards bent from women gripping during childbirth; as long as it hadn't pertained to her it had been merely interesting.

"This ain't no nap, honey." Estelle could afford to be calm because she was not the one suffering.

It was after midnight, muggy with the wind pushing against the black windowpanes, rattling them. Hard rain on the roof, then silence, till the next pain.

"We're almost there now," Estelle said, kinder.

Doll couldn't see her because her knees were propped up, with Estelle between them, and because she was squinching her eyes shut. Sick of circling with her eyes the hoop of gathered mosquito netting overhead. Sick of the knothole shaped like an eye in the beadboard ceiling above the netting.

Then she heard Daniel talking at the foot of the bed. "Is she all right?"

Her first thought was to say, Hell, no, I'm not all right. Get out of here! Ever since this battle with her body had started, some twelve hours ago, he'd been in and out, drinking whiskey and announcing that he'd be back—had to check on a cow having trouble delivering, some such. She looked but couldn't see him at first, then caught sight of him through the vee of her jacked knees, drinking from his glass of whiskey and watching. He looked wet, fuzzy and curious in the hellish sulfur haze from the kerosene lamps placed about the room.

"I could help," he said to Estelle. "I've been pulling calves my whole life."

"Out!" Doll shrieked and snatched her head forward, watching him back, hardy and pain-free, from the room. He shrugged in the doorway and was gone, walking down the hall with heavy heel clinks. Then another burst of rain.

"Looks like it's gonna blow up a storm," Estelle said as if they were talking on the porch.

Another spasm of pain and Doll squeezed the iron spindles with all her might and pushed, feeling the pain curling and rolling in her groin, low and on the verge of gushing. "Never, NEVER, *NEVER*," she screamed.

"I've heard that before. Here comes the head."

"I hate you, Estelle."

"Heard that before too." She cackled. "Bear down."

Like on her wedding night, Doll decided to get it over and done with and figured it wouldn't kill her, having this baby—women did it all the time, dumber, weaker women than she was—and if she overed it she'd never do it again. Growling through gritted teeth, she bore down and let fly the spurry, twisting monster between her thighs.

"It's a girl," Estelle announced, that dry, not a proclamation.

"It's a girl?" Daniel called through the door.

The baby cried, a single broken *waah* sound.

"Ain't all that pretty," Estelle said, "don't know if she's a keeper."

Doll thought Estelle was joking. She breathed out and let go of the iron spindles for the first time since she lay down. Feeling safe in drifting where the pain couldn't go.

Doll named the baby Minnie, after Daniel's mother, who had died when he was eighteen. Upon learning that the baby wasn't a boy, he turned his full attention to his new calves. The baby belonged to Doll.

A great storm swept along the Atlantic Coast for four days after the baby was born. Rain, hail and wind wrapping up along the Georgia and Florida coastlines, Staten Bay became an isolated island for Doll with her crying baby. Daniel was in and out, during the storm, seeing after the household, seeing after his cows; then the last day of the storm, the worst day, he didn't come in at all. When Doll asked Oscar, Estelle, Maureen or Joe where he'd gone, they laughed and shook their heads, meaning this was a common pattern for Daniel and his little wife had better get accustomed to his curious disappearances.

Doll was mad but biding her time. She wouldn't ask again.

When Minnie was six weeks old, that May, Doll placed her in the surrey and set out for her mother's house, stayed two weeks and came home, concluded that Daniel was cavorting and drinking—Maureen said Doll could look for him when she saw him coming—and set out for the flatwoods again.

Come summer, she got home to find Daniel gone; the next morning she met him halfway up the lane: June flies buzzing over the horses stopped parallel, noses to each other's rumps. Minnie whining on the surrey seat next to Doll. The stallion sidled, stamped, swatted at flies with his tail. A mild breeze soughed in the pines. Crisscrossed shadows of branches were stenciled on the knitted grass and dirt.

Daniel brought his left leg up, crooked it on the pommel of the saddle, and crossed his arms. "Well," he said, "if it isn't Mrs. Staten."

Doll had graduated from feeling guilty about wearing her finery in the flatwoods by reasoning that her poor neighbors would not become more prosperous through her sacrifices. Though she did give freely from Daniel's money to the church at Bony Bluff which distributed it directly to the poor. Today, she was wearing the blue dress and locket from New Orleans. No hat, and her thick black hair was spread on her shoulders like a fur stole. Still she wore her old brown hightop shoes; the stylish shoes in the trunk would pinch a dead woman's toes. She picked up Minnie, sat her on her lap, bracing her chest with one hand while patting her back with the other. How Doll's mother held the baby all waking hours and some-times while Minnie slept.

"Say it, Daniel. I've got to get on to Mama's before it gets any hotter."

"How long this time?" He placed his boot back in the stirrup, sat high. The saddle squeaked.

"A while, I expect. Baa's getting married and we're work-ing on her wedding."

He laughed. "Who's the lucky fellow?"

"I don't appreciate the way you said that. It's our preacher and he is a lucky fellow. Bathsheba will make him a fine wife."

"Maybe you'd have been better off married to a preacher." He laughed again. "How long will you be gone this time, Doll?"

"You can look for me when you see me coming. "

"Cute." He snorted, looking off, then looked back.

"What difference does it make? You're never home."

"You can't know that, Doll, since you're not here to check."

The baby sucked two fingers, rattled whining. She was a scrawny baby, like a bird miraculously hatched, and her long white gown made her look scrawnier.

"I've been here," she said. "This time we just accidentally bumped into each other. "

"What's at Mama's that's not here?"

"Mama."

"That sissy lawyer wouldn't be the attraction, would he?"

"Adam is not a sissy and he's not the attraction."

The stallion fluttered his lips, snatched his head around as if to nip at Daniel's left leg, but instead nuzzled the fine broad neck of the bay mare. She danced forward a couple of feet, jostling the surrey. Minnie reared her feathery red head and bawled.

"What's wrong with her?" Daniel asked, turning the stallion full circle and level with the surrey.

"She's teething."

"I meant the mare."

Doll placed the baby on the seat beside her, took up the lines and flapped them. The mare trotted toward the start of the lane. Daniel galloped the black stallion to catch up, slowed to a trot to keep step. Oscar in his wagon, piled high with manure, pulled in behind them, easing along for a minute or two, then veered from the lane to the high green grass under the pines, which was dotted with stray cotton bolls picked after the first frost of last winter. Stubborn in his snuff-brown hat, Oscar kept going, dodging pines, wagon bed grumbling, as if to demonstrate how put out he was with Doll and Daniel for hogging the lane. Fumes of manure lagged and drifted. The whole place and nature too seemed turned in on itself.

"What did I do wrong this time?" Daniel asked.

"Think about it." She turned the surrey north at the road, didn't even glance at him riding alongside.

New corn was pegging in the field on their left, green sprouts fanning in rows with alternating rows of peanuts which would benefit from the shade of the corn stalks. Scattered about the field were Negro women leaning over hoes and children squatting to pluck grass.

"I don't know, Doll. I swear to God I don't know what I'm doing wrong. I'm just being myself."

"That's it," she said. "Giddyup!"

In the flatwoods, at the Baxter house, the three women had finished putting up tomatoes when Daniel came by the next afternoon. From the back porch, where Doll was dumping a dishpan of peelings into the hog slop bucket, she saw him leading the stallion into the lot. The tumbledown slat fence was grown up in thorny careless, dog fennel and briars, then open space where the horses and mules daily tramped the gray dirt. Scattered about were bleached and red corncobs, and strange in the middle of the lot was a broken-back chair with a staved bottom that Doll used to stand on to mount the horses and mules bareback. Crickets chirred in the shimmery heat. Smells of manure and rat-must steamed from the lofty old leaning barn north of the lot that connected by way of a maze rigged from the same brittle boards as the fence. Inside, a horse stamped the soft loam, half a century in the making.

So far, Daniel hadn't seen Doll on the porch.

While the stallion shuddered away flies and drank from the watering trough along the south wall of the barn, Daniel unbuckled the saddle, with keen concentration, lifted it down from the wet galled back of the stallion and carried it to the fence by the lot gate and slung it up and astraddle the top board next to his bridle. Then he looked up and saw Doll standing with the speckled pan circled in her arms. He opened the gate and stepped through, latching it behind him. His green shirt was sweated through in patches of darker green.

"I've got it, " he said, almost to the doorsteps. "You're mad because I never made over the baby, aren't you?"

"You got one right."

"There's more?"

She picked a red tissue tomato skin from the bottom of the blue speckled pan. The greasy ropy dishwater fermenting with table scraps in the slop bucket fumed up in the close fetid heat. She had pricked her fingers quilting and the tomato juice burned like acid. Inside the barn her mare neighed and stamped. The stallion whinnied and trotted twice round the lot, located the maze, zagged through and up the dim barn hall adrift with motes of molded hay.

"I give up." Turning his back to her and facing the water shelf, he dipped water from the bucket to the pan, leaned forward and began laving water to his face, then dried on the towel hanging from a nail on the left wall. Again he dipped water from the bucket and drank straight from the dipper—something she'd never seen him do before because he feared catching pyorrhea. The day would come when she would see him sterilize his hands after shaking with somebody.

"It's simple," she said. "If you can go, I can go."

"Is this about New Orleans again?"

"Partly." It seemed to Doll that New Orleans got farther and farther away. Or, she was pregnant. Or, there was a problem in the turpentine woods. The list went on and on.

"I have to work. I have to *go* to work." He eyed the lees in the bottom of the dipper and dashed out the rest of the water just in case. "For instance, I just rode in with a load of gum to Four-mile Still. Understand?"

Loud kick on the stall wall inside the barn. Wood splintering. One of the horses brayed like a donkey.

"And the other times?"

"You mean my wandering and drinking?"

"Yes."

"Men do that. That's what men do."

In the kitchen on the left, big hands and little hands were clapping. High happy squeal of the baby, Sheba and Mrs. Baxter laughing. All day they'd been teaching her to pattycake. At last she had done it, from the sounds of their carrying on.

Inside the barn, more kicks and splintering wood.

Daniel and Doll watched as the stallion came bucking and twisting up the hall, the bay mare close in behind him. She wheeled, jacked a leg, and like lightning striking, kicked him in the rump.

Doll nudged Daniel with the pan. "That's what women do when they don't like what men do."

When they passed through Statenville the next evening—Doll and Minnie in the surrey, and Daniel on the stallion, riding alongside—the old men on the courthouse porch stood watching.

"Well, looks like he's bringing her home again," one said.

"She won't stay," said another. "Not for long, that gal won't."

Daniel had apparently taken Doll's remark about the horse-mating incident yesterday to mean that she herself had kicked his behind, and likely would kick it again. But finally she understood who wore the britches at Staten Bay and accepted as fact that he would come and go as he pleased, that she could look for him when she saw him coming. The important thing was, she was sleeping with him again and going home with him to Staten Bay.

She could see his thinking in that smug lift of his chin, his back-to-normal proud prancing on the black stallion that had done his thing with her sweet old mare and left satisfied. Same as his master.

She smiled. But inside she was seething. She would find out what or who had the power to lure Daniel Staten away from his wife and new baby during a storm without so much as a goodbye or see you later. The baby was crying now as she squirmed in the seat, Doll bracing her limp body with one arm to keep her from sliding to the floor of the surrey.

Mid-summer was so hot that the freshening of night couldn't turn the heat of the day before. Mornings, the crops at their peak, and even the people at Staten Bay, looked wilted.

Doll, on a mission, set out in the surrey up the lane to have a little talk with Estelle. She had waited till Daniel left the next morning then dressed in the slim brown paisley skirt and silk cream blouse from the New Orleans trunk of pretties. Not that she'd dressed up just to go to Estelle's; she didn't know where she might wind up going—wherever she had to go to find the truth. And she wanted to look fine and ladylike when she found it in case it made her burst out crying or take a swing at somebody.

Her motives were ever-changing: one minute she would tell herself she was just curious about this mysterious man she had married; next minute, she would own up to the fact that she was jealous. Regardless, she had to know or his wandering would eat her alive.

Tender new grass and clover had sprouted through the burned straw in the circular clearing of the cabin. But the trunks of the pines were charred halfway up to their bristly tops, at odds with the green needles and the clear blue sky.

Estelle in her patch of backyard, near the wood-slat chicken pen, was chopping at the dirt with a hoe. With each chop she jumped back. She looked up as Doll drove the surrey into the front yard, stopped and climbed down.

"Old chicken snake," she called out and set her eyes on the snake again. "After my setting eggs."

When Doll came up the red-pied snake was in four neat pieces, each flipping and pitching, tumbling in the scarfed dirt.

"Blasted thing, that'll teach em." Estelle stepped off ground to where Doll was standing clear of the snake, then stood leaning on her hoe, watching the antics of the bloody sections. Already flies were gathering, blowing over it.

"You're back, I see." Her screwed face was dripping sweat onto the tucked bodice of her blue dobby dress.

Doll had seldom seen her dressed up. "You must be going somewhere."

"Statenville." She spat a stream of snuff juice in the direction of the chopped snake. "Got a little something up at the courthouse to tend to. Old patient of mine up and died and had the gall to leave me a dab of money. Bout enough to be a

156

bother and that's it."

Doll could tell she was proud, regardless how little money. A little would mean a lot to her.

"Where's that gal-baby at?"

"With Fate." Doll looked toward the big white house up the lane. "Fate's got her."

"Thought you was fixing to say you'd left her with that Maureen." She moved closer, square in Doll's face. "So, looks like you're off to somewheres too?"

Doll didn't answer. The snake's tail had flipped to the hem of her skirt, giving her the excuse she needed for backing away from Estelle, now trying to read her face.

"Estelle, I need some information."

"How's that?"

"I hope you won't tell anybody I asked, but…" Again Doll stared toward the house. Maureen was sweeping the front porch while Fate rocked Minnie in one of the chairs.

"Y'all ain't still on the outs, err you?" Estelle spat again.

"Who? Me and Maureen?"

"Wadn't who I had in mind, but I figured was who was on yours."

"No. We're okay. She knows who's boss now."

"Then has to be that man you married."

"Yes." Doll spoke lower. "I don't want you to get the wrong idea about me, but…" Doll coughed into her hand.

"Spit it out. Don't, it's gone choke you." Estelle pushed at the four sections of fly-buzzed snake with the hoe blade as if to piece it back together. "I done seen your privates so what else you gotta hide?"

Doll went hot all over. Couldn't speak.

The humid air was heavy with the smells of snuff, chickens, snake and leaching pine tar. Cattle lowed from the woods, the workers in the cotton and corn fields were humming and shouting to one another.

"Okay, you gone make me guess, is that it?" Estelle slapped at a mosquito on her withered face.

"No ma'am." Doll spoke louder, clearer, then lowered her

voice to finish. "I want to know where Daniel goes that's so important."

"We ain't talking work now, err we?"

"No ma'am. I mean I've got a right to know who...what's so important that he would just take off and stay gone till he takes a notion to come home. And me with a baby and doing the best I can."

Estelle laughed, cackling and raring, using the hoe to prop up her feeble body.

"I wish you wouldn't laugh like that, Estelle. You make me feel stupid."

Estelle's laughing dried up. She spat. Piecing together the snake with the hoe. "Well, I can tell you from hearsay that in these woods hearabouts"—she motioned east with her head—"they's a bunch of old camphouses. Menfolks get together to jaw and hunt and drink and what-all else I ain't got no notion. Maybe cook up some deer meat. Play a little poker."

Doll could imagine that, it figured. Same as in the flatwoods, according to the talk.

"Course they's more, if I'm ery judge."

"Like what?"

"I ain't got no more idear where your man goes generally than you do." She eyed Doll with sober concentration. "Can't keep up with my own if I wanted to. But you being a young thing, new at all this, wouldn't be natural if you wadn't curious."

Doll was anxious now to wrap things up, to know or let it go. She was hot in her clingy clothes and wanted to go home, contented to attribute Daniel's strange disappearances to hanging around the camps with the other men. Even if it was more, if he had another woman—women—hadn't he warned her on their wedding night? (Last thing she wanted was Estelle sharing in that shame.) So really there was nothing to be gained by learning where he went and who he saw except to salve her curiosity. But she could sense that Estelle was bent on carrying the investigation farther. On making her point in a big way. She was hooked. Snake forgotten, and the money waiting on her at the courthouse was nothing now.

"I can show you one other place where he used to go and for a fact still do when the notion strikes him or he has to."

Doll felt her heart sink. She'd half-hoped not to know, not to find out. She had to be brave. She'd made a fool of herself already with Estelle and she was bound to go through with it, fool to the end, to get the straight of it. Then she could let it go. Once she learned where Daniel went, what made him tick, she could go on. Doing what about it she didn't know. The baby on the porch in Fate's lap was a good enough reason for doing nothing except taking whatever it was Daniel would do or not do.

"Give me a ride in that fancy buggy there." Estelle hobbled along the log wall of the house to the front porch, leaning the hoe against a corner post. Then she labored on out to the surrey and up onto the seat, tucking in her dress tail.

Doll didn't like the mischievous set of her face. She couldn't take her eyes off that face, those teeny dancing eyes. She got up on the surrey anyway and took the leadlines in hand. Flies were attacking the rump of the mare, making her dance like Estelle's eyes.

"Anybody ask you where we going, just say you giving me a ride to the courthouse. Hear?"

Up to that point, Doll had half-hoped that Estelle was just catching a ride to Statenville, where she was going anyway.

"Pull up yonder and let's go in." Estelle motioned to the hitching post under two grand live oaks behind the courtyard. Square in front of the two-story hotel, which Doll had seen and never considered as a place she might go into, simply because. Well, what business would she have there and her on her way to her mother's or headed to Staten Bay? Two places to stay and never bothering to think about life any other way or how people who didn't pertain to her might actually be staying there, at the hotel. The very word, hotel, didn't fit in her store of words. Conjured up images of strangers and strange goings on. What was she doing here?

Four men in dark vested suits sat on the lower gallery with traveling bags by their rocking chairs. One stood and walked over to the spindled banister and leaned with his legs crossed, facing the other three and talking.

All were watching except the man whose back was turned on Doll and Estelle in the surrey.

"Estelle," Doll whispered, "I don't know what you're up to, but whatever it is, we can't just *do* it here with everybody watching."

Estelle was already struggling down when one of the men in a black fedora dashed from the porch to help her.

The one with his back to them looked around and came down the stairs to help Doll from the surrey. Hands around her waist and lifting her high to show her lightness, his strength. He had red hair and a neat red beard and his eyes were blue as the peeps of sky through the oak branches. He smelled of pipe smoke and was young and handsome but no match for Daniel, who at some point had become a standard for Doll to measure other men.

From inside the hotel came the smells of steeping tea and frying chicken. Silverware clinking on plates, people talking and children playing, their footsteps tapping on the wood floor. A Negro woman called out that she had to clean up some mess, her guttural voice like a stone dropped into the merry chatter.

Estelle with the other man holding to her arm to help her up the stairs was using the railing for support and staring at him suspiciously.

The two men in the rockers stood and nodded. "Morning, ladies."

Doll was almost sure the men were new in town, strangers. She'd never seen them before. Certainly travelers, probably waiting for the afternoon stage.

Looking neither left nor right she made it to the open hallway and stopped, facing the dim stairwell, while gathering her nerve by resting against the cool beadboard walls. Hiding her from view of the people passing along the far end of the hall, going into and leaving the dining room, she guessed, was a potted fern that fanned almost wall to wall.

"Up here! Ain't gone let nobody bite you." Estelle was halfway up the staircase, peering down, childlike. "I ain't got all day."

"Estelle, wait." Doll started for the foot of the stairs, staring up.

Estelle was gone but Doll thought she could hear her witchy cackling and gimping along on the creaky floor above. She felt like she was walking in mud, sucking mud. She had changed her mind. What did Estelle mean, walking off and leaving her? And the embarrassment! What...who...was upstairs? She would never trust Estelle again.

At the top landing, she stopped to peer into a gilded oval mirror between two green velvet overstuffed chairs. Her face was white as ice even though it felt on fire. One sprig of black wavy hair was sticking up. She smoothed it, stepping back, then smoothed her skirt and centered the pearl and rhinestone brooch of the cream silk waistband.

She could refuse to follow. She could go back and wait in the surrey for Estelle, who now that she thought about it had always been more aggravation than help. But if she went back she would have to pass by the men on the porch.

From the far end of the hall, she heard Estelle knocking. No mistaking her brisk but hesitant four raps ending with a half-rap, like a man knocking on a floor with the handle of his pocketknife; after all, Doll heard it almost daily when Estelle came bearing gossip in the form of lessons. And there Estelle stood in the shadows of chairs and tables and lamps and ferns, smaller, gaunter, plainer than she'd ever looked before.

"Estelle," Doll hissed. "Wait!"

Doll walked fast along the hall—she had on the slim bone shoes that went with the skirt which by nobody's measure were the shape of true feet. "Estelle, don't!"

"Open up, Prudie, it's me."

"Estelle, no."

Too late. The door opened and the light from inside cast

Estelle in relief of the shadows along the dim hall.

"Why, Estelle. Why, I never! Come in, come in."

Ringed hands with red painted nails reached through the door and caught Estelle by both hands and led her inside.

"Brung somebody to meet you," Estelle said. "Doll, get on in here," she hollered out.

Doll had no choice. It was too late. What would she say?

She stepped into the doorway of the room and stopped, saying nothing.

"This here's Prudie," said Estelle to Doll. "She awready knows who you are," she added and walked off across the room.

The same hands reached out for Doll's. Claws and talons and rings. "Let me look at you—up close. Daniel's wife. Always causing a stir when you pass through town." She laughed. "Everybody's still talking about you riding through on Daniel's stallion with your dress hiked up to your knees."

Doll was staring into a cheeky rouged face with glittering brown eyes like glass. Brown eyes and blond-blond curls and the largest bosom Doll had ever laid eyes on, especially on a woman so thin. Doll figured her to be about thirty-five or forty, beginning to crinkle under the eyes. She had dense rose-ivory skin, going leathery, and the pink brocade dressing gown she was wearing made her look darker.

"I'm Prude. Prude Purdue." She laughed in a tinkle like bells. "But you can call me Prudie, like Estelle there." She kissed Doll's cheek. She smelled of stale perfume and face power and some kind of hair fixative. No. A closer look revealed the sewn edges of a wig, odor of artificial hair. Loops of silky strings tucked on her long jointed neck. Still, she was beautiful, quaintly fetching in that way of women born beautiful and daily practicing beauty, which the unbeautiful were forever claiming came only from inside.

Estelle was checking out the room, curious as a cat, as if for the first time, but all the while listening and watching the two women through those eyes in back of her head.

There was a faint scent of alcohol and tobacco smoke in

the room.

At first, Doll thought the walls were papered with some dulling black and white pattern, but on closer inspection she saw the paper was composed of posters and pictures and clipped newspaper articles. A younger Prude Purdue everywhere you looked: short fringed skirt, hands on her knees and smiling. Seated at a piano, singing, with her bone-white teeth shining. Teeth a bit large but perfectly scalloped. The headlines of one newspaper article read: "The Untouchable Miss Prude Purdue sings and performs for Macon Gents." Wearing a satiny black corset-like getup with a long plume for a tail, she was posing before one of the leering 'gents,' his cigar extended as if to torch the feather. Her legs didn't look skinny at all.

"Sit down, sit down." Prude walked over to the tapestry loveseat along the wall on the left, sat and gathered her legs under the pink brocade tail of her robe. Holding to one shapely ankle and smiling. Her hair didn't even move.

She sat straight up from the waist and patted the cushion next to her for Doll to sit.

"Prudie calls herself a singer. Sings and plays the piano here at the hotel." Estelle was picking up porcelain figurines from a shelf between the two large windows responsible for the smeary light.

Prude inspected the assortment of rings on each finger. "When I take a notion to. Not much call for a singer in this no-place town." She laughed and patted Doll on the knee. "Unless you go to church, if you know what I mean."

So, what did all this have to do with Daniel? Doll wondered. Was Estelle trying to tell her that her husband spent a good part of his away-time sitting in the hotel, listening to Prude Purdue play the piano and sing? Was it more?

The woman seemed to read her mind. "Daniel likes to drop by now and again. Best chess partner I ever had."

Estelle held up a wooden pawn from the table she was now plundering in the corner next to the window on the right.

"Do you play chess?" Prude asked Doll, twitching her foot

in a pink satin slipper.

"No ma'am. I can play checkers though." Doll was shocked at the sound of her own voice as well as her answer. So dumb!

The woman smiled, her eyes crinkled. "Busy with that new baby, I'll bet."

"Yes ma'am."

"She can talk," Estelle said. "Just a mite on the timid side till she gets to know you." Estelle lifted another figure from the chessboard, examined it and placed it where it was before.

"I'm not...I..." Doll had to talk now. Otherwise this prissy woman would think she was for sure dumb. She couldn't think of a thing to say except, "It sure is hot, isn't it?"

Prude reached over to a cluttered dark wood table on her left, picked up a fan and flipped it open and began fanning both herself and Doll. The fan was lacquered black with a Chinese scene in reds, yellows and greens. Prude may as well have been from China herself for all she and Doll, and Estelle too, had in common.

"So, what's your baby's name? A girl, I believe Daniel told me." She was clearly uninterested, just talking to be talking.

"Minnie." It made Doll mad all over again that Daniel hadn't dignified the child with a name. Plus, the fact that he'd even mentioned either of them to this unusual woman.

"Oh, his mother's name. How meaningful!"

Her knowing that made Doll madder. Hotter. She could easily imagine Daniel enjoying the company of a woman like this. Playing chess, she doubted that. But if it killed her she wouldn't show it.

"Would you like a drink? It's a little early but I like a drink long about noon."

So, Daniel drank with her. He couldn't drink with Doll. That had to be another attraction to Prude.

She stood and archly crossed the room with her silky robe rustling to a dark wood cabinet with doors that opened on front. She took out a bottle of brown whiskey and began pouring a glass on top half full.

"You don't lay off that pison you gonna get down again."

Estelle was perched on a chair before the chessboard, as if studying some move, but studying her rough red hands instead.

Prude laughed. Sipped. Heading stiffly back to the love seat. "Estelle's seen me at my worst, you might say."

A drunk! She didn't look like a drunk. But Doll was grateful for a flaw, any flaw.

Poised again on the loveseat, sitting forward, she reached to the table again, lifted the lid on a small, embossed brass box, took out a long brown cigarette and lit it with a flourish of fire from a matching silver lighter. Inhaled deeply and blew a stream of smoke straight up and layering down. "I would offer you one, sweetheart, but I doubt very much that you smoke."

Her voice had grown raspy and sour. Show over, she glared at Doll. "You thought you'd come here and find one of Daniel's old lady friends. Right?"

"No ma'am. I didn't…"

She broke in, thumping ashes into a clean crystal dish on the table. "Well, I guess you could call me that. As good a description as any. But it's more, us, me and Daniel." She drank again, smoked. "He's the best old boy I've ever known, here to Atlanta, been the best to me." She raised her glass, sloshing whiskey, and mock toasted to Doll.

"He takes care of me." She laughed low in the throat. "Estelle there does too."

Estelle sprang into the conversation. "I brung her here for a purpose, and ain't nothing to do with yore ailments. She's my good friend and she's got a right to know what I know; what I suspicion's another matter."

Prude ignored her. Twiddled the cigarette between the first two fingers of her smoking hand.

"Well, honey, a man like Daniel's got a lot behind and ahead of him." She drank to that, smoked, added, "I'm an old friend of his brother Jimmy's. What's the attraction? I can sing and I like to laugh. I'm pretty and I'm naughty—that's the attraction. *But*, and it's a big one, I never let a man bed me. I'm the Untouchable." Again the mock toast. "Pleased to make your acquaintance."

Feeling almost sorry for the woman and a lot sorry that she had enlisted poor old earnest Estelle in a thing so trite, that they had prompted such a hollow, grasping avowal from Prude Purdue, herself growing old and probably knowing that the game was up, Doll stood. "I'm sorry we bothered you, ma'am."

Estelle stood, wagging her head.

Dark looks all around.

"You're so curious to know, let me tell you that Daniel Staten's a man with little use for people putting on airs. He likes his women hot and feisty and real. Women he can play with. And I'm not talking about checkers. High society types, he has no use for." She drank. "Like his brother did."

"I'm not...it's this outfit." Doll stared down at her silk blouse and brown skirt, the paisley print making her gaze skip. Again, she started to speak, to defend who she was and what she was after. But Prude Purdue no longer mattered. There was nothing real about her. She was just a lonely woman try-ing anyway she could to stand out.

Doll started for the door. "I hope you'll come to see us sometime. See the baby." She meant it. She didn't know why. Relief maybe over what she had at last learned—that Daniel was seeing after his dead brother's mistress or friend or fasci-nating toy. If he was fascinated too...well, she doubted that.

"Aanh!" Estelle waved her hand in Prude's direction, dis-missing her as a waste, then fell in line behind Doll going out the door.

Out in the hall, Estelle said, "I hope you ain't taking none of that to heart."

"I'm not." But part of what Prude had said rang true: Men liked naughty girls, fun girls, but more than all that they liked women they couldn't have.

Summer went and autumn came and the following fall the old men moved from the bench on the courthouse porch to the woodstove inside the commissary across the road, but except for Sheba's wedding, which Daniel attended with Doll, she stayed put at Staten Bay; the American Beauty berries turned from green to vivid purple, shed, and their branches would be turned to switches before she set out for the flatwoods again. But for now: Doll admitted Daniel into her bed and even went out riding with him to check on the cattle and the rising Alapaha, leaving Minnie with Estelle or Fate (she never left the baby with Maureen).

In October, they took the train east from Fargo to Jacksonville, Florida. The railroad line from the North to the South had recently been completed, and more than 100,000 Yankees migrated down to Jacksonville that year. The yellow fever epidemic that summer had killed hundreds of inhabitants, they were told, but still "The Winter City in the Summer Land," as Jacksonville was called, was swarming with tourists. Of more interest to Daniel was the huge naval store—acres of pine stave barrels containing distilled resin, and enough of it to brag about had been sapped from his own pines.

But even Daniel had to admit that meandering along the quartered-off blocks of capped barrels, awaiting export by steamer ships, could get a bit monotonous. So he and Doll made like tourists, strolling the streets of Jacksonville, knocking elbows with strangers and eating in fine restaurants.

It was hard for Doll to miss the eyes other women made at her husband. But thanks to Prude Purdue she was no longer distrustful or overly curious, she was proud of him. If Prude had told him about Doll and Estelle's visit, he never mentioned it. Doll only wondered how the conversation would have gone, whether they could have really *talked*. One other thing she had figured out was, Daniel often visited people he knew—women, men, children—while he was away from Staten Bay on business. Much as he had when he dropped by the Baxter place on his way home from Four-mile Still the time he'd asked Doll to marry him. What went on during his long absences she attributed to somebody or something interesting that had developed from those visits. For instance, hanging with the men out at the camps in the woods. Regardless, he seemed to be settling down, spending more time with her. Like in Jacksonville.

At the beach, a rangy white-mustached older man, seated on a wooden stool with a sketchpad on an easel before him, told them that he worked in a Carnegie steel plant, in Pennsylvania. He asked Doll to pose before the roiling turquoise ocean for him to sketch. All along the beach people gathered to watch while Doll stood in the salt wind and sun with her hair blowing and her skirt tail lifted to keep it from the creeping in-slush of the tide. The man asked her where she was from and she said, "Georgia—Staten Bay Plantation," and everybody laughed at her queer Dixie accent. A tall thin woman with upswept red hair, standing next to the man with the sketch pad, remarked that she didn't know there were any plantations left in Georgia after the Civil War. Surely they had all been burned to the ground.

Stressing each syllable, smiling and twisting, Doll said, "Well, surely not, ma'am. My baby's with one of the darkies back on the plantation this very minute."

The crowd roared. The man sketching her said, "Hold it right there, sweetheart. Hold it!"

Daniel, standing with the crowd, strolled forward, frowning, and took Doll by the arm and led her south along the lace-edged hem of the flaring surf. The crowd followed, and the man kept sketching with his pad braced in the crook of his left arm.

Daniel turned. "The war's over, mister," he said.

Next charcoal scratch on paper, Daniel let go of Doll's arm and wheeled, snatched the pad from the man and slung it fluttering like a bird with all his might into the ocean. The man's eyes followed the arc of the pad out over the sun-spangled water, then Doll and Daniel as they vanished among the sunbathers and umbrellas on the shore.

That evening, they learned that the war wasn't over.

During dinner in their hotel dining room, a newspaperman came and asked for the scoop on the incident with the

Yankees at the beach that day. Said Jacksonville being a major tourist site in Florida, the city commissioners didn't cotton to such disturbances. Daniel, having consumed a couple of whiskeys already that evening, told the story from start to finish, embellishing it with his philosophy on the war and ended up with some prompted remark about his family having owned slaves whose descendants still worked on his plantation.

The next morning the headlines of the Jacksonville News read, "Minor Rebellion at the Beach on Saturday: Georgia plantation owner defends owning slaves."

The hardwoods of the river swamp at Staten Bay thinned with the falling of leaves until the branch that would become Jeff Branch, named after Doll and Daniel's second son, could be seen crooking through the woods to the river where it dumped into a deep gorge. Ducks migrating down with the cold fretted and whipped their wings in the dirty-ice sky and swooped low over the slews fed by the rising river a couple of times a year. Tops of the pecan trees had been fanned free of leaves by the wings of many crows. The patch of silver sugar cane growing between the commissary and the cotton house was cut and ground and kegged as syrup for sopping and sweetening. First frost and cotton-picking time and the whole place revolved around white, frost and cotton, long staple cotton, Sea-Island cotton—a process, a flurry, a mindset that seemed without end but when it did end seemed like a dream of snow. Only the green pines stayed the same, season to season.

Doll could press her hand to her abdomen and feel the baby knot.

She slipped out the door of her bedroom, closing it easy to keep from waking Minnie, who she'd just put down for the night.

It was clear and cold. The sun had gone down as the moon was coming up and halfway up the hall the silvery light in the east appeared to meet the golden light in the west. Daniel would be home soon from duck hunting. The lane was alive with men, women and children going to and coming from the commissary; always more traffic along the lane on Saturdays because the commissary was closed on Sundays.

Earlier, the men had butchered a beef for the commissary—that was the main attraction this Saturday.

Maureen was coming out of Daniel's office, folding a white sheet of paper. When she saw Doll standing in the hall, she slipped it into the waist of her apron-wrap and walked off toward the kitchen.

"Maureen," Doll said, walking toward her, "were you looking for something?"

"Just straightening up before I start supper." She walked on, going through the door of the kitchen.

Always the way of it, but at least Doll let her know she was watching, suspecting. Suspecting what? What was on the paper she had stuck in her apron waist?

In the kitchen, Doll asked her.

"Nothing important." Her back was to Doll standing in the doorway.

She was trying to open a jar of vegetable soup she'd put up that summer.

Now what?

"We're having soup, I see." Doll walked over to the cooktable and stood. She would have guessed fried beefsteak—they always had beef on butchering day. Daniel would expect it.

"Supper'll be ready in about thirty minutes." Maureen was gripping the lid and the jar with the tail of the blue-striped towel hanging from her waist.

The folded paper worked free and fell to the floor at her feet. Before she could stoop to pick it up, Doll walked over and picked it up for her, seeing inside the four flaps of the folds words written in ink. Upside down and therefore unreadable. It never occurred to Doll to open it, though she had every right. Or did she? She simply placed it on the counter next to the jar, meeting Maureen's dreamy brown eyes for the usual exchange: you tend to your business and I'll tend to mine and maybe we can manage this space we have to share.

That night in bed, she told Daniel about Maureen coming out of his office folding the sheet of paper. He had just come back from the quarters, where he'd been summoned to settle some dispute among the Negroes. They lay nestled with Doll's back to him, his right arm over her side and his hand on the mound of her belly.

"Could be she was writing a letter to somebody," he said.

Doll seldom spoke of Maureen to Daniel, made it a point not to. One, it seemed so immature and she was trying to be more mature; and two, no matter what, Maureen always emerged innocent. For instance, only a few weeks before Doll had walked in on Maureen going through Daniel's things in the cherry chiffonier in his bedroom. No she hadn't been snooping; she was "straightening up." And for a fact, his ironed and folded shirts were stacked neater, aligned collars above collars, and the drawer with his personal papers—which Doll herself would never have touched—was organized, postcards from friends stacked with corners squared like fine ironed linens.

What made her skin prickle now was recalling the level standing lettering she had glimpsed when picking up the paper in the kitchen. Daniel's handwriting. Some kind of document or receipt. She lay there trying to decide whether to tell Daniel what she suspected, that Maureen was snooping where she shouldn't be and maybe even stealing.

"Do you really trust Maureen?" she asked.

"In what way?" He tensed slightly.

"In your office. In your personal things."

He relaxed, gathering her closer. "I have no reason as I know of not to."

"I caught her going through those postcards in your chiffonier; she said she was straightening up, but I think she was snooping."

"Let me put it like this, if I had something to hide I sure wouldn't leave it out in the open like that, would I?"

"Well, I wouldn't go through your things."

"I wouldn't go through yours either."

"I don't have any, that's why. I mean postcards and such."

"No letters from that lawyer even?" He stretched his neck his long legs, then pulled closer to her again.

"Nothing you can't see, no." That was true. Though she hadn't been exactly handing over letters from Adam for her husband to read.

"I trust you. If I hadn't I wouldn't have married you. Woman a man can't trust'll make him miserable to the grave."

She didn't know how to get back to Maureen and the folded sheet of paper from his office. She was too sleepy to bother and Daniel always had too many excuses. Besides, she despised women who were always picking for a fight; why would she want to pick a fight anyway? Let Maureen snoop and plunder. But she didn't really believe that Daniel wouldn't ask her about the paper she took from his office. If not, why wouldn't he?

Her eyes sprang wide open, seeing light in the dark. Oh my God! Had Maureen been snooping on her too? Who else would have reported on her mail?

The corn and peanuts had been harvested and the fields were left glazed with silvery bent stubble of stalks and bleached shucks. Doves flocked to the gleanings of corn kernels and peanuts, a thousand strong, pointy-winged and squeaking like rusty door hinges. Red birds darted and lit in the dry sepia reeds of coffee weeds. Shorter days now but the southward arcing sun seemed to shine longer at its evening slant across the fields. Bo Dink would stand each cool clear October day under cover of the pines and measure the birds' increase or decrease for the bossman, who had promised to let him go to the dove shoots after he turned eight. Then he would sit on the rail fence out front, chewing sugarcane and waiting to report to Daniel when he got home.

Bo Dink was eight years and two days old, as he said, the morning of the first shoot. It had turned cold during the night. At daybreak, when Daniel came out with his shotgun and shells, he found the boy waiting on the back steps, bundled up

172

in an oversized coat and carrying a croaker sack and a sling-shot whittled from a forked oak branch. By then, Bo Dink had polished and rubbed the stock of Daniel's shotgun till its varnish was worn dull in patches. Every day he polished it.

Daniel had invited several neighboring men to the shoot, and already they had gathered in the stand of longleaf yellow pines, north of the house, drinking coffee around a fire glowing with pinecones.

Spotted about the field, they waited for the sun to come up and the doves to come in, and before long shots began popping and birds dropping, and Bo Dink was off, scooping them up and depositing them in his croaker sack.

Off and on, throughout the day, Doll watched from the north windows of the house. The only movement across the field were gun barrels swinging round, sun glinting off of them, smoke raveling up and birds raining down from the blue sky, and short-legged Bo Dink scampering across the stubble, picking up doves and putting them in his sack.

Staten Bay rang with silence when they broke for lunch.

Maureen at her station in the kitchen ladled hot thick beef stew into bowls for the men. No longer the snoop but the competent cook. She sliced wedges of crusty brown cornbread and poured rich black coffee into cups on the dining room table. Dreamy-eyed, smiling and aloof she served the men while Doll presided over her table, wife of the host who kept the men talking hunting even while their eyes passed over the two women.

Bo Dink ate unseen at the cook table in the kitchen. Haunting in his silence.

Doll had started several times that morning to bring up the subject of Maureen's snooping, to put her in her place. But she was afraid if she got started she and Maureen would begin to argue about something else—so much to choose from—and she might leave Doll with cooking for the men, Daniel's fine run household in a mess like before when Fate took over both duties as cook and housekeeper. Now Doll thought she wouldn't mention the snooping at all; she figured Daniel had

173

probably corrected Maureen. He was no fool.

Doll's was the honored position. She didn't want to be the cook. She despised cooking. She thought about all those big heavy dinners and breakfasts labored over by her mother and sister and the other women she'd known.

Early frosty mornings, during deer hunts in the flatwoods, they would bake huge waiters of biscuits, fry sausage, bacon and ham—all three meats—cook pots of grits, scramble dozens of eggs and brew enough coffee to satisfy an army.

Then after the men were fed, the women still had to wash the dishes and clean the kitchen and be done in time for the next meal when it all started over again. Like Doll and Maureen had done during the wild fire.

She thought about Maureen then, how they had worked together in the kitchen. How they had ridden out into the midst of the fire to help. How Maureen could have left her to burn alive when she fell from the old plug horse to the ground. Maureen wasn't all bad or even half-bad. She had a heart; she was human. And in her place as housekeeper she would certainly appear to snoop whether she did or not.

Come mid afternoon, that same low sun halting at its easterly slant across the field, the men were shooting again and Bo Dink was picking up doves and putting them in his sack. All merry, with drink in their bellies and gone to their heads, they shot faster, harder, no longer making each shot count. Whooping and calling out, as if warring against friends, not enemies, not birds, and when the sun finally sank it appeared shot and bleeding, hiding behind the treeline of the Alapaha River.

Doll was standing at the window, left of the fireplace in Daniel's room, fire snapping and crackling inside, and outside the guns still going off from all directions, and shot even raining down on the roof. Suddenly she saw Daniel in his brown leather coat walking across the middle of the field, cradling Bo Dink in his arms. Sure the boy had been snakebit or shot, she was waiting on the back porch when Daniel walked up in the yard.

He seemed to read her mind. Shook his head and came up the doorsteps. His face was red, his lips chapped, his pants speckled with beggar weed seed and pronged with cockleburs and sandspurs. The boy's worn brown borrowed boots, sizes too large, were loose and dangling.

"Asleep," Daniel said, bypassing her on the porch and starting up the hall. He smelled gamy, of whiskey, smoke and cold. Surprising Doll, he carried Bo Dink into the bedroom between his office and the dining room and rolled him from his arms onto the patch-work quilt covering the bed. The boy curled like a new puppy, back to Daniel, and slept on.

The following Saturday, Bo Dink was back, rearing to go to the cornfield. It was a cold gray dawn with light rain falling on the dried shucks, stubble and stalks. Solid beige and sodden from one end of the field to the other. Daniel took the croaker sack from Bo Dink and handed him the shotgun. He carried it barrel down, grinning as he walked off with Daniel across the yard and fields. The shotgun was almost as long the boy and caused him to list right.

Middle of the morning, the men were still shooting and the field was littered with dead birds. Then the rain came harder, dropping straight down from the muddy gray sky like a shot-up roof, and they had to quit, though the air was loaded, squeaking with doves. Only when they got done shooting did Daniel send the boy out, and only for his own birds.

Following Sunday meeting in Statenville, after Thanksgiving, Doll left Minnie with Estelle and went with Daniel to the race track on the Highland Plantation, five miles north of Statenville. They rode together in the surrey—rare for Daniel— the black stallion tied and trotting behind. About once a month, select men from the community would meet at the Highland and race, drink and fry fish. Rare too was this invitation to the women and children to join them.

It had rained on Thanksgiving Day, turned cold the next and colder the next, but now the sky was blue, deep and blameless, the air was thin and mild. Sun sparked in the pines each side of the road, drawing the tangy tar from the needles. In the west a half moon hung like a broken mother-of-pearl button.

At the lane to the Highland, a cotton plantation owned by Nolan Vincent, Daniel pulled the surrey in behind a wagon loaded with children on patchwork quilts. All freckled, squinting in the sun, staring back at the surrey. Doll guessed sharecroppers. A black buggy pulled in behind the surrey, adding to the screaking of wheels and the clopping of horse hoofs.

On the left was the bare-dirt racetrack, a lane of live oaks with branches meeting overhead. Already men on horses were trotting in the paisley shadows parallel to the buggy lane, up to the main road and back to the big house: a two-story white Colonial with an open crescent gallery and hovering bushes of blue hydrangeas below the spindled banisters. More men on horses crossed the oak-shaded yard, from the barn on the right to the race track on the left, spotted dogs switching their tails and waggling among the horses, and children chasing from the barn to the porch. A dozen children at least, about half of them belonging to Bee and Nolan Vincent. Bee was white-headed but not old, tall, slim and handsome in a navy skirt and white blouse with rolled sleeves. From the porch, she scolded the children. A little girl in a rose print dress bellied up on the banister to Bee's right and flipped bottom side up into the hydrangeas, white bloomers shining. Bee reached for her, missed, shook her head. The little girl crawled out from the bushes and skipped off toward the other children at the barn. A slim Negro woman came around the house at a trot and chased after the little girl with a switch. Five women grouped under the oak on the sideyard stopped talking to watch, then went back to talking again.

Bee smiled and waved at the visitors unloading at the barn. The children on the wagon hopped down and quickly mixed with the others, squealing and trailing along the worm fence that separated the yard from the fields and woods. Daniel, with Doll by his side, led the eager stallion over to the watering trough at the well where Nolan, a short man with curly dark hair, stood talking to a rangy blond man.

Lately, it seemed to Doll, when men got together, they broke into conversation with talk about the "New South": big government's notion that industrialism would break the cycle of rural poverty. Textile mills were the answer, some said; just like the governor when he came to the flatwoods. Only this time the idea was to move more people to the city and put them to work in the mills. Daniel said moving wouldn't be much of an improvement if a man wasn't happy; Nolan predicted the campaign would falter; the blond man agreed, said it was best all round just to ride it out, these hard times.

"I doubt you three gentlemen are who they have in mind," said Doll and walked off with them watching. She felt like a hypocrite saying that. She'd been a landowner too, and she was hardly suffering now at Staten Bay. But she had said it for the hand-to-mouth sharecroppers in the rickety wagon ahead of them coming up the lane to watch the big shots race. She'd said it for herself before this beneficial marriage to Daniel Staten, and for who she could be again with a single slip of the tongue. Like the remark she'd just made. She could be poor again and she wouldn't even have her old homeplace.

She started toward the porch to speak to Bee Vincent, on her way speaking to the huddle of strange women to the right of the porch. Only one she knew from Big Meeting at Bony Bluff, when all the area churches came together at the end of harvest time, a tall pale blond in a two piece tapestry dress that seemed to weigh her down.

Bee stepped up the banister, leaning out. "Daniel's racing today, I see." She had stern blue eyes contrasted with a tender smile.

Doll looked back at Daniel now astride and trotting the stallion toward the oak-lined racing lane. There was a smell of rotting leaves and oak mold in the shady grassed yard.

Bee placed her hands each side of her mouth and shouted out, "Fred, you boys, you're gonna break your necks on those Tom Walkers."

Three boys on six-foot stilts were stepping over the worm

fence and back. Cheeks pink as apple blossoms against the overhang of blue sky.

"I declare," said Bee, shielding her eyes with one hand. Then, hand down by her side, "How's that baby, Doll?"

"Good, growing like a weed." Only Doll and Bee were without hats. The grouped women were eyeing them, talking with their heads bowed.

Like Doll, Bee didn't socialize much away from their plantation. No time and no need, what with the company of family members and hired help.

The little girl in the print dress came back up on the porch. Bee paused talking only long enough to spank her bottom as she flipped over the banister again. Then Bee leaned with her forearms propped on the banister and clasped her rough, veined hands.

"Isn't that some of your bunch, Doll?" she asked and nodded toward the lane.

"Maureen and Joe." Doll watched them walking toward one of the oaks about halfway up the lane.

"Nolan took dinner with Daniel a while back. Says she's a Jim Dandy cook." Bee never said anything about anybody if she couldn't say something good but true.

"You know, she used to cook in some eating place in Louisiana before she came here," Doll said.

"What Nolan said. Said her Daddy had trained her to cook—mostly Creole, kind of food I just love but never get here."

"She never mentions her Daddy, never mentions family at all. She had some sort of run-in with the owner of the place where she cooked. Then Joe got in trouble, she said."

A confounded look crossed Bee's sharp features, then just as quickly vanished. She stood tall and folded her arms. "A bad thing, him killing that fellow and them having to leave home. We think the world and all of Joe."

Doll was stunned by that bit of news. Wanted to ask more but could sense Bee had ended the discussion and was now deliberating over what had been said. Besides, the race was about to start.

Everybody at the barn and along the lane began gathering under the oaks parallel to the racing track. The women in the group on the sideyard wandered out too, now obviously not staring at Doll, or so she thought.

One sniggered and the decorated heads drew together, whispering like schoolgirls, sneaking glances at Doll. Or was it Bee?

"Enjoy the races, ladies," Bee called out.

"Do you know them?" Doll asked low.

Bee was smiling, staring out toward the racetrack. "Not really. I've seen them around. Fancies themselves society types."

Doll was trying to think of something to say to console Bee—everybody knew how Nolan flirted. He never tried to hide it. Any woman who took him seriously ran the risk of making a fool of herself. Not only because he was harmless, but because Bee didn't take him serious. She came out shining every time.

"Don't let them bother you," Bee said and stepped away from the banister to speak to a brittle-looking old woman standing in the front door. A black cat slunk out of the house and rubbed against the legs of a wicker chair, then sat forming a base of its haunches for its tail to wrap round.

Using Bee as an example, Doll crossed the yard with her head high, dodging a couple of boys in knee britches and suspenders dashing toward the track. Adding a smile, she walked up the buggy lane until she reached the shade of the second oak, the first oak being occupied by the women from the yard.

Okay, so what was new about the fact that Daniel had a reputation as a lady's man before they married? He'd never denied that. If she had to guess she would have guessed that Daniel had courted and jilted one of them. She was used to that. Not the pale blond with no eyelashes, she wouldn't have been his type. Probably the cute brunette in the rose dress with an exaggerated bustle. Or was it her behind? Doll smiled.

"Society types," she said low, recalling what Prude Purdue had said about Daniel having no use for society types.

The men at the start of the track were sitting their horses, milling, talking, swapping bottles on the side away from the spectators. Sun shimmering on their white starched and ironed broadcloth shirts. Nolan in a black vest stepped out from among them and welcomed everybody to Highland Plantation, told a few jokes, got everybody laughing, then switched to a speechy voice, announcing who would be riding in the first race. "Got two men hailing all the way from Douglas. Neighbors, you might say."

The two men identified themselves by reining their horses away from the others and walking them over to where Nolan was standing, side-stepping, then lining up next to each other while Nolan finished introducing them. He had his thumbs in his vest pockets, the gold chain of his pocket watch throwing spasms of sunlight to the trunk of the first oak and the women standing round.

"Old Warn's the one with the good-looking wife there." He nodded to the tall pale blond and she nodded back.

Leave it to Nolan to play up to the woman who was least attractive.

A man in the group at the start of the track yelled, "You think they all good looking, Nolan."

Everybody laughed.

Somebody up the line of oaks yelled, "Quit messing around, Nolan, and let's get on with the race."

Nolan laughed, made some jab, then switching back to serious reminded the men that there were woman and children present today. "No cussing and swearing," he yelled. "No drinking. That is, unless you offer old Nolan here a swig first."

More laughter. A horse nickered. Wrapping up, he warned the children to stay off the track. "Don't, your mamas and daddies are welcome to use that cow whip hanging on the hall tree up at the house."

That said, he labored at a slow run to the other side of the track, turned, twitching his pistol from the holster at his waist, cocked and fired it into the air. The women squealed; scattered tittering reverberated along the line of oaks. The first two riders sprinted off up the track, tilting forward and whipping their horses with their reins. Dirt clods spun from the horses' hooves.

The grouped women began moving closer to Doll's oak. She walked off, under the pretense of following the racers in order to see. When they turned at the end of the track, coming strong and fast, the crowd shouted and clapped. Doll kept walking. Seeing ahead Joe's red-checked shirt and Maureen's pearly cream blouse.

Joe, tracking the racers with his drooped blue eyes, spotted Doll and waved. Then moved away from the humped roots where Maureen was sitting and shouted at the two men, almost shoulder to shoulder, whipping their horses past.

Doll stepped among the roots and sat next to Maureen and rested her back against the trunk. "I didn't know you and Joe were coming," she said.

"Joe's a fool about racing." Maureen leaped to her feet, clapping for the two horses skidding toward the finish line. Too close to call.

Next up were Nolan on a roan plug and Daniel on the sleek black stallion. After much clowning, the unmatched pair was off. Nolan suddenly stopped a quarter of the way up the track, said Staten started before the gun went off.

"Ahhh," everybody said.

"You lying son-of-a-gun," said one of the men at the starting point.

Daniel smiled, turned the stallion, sitting high and straight in the saddle. His reddish beard was groomed, his hair streaked with comb marks. He pranced past Nolan on the hay-bellied roan, still running his mouth to the crowd.

"Calls hisself a ladies' man," Nolan said, moping the roan in behind the stallion. "No offense, Doll." He cut his eyes quick at Doll. "Staten, can I have Doll?"

The crowd laughed.

They started over. And over. Nolan joking, till finally they made it to the end of the track and back. With Daniel winning of course.

The entire county would turn out for Nolan's funeral, a few years later. Nolan made them laugh. According to Bee, at home, after he got done entertaining at church and fish fries and such, he would clam up and dare her or the children to even speak to him.

The group of women now stood one tree up from Doll and Maureen, seated together high at the base of the number four oak.

"You know them?" Maureen asked.

"Know who they are. Sort of. Saw that blonde woman at Big Meeting at Bony Bluff."

Daniel and another man passed, whipping their horses, keeping stride. Maureen jumped up, shouting, "Go, go!" then stepped out to the middle of the track with the other spectators to watch the racers' progress. Then the crowd parted and Daniel and the stallion streaked past on their way to the top of the track—winning, of course. Everybody clapped, whistled and whooped.

No, not the brunette, Doll decided. Her nose was too long to suit Daniel. Maybe the smaller woman with dark skin and a fawn hat piled high with peach flowers. Doll figured Bee knew and that was why she'd said not to pay them any attention.

Maureen sat down next to Doll. "Guess nobody ever taught them it's bad manners to stare."

Doll felt strange having Maureen on her side, Maureen talking about manners after all but spitting in her face. Could she trust her now, could they be civil? Or friends like Doll and Estelle? She examined the ripe bisque face, the gleamy dreaming eyes. She was smiling, a sly smile, looking out at the track. Doll doubted it would work but decided to try her by confiding. "I think Daniel may have courted one of them." She waited, then added on second thought, "Before we were married," for the purpose of maintaining proper distance and pride. Just in case.

Maureen switched her eyes toward the ladies. Didn't move a hair till Daniel and Joe rode past with their horses' bodies perfectly paired and legs scissoring in synchrony.

Daniel was a favorite; the crowd cheered for him. But Joe was a close second: Joe the legend, the Joe with the guts to walk right up to a black bear every bit of six feet tall and weighing six hundred pounds if it weighed an ounce and stick his rifle barrel to its back and shoot. The bear grew with each telling.

Had he really killed a man? Doll couldn't imagine that. But she knew Bee wouldn't have said it if it weren't true, and Joe would have had good reason. She wondered if he would be happy now to go back to some city, pulling regular wages on some regular mill job. Doll thought he should have that choice—if not New Orleans, then somewhere else. Maureen should have that choice too.

The clean fall air, sweetened with oak moss, was suddenly undercut with the smell of frying fish from up at the big house.

Doll could see Bee standing with her arms crossed under the oak nearest the house, and on down the line other people, then the women at the next oak creeping closer. Maureen was standing with the crowd out on the track, watching Joe and Daniel galloping their horses to the finish. Too close to call.

Doll waited till Maureen came back and settled in above her on the humped and flaring roots of the oak. Then she called out to the women, "Would you ladies like to join us?"

They sauntered over, smiling, lifting skirts and stepping high over the roots, and seated themselves with their perfumed finery spread like fairytale princesses. Maureen, plain and tall and at the peak of the pyramid, was fairest of them all.

But it was Bee who stole the show in Doll's eyes. She would handle them all with Bee's special brand of beatific obliviousness.

Two days before Christmas and Staten Bay was humming with the holiday spirit. Since Thanksgiving the weather had been switching back and forth—warm, rain, cold, warm, rain, cold. The rest of the year the men worked on outside, regardless of the weather, but Daniel had sent them home to celebrate Christmas. The cotton had been picked, the corn gathered, and head-way had been made in the turpentine woods, scraping the hardened runs of gum from the catfaces of the slash pines; the chipping could wait—*have to put on that healing streak soon*—and spring dipping seemed a long ways off. The greedy rang-ing cattle lowed, foraging for foliage, but for now they would have to make do and pay for their feasting during the green seasons by cleaning up the singed briars and brambles in the wintering woods. Neat wheels of pinestraw had been raked away from the pines in windrows before fire had been set to the woods, and the clean bare circles accented the hottest burns, the first grass that would show green through black in early spring. All pressing work behind them, Daniel had sent the men home to celebrate with jugs of whiskey that he and his friends, likewise celebrating, had cooked off in the cane-syrup kettle. No let-up for the women inside, they worked on, cook-ing for Christmas while dodging their likkered-up men, whose drunken brawls were viewed as normal, even festive, just men being men, part of their Christmas celebrating.

Daniel gave Bo Dink a cloth bag of marbles and a silver dollar, on the eve of Christmas Eve, and took him to Valdosta to spend the money. All on candy, which he ate on the way home. He was so sick he looked drunk when he got back to the quarters.

While Daniel passed out candy to the other children, Bo Dink stood at the back of the present-packed buggy and puked. His eyes were rolled up in his head; his pockets were bulging with candy and marbles. All laughing and jabbering, the women gathered around the buggy full of Christmas from the bossman. Fate, stealing the show in her red headrag, started around the buggy with a switch. An old man with a rising on his neck poked out on one of the porches, sat in a cowhide rocker and leaned on his cane, grinning.

It was a mild gray day, threatening rain. Cone-shaped green cedars stood out from the backdrop of bare hardwoods and russet bristles on cypresses. Smoke rose from the chimneys of the shanties and curled up into the muddy clouds. Damp-dirt and damp-dog smells and smoke. Till the candy: scents of lemon, licorice, strawberry, cherry, grape...

Daniel called out to Fate from the circle of children. "Fate, let him alone, why don't you? He's miserable enough as it is."

"Old greedy," she said, fanning the switch at Bo Dink, parrying, dodging, going for the touchy creases behind his knees. "Fraid he have to divide up with the other chirren what he fraid of."

Daniel thumped a little girl on the noggin; the children laughed and squealed, dodging him. Then pulled back in for more candy. The old man sat forward and knocked on the porch floor with his cane. "Leave that boy be, woman," he shouted.

"He have a whipping coming, shore nuf."

"Uh huh," the other women chimed.

Warming up to the bossman in the quarters, the working men wandered out with their gift jugs of shine and sat, watching and chuckling, justified in drinking and hanging around the house and it broad daylight. Long as the bossman was laughing, long as it was Christmas. Still, they lifted the glass jugs easy and quick to their lips, swigged and set them on the floor between their feet without a sound.

Blackbirds, a hundred strong, slewed south over the cornfield and swooped down like wind-borne cloth.

Daniel was passing sticks of licorice to the outstretched hands. The children were laughing and shouting, "Me, me, Mr. Daniel. I ain't have one."

Fate now stood before the puked candy on the dirt, facing Bo Dink with the switch. "Wadn't for Mr. Daniel, yo behind be grass," she shouted. "Now, hand it over."

"What, Mama?" He was leaning with his head against the backend of buggy.

"That candy, that what."

The women laughed.

"I done et it."

She switched his legs, he danced. Pulled from his right pocket a hard red cherry candy with lint on it and gave it to

her.

"The rest of it," she demanded.

He halted with his eyes meeting hers, as if to refuse, but fished the rest of the candy from his pocket and handed it to her. He patted the bulge in his left pocket. "Marbles Bossman give me," he said.

Fate turned away, walking toward the children flocked around Daniel. "You babies look ahere." A girl and a boy reached out for Bo Dink's candy. "Old greedy gut like to eat it all up."

"Fate," said Daniel, wadding a brown paper sack to show the children it was empty, "I wish you'd let him have it."

She ignored him.

"Fate," he said again, same tone, "you want your Santy Claus, you better give that boy back his candy."

Exaggerating a fast trot toward the back of the buggy, spurred on by the laughter of the women, and the men, she handed Bo Dink his candy.

Revving up as Santa Claus, at home, that evening, Daniel presented Minnie with a doll that had a cloth body and was dressed in a long white gown. The doll, bought because its coral-tinted porcelain face reminded Daniel of Minnie's, made her sad rather than happy. One look at the doll's turned-down mouth, and Minnie took on the same doomed expression, primped up and cried.

Seated on his bed, across from Doll with Minnie on her lap, Daniel held the doll face-out and in one hand. He watched, puzzled, as Minnie cried on Doll's shoulder. Doll patted her back, rocking and shushing her.

In the corner, left of the fireplace, a tall, bushy woods cedar was decorated with strings of popcorn and cranberries. The room smelled of cedar, essence of Christmas. That afternoon Minnie had picked up a shed cranberry under the tree and poked it up her nose and Estelle had forced her to inhale snuff, making her sneeze. She cried and Estelle told her to hush, that next time she'd be more heedful of what she poked up her nose.

"Why is she crying?" Daniel asked Doll now.

She told him about the incident with the berry, adding, "Maybe she's still upset about the berry. Or could be she's crying because the doll has a sad face."

Daniel turned the doll like a puppet. "By God, she does." Then he placed the doll face down on the bed, got up and left the room to deliver more gifts: disappointed in Minnie's reaction to the doll, but too full of Christmas spirit to slow down.

After Doll got Minnie to sleep that night, she went into Daniel's room. She stopped in the doorway, watching him reading and dozing in the wine brocade chair to the right of the slow oak fire. His chin dropped, waking him, and he looked up, face spreading into a smile.

"Just Doll," he said low. "How long have you been waiting for me?"

"*Waiting?*"

"Under that mistletoe." He pointed to the doorframe over her head and the brittle green sprig with clear waxy berries.

She closed the door, crossed the room and kissed him on the crescent of fire-warm cheek above his beard. She could smell whiskey on his breath. "I'm not still mad about you sending the men home with whiskey if that's what you think."

"Good." He pulled her closer, kissed her lips. "It's harmless fun."

"Not for the women, it's not." She straightened up and sidestepped over to the hearth, took the poker from the stand and began punching at the seething red heart of the log, then held out her hands and watched as it ignited into an even row of flames.

He started reading again, magazine folded over to column-size and close to his face, but she could tell he was thinking about what she'd said and probably hadn't given much thought to her brooding about the whiskey in the first place. Anyway, as he said, she just didn't understand the ways of men or the workings of a plantation. She'd found since marrying Daniel that for the most part he treated her brooding spells as lapses into deep thought and stayed out of the way until they were spent and she never really changed his thinking anyway. A waste of emotion, brooding.

A cold front had pushed a quick rain through Georgia that evening, then south across the Florida line, leaving behind a fresh flock of mallards and a bright vaporous chill. By Christmas night, Doll thought, there would be a hard freeze.

She stood staring at the hump-backed mahogany clock on the mantel, listening to it purring and the purring of the fire. Only eight o'clock and already dark out and she felt drowsy too, was tempted to go to bed. Then she looked back at the brass bed, to the right of the door, and saw all the commissary wares waiting for her to make gifts of them. Tomorrow her mama and Sheba and the preacher would be coming and she had to wrap their gifts at least. Right after Thanksgiving she'd started spotting and Estelle had warned against going on long trips, so she hadn't been able to go to Valdosta and Christmas shop with Daniel. Estelle had also warned against her sleeping with her husband—big ole man like that, she'd said. Doll smiled. Really she'd been glad to shop at the commissary: for Sheba, she had picked out the woven leather horse blanket that she had admired when she first came to Staten Bay, though she figured like herself her sister would think it too finely crafted for the back of a horse or mule.

She looked left at the paint-black window and the bushy cedar before it. The tree breathed green into the parched-oak scent of the room. Then she tiptoed from the fire to the bed and sat, making for herself a nest of green and red Christmas paper, ribbons and gifts-to-be. She yawned. The combined fluttering light and sizzling and warmth of the fire made her want to sink back into the cloud of feather bedding and float off to sleep, taking with her into a dream this vision of the fine, handsome man before her now deep in sleep with his head back on the chair and his magazine open on his lap. One boot crooked and resting on his knee, hands loose on the chair arm. Long fingers that looked stained but clean. Skin, hair and beard copper, a copper-toned portrait of a satisfied man, white shirt glowing in the yellow light of the lamp on the table between the front window and his chair.

Doll was satisfied too. Satisfied to stay home, to wait, sometimes. Other times she reminded herself of the women in the flatwoods whose husbands roamed wherever, whenever. And where did the women get to go but Sunday meeting? Her daddy, in particular, would sit out on the porch, when he was home, rocked back to the wall in a straight chair, and wait for the next neighbor or stranger passing by out front to stop and ask if he wanted to go with them. He'd say, Just a minute, let me get my coat. He never asked where they were going or when they were coming back, and summer or winter he wore that coat when he left the house, because in the pockets was the little bit of money he'd earned the week before and would squander on whiskey or lose before whoever picked him up delivered him home again.

She was wrapping her first gift, a sheepskin rug for her mama, when a series of pistol-like pops sounded up the lane. Then another.

Daniel was on his feet at the window, trying to stare beyond the mirrored glare of lamplight.

"I knew you shouldn't have given them whiskey, Daniel," Doll said. "It's been nothing but trouble all week."

He laughed, surprising her, still peering out with his hands like blinders each side of his face. Usually, he got upset with the Negroes when they misbehaved. "Come on," he said, turning and tilting his bearded chin up.

"No." Doll shook her head. "They're drunk and I'm not going out there. I'm on Fate's side about this."

He laughed. "Fate's drinking too, don't let her fool you. Now come on out on the porch with me, I want you to see something special." He crossed the room to the bed, reached out and caught her hand, then waited till she stepped to the floor in her white dressing gown, black hair like a shawl on her shoulders.

On the edge of the front porch they stood, watching about halfway up the lane what looked like many elves with lit wands grouping then dashing out into the trees each side of the lane, leaving a centerpoint of sputtering sparks and slashes of fire; then triggered by a burst of noise like a dry grass fire, the rocket exploded into the frosty night sky, showering down sparks, brighter than the myriad stars—all except for one star, larger and spiking like a sun-shot mirror. Again the elves with lit wands grouped in the lane, dark faces burnished by the flares.

"Bo Dink, that you?" Daniel called.

"Christmas, boss!" Bo Dink called out and lit a long string of firecrackers. POP POP POP POP. The sky lit up with pagan and divine starshine.

"Don't tell me Bo Dink is drinking too?" Doll whispered. She leaned into Daniel, shivering and hugging her body. He placed his right arm about her shoulders and pulled her close, but his eyes never left the play up the lane.

Sparks rose and settled in the tops of the tall yellow pines like lightning bugs. The torches came together and moved down the lane, almost gliding, toward the front of the house.

"Who's behind the torches?" she asked.

Daniel was smiling, grinning, nodding. "Just listen. Watch and listen."

With the flares floated a sudden song, a shrill, sweet, mangled song of Jingle Bells, and children's voices pealed like bells in the thin pearly light of the sky. Smoke from the torches and the vapors of their breath carried on the cold air. They had stopped at the fence, lined up and were singing to the top of their lungs, scream-singing, with torches swaying in time.

There was a slice of moon in the sky somewhere, maybe beyond the western peak of the roof, spattering shadows and misting the world with its white light, but it appeared dim in contrast to the torches and the fire-lit faces, just a light.

Bo Dink set off another round of fireworks, this time fire-crackers, followed close by a bottle rocket. When the rocket went up, sputtering, whistling and arcing out over the north field, he ran down the lane at a shambling gait, pale shirt capturing the skylight as he cleared the shadows of the trees, and on toward the children now singing Silent Night. One little girl was cradling a shiny-faced Christmas doll in her arms, almost like the doll Daniel had given Minnie.

"Christmas, Boss!" Bo Dink shouted and stepped up to the gate when they were done with the song.

"Christmas, Boss!" they all yelled, laughing, whooping and scattering.

Daniel laughed and walked down the steps. "Looks like you're gonna pull through from eating all that candy." He began fishing in his pants pocket, rattling change as he went.

"Daniel, don't," Doll whispered but it was too late; he'd already reached across the fence to pass a coin to Bo Dink.

Bo Dink backed away, turning and skipping to catch up with the other children. "No suh, boss," he called out. "This our Christmas to you."

Inside again, seated on the edge of her bed, in the firelight, Doll held up her heavy glinting hair for Daniel to hook the silver serpentine chain of the locket he had bought her for Christmas. He kissed her neck. She let her hair go, smiling, watching the firelight flicker on the silver heart coming to rest above the vee of her breasts and the eyelet trim of her white nightgown.

She loved pretty things—those pretties he brought—but didn't really love jewelry. It was a waste, served no purpose other than to make restitution for some sin of the giver or to show payment for services rendered by the receiver. She would never tell him how she felt about his gift jewelry. She would never tell him she liked rendering those services so much that she should probably be buying him jewelry.

But he knew. "That hot skin," he said, settling beside her, on her left. He peeled back her hair over her ear and whispered, "Soon as the baby's born, I'll take you to New Orleans."

Then he kissed her on the mouth and slipped one hand down into the bodice of her gown, cupping a small but ripe breast. "To hell with New Orleans," he whispered, "I'm gonna keep you right here in bed for about a month."

Doll would never have confessed to Estelle that she liked sex, that she liked this big man. Craved was more like it.

They lay back, at first talking about Bo Dink and the children and their Christmas gift to him, then drowsing in silence, holding each other and staring into each other's crossing eyes. Nose to nose and not speaking. Listening to the fire sing and snap with its heat on their backs. Feeling their second child between them like a smooth round stone.

The log burned through and broke in half and glowed brighter, a white-hot heat, just before it turned to chunks of live red coals then powder and ash. The whole house ticked with cold and time and silence—it could have been anytime but it was now—while they slept. The star in the east shone brightest.

On Christmas Eve, Mrs. Baxter came, bringing two pecan pies and Sheba and the preacher, who were now living in Waycross, a big little-town thirty miles east of the flatwoods. The house smelled of cloves and nutmeg from Maureen's wine-steeping fruitcakes. Sweet potatoes for tomorrow's candied yams were baking, a slow wafting of the syrupy tar dripped on the hot floor of the oven. Mrs. Baxter and Sheba took over the baby, as Maureen had taken over the kitchen, leaving Doll to entertain the preacher before the fire in Daniel's room, then he happened by and she left him with the preacher on the excuse of seeing to their sleeping arrangements. She absolutely could not sit there another minute with the solemn, rocking preacher while all about the house Christmas was going on. She stood in the hall, breathing in the cold air.

The weather was holding, hard cold and bright on Christmas day.

Maureen came early to cook: hen and dressing, turnip greens, candied yams with wedges of Florida oranges, a gift from Daniel's daddy's first cousin Hayward and his wife Odessa, visiting from Bartow, Florida. Tall man with a paunch, Hayward looked nothing like Daniel, or Daniel's father in the picture in the office. Booming about the cold house, Hayward

192

told stories about the eccentric Statens, which Daniel under-cut on the sly, calling Hayward "the lying Staten"—there's one in every family. He seemed to prefer the reserved family image conferred by the safe silent pictures in his office, or didn't care at all about family. Stories were lies and he was a man of truth and measured other men by their truths.

A week later, Doll was sitting on a quilt spread before the fire in Daniel's room. Minnie, seated before her, was undressing her Christmas doll after Doll had just dressed her. Minnie picked up the doll by her feet and began banging her head on the floor.

"No, no, no," Doll said, laughing. "I hope that's not how you're gonna treat the new baby."

"Ba-be," Minnie said and gnawed on one of the doll's hands. Her flat blue eyes stretched when she opened her mouth.

"Yes, ba-be. Love the baby." Doll took the slobbery doll and placed it in her own arms. Rocking side to side with her legs crooked under her.

Minnie crawled across the room, toward the closed door. Maureen started to open it from the other side.

"Wait!" yelled Doll. She jumped up and ran to Minnie, picked her up facing out with one arm about her waist and the other under her bottom.

Maureen came in carrying a stack of folded clothes and began placing them in the drawers of Daniel's cherry chiffonier. On top was a hatbox with a foxhunting scene.

"You're wet again, girl," Doll said to Minnie, then carried her over to the pallet before the fire and laid her down. "Bring me a diaper, will you, Maureen?"

Maureen went out, came back and handed the folded white square of cloth to Doll, then walked over to the window next to Daniel's chair, right side of the fireplace. She raised the window and took a piece of split oak from the stacked wood on the scaffold. She placed it on the fire and punched it up with the poker. The fire popped, hissed, purred.

The men had killed hogs that morning and the greasy smoke

from the pot where they were cooking off lard had filled the hall and seeped into the room. The whole house smelled of sage and pepper used for seasoning sausage.

Doll was amazed at how little thought she'd given to Maureen since trying to chum with her at the racetrack after Thanksgiving. And sad, she felt suddenly sad that she had been forced to appear so aloof and lordly with the hired help. But really they were simply tending to their own business, staying busy and out of each other's way. It worked. Worked so well that they seemed almost oblivious to one another. Maureen cooked and kept house, Fate washed, and Doll tended the baby. Doll was shocked to feel that Maureen no longer mattered; she'd never felt another human didn't matter, not in her whole life. It had been easier to hate Maureen when Maureen had been the one to treat Doll as if she didn't matter.

After dinner yesterday, she had walked with Minnie down to the cotton house. Lint on the cold sunny air in front of the house, they had stood watching the women on the porch batting seeds from the new cotton with their wire brushes, then walked on around the curve to the neat square bungalow where Maureen and Joe lived. All was quiet inside—dead grass yard and a dead pomegranate tree outside. Maureen had probably been home, had probably seen Doll looking and not caring enough to walk up to the paneled wood door and knock.

Changing Minnie's diaper, Doll watched Maureen, sideways and leaning to place the poker on its stand on the hearth. As always, her dark hair was parted in the middle and caught up in a bundle on her nape. In the backlight of the fire, through Maureen's long brown skirt, Doll could see that her abdomen bulged—that unmistakable baby bulge even on so large a woman.

"Maureen, you're expecting, aren't you?"

Maureen got still, staring, frozen before the fire.

"I'm sorry I hadn't noticed before now. I should have said something." Actually Doll wanted to tell Maureen to say something—let's talk.

She just stood there.

"Do you miss New Orleans?"

"Not really."

"I heard that your daddy taught you how to cook."

"Yes."

Maureen seemed meek, trembly. Not at all bold or threatening, probably couldn't really afford to have a baby right now. Doll would speak to Daniel about paying her more, her and Joe.

"Is he still in New Orleans?"

"No, he died."

"The rest of your family, are they still in New Orleans?" Doll fastened the safety pin on the diaper and sat the baby up.

"Joe's my only family."

"Your mama's not living?"

"No."

"What about brothers and sisters?"

"Joe is my brother."

Doll was in the act of lifting Minnie under her arms and paused only long enough for her heart to resume beating, then stood with the child and went out the door and across the hall to her own bedroom. She sat in one of the wicker rockers and began singing Minnie to sleep, which was a long time coming and Doll could barely force herself to sing. Minnie hummed along with her fist in her mouth, staring up at Doll with those bird-egg eyes. The counting song of fleecy white sheep leaping over fences came forced and sad, a melancholy lullaby that left Doll hollow and aching.

Even after Minnie fell asleep, warm and close, cheek to Doll's heart, she still sat, no longer singing or rocking, but seething, bleeding inside. Her hurt pride wasn't at the center, it was somewhere at the side, but was jarring loose sparks of humiliation from her heart to her head: those women at the races knew about Daniel's old-testament style wife and concubine. Bee knew, or had she guessed? No wonder the men from the dove shoot were cutting their eyes from one woman to the other. Did Estelle know? Prude Purdue? The old men on the courthouse porch always calling out to Daniel when he and Doll passed? She had to stop there with listing everybody who might have known what a fool she'd been or she would be left with nowhere to go inside her head or out where she might not bump into one of them.

She couldn't hear Maureen anywhere in the house, but heard Daniel stamping mud from his boots on the back doorsteps, then striding long with his boot heels tapping up the hall to his office. She stood and crossed to her bed and eased Minnie down in the middle and took the folded quilt from the trunk at the foot and spread it over her. Then she tiptoed out, closing the door behind her, and headed for Daniel's office.

He was sitting behind his desk with a pencil in his hand, staring down at an open green ledger.

She stopped in the doorway, then walked on toward the desk. "I thought Joe was Maureen's husband."

He looked up, his eyes green as the globe of the lamp on his left. He looked down again, writing, saying, "He's her brother, I think."

"You *think?*"

"I know he is. Why?" He kept writing.

"Well, who's the daddy of her baby then?"

"What baby?" No indication that he knew, that he cared anymore than he cared about the wine clothbound book about to drop off the right corner of the desk.

"Look up, Daniel. Look at me."

He looked up and reared in the chair, twiddling the pencil between thumb and forefinger.

"Is it your baby?"

The book on the corner of the desk hit the floor.

"I'm not the only man on the place, you know."

"Don't tell me it's your dead brother Jimmy's."

"I'm not...I didn't...I said I'm not the only man on the place."

"So, it's not your baby?"

"I wish I could say no."

"You've just said yes."

"How can I make it up to you?"

"I need to think about it. I doubt there's room for your two separate families under this roof."

"I'll get rid of her." He flipped the pencil to the desk. It rolled to the floor with the book. "I'll let Maureen go."

"I was afraid you'd say that." Doll turned and stepped to the door, stopped and said, "I'm taking Minnie and going to Mama's first thing in the morning."

Chapter 8

Two days later, he rode up to Mrs. Baxter's on the black stallion.

As much as Doll had thrived on love, she now thrived on hate, emotions slipping just that quick over some line that nobody could explain and what she'd thought for the past two days was: All this time; this thing with Maureen has been going on all this time and I didn't even know it. All that time wasted on love when she could have been hating, which hurt like hell but made a lot more sense—misery did—was a lot more satisfying. Hating was safer.

Mrs. Baxter had been standing clear, letting Doll rant till she wore herself out.

From the parlor window now, Doll watched Daniel dismount and loop the reins over a paling on the gate.

"Mind Minnie for me, Mama," she said and crossed the room to the door.

Mrs. Baxter was rocking before the fire, reading a letter from Sheba, while Minnie played with a cord ring of sewing thread spools at her feet. "Don't stand out there in the cold. I can take the baby to the stove in the kitchen and y'all can talk it out in here."

"No ma'am. It won't take that long."

Doll met Daniel on the porch. They just stood there. His brown leather coat was buttoned up. He was wearing a dove felt hat. He looked pale in the dove hat, in the open gray light of the winter sky. Hands in pockets. About ten pounds thinner and tired looking.

Across the road, the cold pines rustled in the laying wind made visible with woodsmoke from the chimney. Dark would come with a finger snap, a door slam.

"I miss you, Doll."

"Maureen's your mistress, isn't she?"

"That's ridiculous; you know she cooks and keeps house for me."

"Nice—a mistress who can cook and keep house. One of your trips to New Orleans you just brought her home, same as you did me when you went to Four-mile Still."

"You know better, that's different—you're my wife." He reached for her and she backed away, gathering her white knit shawl about her shoulders. "I first met her at this café where I liked to eat."

"I don't care," she snapped.

"Well, I do. I should have told you before…"

"Before we were married or before you began skipping bed to bed."

"I didn't. I swear. Not like that." He stepped closer as if to warm by the heat and beauty of her. "The owner of the café later hired a chef, this man, and she was all up in the air over it. I spoke up for her to the owner, said I'd take her home to cook for me if he didn't treat her right."

"You're getting the facts all crossed up, aren't you, Daniel? Liars'll do that." She started to go inside but he grabbed her arm; her shawl slid from one shoulder and she caught it. Glaring at him.

"Anyway. Later on, I met Joe, took a real liking to him. One thing led to another and next thing I knew…"

"Spare me."

"Then next thing I knew Joe had shot this big-name politician for cheating in a card game and the law was after him. That's when I brought them both home with me to Staten Bay."

"I'll be going inside now, Mr. Staten Bay."

"I want you back, Doll. I'll do anything." He took his hands from his pockets and started to reach for her but kept them raised like somebody giving up to the law.

She stood her ground, crossing her arms. "Build me a house then." As much as she still loved home here she had no intention of moving in with her mother and her with two babies to clothe and feed and crowd into the small house. She had no intention of letting Daniel off that light. Though she'd like never to see him again on earth or in hell.

He laughed. His face lost its tight look and the light of hope welled in his eyes. "All right. A house. You want a new house, I'll have the lumber sawed."

"A house of my own. Just up the road from you. Under the oaks across from the quarters."

He looked off, sighed, looked back. "Doll, you can't live by yourself, you know that. Let's go inside, I'm freezing."

"When you get it built, let me know." She started up the hall.

"I thought I'd stay the night," he said, "if that's okay."

"No, it's not okay." She stepped through the door on the left and slammed it to make the dark.

Mid-march and he was back. Standing where he stood before. About the same time of day. Wind blustering through the woods, howling around the house. Cold still, but yellow jasmine was blooming in the great pines, the sap was rising, a winey smell.

Doll was huge, incredibly huge, huge to the point of waddling stomach-first, like a child pooching out her belly for a laugh. The hate in her heart was thinning out, but was yet to be refilled with love for him.

"Your house is almost finished," he said. "You'll want to see it, I imagine."

"When it's ready for me to move in, come get me." She turned to go up the hall.

"Can I see Minnie?"

"Mama, bring the baby here," Doll called through the door on her left.

"Doll," Daniel said, "it's almost night. Let me stay."

A dogwood tree in the left corner of the fence was dripping sap like water from a branch nicked by a squirrel's teeth.

"Doll, listen to me. You're gonna have that baby anytime now. You need to be home, at Staten Bay, where Estelle can see to you."

"Adam's sending a doctor out from Homerville. You'll get the bill."

"Adam, huh?"

"Yes, Adam."

"He's not the daddy of this baby, I am. I won't have him hanging around you."

Well, Adam was hanging around every chance he got: solicitous, entertaining, annoying in his eagerness to please Doll. He made her feel like she was awaiting an operation, not delivery. Doll didn't need him, had lied about him sending out the doctor. She'd arranged for that herself.

Really, she was about as furious with Adam as Daniel. Sometime back, according to Adam, he had done some private investigating on Maureen and Joe and had learned through his lawyer-buddy-system about Joe having shot dead that New Orleans big-shot. That had been bad enough, Adam snooping around without asking her, and the two of them such long-time friends. But what enraged her most was Adam having heard all the talk about Maureen being Daniel's mistress and never saying a word to her.

"I was trying to protect you," he'd said. "To give Staten the benefit of the doubt."

She doubted that.

The only reason she told Daniel that Adam had arranged for the doctor and not she herself was because it seemed more hurtful, and weren't her days spent trying to come up with ways to hurt Daniel as he had hurt her? It was a sorry way to spend her time, granted, but it was an obsession and her only pleasure.

Mrs. Baxter stepped out the door with the baby wrapped in a quilt, pinkish head peeping from beneath the patchwork of cloth-scrap stars. Her nose was running. Mrs. Baxter wiped it with a handkerchief. "Hey, Daddy," she said, baby-talking, and lifted one of Minnie's clinched fists to wave. "Da-dee. How you doing daddy?"

He took the child swaddled in quilt. She reared back, whimpered. Mrs. Baxter caught her and laughed.

"My own daughter," he said. "Doesn't even know me."

"You know daddy, don't you, sugar?"

She clung to Mrs. Baxter like a lizard.

"Doll, I can't believe you'd do this to me."

"Good evening, Daniel." Doll passed through the door, hearing Mrs. Baxter talking to Daniel on the porch. Repeating almost word for word, baby talking, even as the stallion clopped up the road.

Inside, Mrs. Baxter said, "I know it's none of my business but..."

"Right, Mama."

Baby-talking to Minnie again. "Looks like Daddy's gonna be cleaning stoves the rest of his born days."

When Daniel came again, only days later, he didn't try to stay or to get her to go home, but to see how she was faring—she still hated him, that's how she was faring. But when he came, a month later, she seemed to have gotten over it or at least her hate didn't seem so vivid in view of the fact that she was holding his own flesh and blood new-born son. To his surprise, she hadn't given the baby away or anything like that.

Not that she was friendly.

But to his relief she was going home.

Doll in the surrey with two babies now, and Daniel on the stallion, they passed through Statenville on their way to Staten Bay.

The old men had just moved from inside the commissary to the courthouse porch. Talk was, about 50,000 Americans looking for homes had ridden or ran to claim land somewhere Out West during a government-sponsored race. Hard to believe, when right here in Echols County, the best place in the world to live, thousands of acres of prime pinewoods, fields and swamp was home to less than a thousand people. Pale green shoots of new growth on the ancient oaks, dead leaves raining down on the cow paths and people taking in the soft spring air of the courtyard after a long hard winter.

Doll spied Prude Purdue on the upper gallery of the hotel. Leaning on the bannisters, watching. She waved but Doll didn't wave back. She hated her too. Oh, yes, Prude had known about Maureen and Daniel. She'd been in on it from the start. But she had to hand it to Prude, at least she had more than just sex with Daniel—providing what she'd said was true. Doll had had nothing but sex with Daniel. They'd never even played checkers together.

The old men on the courthouse porch wagged their heads, but waved at the odd family. The baby in the surrey was squalling and kicking.

"You bout wore out that horse, ain't you, young man?"

"How you, Herbert?"

"Fair to middling, what about you?"

"Never finer. Got me a boy. Hold him up, Doll, will you?"

Doll kept her hands on the leadlines, her eyes straight ahead. "Giddyup." The bay mare spirited south at the crossing.

Daniel laughed, circling the crossing, then swung round into the surrey tracks. "Mrs. Staten's in kind of a hurry to get home."

"That new house, I reckon so," said another.

"Be seeing y'all." Daniel kneed the stallion into a gallop.

"She's good-looking, I can say that much."

"She won't stay." All agreed.

"Yeah she will. She's got her own house now."

"Not unless Mrs. Baxter moves in, she won't."

"You got a point there."

"I was him, I'd go get her my ownself and be done with all this gallivanting."

"Had him two women, they say. How come her to stay in the flatwoods long as she did this time."

"Lucky sonofagun!"

"Lucky he ain't kilt dead, you ask me."

Doll had expected a cabin like Estelle's maybe, but she never expected a replica of the big white house at Staten Bay. There was even a rough-pine barn south of the house, smaller than Daniel's but with a shelter on front for the surrey.

She turned the surrey down the raw cleared lane circling the oak grove that separated the quarters across the road from the house. Oscar, happening up in his wagon as though summoned by some spirit, pulled in behind the surrey; Daniel rode next to Doll, as near as the stallion would allow. He watched her face for some reaction to the house he'd had built for her—close enough but not too close, in both proximity and design. She figured he was thinking that once she got over her mad fit—this *thing* with Maureen—he would move in here, or Doll would move in there, and he wouldn't have to suffer major readjustments, nor could either woman claim that she had been slighted or favored.

Doll had hardly spoken to him since he had gone to the flatwoods for her and the children the evening before. She didn't bat an eye now. Was a bit pale, but still with that same trim jaw and pointy chin, still mad, which gave her a haughty, impenetrable porcelain demeanor.

The quarters' dogs gamboled behind and ahead, flews of the spotted hounds aquiver with excited whooping. Oscar shouted and cracked his whip at them, but Daniel seemed not to notice. The baby hadn't let up crying since Doll had nursed him a couple of hours ago. He was lying in an oak-strip basket on the surrey seat between Doll and Minnie, who like Doll, had grown used to the noise or had given up trying to pacify Little Dan. His crying outvoiced the dogs' barking, the whip's cracking, the shouting, screaling and clopping.

Doll stopped the surrey in the live oak shade at the picket gate and saw Fate in her red headrag waddling up the hall toward the wide front porch. Under the barn shelter, Aldean was sharpening knives and tools on a whetrock. South of the house, Lottie was drawing water from the new brick well. She left the bucket on the mortared well rim, crossed to the fence jamb and picked up a peeled cane, came out the gate and began chasing the dogs toward the quarters. Their running bodies blended into the paisley shadows of the oaks.

"Got you some help," said Daniel to Doll. He tilted his dove hat up, grinning and gazing at the house, then at Doll for her reaction.

She stepped down from the surrey, handed the leads to Daniel, who handed them to Oscar as he walked up from the lane where he'd left the mule-faced horse to doze in the west-bound sun. Minnie sailed from the surrey into her mother's arms and latched her thin legs around Doll's waist. Daniel picked up the basket with the squalling baby and lifted it down. Two coon-like feet kicked high.

"You ever heard a better set of lungs, Oscar?" Daniel held the basket for Oscar to see.

Oscar's rucked upper lip was stained with tobacco juice. "Ain't much else to him though is they?" Oscar laughed, squinted down into the basket.

Daniel reared his head and laughed. "Hey, that's my boy you're talking about. You just wait. Give him a couple of months."

Oscar scratched in his thatch of brown hair under his hat. Reset it. "Chip off the old block, huh?"

"Chip off the old block," said Daniel, solemnly peering down at the plump, fair-haired fit-pitching baby.

"What ails him anyhow?" Oscar asked.

"Colic." Doll stepped between the two men, took the basket from Daniel, carried it through the gate and up the steps and set it on the porch where she'd left Minnie sucking on her fingers.

A mockingbird graced one of the fence palings, doing a bad imitation of a bobwhite calling from the woods behind the house.

Fate and Lottie unloaded the surrey, carrying Doll's things into the first room, left side of the hall.

Daniel moved into place beside Doll, one tan suede boot

out before him and hands on his low slim waist. "Your house, Mrs. Staten. How you like it?"

Holding the baby on her shoulder now, Doll walked down the hall walled in hand-planed virgin heart pine and looked into the room where Lottie was unpacking her New Orleans trunk at the foot of the same white iron bed Doll had slept on at Daniel's house, placing her clothes in the same oak chest from Daniel's and the chiffonier from Daniel's—all set up in the exact same spots of the room as at Daniel's. Even the two wicker chairs sat in the southeast corner under windows like the ones where she used to look out and watch Maureen coming and going. The same blue rug but without the kerosene stains. The Seth Thomas clock from her old room now sat on the mantle of her new room—she would wind her own clocks from now on. New paint and green lumber smells, Fate's lard cooking and harsh lye. No lavender or beeswax, like at the other house, and Doll was glad.

She stepped inside with the baby in her arms and Minnie hanging to her skirt tail. "Excuse me while I nurse this baby," she said to Daniel and Oscar and closed the door on their grinning faces.

While nursing the baby, sitting in the deep-seated wicker rocker from her look-alike bedroom at Daniel's house, she wondered if he had set up a room for himself across the hall. If he'd intended all along to build this house for them, himself and her, leaving Maureen at the other house. What did it all mean?

She was still wondering, still nursing the baby though he'd long been asleep, one fist curled on her white breast, when she heard Daniel's stallion trotting up the lane. She got up and placed the baby in the center of her bed. His downy head rolled to one side, his bottom lip quivered. The tiny trench between his pert nose and upper lip was dewy with baby sweat. He was a pretty baby, but also a crybaby.

Leaving the room on tiptoe, she could see through the open door of the room she supposed Daniel was hopeful of calling his own, a small square table with two facing chairs set up

206

before the fireplace. On top was a chessboard with all the quaint figures set up and waiting. She walked up to it and stood staring down. Then she laughed in her new bitter voice. Then she picked up the pieces one by one and began pitching them into the cold clean brick bed of the fireplace. Kings, pawns, queens, whatever the hell they were called. Wooden board last for starter of a long winter fire.

After supper, and still not dark, Doll sat on the porch and rocked Little Dan.

Minnie, exhausted from the trip and the excitement of the new house, was already asleep in the narrow middle room next to Doll's. Fate and Lottie had gone home. Before Lottie left she had set a bucket of smoldering rags in the front yard for the westbound breeze to carry the smoke down the hall and fog the mosquitoes.

Dreamlike and ominous, in the afterlight of sundown, was a luminous thunderhead in the east that made the dusk like morning. It grew and brightened before her eyes. The evening was hot and still and edging toward a slow dark heat.

Across the road, more smoke, smoke and open fires and the high-pitched squeals of children, a hurt dog's yawping, and the low gibbering of men and women walking home from the fields between Daniel and Doll's separate houses. Babies in the quarters cried as if in echo of Little Dan, now squirming his way up Doll's shoulder. His fingers were hooked in her hair like combs.

"Hush, baby," she said, then sang till she realized her song had long been lost in his crying. She lay him flat on her lap, head on her knees, and checked to see if was wet. Dry. When had she fed him last? An hour ago. She placed him on her shoulder again, rocking, patting, staring out at the raw-looking lane, the smoke layering in bands from the quarters. There were an even dozen live oaks and that many stumps in the grove, like stools to sit on—a peaceful thought. At her mother's house, the evening colic spells hadn't seemed as prolonged and traumatic. Of course, grandmother and mother had swapped off rocking time, and Doll would take Minnie for walks, safe in the knowledge that her mother was in charge, that the baby, despite sounding as if he might die any minute, was alive and safe.

Oscar in his wagon turned down the lane. Elbows on his knees, horse plodding along, he stopped next to the oak at the gate. Spat off the side and wiped his screwed mouth with the back of his hand. He said something, but Doll couldn't make out a word for the baby's bawling.

"I can't hear you, Oscar," she said loud.

He eased down off the wagon, came on through the gate to the edge of the porch and squatted, peering up at her and the baby. "Mr. Daniel told me to check on you along and along," he said.

Doll didn't want Daniel there, but it made her fighting mad that he'd sent Oscar rather than come himself. She placed the baby on her lap again.

"Tell Mr. Daniel I don't need his help."

Oscar took a broomstraw from the bib pocket of his overalls, stood, and began picking his teeth as he poked on back to the wagon. He got in and drove away up the north curve of the lane, then straight across the road to the quarters where a sack race among the children was in progress.

Doll got up and paced a T from the porch to the hall.

The baby's crying in the hot hollow house made her feel doubly desperate and alone. She went into her bedroom, placed the baby on the bed and lit the lamp. His pudgy legs pedaled in the kerosene-fumed air.

She leaned over him, hands each side on the fluffy white bed and pressed down, rocking him. He gnawed a fist, closed his eyes, opened them howling. To keep from waking Minnie in the next room, she picked him up and went out on the porch again. Only the light of the fires across the road—now and then a flambeau or two moving through the dark—except for the light through the window of her room.

She lay Little Dan on her lap and rubbed his tight tummy; she'd seen her mother do that and it had worked. He bawled louder.

"Poor baby. Did I do this to you by eating Fate's cooking?"

Black dark, and still she stayed on the porch to keep Little Dan from waking Minnie.

Through the silhouettes of oak moss and leaves she could see the stars twinkling, and below, lightning bugs drifting like stardust. It was cooler now and she'd covered the baby with a flannel blanket, held it close around the back of his ball head.

He dozed off, woke up recharged and bawling.

Again Oscar came to check on her and again she sent him away. Watched the flame of his lantern dwindle out up the lane like the white thunderhead in the dusk.

It was midnight when he came again. This time when the wagon stopped, the lit lantern on the yonder side dribbled down and around and up to the gate, through the gate, up the walk and doorsteps, and onto the porch.

"Well, honey, you got yourself a crier shorenuf, ain't you?" Estelle set the lantern on the floor, came over and took the baby from Doll. She smelled of dust and wool, like an old rug.

"Go on home," Estelle called over the baby's capped head to Oscar. "Get my bottle of paregarc and bring it back here." Then to Doll, "You go get some shuteye, you hear? You trusted me enough to bring that lil ole speckled gal of yours in the world, reckon you can trust me with this hyenie here."

"I don't think I could sleep, Estelle, not and him crying like this."

"I'd of been here before now but I had to see to Maureen—had herself a girl this evening, was a long time coming."

Doll stood and Estelle took her rocker, angling it as if a different vantage was called for to tolerate the baby's bawling.

Doll fell asleep to the baby's crying. Woke the next morning with him sleeping beside her. She could hear Fate in the kitchen talking to Minnie. Then Minnie's wobbly footsteps along the hall.

"See you don't wake yo mammy now," Fate scolded. Then, "Bo Dink, you better get them eggs on here fore I take a stick to you. And I ain't seen sign one of that buttermilk you belong to bring in from the well."

The doorknob turned and Minnie's sharp freckled face peeped in. Her blue eyes were wide and spoked.

"Come here, baby," Doll whispered.

She sidled through the door, looking back, then scampered over to the bed and climbed up. Slipped to the rug and started over again.

"I want Mama," she said and scrunched close to Doll.

"Me too." Doll kissed her grits-smeared face. Minnie called her grandmother "Mama" because Doll did.

Little Dan opened his huckleberry eyes, blinked, whimpered, bawled.

Doll nursed him while Minnie let his hand make a fist around her finger. Pumping his arm up and down.

"Is he gone cry again, Mama?"

Doll laughed. "Probably."

"Let's give him to Mr. Staten."

"Mr. Staten?" Doll laughed.

Then she cried. Not loud and not long, and if Minnie noticed, Doll couldn't tell.

"Run play with Lottie's girl, okay?"

Minnie climbed halfway down and fell on her bottom to the rug. She got up laughing and ran out of the room, leaving the door swung wide.

Doll played Minnie's calling her own daddy Mr. Staten over and over in her mind. Regardless how much she hated him, she didn't want her children hating him. She didn't want their daddy to be part theirs and part Maureen's baby's. This whole business was a nightmare. The games between them, or among them if she counted Maureen, shouldn't involve the children. She felt petty thinking it, but couldn't help it—Daniel had apparently stayed with Maureen during the birthing of her baby last night and that said it all about his divided loyalties. Another victory for Maureen.

The baby was sleeping again with the nipple of Doll's breast in his warm mouth when Daniel suddenly appeared in the doorway. He was wearing a green shirt and light pants. No hat, and his green eyes beamed. He stepped inside, closed the door easy, and came over to the bed and sat, staring down at the baby, at the breast. Whispering: "I believe somebody's been making up lies on my boy. You're no crybaby, are you Little Dan?"

He tilted forward, propped on one elbow, and kissed the baby's forehead, then Doll's breast. She grabbed his fair wavy hair and yanked up. Hard. He sat back, smoothing it down.

"I've done everything you said, everything I know to do. How much longer, Doll?"

He didn't mention that Maureen had just had a baby—his baby—and probably he never would.

Confident her son would quell the question Daniel had just asked, Doll lifted Little Dan away from her breast. Eyes still closed, he wailed as if placed on earth for no other purpose.

Night again, and again Estelle came with her paregoric. Thunder and lightning, the house abloom with linking florescence, Doll lay in her bed listening to the baby's crying broken only by thunder booms and rain pelting the roof. Doll had ordered Estelle not to dope the baby until she absolutely had to. She knew too many women in the flatwoods who had started out taking paregoric for menstrual cramps, then taking it for backache and headaches and no aches at all.

She slept, woke with the baby nestled close. Sun streaming through silent windows.

She was rocking the sleeping baby, that afternoon, when she glimpsed Lottie standing in the doorway with the left side of her head leaning into the jamb. Something about her head looked unbalanced, warped even. Her quick dark eyes were gleaming with tears.

Doll stopped rocking. "What's the matter, Lottie?"

She turned her head sideways, revealing the stubble of a

lopped braid.

"What happened to your hair?"

"I come to tell you I want to go back to the fields." She covered her face with her hands, sobbing.

Doll stood and eased the baby down in the middle of her bed, then crossed over and placed her arms around Lottie. She felt stiff, feverish. "Did Fate do this? Did she whack off your hair?"

She nodded, sobbing on Doll's shoulder like a child, but being a good head taller than Doll, she had to duck way down.

Doll walked her out into the hall, closing the door softly behind her, then on toward the kitchen at the end of the open back porch. Fate was standing in the kitchen doorway with her arms crossed in a huff. Avenged and not making any effort to hide it.

Lottie stopped walking but Doll didn't. "Fate, you oughta be ashamed of yourself," Doll said.

"I catch her with my man again I gone cut her throat."

"Keep it down, Fate, the baby's asleep," Doll said. "Now, I'm not going to have you jumping on Lottie every time I turn my back. I seriously doubt she did whatever she did with Elkin by herself."

"I didn't," said Lottie, inching closer and sobbing openly. "I never have a thing to do with that man."

"You a lie and you know it," Fate shot back but stayed planted in her spot before the door. Toes of her punished black shoes pointed out. "I catch him coming out of yo house this moaning. See him with my own two eyes."

"I send him home," Lottie bawled. "I say I don't want no more trouble and he have to go."

"You a lie."

"Shh! The baby," Doll said. "I believe her, Fate. Now, you go fight with Elkin all you want to, but you better not lay another hand on Lottie. You hear?"

"Yessum." Fate's lips looked bee stung. She turned and flounced into the kitchen, slamming the screen door behind her.

The baby woke up and while he cried, and Lottie cried, Doll made her sit in a chair on the back porch and commanded Fate to snip off the other braid and put it in her apron pocket. Then she handed the baby over to Fate and evened up Lottie's hair, brushing it high on her high forehead with a gentle part on one side.

"Lottie, you look even more beautiful with short hair, I promise."

Lottie had overed crying and was sitting silent and resigned. The baby was warming up for his evening screaming session. As punishment, Doll made Fate hold him, then for further punishment made her follow the other two women into the bedroom and watch as Lottie faced the mirror and a slow smile spread over her pretty face.

Back in the hall, while Doll nursed the baby, she made Fate sit in the chair while Lottie whacked off her hundred-and-one stuck-up braids. Black braids formed a knotty mat on the floor. Fate looked like a man going bald when Lottie got done and started to cover her head with her red kerchief.

"No. You're not going to cover your head. Not till Lottie's hair grows out," Doll said. "Now take Lottie's braid home to Elkin and tell him next thing you're going to cut off won't be hair."

After a month, which seemed like a year, Doll agreed with Estelle to give Little Dan a couple of drops of paregoric each night. Only at night. Days, with the help of Lottie and Fate and Estelle, she tolerated the baby's crying. Four women to tend one tiny baby with a big name like Dan. Soon, Doll found herself walking the house with the bawling baby and watching from the back porch for the sun to set behind the pines along the river and signal time for the baby's dope.

Would he grow up to be a dope fiend like those women in the flatwoods? No. She placed the paregoric in a spoon and milked a few drops from her own breast and dosed him. Nursed him in the rocker in her bedroom. Placed him in the oak cradle between the foot of her bed and the windows over the porch.

Then she went to bed herself, before good dark, to sleep till Little Dan's next four-hour feeding and crying session.

She dozed and woke to hear the wagon wheels trundling along the lane—Oscar on patrol. Slept and woke to a warm body sidling close.

"What?" She sat up.

"Don't wake the baby," Daniel said and pulled her down, clamping her with a long hairy naked leg. His penis hard against her left hip.

She stiffened but grew hot and light, toes to head. She was trembling, and there was a metallic mist in her mouth. "You must have gotten rid of Maureen after all."

"Shh! The baby," he whispered and stopped her protests with his lips, a lukewarm kiss, whiskey-sweet.

She bit his lower lip.

"Damn!" Loud whispering. The leg gathered her closer, half his weight on her now.

She could speak at a half-shout and wake the baby and be rid of Daniel, she knew that. But she'd also wake Minnie. And for a fact, she wanted this man inside her, moving, thrusting, as he was doing already.

This was armistice. Time enough tomorrow to resume the war.

The next night he came, and she was ready. Craving satisfied and strengthened by her resolve to oust him. Told herself she'd used him too, and it was as much her fault as his. Another fact: she did not intend ever to be his wife, to be wifey, again. She couldn't trust him.

When he crept into her bed, this time, she was fully awake and fully dressed and laced up where it mattered in the corset from the New Orleans trunk.

His hand felt up and down, under the skirt of the blue dress and the matching petticoats. He sighed and began trying to unlace, tug open, tug down, tug up, but the corset held fast. The ribbed boning was one with Doll's ribs.

"Take it off," he whispered, panting. "Please, take it off."

214

"I'll wear it to my grave," she said.

"But last night...remember?"

"Last night never happened. Understand? You can come by and visit the children and that's it."

"*Visit?*" He sat up, spoke up—a man's reaction by rights. Damn waking the baby, I am justified. "Don't you lie there and tell me I can *visit.*"

She sat up. "I'm sitting up, Daniel. YOU CAN VISIT."

He leaped from the bed, pulled on his pants, stepped into his boots, stamping his feet down inside them as he crossed to the door and opened it. "By God, I'll show you!" Slammed it.

The baby slept on, halleluia!

The high sun was barely shining through the east windows when Doll opened her eyes, thinking, feeling first the squeeze and pinch of the corset—she needed to pee—then terror. Her breasts were full and throbbing hot. From the front porch came a rhythmic *shish shish,* plus the eye-burning odor of scalding potash. Lottie scrubbing the floor, she supposed. What time was it?

"Oh my God! He hasn't cried" Doll said. "That paregoric has killed my baby."

She doubled over to the foot of the bed, corset cutting off her breath. She could see the oak cradle was empty, baby and blanket gone.

"Fate's got him." She jumped to the floor, twisting her ankle, limped on toward the closed door.

"Fate," she yelled, limping on down the hall toward the kitchen. "Fate, you got the baby, right?"

Fate floated in her long gray skirt from the kitchen to the back porch. Empty-handed. Her face round and blameless, her hair sticking up, skin light and tight over marked cheekbones. "Why you be carrying on so?"

"The baby's gone."

"What *gone* you talking bout?"

Doll wheeled with her petticoats swishing and Fate bounding behind her up the hall to the front porch. "Lottie!"

215

Lottie stopped pushing the cornshuck scrubber, stood tall with her bare bleached feet rooted to the sudsy wide boards.

"Where's Estelle, Lottie?"

"Miss Estelle ain't set foot on the place to yet," Lottie said, then yelled out to Bo Dink under the barn shelter, "Bo Dink, you see Miss Estelle?"

Bo Dink, shelling corn to take to the gristmill, quit turning the crank and cocked his head. A few golden kernels rattled into the tub between the sheller legs; the sheller spat a white cob to the pile growing on the ground ahead. "Not this moaning, I ain't." He stared out at the road and a wagonload of gum barrels rumbling past, then started cranking the sheller again.

Fate called from Doll's bedroom. "Lawd, Miss Doll! That baby shorenuf gone."

"Where's Minnie?" Doll met Fate in her bedroom doorway, coming out.

"She out feeding the chickens last time I look."

Favoring her good foot, Doll set off down the hall again, stopping on the back porch. Minnie was standing next to the chicken yard, shelling corn from a cob and punching it kernel by kernel through the diamond wire to the cluster of frantic chickens. She had on a blue dress with a tucked bodice, hand sewn by Mrs. Baxter, and brown shoes with buttons on the sides.

Doll spoke low to Fate standing behind her. "Don't upset her. I've got to pee."

She dashed down the hall to her bedroom, and with lightning speed shucked the corset and was seated on the square oak stool, peeing into the chamber pot inside, when Fate waddled in.

"Don't you fret, Miss Doll. Anybody stole that boy be bringing him back by nightfall. Ain't nobody but a mama put up with that fuss."

On the blue rug, left side of the bed, Doll was circled round by a confection of petticoats and blue skirt. "Or a daddy," she said, suddenly smiling.

"Nome, ain't no daddy gone put up with that fuss."

"Daniel got him." Doll stood, kicked off the corset wrapped around her feet, then got down on her knees and elbows looking under the bed. She had to push aside the shiny paired shoes from New Orleans—which she'd only lately grown to tolerate on her feet—to get to her old brown hightops.

Fate picked up the corset, looked at it, shook her head and laid it on the bed. She lifted the chamber pot from the oak stool, mumbling, "White folk ways be a mys'try to me."

"Fate, listen, don't say a word." Doll was sitting on the rug, pulling on her shoes but not lacing them. "Not word one to anybody except Estelle. Just tell her to check on the baby from time to time till I get back." She got up, hurrying from the room, talking back to Fate. "No paregoric, tell her. Now go tell Aldean I said hitch up my surrey, then get Minnie inside and tell her we're going to Mama's. Pack up our things and I'll be right back by for them."

She was waiting outside the gate when Aldean brought the surrey around, and already stepping up by the time he stepped down. He turned to help her up just as she was whipping the mare into a trot up the lane. At the road, she hauled back on the leadlines. She had to pull herself together, she had to act calm. Otherwise what she would do, what she had to do, wouldn't work. She sucked in, closed her eyes, opened them and turned the mare south, stepping high but at a saucy gait as if to set an example.

Shoelaces still untied, Doll stopped the surrey before Daniel's front gate, sitting, listening to the baby crying inside.

When Daniel stepped out to the porch, she reached beneath the seat, picked up the lace-edged parasol he'd bought to match the blue dress, stepped down daintily but in great pain from the twisted ankle and her engorged breasts. She popped open the parasol, dome of blue sky overhead, same shape and shade of the parasol, and the blue lace border like a veil over her blue eyes. Iridescent mosquito hawks with lace wings hovered and buzzed above the quivering bay mare.

Daniel walked out to the gate, ironed white shirt, black

pant legs stogged in his black boots. His bottom lip was scabbed with dried blood. "Well, Mrs. Staten, you're looking fine and fit this morning."

"Thank you, sir."

"I guess you're here to *visit* my son."

The baby's crying sounded from back to front of the house. Or was it both babies crying, Doll's and Maureen's?

"No," she said. "I've decided you're right. A boy needs his daddy. I just came by to tell you that my daughter and I will be gone for a few days."

He looked frozen in his cocked stance. "I guess you're off to Mrs. Baxter's again."

"Mr. Burkholt, my attorney, sent word he'd like to talk to me about a private matter."

"What private matter?"

She lowered the parasol to cover her face, turned and stepped up into the surrey, marring her image, she thought, with one untied old shoe. "It wouldn't be private if I told you, now would it?"

The baby's crying sounded closer—in Doll's old room. No, both babies were crying, a chorus of crying.

"Doll, it won't work," he said. Then behind him, "Take those babies to the kitchen, Maureen." Then to Doll again: "As I was saying, you're not taking the boy back over there. You can stay here and you're welcome to, you and Minnie, but you're not dragging my son off from home again."

She snapped the parasol shut and picked up the leadlines. "Tell that fool in yonder, if she'll burp him, he might get rid of some of that gas. Giddyup." She wheeled the surrey round and with it the cloud of mosquito hawks.

Chapter 9

From the time she left her house on Tuesday, till she got back on Friday, Doll was seldom out of Oscar Bowen's sight; he was seldom out of hers, as well, either as a roving object behind her surrey on the road or a picture of an old wagon with a stubborn man scooched low, brown felt hat over his eyes, at Mrs. Baxter's house.

The picture came to life only for the subject to spit, then went still again.

Leaving Minnie with her mama, who was wringing her hands over Doll leaving the baby with Daniel and speaking too high and bright to comfort the big sister, Doll set out in the surrey for Homerville, some ten or twelve miles northeast through the woods, spurring Oscar's wagon into motion.

At Mrs. Baxter's he parked the wagon in the woods in front of the house; on the road he lingered on the curves, white horse clopping and wheels screaling behind, but seldom really out of sight. Which seemed to him not to matter in the least; he was there, Daniel's man, idle or traipsing after that fool woman when he could have been home working.

"He's like a good dog," Mrs. Baxter said earlier, peering through a lace curtain on a window in the parlor.

"Just loyal to the wrong side," Doll said.

Mrs. Baxter turned. "I think this *side* business is getting out of hand."

"Any suggestions?"

"No. But I'd think twice about using a fine boy like Adam."

"I'm not using him."

"That's worse." She went through the door and up the hall to the porch and shouted out. "Mr. Bowen, you come on in here and I'll make you some breakfast."

The hat over his face never moved.

Never moved later when Doll strolled out of Adam's law office, holding his arm and talking. She was convinced that Adam had had her best interest at heart by not telling her what he'd heard about Maureen and Daniel; after all the rumor had been only a rumor, as far as he knew, and really his not telling her had been a kindness. She was almost over sorting people into those who had known and those who had not. Adam's snooping into matters concerning Maureen and Joe without first asking Doll seemed more of a betrayal now. Plus, his doing that had revealed a seamy side of his character that made her suspicious of what else she didn't know.

They strolled on up the tree-lined main street of Homerville, past neat little clapboard houses and the two-story courthouse at the junction. The ornate round clock in the tower registered the time at 12:15. When Doll had set out at first light, fog like a mist from last night's moon had cooled the summer sun. Now the fog had burned off and the sun was blazing straight down on the crisscrossing buggies, wagons and timber carts, and people on foot heading to and from Tommy's Diner southwest of the crossing. Down the street, a train whistle sounded, then its bell. There was a far-off ping and whine of a sawmill from the pinewoods.

Inside the diner, Doll sat facing Adam across the table and the open window featuring a view of the courthouse. Adam picked up the hand-written menu, reading while Doll watched Oscar's wagon pull up into the pine shade of the courtyard. He reached back for a tin bucket, pulled out what looked like a baked sweet potato, peeled and ate it.

The heat of the low room enhanced the smells of frying food and burning oak. An occasional whiff of hair tonic when men in suits passed on their way to another of the close-set square tables covered with red-checked cloths. Doll sipped her iced tea, not too strong, not too sweet, just cold going down and fooling her into believing that it cooled her fevered throbbing breasts. She had to wear rags in her bosom to keep her milk from soaking onto the pink New Orleans' dress. She missed the baby.

"Let's see," said Adam, standing the menu on the table before him. "Thursday special—chicken and dumplings."

A fast-talking tall woman in a red checked apron, sidling between tables, stopped next to Adam. "Hot enough for you, lawyer?" She cackled, looked at Doll, then down at her pad and poised pencil.

Adam grinned up at her, nodded. "Any hotter and Tommy can quit shoving wood in that stove back there." Then to Doll, "Special okay with you?"

"Okay." Tomorrow she would go home, before her milk dried up.

"Be right back with more tea," the woman said and sidled away.

"I've got news for you," Adam said to Doll.

"I hope it's good news."

"You be the judge; some people around here think it's not such good news."

"What?"

"The governor has finally located the spot in South Georgia for his cotton mill."

"Where?"

"Twenty-five miles west of the flatwoods, in Lowndes County."

"Adam," Doll said, "it seems so long ago since we staged that party for the governor. I feel like somebody else."

"Don't tell me you wish that cotton mill had been built in the flatwoods."

"I don't know. I only know it's an option poor people don't have as it is." She sipped her tea. "So, tell me what you've been up to since I saw you last."

"I just got back from Atlanta," he said. "Went for the new State Capital dedication on Independence Day."

"They say the dome is gold. Is that true?"

"It's gilded—a golden cupola. Talk about a sight!"

"Mama read about it in *National Geographic*. She saved the article for me." Doll drank, set her glass down. "I love this, I absolutely love this ice."

"Rare at Staten Bay, huh?"

"Daniel has an icebox, I hear."

He reared in the chair. "So, tell me about it."

"What? The icebox?" She smiled, stood her elbows close together on the table.

"Life at Staten Bay, what else?"

"I'd bore you."

"I doubt it."

"I don't regret marrying Daniel if that's what you're asking for."

"I guess it is." He sat forward, arms crossed on the table. "I guess I wanted you to say you wish you'd married me."

"You never asked."

"He beat me to it."

"I don't think so, Adam. You know what I think?"

"What?"

"That you were relieved."

He shook his head. "I don't get it."

She could tell he did. "I think you like me, even love me, but not like that. You want me with you, but only now and then."

"Now more than then. I miss you."

"I miss you too. I miss Brice."

"Friends forever," he said and placed his right hand, palm up, in the middle of the table.

She covered it with hers. "Well, friend, let me tell you. I've left my two-month-old baby with a mad husband."

He sat back, dragging his hand away. "You're serious?"

"I'm serious. I want you to turn your head slow, like you're looking at something across the room. But look through the window behind you at that man in the wagon with his hat over his eyes."

Adam looked. "I see him. What about him?"

"Daniel's man. Sent to watch me."

"Oh, yeah, from the wedding." He clasped his square hands on the table. "I get it. You're here with me to make Daniel jealous."

"No. Not altogether. I mean, I guess it looks like that. But I'm not living with Daniel anymore, I can't trust him. I have my own house now, and I want to find a way to live on my own. To have an everyday life that doesn't concern him." She tried to read his face. How much did he know already?

"Doll. Look at me."

"I am." She had to trust somebody.

"No. Open your eyes. Look at me close and listen with your eyes and ears. You *are* his—no matter what."

"You don't know..."

He stopped her. "No listen. A man like Daniel Staten calls the shots. He bought and paid for you, and in the bargain got your homeplace."

"No, he paid off the mortgage and taxes is all."

"I wonder if you know how much land he's bought up in Echols and Clinch County just since you married him. How many head of cattle he owns, how many crops of turpentine he's boss over. Are you aware that your homeplace borders his other land? Remember that joke in these parts I told you about. The one where they say—no I think he said it himself—'I don't want to own all the land, just the land bordering my own.'"

She waited till the waitress had set both plates of runny chicken and dumplings before them, then stood up. "I don't like you sneaking around, checking on stuff concerning Daniel or me. I thought I made that clear. And, I don't like what you're implying either. Daniel has his faults, but he didn't marry me to get my homeplace."

Adam tugged at her hand. "Please sit, Doll. I'm sorry. And truth be told, I believe he married you mainly for you. You're pretty and sharp. You have that unnamable something that makes men grovel."

"I hate that."

"No, you don't."

"I do."

"It's the only real weapon you have. For now. But if you're smart you'll grow out of it before it's gone."

"How can I when I don't know what it is?"

"Just listen with your eyes and ears." He started eating, broth with his spoon and dumplings and chicken with his fork. "Eat up," he said. "You don't want me to miss my first big case in court, do you?"

The chatter and laughter in the diner was growing louder, clinking of spoons and forks on plates. "I wish I could understand what makes men tick."

"Sorry," he said, looking up from his plate, "I didn't hear what you said."

She repeated it.

"You mean men like Staten, not me. Am I correct?"

"Men in general."

"Well, I doubt you can put all men in the same pot. I'm on the side of right and from all accounts, Staten's not."

"So, that's it—honest men and dishonest men?" She sat back, serious and determined to get an answer. "That's not what I had in mind."

"Men like your husband want power, power over women and men."

"And you don't?"

"I don't. I just want to be the best I can be and live a good life." He blotted his mouth on his napkin, then tucked it under the edge of his plate. Left side of his plate as was proper.

"Where do women figure in with you?"

He crossed his arms and stared down at his lap. "When the right one comes along..." He left the answer open.

She waited.

No answer. Then a minute later, "You're on the money when you say that I was relieved when you married; I didn't want to marry you. I feel guilty about that, given the way things have turned out." He continued staring down. "Truth is, you would have upstaged my life. Destroyed the order I was working toward. What I have now."

She sat forward, tilting toward him. "Thank you, Adam."
She smiled. "You are a good man, and the best friend any
woman could have."

"But not a man, not a good friend to a man?"

"I don't think that, really I don't. But man to woman is a
whole lot different than man to man or woman to woman."

"The point being?"

"Daniel and I were about right for each other. A matched
pair?

"I heard that *were*."

"Yes, were. When I get wise to the ways of men—men like
Daniel—we might try again. I don't see that now. But I do
wonder if bliss isn't sometimes enough. If bliss between two
people, you know what I mean, and I'm not talking about
love, doesn't make for the longest lasting marriages. I can't
imagine anything else holding up."

He laughed. "Now, that's a woman talking." He pulled
the gold watch from his dark vest pocket, checked the time
and put it back.

"No. I think that's where men and women are on level
ground, not thinking but feeling." She could tell he had no
idea about this feeling over thinking.

"Time to go." He stood, sliding his chair up to the table
just so.

On Thursday morning, Doll and Sheba woke in their girlhood
beds to a quick rain shower. Minnie was sleeping with Mrs.
Baxter. The house was dim and still, no sound except for the
rain.

Sheba sat up. "I say let's go back to sleep. Forget about
cleaning the cemetery." She had come over from Waycross the
evening before to stay for a couple of days.

"I hope Oscar Bowen drowns out there."

"Oh, my God!" Sheba stood on the floor in her old white
sheeting gown. "I forgot about him."

Doll rolled over, facing her. "You wouldn't if he was shad-

225

owing you night and day." Her breasts were throbbing, milk wicking into the cotton eyelet bodice of her gown.

"How did your life get so complicated?" Sheba sat on the edge of her bed. Her stout calves were hairy, her big feet flat.

"I married Daniel Staten."

Sheba dropped to her knees, laughing, praying. "Thank you Lord, thank you for sparing me." Then to Doll, "I always wanted to be you."

"Now you're glad you're not, right?"

"Wrong. Peter's a good man but he's about to bore me to death. Wife of a preacher's always being watched for slip-ups."

Doll thought about what she'd said to Adam about bliss—she shouldn't have said something so verging on the subject of sex. But it was true. She wouldn't say it to her sister because from what she'd just said about Peter boring her to death meant she had never felt that way with him. Was she better off for not having it? No, she knew what it was, what she wanted, even if she'd missed out on it. What a mystery! This double-sided bliss that made for misery as well as joy.

The sun was already out by the time they finished break-fast. A wet sheen on the trees and vines. Tiny droplets clung to the pine needles like crystals. And Oscar Bowen sat steam-ing in the sun.

When the buggy with Mrs. Baxter, Doll, Sheba and Minnie started south toward Bony Bluff, he pulled in behind them on the rain-packed road. On back of the buggy was a grubbing hoe, a garden hoe, a brush broom and a vine basket of deviled eggs and fried chicken. Perched on Mrs. Baxter's lap, Minnie was wearing a pink bonnet that made her face look small but grownup. Doll, who was driving, kept whipping the leadlines on the roan mare, taking the curves fast.

"I guess we're trying to lose him, right?" Sheba, next to Doll, looked back. "I don't see him. Yes I do, now," she added.

"Giddyup," Doll said, clicking her tongue and snapping the lines.

"What difference does it make if he comes along?" Mrs.

226

Baxter on the other side of Sheba called out. "I say we let him help us hoe up that mean old Johnson grass from the graves." She was wearing her straw hat with the big red rose, meaning she was mostly going to boss the cemetery cleaning and mind the baby.

"Giddyup." The mare was now trotting, sun streaking her muscled flanks. "I'm gonna lose him if it's the last thing I do," Doll shouted.

Sheba turned again, eyeing the straight stretch of road behind them. The wind flapped the brim of her hickory-stripe bonnet on her coarse, florid face. "I think you just did."

Still Doll kept driving the horse faster.

"Okay, Doll," Mrs. Baxter said, "that'll do."

Doll hauled back on the lines, slowing the mare and listening behind. "I think I hear him," she said.

Sheba looked. "You do. Coming round the curve like a turtle."

"That does it!" said Doll. "Mr. Hamilton always said if anybody messed with us to come to him."

"Doll," said Mrs. Baxter, "I'd ruther you didn't."

Doll turned the buggy left down a woods road, wet branches slapping and dog fennels scratching under the straddle. Mosquitoes buzzed, lit and bit.

"I'm taking the shortcut to Mr. Hamilton's house, giving Oscar one last chance. If he follows it's not my fault."

"He'll see your tracks right after this rain," said Sheba, "and follow for sure."

Doll steered the mare around a gopher hole with dredged white sand on loam, then through a cove of crabapple trees with clusters of tiny pink blooms that looked like roses, smelled like roses. Bees buzzing over them. "Way I figure it, he's wet already, probably hungry. Won't take but one or two more run-ins with nature and he'll head on home."

"Doll," said Mrs. Baxter, laughing weakly, "I'd as soon you didn't bother Mr. Hamilton over this."

Minnie said, "Baa baa." Sheba kissed her cheek. They laughed.

227

Doll followed the three-path trail through the woods, checking the sun at eleven o'clock to be sure she was traveling north-northeast. Sunshine strengthened the green smell of the leaves, pine tar and camphor.

Through the trees and vines they could see the rusty pebbled tin of the many-gabled roof and the south side and front of the big old sagging house. Even the huge twin magnolias looked saggy, their waxy leaves curling in over brown seed pods whose red berries the squirrels had snitched, and the white-washing applied for the governor's visit now showed only in the wood graining and knotholes, odd streaks and swirls like fancy embossing on the brittle heart pine walls.

The buggy suddenly popped out of the woods to the dirt yard closing in with vines and scrub, facing the south side of the house and the outhouse behind, where Mr. Hamilton was standing in the doorway pulling up his suspenders. He was a tall handsome man with strong tanned arms and face and silver wavy hair like a light.

"Oh, no," Sheba whispered, "we've interrupted him in the outhouse."

"I'm never gone live this down," said Mrs. Baxter. She moaned and hugged Minnie closer as though to hide herself.

He stood for a minute, squinting at the buggy with those beaming blue eyes, trying to figure who had the gumption to interrupt his morning and trespass through his woods. Then recognizing the three women, he grinned and came walking over to Mrs. Baxter's side as Doll halted the buggy in the middle of the yard and waited.

"Hey, Mr. Hamilton," Doll said.

"Well, I be doggone!" he said. "If you girls aren't a sight for sore eyes this morning." He goosed Minnie in the ribs and she scrambled over into Sheba's lap. "Sheba, Doll," he said. "How y'all doing?"

"Good, and you, Mr. Hamilton?"

"Getting by," he said and laughed.

Mrs. Baxter smoothed her green-checked skirt and squared her hat with the rose on the front like a big eye.

"You've put on some weight since I last saw you, Mr. Hamilton," Doll said.

He looked down at the pooched but smooth firm belly under his white shirt. "Been eating good," he said, and winked at Mrs. Baxter. Then he leaned over her, patting Minnie on the crown of her bonnet with his right hand while pinching Mrs. Baxter on the thigh with his left.

She laughed. Her face was as red as the crepe myrtles lining the lane to the left, in front of the house. Was as red as the peppers on the bushes in the garden behind the house. From the woods came the trundling sound of Oscar's old wagon, about halfway there.

"Mr. Hamilton," Doll said, looking back, "I hate to cut it short, but we're in kind of a hurry. Remember after Daddy died you said if anybody ever messed with us to let you know?"

"I do," he said, and placed one arm on the seat behind Mrs. Baxter's red neck and leaned in to her like he was warming by a fire.

"Well, hear that wagon coming through the woods yonder?"

He listened. "I do. Who is it?"

"This fellow's been hanging around Mama's house. Setting out there day and night and worrying the dickens out of us."

"That a fact?"

"Now, Doll," Mrs. Baxter said and tittered like a girl, "he's not all that bad. Oscar's kind of nice, really. Just gets carried away when he sets his mind to something."

Hamilton stood straight, about six-foot-six with his broad shoulders squared and his fine head high. "Messing with you, huh?" he said to Mrs. Baxter.

"Doll!" she said.

They could hear the wagon getting closer.

"We're on our way to Bony Bluff to clean the cemetery," Doll said, "and he's following us."

"Well, you ladies go on. I'll take care of this. I doubt he'll be bothering this pretty lady here anymore." And this time he actually, and right out in the open, hooked an arm about Mrs. Baxter's shoulders and squeezed till she grunted.

Doll caught her breath. Of all people...her mother and Mr. Hamilton...misery and joy of bliss at their age. "Thank you, Mr. Hamilton," Doll said. "Be coming to see us." She turned the buggy up the lane, whipping the mare into a saucy trot.

"Mama?" Sheba said.

"Mama!" said Doll.

"I just cook for him on occasion is all."

"Good of you," said Sheba, "looking out for that wore-out old widower."

Doll looked back, seeing Oscar's wagon stop in the yard and Hamilton strutting round with both fists balled. "And here I've been worried sick over you, Mama, being lonesome and all by yourself."

Doll and Sheba were hoeing sprigs of new grass from their Daddy's grave when they saw the mule-faced horse plodding along the road, north of the iron fence.

Oscar in the wagon was hunched over with his battered brown hat pulled low and a red kerchief over his nose. He turned in under the pines before the solemn white churchhouse and stopped. Close enough for them to see that his left eye was swollen shut; his jawbone had been reshaped from square to round. His dingy white shirt was crusted with dried mud and his right ear was leaking blood, red as Hamilton's peppers and Mrs. Baxter's face.

Doll was in fits by Friday morning. Not only from the agony of her burgeoning breasts, but from the urge see the baby. It was all she could do not to work the mare into a lather along the sun-beamed straightaway from Statenville to Staten Bay, and then all she could do to keep from bypassing her own house and going on to Daniel's. No, he had to bring the baby to her; he had to turn Little Dan over to his mother and admit his error—no, *crime*—in kidnapping him. Surely, by now, Daniel would be exhausted from hearing him crying. Maureen would be crazy with two babies on her hands—at her breasts. Doll smiled and turned the surrey down her oak-shaded lane, glad to be home and glad she hadn't given into the urging.

Rags in her bosom sopped with milk, Doll sat out on the front porch of her own house on Friday night. Watching the yard fires across the road. Listening to the katydids shrilling in the oak grove, the mixed talk and lone shouts in the quarters, and now and then a cow lowing from the woods. Minnie had stayed with her mother, so Doll was waiting alone. At sundown she had lit a lamp on the table to the right of her chair, and as the sun sank behind the house she had become one with the circle of yellow light. Moths and beetles darted at the hot globe, down the glass chimney and into the flame. The bitter scorch of burning bugs claimed the clean sagey smell of cooling earth. In the east, a full moon rose above the ragged line of pine tops, casting long lonesome shadows on the dirt of the lane and yard.

The wheels of Oscar's wagon, now as familiar as Doll's own breathing, sounded up the lane. She expected him to drive on through, checking as on other nights, but he stopped.

"Whoa." He stepped down and walked through the gate and up to the edge of the porch.

"Mr. Daniel sent me to bring you over there." Oscar nodded in the direction of Daniel's house. He seemed to be winking at her with his left eye, now ringed in shades of brown and blue. His jaw was the same color, and his right earlobe looked dog-gnawed.

"Tell Mr. Daniel I have no time set to go over there."

He moseyed back to the wagon, got on. "Hum up there, Pokey."

She could never remember him calling the gelding by name and only seldom signaling other than by swigging in air at the corners of his lips. Decided it was his way of showing how irritated he was with playing detective and messenger.

She sat still, not even rocking. Waiting. What if Daniel didn't come? What if he never came? She smiled. Of course, he would come.

231

Earlier, Estelle had come over to report that Little Dan, who had been wet-nursing from Maureen, was otherwise crying most of the time, just as Doll had figured. Doll was staking her tomatoes in the garden behind the house. In the flatwoods, tomatoes had been grown mostly to look at—fat red orbs of ornamental fruit. She'd never tasted one till she came to Staten Bay, then talked her mother into growing them. Had found that she craved the acid-sweet flavor, often even ate them sun-warmed and juicy straight from the vine. Still, Aldean, who tended her garden, refused to touch the tomatoes because he believed they were poisonous.

"That Maureen's about to dry up, looks like. Both them babies at once." Estelle leaned close and made a pained face. "Course with them big ole bosoms..."

"I don't want that." Doll tied off a tender branch with a strip of sheeting wound round a cypress stake driven into the dirt at the base of the hairy stalk.

"Won't last that long, honey. Now he knows you're home, he'll bring that baby back."

"You sure?"

"Here," she pulled a small brown bottle of paregoric from her apron pocket. "Take you a dose for your titties before you go to bed."

Doll took the bottle, dropped it in the pocket of her old brown skirt. Bending made her breasts throb like boils; working her tomatoes helped to ignore it.

"Old tooth dentist come by while you was gone."

"Did you let him pull that tooth?"

"Not so you'd notice." She cackled. "Yep, Mr. Daniel can handle the coloreds and the timber and the cows, but a lil ole bitty baby...he ain't got nery notion." Estelle kicked at the good black dirt with an old brown hightop. "You wanta get Aldean to haul you in some leaves once these tomatoes is done bearing." She was always thinking a season ahead.

"Estelle, you know Daniel's the daddy of Maureen's baby, don't you?" Doll wiped her tarry hands on her skirt. The tar smelled like smushed green bugs.

"Could be. Could be the man in the moon's. I'd lay it to him, though." The sun at four o'clock was shining into those terrible colorless eyes scanning for the moon. "But one thing's certain, wadn't no more to him than one of them whore's in New Orleans."

"She is from New Orleans, she told me that."

"Yep, that's where she come from awright. Bout three years ago, he brung her and Joe both in from one of them trips. Didn't offer no explanations that I heared tell of—you know how he is about people messing in his business. I got my doubts she was a whore though. Course I ain't never seen one as I know of."

"I believe she's his mistress," said Doll. "Just so happened she was a cook. Main cook, from what I gathered, at a café where Daniel liked to eat. She had a run-in with the owner over some chef he'd hired and Daniel decided, sort of, to bring her here and let her cook for him."

"Well, I be dogged! A cook."

Doll thought about telling her about Joe killing a man and Daniel helping him dodge the law. Then decided against it, not because she didn't trust Estelle. She just thought something like that was better left secret. Too many people knowing might cause a leak and Joe could still be picked up by the law. It bothered her enough that Adam knew, though she trusted him only a little less than Estelle. Estelle would have no one to tell that mattered; Adam had plenty of people in high places to tell. Doll couldn't say why she cared; she just liked Joe. She didn't understand his loyalty to Daniel exactly but neither did she understand her own. After all, she'd bawled Adam out for snooping into Daniel's business.

"You wondering how come him to marry you and him with all the good food he can eat, plus all the you-know-what when he takes a hankering for it."

"Yes ma'am, I have wondered about that." Doll was kneeling in the dirt, gently gathering branches to the stake.

Estelle took a white strip from the basket at the start of the tomato row and wrapped it around the branches in Doll's arms. "Quit wondering. A man like Mr. Daniel would see a wife one way and a mistress another way, what I think." She tied a loose knot, stepped back. "Word is, he aimed to settle down. Went looking for a wife to have his sons."

Doll let go of the branches. Stood. "That makes me crazy, Estelle—him thinking of me like a sow."

She held up one hand. "Hold on now. Way I see it, he fell head over heels for you. Then he couldn't just chunk Maureen out. So all was left was to try and keep her on as his cook and housekeeper, and being a man and dumb as they come, he expected the two of you to live happy ever after with his set-up. I got all ideas when he married you, he set his mind to keeping her in the kitchen, but not in his bedroom."

"Well, he didn't." Doll picked up her basket and started toward the back porch, talking to Estelle hobbling alongside. "Much as I despise her, I feel sorry for her. How Daniel's used her."

"I'd say it's tother way around; I figure she aimed to get shed of you by getting in the family way."

"What do you reckon Joe thinks about all this?"

"Just cause I can lay hands on a little paregarc don't mean I'm God."

Bittersweet taste of paregoric on her lips, that night after Doll gave up waiting on the porch, she floated off, fully dressed except for her shoes, into a fuzzy skimming sleep in which she dreamed she heard her baby crying, far off but growing closer. Very close. She opened her eyes and saw Daniel standing in a chute of moonlight at the foot of her bed, cradling the crying baby in a white blanket.

"You win again, Doll." He stepped around to the right side of the bed and laid the baby gently beside her.

She propped up on one elbow, opened the blanket and placed a hand on the baby's body. Then sat up, unbuttoning the bodice of her dress and lifted him to her breast. He sucked, cried, sucked, spread a warm hand open on her breast possessively.

Daniel stood watching in the lit and swollen silence.

Doll could feel herself going warm with gladness and sorrow: gladness over seeing, touching, her baby again; and sorrow because there was something final in the way Daniel simply stood there and she didn't feel even half as triumphant as she'd expected. At some point they had switched places and now Doll was in the wrong, had gone too far, and not the other way around. She thought she might cry and she wanted him to go.

"You can go now, Daniel," she said, not meaning it to sound like a dismissal, but it did.

"Thank you, Mrs. Staten. I was just about to."

She couldn't see his eyes, she couldn't see his face, only the outline of his tall straight body in the moonlight. Standing so, he usually cocked his hips and placed his hands on his waist, but not this time. His arms hung loose alongside.

She gathered the baby closer, for comfort, crying but not out loud. She could feel his tears on her breast, or was it her own? "You had no business kidnapping my baby," she said, and again her voice sounded petty, more hostile than she felt.

"I had no business doing a lot of the things I've done."

"Amen to that."

"Most of all for thinking I could make up to you." Then he turned and started for the door. "You can take off your corset now, Just Doll. The next move is yours."

Chapter 10

Pregnant again, Doll looked on throughout autumn and fall and winter while Daniel visited his son, whose crying waned, paying scant attention to Minnie and no attention to Doll's condition.

It was 1890, and there was a new president of the United States, Benjamin Harrison, and Doll had another spring baby, another boy, who she named Jeff, and still Daniel visited daily, carrying the boys out to the porch to play with them. Gradually wandering from the porch with them until one day he put Little Dan on the saddle before him and rode off on the black stallion. Stayed gone and stayed gone. Came back and handed him over to Doll.

Women in Wyoming were now allowed to vote. The Southern states were likewise preoccupied with new voting regulations—literacy testing imposed on Negroes, specifically in Mississippi, but not illiterate whites; property qualifications and poll taxes—anything to keep the Negroes from exercising their rights. Jim Crow laws separated the Negroes from the whites in public places. Trumped up crimes against Negroes resulted in lynchings.

Doll read all that from her various magazines and newspapers, plus listening to the wireless, but had trouble putting it into perspective. None of it seemed to apply to Staten Bay, even news of an economic downturn for farmers didn't seem to pertain. Hoping to lower costs by buying supplies at reduced prices, obtaining loans at rates below those charged by banks, and building warehouses to store crops until prices became favorable, farmers' alliances were forming throughout the South. Farmers wanted the government to regulate or take over railroads to lower farmers' transportation costs. Businesses were failing, farm prices were falling, railroads were going bust.

The "New South" was impoverished, with the lowest income and educational level in the nation. Had he been elected president, could William Jennings Bryan have turned everything around?

Doll longed to discuss all this with Daniel. Daniel would know.

Often, but less often than before, Doll went to Mrs. Baxter's Half the time Minnie, five years old now, stayed with her grandmother when they went there, and it all got too complicated, the goings and comings and visitations and Doll was lonely for a man, for her husband.

She went to Waycross to visit Baa; she went to Homerville to visit Brice and Adam. She made the rounds of places she'd already been, but she never went to New Orleans, her Promised Land. Wasn't even sure now that she was free to make the journey, now that she wasn't pregnant or nursing or shackled by the foot to the chain of duties involved in running her own division of Staten Bay, that she wanted to go to New Orleans. She had thought about it, maybe she and her mother, chaperoned by Adam, and pored over pictures of gardens and quaint houses of pink and purple and green in a recent issue of *National Geographic;* a picture of a famous café with boughs of cerise bougainvillea draping wrought iron balconies at the end of a cobblestone alley. Daniel may have walked there. Maureen may have cooked there.

Her interest turned to stone and her eyes glazed over from imagining the hard truths of so glimmering a destination: She and her mother, both spinsterish, joining the throngs of tourists, eating their way along the streets of New Orleans, gazing into windows of houses and shops with longing, not so much for what they could or couldn't buy but with longing to belong, to stop time and experience the rapture of finally being there. And Adam, poor Adam, almost spinsterish himself, anointed as guide and protector—he wouldn't even know how ludicrous he was, just another tourist, how he'd been duped into believing he stood out in so grand a city, that he was somebody, same as at home in Homerville.

Such thoughts made Doll drowsy with dullness. She felt old and listless. She saw Prude Purdue, all dressed up, crossing from the post office to the courtyard, while passing through Statenville in the surrey on her way to one or the other of her somewheres, and she believed she caught a glimpse of herself: pretty, naughty, withholding. A rocking sensation.

Doll sat at the crossing and watched Prude in pink, her best color, walking with skirts lifted along the cattle path under the oaks toward the hotel. Suffering her own aloneness, Doll imagined that Prude was lonely too. Did Daniel still visit her, sit in the dining room and listen to her sing and play the piano? Play chess and drink whiskey with her in her room, memorial to her days when she was truly young and her company was desired? Had he grown numb to the games of his bachelorhood?

Whipping up the leadlines of the surrey and setting the roan mare trotting, Doll headed right at the crossing, then right again along the road behind the courtyard, eyes on Prude now going through the front door of the hotel. It was a warm winter morning, a mock spring in South Georgia, making bearable the cold and rain generally swapping off weeks, but nobody was sitting in the rockers on the porch. In fact, and it was almost eerie to Doll, there was nobody out and about in the area around the courtyard and hotel. The mare's hooves clunking and the faint rattling of the surrey, the creshing of the wheels, were the only sounds to be heard. Not even a bird singing or a cow lingering and lowing from the cluster of oaks in the courtyard where they came up each evening and stayed the night.

Having had in mind to stop and visit with Prude Purdue, Doll drove on past the hotel, taking the courtyard square and coming out on the sunny road home, home to Staten Bay.

She had no notion of going back to revisit girlish comparisons to Prude Purdue. She had family and friends and things to do; she had children to raise and a place to keep up. Daniel had done her wrong and maybe she'd done him wrong, but she wouldn't dwell on that either. As for Maureen, who was still at Staten Bay, still in the cottage next to the cotton house, she had ceased to be either threat or rival.

Doll had been smart not to leave Staten Bay, giving up what was rightfully hers and her children's, just to punish Daniel for his wronging her with Maureen. Other women she could call by name—maybe Prude Purdue or Maureen herself—might have left on principle, or clung to their hurt like a trophy. Doll had come close when she had decided to return to Staten Bay after learning that Maureen was pregnant with Daniel's child. But whether by instinct or reason she had done the practical thing—her children had a father, figurehead as well as provider. Doll was yet to meet anybody fed or clothed on principle or pride.

Not that her motives for staying had been all pure, all practical. Life without at least being able to see Daniel would have been a fate worse than nakedness or starvation.

Mrs. Baxter came to Staten Bay, Sheba came, and Adam and Brice, but Doll still longed for company. Daniel's company. Hated herself but longed for him so much that she began dressing up each morning—no corset—and waiting without appearing to wait.

More than once Adam was there when Daniel came for his daily visit with the children. He was so civil toward Adam it made Doll itch. Gone were Daniel's rooster preening and mocking remarks. He no longer cared. Adam's being there in his smart dark lawyerly suit no longer bothered Daniel. He treated him like a brother-in-law. No, like another woman or a preacher come calling.

One spring morning when Daniel came stood out in Doll's mind as most irritating. His signature light cotton pants were stained with dirt and pine tar; he was wearing an old tan-striped oxford shirt, tail loose, pant legs stogged in his slim brown boots.

Doll and Adam were sitting on the north end of the front porch, waiting dinner, talking and taking the morning air. Bobwhites called crisply from the pinewoods and mourning doves cooed in the planted fields close by. Moss swags in the live oak shading the porch and half the front yard were alive with keening insects. From the kitchen Fate's heavy flat footsteps and her usual grumbling over cooking, a dish shattering, a skillet raking across the grates of the iron stove. It was June and cool mornings would break into sudden heat, the thought of which made Doll fan her face with a hand fan pasted to a flat wooden paddle, as Daniel rode up on the stallion.

She always felt hot when he came.

One long leg, which she could picture naked and hairy, marked with muscle and sharp shinbone, swung over the saddle and he stepped to the fresh swept dirt. He seemed not to have seen Adam and Doll rocking on the porch, in plain view, as he hitched the reins to the medium-long pole supported by same-size end posts in the sun-laced shade of the oak.

The stallion neighed and stamped and swatted at flies with his luxurious tail, watching Daniel stamping his muddy boots on the brick walk leading up to the porch. Daniel's prominent brow and perfectly symmetrical features a study in great faces. No hat and he nodded to Doll and Adam as he strode up the porch steps.

Doll wished he'd ridden on by, having seen Adam on the porch with her. It would have been the gentlemanly thing to do, under the circumstances, what Adam certainly would have done, other way around. She wished he didn't make her face burn so; her heart was beating way too fast, felt sore and quickened with surfacing fire like stark fear. A slow fever was building in her groin. And yet she'd like to see all over again him riding straight in the saddle, one with the wild virile stallion. But most of all, she wished she wasn't drawn to comparing this man, her husband, to her friend Adam, who could not help being born pale and pock-faced, soft as a woman.

Adam's face was too square, his black eyebrows too bushy. She'd never before noticed how his ears stuck out. Daniel's ears were the peach shell ears of Doll's children. She loved those ears.

"Morning, Doll. Adam." Daniel stood, one hip cocked, on Adam's right, facing the open hall and the light breeze flowing through. Smells of cooking: frying chicken, early garden peas in cream, cornbread and steeping sweet tea.

Adam stood and shook his hand, then sat again.

"It's been awhile," Daniel said. "Good to see you."

He walked off in long measured strides down the hall, boot heels setting solid but easy on the floor. She hoped he noticed through the open door, right side of the hall, Adam's packed traveling bag on the bed Daniel had intended for himself when he built the house for her. Then he'd know that Adam would be leaving soon, but then he'd know that Adam had stayed the night before. Then what would he think of her, his legal wife, having another man sleeping directly across the hall, an old boyfriend at that? She hoped he thought the worst. She hoped he was jealous but didn't doubt he wouldn't be.

Adam said something to Doll but she missed it. "Sorry. What did you say?"

"I said, looks like it might rain this afternoon."

"Oh." A cloud out of the west covered the sun balancing above the pitch of the roof. Doll had felt the shadow as the eclipse of Daniel's presence. She could hear him talking to the children on the back porch. Them acting out what Doll felt like doing every time he came: squealing and hugging, latching onto his leg.

This was Doll's favorite time of day. What she lived for. She despised Adam for being there. She despised his black bristly mustache. Listening to her family, of which she was absent as a member, she investigated Adam's mustache, as if he'd just grown it. So silly, a mustache: bristles growing between his boyish nose—which seemed to get smaller, more pug, every time she saw him—and his full reddish upper lip.

He looked like a hog. Yes, a black hog in his black suit

with black hair even on the tops of his soft white hands.

She could hear her family out in the back yard now, the boys' croaky voices, Minnie's bright chatter.

Adam seemed to read her mind. He stared at her, his brow wrinkling below that womanly widow's peak. Why did his nappy black hair grow so low on his forehead? She'd never noticed that before.

"Shall I leave?" he asked.

Shall.

"Of course not, and it right here at dinnertime." She sat forward, breaking the spells cast by both men. "Fate's just now putting it on the table."

Daniel went away to New Orleans, stayed gone three months—on business?—came back with clothes, shoes and toys for the three children. A wheel for Dan, a little red wagon for Jeff, and a trunk full of pretty dresses for Minnie, plus a hand mirror and a brush, silverplated.

Nothing for Doll.

He was in the guest-room/parlor with the children while she waited on the back porch, that fall morning he got in from New Orleans. Aldean was banking the newly dug sweet potatoes between layers of dirt and straw, creating cone-shaped mounds next to the wash shed. Soon the cold would come and the otters, coons, and possums would start putting on fur and Aldean would be about his trapping—potatoes banked, winter garden in—all chores behind him. He was a good man, dependable and quiet, and as loyal to Doll as Oscar, out front waiting in the wagon, was to Daniel.

Daniel walked out of the room to the hall, all three children following. Dan clinging to his leg. "With your permission," he said to Doll, "I'd like to take the children to my house for awhile."

No mocking "Mrs. Staten" or "Just Doll" attached.

God, how she missed being Just Doll!

"Help yourself," she said.

He scooped Jeff up, hefting him in his arms. "You're getting heavy, boy." (Jeff had Doll's hair, wavy, black, thick and shiny and he would test her as by fire.) Daniel was striding up the hall with Dan, four years old and tall for his age, striding in his daddy's boot steps. Minnie skipped after them, then turned, racing back to Doll and hugging her about the waist. "Come on, Mama. Go too."

"No." Doll pressed Minnie's head to her body. "Go on, have a good time."

She stepped back, peering up and pleading. "Can Dimmie come spend the night?"

"Of course."

Just as Minnie always tried to stay with Mrs. Baxter when they visited, she tried to make everybody stay with her when they came or when she went. Especially Maureen's Dimmie, who was like a sister.

She skipped down the hall to her daddy, waiting on the front porch with the boys, watching Doll. He looked mellow, handsome and subdued in his dark vested suit. He stood Jeff down beside him, reached into his coat pocket and pulled out a black velvet box. "Minnie, here," he said and handed it to her. "Go take this to your mama."

"Look, Mama," she called, smiling, coming on. "Daddy brung you a present too."

"*Brought*, Minnie." Doll took the box, sprung the lid open. Inside lay a gold oval watch on a chain.

Eyes locked with Daniel's, she slipped the chain over her head, dislodged it from the ball of hair on back and pressed the watch to her bosom as it fell. "Thank you, Daniel."

"You're welcome, Doll." Again, he turned to go.

Doll walked down the hall, speaking to his back. "Wouldn't it be something if both sides at war could settle up and see their own faults and call it quits?"

He stopped but didn't turn around. "It'd be something alright."

The boys were already on the wagon and Oscar was fussing at them. Minnie stood out in the yard watching her mother, watching her daddy.

"I miss you, Daniel."

"I miss you too, Doll."

"Nobody laughs like you. Nobody says my name like you."

Then he turned, facing her.

Her hand was still on the watch. "If I could have anything I wanted, it would be your calling me Just Doll again."

"Daddy," Jeff shouted from the wagon, "make Dan let me sit here."

"Y'all shut up," Minnie yelled, still watching the porch.

"Don't say shut up, Minnie, it's not nice," said Doll with her eyes on Daniel.

"I want you back, Just Doll," he said, stepping slow across the porch to where she was standing. "I want to settle up and see my faults and call this war quits."

One more step, hers this time, and she was in his arms, crying. Minnie was crying, the boys were crying and even Daniel was crying.

Their first cold night back together, Doll lay on Daniel's left with one leg crooked over his lower body. He smelled of soap and the two of them combined, their loving. A low fire purred in the fireplace, the clock on the mantel ticked. Perfect peace.

Her face was cold, but her body was warm. His left arm was under her neck, his hand stroking her back, the slope of her buttocks. Perfect peace and contentment, deathlike after feeling so alive.

In the room down the hall the boys were laughing, knocking about. Jeff coughing. She should get up and check on him. He stopped coughing.

Daniel, sensing she might go, rolled toward her, pulling her face into his hairy musky chest. A gland there in the hollow between the ribs she was made from.

"I should go," she said.

"It's just a cold." He kissed the top of her head.

They hugged tight, rocking, shaking the bed.

The door opened. They went still. Coughing.

"Mama," Jeff said.

"Mama's busy," Daniel said.

Doll laughed. "Daniel!"

Jeff was standing next to Doll's side of the bed.

"I'm gonna knock some heads together if you boys don't cut it out."

Jeff crept from the room, closing the door behind him.

"Daniel, that's no way to talk to children."

Racket down the hall, Jeff crying.

"You've spoiled them rotten."

Doll grew numb, drowsy, drunk on her husband's musk.

"You don't see Dimmie and Minnie behaving like that," he said.

Doll loved hearing him speak well of Minnie; she loved hearing him couple the two names—sisters. They were sleeping together in the room across from the boys' room. Maureen never protested Dimmie staying with Daniel while she stayed at the cottage, alone now that Joe was gone.

The law had finally caught up with him and he had been sent back to New Orleans where he had been tried and convicted of killing the politician caught cheating in that card game. Daniel with all his influence and effort hadn't been able to change the outcome. Joe had gone to prison. It had been all Daniel could do—and Doll never knew exactly what, only that his three-month stay in New Orleans had been business after all—to keep from being prosecuted himself for helping Joe escape and keeping him on at Staten Bay even knowing he was a murderer.

They discussed in low tones what had happened. Tensing in Doll's arms, Daniel said he'd like to meet the sonofabitch who had turned in Joe.

"Why didn't Maureen leave when Joe left?" Doll asked. "Seems like she'd want to go back to New Orleans."

"Does it bother you that she's still here?"

"She's not—not as far as I'm concerned. Not in my kitchen."

He sighed. "Fate's cooking will be the end of this family."

"It just takes getting used to."

"I don't need food." He pulled Doll over on top of him.
"I'll make Maureen go, if that's what you want."

"No. She might take Dimmie. It would kill Minnie to lose
Dimmie."

"Me too."

"She looks just like you."

"Jeff looks like you."

"Dan looks like you."

They laughed. "What you say we make another baby and
see who he or she looks like?" he said.

"I think we should just practice for a while."

But they did more than practice. Or as Mrs. Baxter said, every
time Daniel hung his pants on the bedpost, Doll got pregnant.
This time the baby was a girl, a darling with rosy cheeks and
angel-white curls, Zillie, who looked like neither her mama
nor daddy, but like a kiss blown by both of them, or an image
formed in expression of their purified love and contentment.
Happy times at Staten Bay, the kind of happiness Doll knew
couldn't hold because if it did it would probably end up making her and the rest of the family as miserable as unhappiness
would. So, she just took it as it came: life.

"Mama! Mama!" Minnie, ten now and always in charge,
popped through the kitchen door. "Zillie's out there in the
rain, barefooted as a yard dog." Her face was freckled and
her brown hair was straight and limp, but she had about her
an air of gladness that drew everybody to her.

Doll, trimming Jeff's hair, dropped her scissors on the round
table and dashed out the door. Pulling her sweater close against
the chill rain blowing onto the back porch. "Where?" she asked
Minnie, following up the hall. "Why didn't you get her in?"

Even asking, Doll already knew where, could see Zillie's
bright head bobbing along the lane. She stopped on the front
porch only long enough to slap Minnie across the face. "You
were supposed to be minding her." Then set out running
through the rain.

"Zillie! Zillie! Come back here."

Spying her mother behind her, Zillie toddled on toward the road, laughing as she splashed headlong through the clean dimpling water standing in sandy ruts. This was a game now.

Estelle, standing on her front porch, urgent and strained, hobbled out and across her muddy yard to meet the child.

Only seconds ahead of Doll, Estelle scooped Zillie up with filthy feet kicking. Her white gown was mud-flecked, wet and stuck to her cherub body.

"Sometimes I wonder about you," Doll said to the child, taking her from Estelle. "Estelle, you get in out of this rain before you catch your death."

"Put her in a hot bath." Estelle rushed off limping toward her cabin with her gray bonnet pulled closed at her throat.

Two days later, Zillie was wheezing and running a fever. Doll and Estelle took turns sitting up with her. Plastering her chest with mustard poultices, trying all they knew to sweat the fever.

Days were long, nights were longer.

Saturday, midnight, Doll had sent Estelle home and was sitting in Daniel's wine velvet cushioned chair next to Zillie in Daniel's bed.

She lay curled on her side, facing Doll, with her right fist loosely clenched under her chin. Her plump bottom lip was cracked and scaly, chapped from breathing through her mouth. Silvery ringlets spread on the white pillow, she was wheezing. Sounded like a kitten purring.

Was she getting better? Worse?

Doll sat forward with her elbows on the chair arms, left hand holding the right as if to stay it from reaching out to test Zillie's forehead, as she'd been doing about every five minutes. Her hand felt hot now without even touching Zillie.

Wind howled around the north corners of the house and puffed down the chimney whipping the flames of the burning log. Smoke rolled up to the mantel shelf but sucked down into the fireplace before Doll could get up to shove the log further back. The room smelled of the camphorated oil Estelle had rubbed into Zillie's chest till it looked blistered. Made Doll's

247

eyes burn, and the wind...if only it would quit howling. Her nerves felt raw from trying to breathe for Zillie, from watching Zillie. From being unable to help her.

The door eased open and Doll turned to see Daniel. "I want to sit with her awhile," he said.

Doll shook her head no. "I couldn't sleep anyway. Go on back to bed."

He stepped inside and closed the door. "I can't either."

Standing by the bed, he lay his hand on Zillie's forehead, covering her long-lashed eyes, her smidgen nose and half her face. "Still burning up." He was dressed in the same clothes he was wearing before he went to bed—*if* he had gone to bed. He was wearing his boots and the tail of his indigo chambray shirt was wrinkled and untucked.

As much as she hated nights alone with Zillie, and being the only person in charge, she wanted Daniel to go. He loved Zillie too much and when he was in the room Doll felt responsible for him too. He wore her out with his questions, his needling. So far, he hadn't blamed her for Zillie having gone out to play in the cold. Unlike Doll, who had blamed Minnie—she had that guilt to heap on her burden.

Zillie tossed her head, coughing, coughing. But slept on, this time gasping for air, her chest under the white gown rapidly rising and falling.

"There has to be something," he said. "What does Estelle say?"

"We're doing all we can."

"That's not enough."

Doll felt angry suddenly. "Tell us what to do then, Daniel."

"I didn't mean..." He placed his hot hand on her shoulder. "I'm going to get her some water."

"Don't wake her, Daniel. She needs to rest. When she cries her breathing gets worse."

She hadn't meant to scold him. Spoke in a kinder voice, "She's already had water."

"I'm going after Doc Hill."

"Tomorrow. If her fever hasn't broken by tomorrow..."

The next day, Sunday, Daniel rode in the ongoing rain to get Dr. Hill from Statenville.

Late evening, cold rain falling still, the two men got back to find Doll rocking Zillie bundled in a quilt before the fire in Daniel's room.

The boys, bored with staying in, were playing in the hall, in and out, slamming doors, leaving them open, while Minnie stayed in the kitchen behind the cattycornered cookstove. Sitting in the corner on the warm floor with her knees up and head down on them.

Doll laid Zillie on the brass bed—she was hectic-red, wheezing and limp—and opened the quilt for the doctor to examine her.

"Got yourself a sick baby here," the doctor said. He was a stout man, looked stouter as he sat on the edge of the bed next to Zillie. He placed a hand on her forehead, testing backside, frontside, this child too angelic to be real in the first place. "Pneumonia's my guess." He leaned down and took a stethoscope from his black bag on the floor, centered the cup on her chest and listened, gazing between Daniel and Doll at the rolling fire in the fireplace.

"Let's get her over to the hospital in Jasper," Daniel said.

One of the boys rammed the closed door, hollered out, then ran up the hall, whooping and laughing.

"I wouldn't run a risk in this wet and cold," the doctor said. "Better to wait and hope the fever breaks. Ain't nothing they'd do we can't do right here." He hung the stethoscope over the top rung of the bedstead. "Doll, go get a big kittle of water boiling. Daniel, go get Estelle to help me set up a mist tent. And make them boys out there settle down, will you?"

Going out the door, Daniel nabbed Jeff by the ear as he passed up the hall. "Get in here, boys," he said. He towed Jeff by the ear, Dan following into Doll's room.

From the dim hall, Doll could hear Daniel's belt strip from the loops of his pants. The lapping of the belt and the boys wailing. It was almost dark now and a sullen raw cold had settled in with the rain beating down on the roof and gushing from the gutter over the watershelf.

Bo Dink, a grown boy now, was sitting on the back porch davenport, staring out, waiting to drive Fate home in the surrey. Other than Doll, only Bo Dink was allowed to drive the surrey. He was so short and wiry and dark that Doll almost walked past without seeing him.

"Bo Dink, why don't you take the surrey and go on home?"

"No ma'am," he said. "I gotta keep the fire going in the smoke house, bossman say. Sides, I ain't leaving till Miss Zillie out of the woods."

"Well, at least go in the kitchen where it's warm then."

He looked up and Doll saw that his great eyes had gone liquid, tear-streaks down his ashy face.

A few weeks before, he'd found Zillie smearing soot from the washpot onto her sheer face, arms and legs, to look like Bo Dink, she said. Daniel had scolded her, bathed her, kissed her. Hardly a night passed that she didn't end up sleeping with him—hardly a day passed that he didn't take her out riding on the black stallion. But it was Bo Dink who had watched over her—her guardian—since she started to crawl and crawled through a loose board in the floor and underneath the house that the boys had practically wrecked. Bo Dink hadn't been watching the day she got out in the rain and now Zillie was sick.

"Go on in there and see her, Bo Dink." Doll had to swallow back crying to speak, went on into the warm lit kitchen. It smelled of oak smoke and fish.

Fate was standing at the counter, cleaning brim to fry.

In spite of and because of the rain, Lottie, who had kept her hair cut short ever since Fate had lopped her braids, had taken her two boys and set out fish baskets in the swollen branch and river. Brought a mess to Miss Doll.

"Fate," Doll said. "Dr. Hill needs a kettle of boiling water."

Fate's hair had grown out and her entire head was sprigged with braids. She wore her red headrag around her neck, a curse forever. She nodded toward the stove, at Minnie sitting behind it with her head on her knees.

Doll walked over and stood next to the copper water tank. "Get up, Minnie."

All legs and freckles, she stood.

"Now come here." Doll stepped over to the cook table.

Minnie crossed her bony arms, walking out and around the water warmer on the side of the stove.

The boys were wailing louder, in unison now.

"I wish he wouldn't do that," Doll said to Fate.

"They be asking for it the live-long week." Fate turned and spoke, then faced the paint-black window with rain sliding down the glass. "Lawd, ain't this rain never gone quit?"

Minnie stood before her mother.

"Can I have a hug?" Doll said to her and reached out. "I'm mighty sad about Zillie. Tired and sad and sorry I slapped you."

Minnie began crying. "Why's Daddy beating the boys like that?

"Same reason I slapped you," Doll said. "Listen, Zillie was already sick and you know that. Might of got pneumonia anyway."

"Pneumonia?" Minnie started squeeze-crying, touching knees with Doll sitting in a chair to keep from dropping.

"Now, I won't have any of that. Understand? Last thing in the world I need is crying. I want you to do something for me."

Sniffling. "What?"

"I want you to put on your daddy's old rain coat and boots and go get Dimmie."

Maureen still lived in the cottage down the fork in the lane, beyond the cotton house, she and Dimmie.

Fate turned again, holding up a withering blue brim with clouded eyes. "Miss Doll, no ma'am. You send Miss Minnie out and she gone come down with it too." She wiped her leaking eyes on the corner of her red neckerchief, shaking and crying but not out loud.

"Hush, Fate, I know what I'm doing." Doll shook one of

Minnie's arms. "Now go get Dimmie. Say please and thank you to Maureen and see to it that Dimmie bundles up good in Joe's old rain coat. Okay?"

"Yes, ma'am."

"Miss Doll..." Fate held out both hands coated with fish guts, scales and blood.

"Hush, Fate," Doll said, smiling at Minnie. "Now you listen good to the rain tapping on the coat hood. Listen for Mama. And when you and Dimmie get back, I want y'all to sing everlast one of those songs y'all sing for Zillie everyday."

Doll let go of her arm. Stood and said, "Put that water on to boil, Fate, like I told you." Calling up the hall as she went out. "You boys, I've heard enough of that. No more crying tonight." Stifling her own crying likewise.

The doctor, Estelle, Doll and Daniel rotated from the steamy bedroom to the kitchen for coffee, slipping in and out of the room with the cold. But Dimmie and Minnie, standing before the fire, kept singing. Singing to drown out the rain that wouldn't stop. Mostly church hymns, mixed with nursery rhymes.

Hoarse, at midnight, they were waved out of the room by Doll. "Go to bed, girls."

Sudden quiet, raindrops hissing in the fire like spreading-adders.

As they went out the door Fate came in. Stepped up to the bed, holding her big rough hands before her, staring down at Zillie, sleeping sweetly but wheezing.

The mist tent, rigged with a white sheet over the back of a chair, had terrified Zillie so that Daniel had yanked it down. It wasn't working anyway, the doctor said. Best to keep her calm and still.

"Miss Doll," Fate said and started crying in spite of herself, "I dream I see you come carrying yo baby in a white dress." Her voice rose, hollow, laden and monotonous. "Her laid out in yo arms and you coming up the lane."

Doll was rocking before the fire, staring into it. "Go lie down in my room, Fate."

Daniel standing by the bed placed an arm about her shoulders and walked her out. Minutes later, Doll could hear him crying on the front porch, sounded like he was choking. The doctor came in, listened to Zillie's chest with the stethoscope draped over the brass bedstead. Daniel came in—no sign of crying.

Doll could smell whiskey on both of them.

The doctor stood straight, folded the stethoscope and this time placed it in his bag. Pulled the sheet up over the cherub body, cheeky face and silver ringlets.

Doll stopped rocking. Got up and went out, down the cold damp hall and into the kitchen. Estelle and Fate were sitting at the table. They looked up when she came in, then stood and hugged her. Not a word, not a tear, just the three of them with the fire in the stove ticking like the rain overhead. Then they heard Daniel's broken wailing from the front room, the eeriest, most unreal sound since time began.

Just when Doll thought she would never laugh again—would never hear laughter again—that the sun couldn't shine without Zillie—Mrs. Baxter came bringing sunshine and summer to stay for awhile: ordering everybody around with that laugh that said, "People get born and die and the living go on living, but only if they laugh. When laughing dies, people die. Now get your buckets and let's go blackberry picking."

But Daniel didn't laugh.

After burying Zillie to the right of the walnut tree in the field northwest of the big white house, he seemed done with them all—boys bedamned, Minnie and Doll bedamned. He would ride off on the black stallion in the morning and come home falling-down drunk just in time to get up and go again.

One evening, at sundown, Minnie and Doll watched from the kitchen window as he rode out toward Zillie's grassing-over grave. Doll could tell by the loose way he rode in the saddle that he had reached his peak and would soon start to slide. He was carrying a shovel, right hand centered on the handle and hanging down. Left arm hugging what looked like a squat pottery jug. Reins dangling, and it was apparent that the stallion was on his own but expected to know what Daniel had in his soused mind. Burnished black and glistening in the topaz sun, the stallion wandered and grazed and started with his head high when Daniel scolded him, kneed him. The red cattle nosing into the rank green grass likewise lifted their heads, sun mirroring off their wide somber eyes.

"What's he doing?" whispered Minnie as if he might hear her.

"I don't know."

"He's not fixing to dig Zillie up, is he?"

"No, silly." Doll laughed and ruffed her lank brown hair. Who did she look like? Not Doll. Not Daniel. Dimmie looked like Daniel.

But Doll was holding her breath.

Leaning, he turned the horse and walked him back toward the house, stopping midway between the house and Zillie's grave—a straight shot—dismounted with the crock and the shovel and began stepping off ground to the east, lining up with the chimney in his bedroom, it seemed, facing ahead, then looking behind at the line of sweet gums and oaks angling with the branch. He stuck the point of the shovel into the dirt, set the jar down, and placed his right boot next to the helve.

"He's digging a hole," Minnie said.

When gray dirt turned to clay, maybe a foot deep, he dropped the shovel and picked up the crock with both hands and stood it easy in the hole. He stepped back and sighted for landmarks again, then began shoveling dirt onto the crock, topping the spot off with the sod clumps and packing it in. Back at the stallion he took a flat bottle of whiskey from one of his saddlebags, uncapped it and drank to the setting sun and Zillie.

"What did he bury?" Minnie asked.

"Money, more than likely. Sold some cows or sold a load of gum, one."

"Let's don't forget where it is in case..."

"Hush now."

If not for Mrs. Baxter taking over the mood-setting of the house, Doll thought she couldn't have stood it. But really she was saved by the very same activities that used to anger her so: Daniel's carousing and drinking. Till he came home and parked himself on the front porch with a pottery jug of moonshine whiskey. Then his pastime turned to scolding the children; he would threaten the boys if they spoke above a whisper, dared Dimmie and Minnie—as well as Mrs. Baxter—to either sing or laugh.

The mailman came by one morning and announced that Theodore Roosevelt had formed a group of volunteers called "the Rough Riders" to sail to Cuba and put an end to the Spanish-American War. And Daniel informed him that his news wasn't news—his news never had been news—was only an excuse for stopping by to make eyes at his wife.

Boots crossed on the porch post in front of his rocker, Daniel would call Bo Dink to him, whispering while digging money from his pocket.

Bo Dink was eighteen now, but was hardly taller than when he was twelve. He would leave with the dirt-colored jug empty and come back with it full. Daniel and his buddies would get together after canegrindings and syrup cookings and run off a kettle of shine, then store the jugs of whiskey in the cribs and barns (Daniel had almost taken on the ways of the other local men and quit bringing whiskey into the house).

Then one evening when Bo Dink came trotting up the lane and onto the porch with his whiskey, setting it down next to his chair, he turned to go and Daniel grabbed him by the arm. "What you mean, boy, turning against me and digging up my money after all I've done for you?"

"Nawsuh! Nawsuh! I ain't turn on you, Mr. Daniel. Ain't *seen* no money but what you give me." He yanked free of Daniel's grip, set to lunge off the porch.

Daniel jacked his right leg and kicked him in the seat. Bo Dink jumped to the ground sprang up running toward the lane, looking back.

In the field, north of the lane, the Negro women chopping cotton stopped to watch.

"Daniel!" Doll stepped from the entrance to the hall, coming on.

"Don't you come out here sticking your nose in my business," he shouted.

She could hear the boys playing out back under the grapevine; Minnie and Mrs. Baxter were in the kitchen making a pear pie.

"What in the world's wrong with you?" She walked over to his chair and reached down and picked up the dun crock of whiskey.

He caught her by the arm and shook it the same way he'd shook Bo Dink's arm. His other hand flew up, formed a fist. He glared at her, face red around his graying beard.

"Your mind's poisoned, Daniel. Let go."

He let go of her hand and dropped his head. Placed both hands flat on his thighs. "Go away, all of you. You're good at going, so go."

"No."

He shouted. "I said GO."

"Okay, I'll go. But I'll be back. I love you, I know you love me."

"Shoot!" He swung his head, laughed. "I loved that baby-girl out there." He nodded toward the field on his left, just off the porch and over the fence. "I loved her and what did it get me?"

"I loved her too, Daniel." Doll set the whiskey on the floor. "Look at me."

He was the same proud tall man she'd married, but now his chin jutted and his gaze looked more critical and intense from years of frowning.

"I loved her too, but I've got other children I love. I've got you." She was almost crying—almost. "I miss you. I miss you loving me."

"I'm old, I'm an old man."

"Old is time. Old is Zillie cause she's dead."

"I died with her. That part of me did."

"Why is it you can love only one person at a time?"

He was still sitting on the porch with his feet up but not drinking when the surrey packed with his family rattled from the barn to the fork and mixed into the shadows up the lane. Mrs. Baxter was driving. The fringe on back was ripped loose and hanging like a slatternly woman's skirt.

Eyes on the lane, he watched them go, watched, he imagined, Doll among them leaving for the last time.

He reached for the crock of whiskey, changed his mind and left it there. His fair head not even resting on the chair back, only his arms at rest on the arms of the chair.

Aldean, home from the gristmill, drove the wagon down the lane. It was loaded with sacks of cornmeal and grits for the commissary. He waved to Daniel, turned left at the fork and on toward the commissary.

Doll stepped from the hallway. "I see Aldean's back from the gristmill," she said.

Daniel glared at her. "I thought you went with them," he said.

"I'm not leaving you, Daniel. I sent the children to the other house with Mama till we get you straightened out."

"You're expecting too much if you're expecting that." He gazed out at the oak, its bushy top lit by the sun peeping over the roof. Recrossed his boots on the post. "I'm too far gone to straighten out. Don't even want to straighten out."

"Well, you will." She walked over, pulled up a chair and sat beside him. "You will because you love me and you love that surrey full of mean boys too. Even Minnie—I know you love Minnie."

"I never said I didn't love Minnie. It was you made her feel like that."

"I didn't, but I'm sorry if you thought I did."

"I'll make it up to her, I'll try." He raked one hand through his thinning bronze hair. "Bo Dink...I declare."

"He'll be back—you know Bo Dink."

"I'm a fool about that boy, you know it. Couldn't think

more of him if he was white and one of my own." He cut his eyes at her, speaking in that high proud monotone of his old sober self. "No, he's not mine, if that's what you're wondering. Dimmie's mine and I'm not denying it." He raised his right hand as if to swear or halt any interruption. "I'm not even denying that Maureen was my mistress before we got married. After that I didn't have anything else to do with her till you left that summer after Minnie was born."

"Much as I still despise Maureen, I'm glad you did."

"What kind of trick is that?"

"No trick. I'm glad because we wouldn't have Dimmie if you hadn't."

"What are you up to?"

"Quite a bit actually." She locked eyes with him. "They say Jacksonville was almost destroyed by fire a while back. Forty years after the war and it burns again."

"They'll build it back," he said, "it'll prosper."

"Yes." She stood, unbuttoning her white blouse at the neck. "I wouldn't mind going with you to Jacksonville again."

"What're you up to?"

"Here on the porch, or in the house?"

"Cut it out, Doll. Elkin's out there at the barn. No telling who-all's at the commissary, could be a drummer dropped by."

"Then we better go on in, hadn't we?"

He placed both feet flat on the floor, grinning, shaking his head. Started to rock but stood instead. She led off across the porch, down the hall.

"Lordy me!" he said, laughing.

"Lordy me, I say," she said laughing too.

"I'm an old man," he said, passing through the door to her room, looking around for her.

She popped out from behind the door, naked and at his mercy.

Chapter 11

Doll could feel the faint swell below her crossed arms and the sore rising of her breasts above. She didn't want to be pregnant now—if she was. It seemed that people were just passing through only long enough for you to get to loving them, then gone as if they never were, or were somebody you had dreamed up for the sole purpose of bringing suffering. Love was dangerous suddenly: a child or husband might be with you one day and gone the next and leave you gnawing on the corner of your pillow to keep from crying out questions in the middle of the night. Then morning, there was always morning

Jeff, tall for twelve and with a mop of glossy black curls, had run ahead to tell Doll that his daddy had been thrown by the stallion.

Doll was standing on the top porch step, holding her breath in the inching shadow of the porch eave, watching the wagon moving slow through the sun warp, dreamlike in the heat along the lane. The black stallion was tied and prancing behind.

"How come he's tied up behind the wagon like that?" Jeff asked in a quacking voice.

"Hush, honey." She wanted only to be quiet, still and quiet.

Dimmie and Minnie had been out by the cotton house picking Brown-eyed Susans from the patch growing wild there. Holding bouquets of the bright yellow flowers they stood this side of the barn watching the wagon rocking through the spurry pine shade, halfway mark of the lane. When they spied Doll, they ran lifting their skirts to the gate and through the gate and in a flash were on the porch step, one on each side of Doll.

"Where's Daddy?" Minnie appeared tight with excitement more than concern. She had lips like the thin pale rind of citron and her face was made up of meeting freckles.

"In the wagon, Minnie?"

"Why?" Dimmie smelled like warm honey. Fresh-faced and straight as if posing for a picture, she held the bouquet out in front of her. Her red-gold hair was damp with sweat and Doll imagined her wondering where she fit in all this.

"The stallion threw him."

Having brought the news that the stallion had thrown Daniel while jumping a ditch, Jeff walked off down the hall, mum and waiting for Mama to fix this. Dan was sitting perched on the side of the wagon, staring down at his daddy inside. He could have been Daniel at that age—that monotonously serious, that cleanly handsome.

"Mama?" Minnie placed her head on Doll's right shoulder and began to cry.

At least she was showing some feeling, back to normal, after worrying Doll to death by acting so growny and addled. Yesterday, Oscar had picked her up from Mrs. Baxter's on his way home from Four-mile Still, and all morning Doll had been collecting clues from giggled secrets between the two girls. She would have a talk with her mother about letting Minnie traipse all over the flatwoods when she went there. Had to be a boyfriend at one of the sawmill camps and with Minnie's lack of looks no telling what she would settle for. And just as well—this was as pretty as she would ever get—she was at her peak. Doll had quit preaching that pretty is as pretty does when life began to make a liar out of her.

No. She did not want another child to raise; her hands were full, her house was full. And now Daniel...

Oscar was driving the wagon with his notched brown hat pulled low, his mouth working as if mumbling a prayer or chewing, and Elkin sat on the floor of the wagon bed next to Daniel, whose body was stretched flat and bound with strips of white sheeting to the board where they had laid him. Estelle was coming at a run up the lane behind the wagon, flagging what was left of the bed sheet. And out of the noon shadows of buildings and trees, there seemed to converge on the lane and in the yard every man, woman and child who'd ever worked or played at Staten Bay.

The wagon had to be moving faster than it seemed, Doll thought, otherwise how could Estelle be running? Something was wrong, out of kilter. The wheel of the clock that made the hands move north, south, east and west, dictating time and space between the flatwoods and other places, had relocated to Staten Bay and Doll hadn't even noticed. There must have been something going on out there in the world right then, something that would mark time for humankind, but all that mattered in Doll's world was this wagon spiriting up the lane and halting time.

End pointing north and front pointing south, the wagon stopped sidelong at the gate. The stallion, black hide glistening in the sun, still pranced and swung his head as if the wagon still moved. The moss in the oak stirred in a pulsing breeze. Dan in suspenders and gray britches hopped off the wagon; he wore his boots like his daddy, pants legs tucked into the tops. Solemn men gathered at the back of the wagon. Then Maureen and her two rambunctious boys, seed of the sour farmhand Daniel had hired on to grow corn at Staten Bay.

"Easy now," Oscar said, standing at Daniel's turned out muddy boots while four men on each side of the board slid it out and lifted it and carried it like a tray of eggs through the gate and up the walk and onto the porch. They stopped briefly, exchanging looks, when they got to Doll. Daniel's face was splotchy white but pure gleaming as ivory, his beard crusted with dried mud, his green shirt and light pants crusted with mud, his eyes closed but twitching as if he were playing asleep or afraid to open them. Dan stepped forward and hugged his mother close, but formally, then stepped back with the other men. She nodded to them and followed as they carried Daniel on into the hall and then his room, and placed the board head to foot of the bed as he had slept.

Minnie and Dimmie trailed, bouquets of flowers trembling, wilting. No questions now as if they knew the answer.

They all knew.

"Y'all did good," Doll said to Oscar and Elkin, standing behind her as she stood before the bed.

Somebody pulled up a chair for her to sit but she remained standing, peering down at Daniel on the wide pine board, on the summer-white seersucker bedspread.

"His neck's broke, isn't it, Estelle?" Doll hadn't seen her come in, just took for granted that she would be there. She always was, through birth and death, she was always there.

"Yes um," she said, and moved to Doll's right. "Looks like it."

The room was full of people, moving, coughing. Only Maureen was still and quiet, standing in the doorway she hadn't set foot inside in years. Somebody was crying out in the hall. Jeff, Doll supposed, but could be Dan because he was no longer in the room.

"Daniel?" Doll said loud. "Can you hear me?"

His eyelids twitched but didn't open. He smelled of sour mud from the ditch where he had fallen and a button had popped loose from the fly of his light twill pants. But he still looked important and dignified, in his stillness he looked dignified, more dignified than the best posed pictures of his brother, the senator, or even President Roosevelt.

Estelle placed one shaky speckled hand over his face. "He's breathing but it ain't much."

"Is he suffering, Estelle?"

"No. He'd be all drawed up and moaning if he was."

"Not if he's paralyzed, he wouldn't."

"He ain't suffering." Estelle placed a hand on Doll's shoulder then stepped away.

"Somebody go get the doctor, okay?" Doll only said that because she always said that, or somebody always said that—after the fact.

Oscar went out with his hat in his hands and his head

bowed. The rim of his hat had worn a groove around his sweaty graying hair and his forehead.

Again, she could hear either Jeff or Dan crying in the hall. She decided Jeff. "Will somebody go check on Jeff for me? He's taking this hard," Doll said.

Another person left the room. She didn't look back to see who. They were all glad to do her bidding, all eager to go. She took Daniel's cold, curled right hand and clasped it in hers. "Just open your eyes, just for me, that's all I ask." She started crying and through the tears saw his eyes open halfway and fix forever in a blind man's stare.

She placed her face on his chest, ear down and listening for one more heartbeat, then she sat, pleating her dobby-striped blue skirt, sensing more than seeing Maureen standing in the doorway as before.

"Go to the house, Dimmie," Maureen said. "I left a roast on. See the boys don't get into anything and me gone."

Dimmie placed her flowers on the bed by her father's side and before leaving the room kissed Doll on top of the head. Her last name was Staten and she knew that and that she should be allowed to stay with the woman who'd half-raised her. To stay with the man who had given her his name and made provisions for her forever. All he had to give her because he didn't know how to give his love. That had been Doll's department.

As for the girls, they had always accepted that there was more blood than friendship between them.

Minnie's bony arms wrapped around Doll's shoulders from behind and squeezed.

"I don't know why, baby, so don't ask," Doll sobbed. "I don't know anything, so don't ask. I can tell you I love you but I can't tell you why or what it means." She reached up and caught a hand, clammy but warm with life.

Done with crying, Doll added, "Now go tell Estelle I'll need a few more minutes, will you?"

Slowly Minnie took back her hand, and slowly walked from the room, easy to keep from shattering the death pall and the heat and the tension between the two women.

Doll watched Minnie go. Eyes locking with Maureen's eyes. She was still beautiful, especially her pale skin. But she'd grown heavier, coarser, poor. Wife of a farmer, why wouldn't she be poor? Doll saw her almost every day, though Maureen no longer cooked and kept house for them. Hadn't for years. She and her family still lived in the cottage where she and Joe had lived. She'd become only a shadow at Staten Bay, ghost of the woman she might have been, knowing there were two reasons and two reasons only that the man she loved had kept her on the place: one, her husband was the best around at growing corn; and two, Dimmie...

Dimmie was every bit as loveable as her mother was hate-able.

"Why are you here, Maureen?" Doll asked.

"You know why."

"Please have the decency to go."

"Please have the decency to go yourself." Her tone was that of the old Maureen but with a catch in her voice. She stepped from her spot in the doorway to just inside the room.

Doll was struck anew by the bluntness, the grit, of her husband's ex-mistress. But also her pleading wet eyes. This proud woman pleading.

She placed her right arm protectively around Daniel, as far as she could reach and still remain seated. If she stood she would faint. Her face felt white and prickly and yellow sparked before her eyes.

But she did stand, then turned, facing Maureen. What was a moment out of a lifetime? "I want you to know I would do the same if Daniel was alive now," Doll said. "I could do that now."

"That's kind of you. Thank you."

"Don't take it for weakness, Maureen." Doll was standing level with the other woman; she felt level. "He's Dimmie's father and that's your only right."

"Can we stop now?" Maureen was staring at the bed, at Daniel, ready for Doll to go.

Can we stop now?

Maureen's devotion to Daniel even dead came as a jolt to Doll. She thought about the times, and there were many, that Daniel had wanted to send her away, and Doll wouldn't let him. She remembered the times, and there were many, that she had prevented him from doing other things that would have been small or cruel. He had never come right out and thanked her for stopping him, but there had been that bond between them. Without saying so, and certainly without letting anybody else know, he had relayed his need for her to decide for him. He couldn't get any further with his own decisions; simply couldn't do some of those things that were just a glimmer in his mind, but he'd known the rightness of them when she had done them, and let her have her way, and the right thing had been done.

Just as Daniel had brought out the worst in Maureen, he had brought out the best in Doll, she decided. If she was any judge, he had taught her by example to be bigger than she was, to sort right from wrong but not play God by trying to make people around her who she thought they should be, not to lord her power over them, while at the same time overlooking, if not always forgiving, the trespasses of those depending on her, talking about her, judging her. If duty had been Daniel's greatest strength, hers was love.

But could she love Maureen? Could she forgive Maureen? Could she walk out of this room and by doing so not say, You win?

She had to.

Facing this haughty woman before her, Doll was suddenly flushed with feeling—be it pity or compassion. Look at how much she had sacrificed, how little she had gained. How belittling to know that the man she loved—and Doll did believe she had loved Daniel—had allowed her to stay mainly because it was easier than making her go. That was the truth of it.

Whether Maureen had left New Orleans in hopes of becoming Daniel's wife, or to protect her brother, she had given up her profession as a cook and maybe someday owning a fine café and being somebody in an exciting city. Doll, who had never traveled and couldn't cook, could certainly appreciate that. Cooking was an art and a gift, but it was hard work too. And then she recalled Maureen saving her when she fell from her horse during the wildfire after she and Daniel were married. Maureen could have left her there to fry and who would have been the wiser? But the greatest sacrifice, the most tragic and telling, was her having stayed on after Joe had gone, her having stayed at Staten Bay where she was scorned instead of respected, whether for her daughter or to be close to Daniel. That was love beyond which Doll was capable. And even if Maureen's motive for staying had been revenge, to make Doll and Daniel both suffer seeing her every day, her bearing up had been a test of strength and will and not to be slighted.

One more glance back at Daniel on the bed and she walked up to the winner. "We can stop now." She touched Maureen on the shoulder. Neither moved for long moments.

At length Doll went to the door. All that she and Daniel had started alone and together at Staten Bay was waiting for her, dragging on her strength.

She was up to it now. She touched the watch hanging from the chain around her neck and stepped out into the hall.